Like We Used To

JAMIE CLUFF

For mom.
Thanks for always being the number one supporter of
my dreams. Who knew the dreams would come with a
few f bombs and a couple of sex scenes, huh?

Author's Note

Although *Like We Used To* is a fictional story, I understand as a reader, the importance of knowing what triggers to expect before walking into a novel that has them. *Like We Used To* is an adult romance novel, and thus, has adult language and explicit sexual content. Parents may want to preview the contents before allowing readers under the age of eighteen to proceed.

Additionally, this story centers on a widow who moves forward into the dating world five years following the death of her beloved husband. While we do not witness him dying on the page, his death, including the details of the family's time in the hospital, are written in extensive detail in Chapter 18. Take care of yourself, dearest reader.

Chapter One

Now

From: Marjorie Winthrop
To: Quinn Clark
Subject: Syllabus Concern

Dear Ms. Clark,

    I am emailing you today to raise a concern about your ELA syllabus as it pertains to my Dalton. You state: "Late assignments will be docked a minimum of ten percent (10%) per day, whether the absence is excused or unexcused. After ten days, the assignment will be given zero credit. Extenuating circumstances will be evaluated on a case-by-case basis" *and I simply find this absurd. These are children! Not only are you docking credit for the assignment being late, but that only gives him ten days to make up work that he's forgotten about. Please consider amending this portion of your syllabus to accommodate children who are still learning to be responsible.*

    Sincerely,

Marjorie Winthrop

I roll my eyes into a new dimension reading the latest parent email in my inbox. If someone were to ask what the most difficult part of teaching is, they'd be surprised to know that most teachers will never answer "the students," and instead answer, "the parents." As an eighth-grade teacher, I always get a few parents a year who refuse to acknowledge that their kids are growing and need to be pushed to take more responsibility over their education, but Marjorie's email is particularly irksome. In what world is it unreasonable for students to lose credit on an assignment *after* the due date?

I pull out my phone to text my friend Sybil. We taught together in Kansas City for the last twelve years, but with my recent move, I miss confiding in her about the intricacies of teaching secondary students. My best friend, Dani, teaches fifth grade, but it's different at this level. Students are expected to do more at this age, and their parents have to learn to loosen the reigns. I've only been in this new school for a few weeks, and while I like the staff, I haven't connected closely with anyone just yet. I type out a message that includes a screenshot of the email, then take a deep breath to regain my composure before I begin typing out a response to the email. Before I start, my phone pings with a notification from Sybil.

Got this parent email today and knew you'd get a kick out of it. img.png

Yeesh. Looks like the parents in California are just as unhinged as the ones in Kansas.

"bUt He'Ll LoSe PoInTs." As if that isn't the purpose of a late work policy.

GIF of SpongeBob's beak nose

You mean my kid has to be held responsible?

Teachers are the worst.

Total bitches. Maybe we should pay them less?

I laugh and tuck my phone away. As a teacher, my response has to do three things at once: Marjorie has to feel like her emotions have been validated regarding her son growing up; I have to hold the boundaries and expectations for my classroom; and I have to offer a solution so she still feels like she has some semblance of control. Parents are protective of their kids, but usually their issues lie in refusing to acknowledge that their kids are getting older and need them less and less—I should know, I'm in the same boat with my own kids.

From: Quinn Clark
To: Marjorie Winthrop
Subject: Re: Syllabus Concern
Hello Marjorie,

Thank you for the email concerning my late-work policy. I understand that this is a big change from previous years, and that the policy may sound severe. However, it is my duty as an educator to prepare students for bright futures and teach them the importance of responsibility and punctuality in their assignments. I am sure, based on Dalton's previous academic records, that he will have no problems excelling with turning his work in on time. To help ensure that students are aware of when assignments are both assigned and due, I post a calendar to Google Classroom every week that students and parents may reference. Please let me know if you have any other concerns that I may address.
Best,
Quinn Clark

I hit send on the email and see I only have fifteen minutes before my planning period is up: my cue to head to the staff bathroom before I'm forced to hold my bladder until lunch. When I head back into my classroom, I take in the décor in the new space. Where I once only had cinderblock, I now have a window on two walls that allow my potted plants the light they need to thrive. I'm on the second story now, instead of the ground floor, and the posters I made for literature devices in popular song lyrics look at home in the new room. Even though it's been twenty-three years since I attended Pine Grove Middle School, the nostalgia overwhelms me. It's a strange feeling having so many memories somewhere, only to then occupy the same space as an older version of myself.

My classroom phone begins to ring, and I see it's the school nurse, which can only be one thing since I'm student free at the moment: one of my kids is in her office.

"This is Quinn," I try to sound chipper.

"Hi, Quinn, this is Shauna in the nurse's office. I have Sawyer in here with me."

Shit.

My heart rate spikes, because Sawyer is generally not a kid who needs the nurse unless he's violently puking or something is really wrong.

"Is he okay?"

"I think its best if you come down here and be prepared to take him home."

"Okay, let me call the front office to get coverage for my last three classes."

The office sends in a paraprofessional who always seems to have it together—thank God—so I leave her with the assignment on punctuation marks and fly out the door. I have to go down a flight of stairs inside, then up a flight of stairs outside, and into the other building before I finally reach the nurse's office, but I swear I've done it in record time—I could probably even beat my thirteen-year-old self with my pace. Finally, I see Sawyer who has an icepack pressed to his eye.

"Hey, bud you good?"

Shauna strides over, and I can tell that she wants to put me at ease. "He got a black eye during P.E. I tried to look at it, and it seemed like it responded fine to my light, but he said his vision is blurry. You may want to take him to the doctor."

Sawyer looks up at me, and I see the tears well in his eyes; he's embarrassed. The middle-school teacher in me has a unique sense of empathy for the phase of life my children are in. Being a new kid, at a new school where your mom works, and then getting a black eye in P.E.? The poor kid is probably mortified.

"Okay, can he stay here for a few minutes while I make a few phone calls and try to get him seen today?"

She ushers me out and toward the school lobby where the cell reception is the best. "Of course! And I'll get my TA to go collect his stuff from the gym."

After being told that his pediatrician's office can't see him till tomorrow, but still not wanting to wait that long for some type of professional to look in his eyes, I settle on calling Eye Care of Pine Grove, where Lydia, the receptionist, peruses her computer to see if she can squeeze us in.

She lets out a sigh of relief, causing me to do the same. "Dr. Thomas has an opening in thirty minutes if you can make that? He would at least be able to tell you if you should consult further with a doctor or an ophthalmologist and run some basic tests to assess your son's vision?"

I tell her we'll take the appointment. Something is better than nothing at this point, and I head back into Shauna's office. Helping Sawyer to his feet, Shauna's TA trudges in with all of Sawyer's stuff. Realizing I'm about to leave without my other child, I ask the office to call Wyatt out for the day so I don't have to come back here after the appointment. She'll be disappointed—she's my school lover, but maybe I can persuade her with an early movie night or something.

"Sawyer!" I hear her before I see her. "What happened, are you okay?!"

My kids are Irish Twins, just eleven months apart, and most people have assumed they're fraternal twins their whole lives because they are inseparable. When they were toddlers, they were so joined at the hip that Preston and I would often find them curled up in each other's beds because they didn't want to be apart. After a few months of that, we gave up and bought them a queen to share. Now, they have extremely different interests, but they are still wildly protective of each other.

"Yeah, I'm alright. But things are a little blurry in this eye." Sawyer points to his left eye and winces.

We make it to the car and load all of our bags into the trunk. I pull out a Gusher fruit snack from the box I keep in the car and pop them into my mouth.

"What type of snack is that mom?" Wyatt peers over my shoulder. I have a habit of categorizing snacks—always have. Sad snacks? Pop Tarts. Happy snacks? Sour punch straws. Hangry snacks? Anything I can find within reach.

"This is a your brother got a black eye in PE and I need him to tell me the whole story right now snack." Both kids groan at my attempt at humor, but it opens the window for Sawyer to tell me what happened.

"It wasn't anything mean," he begins. "We're doing volley-ball right now, and when Jaxon came down from the spike, I was right there for his elbow to land on. It could have happened to anyone." He shrugs it off like it's no big deal, but I detect an undercurrent of humiliation lacing his voice.

"Did anyone laugh at you?" I hedge, knowing how malicious and cruel middle school kids can be.

"A few of them, but this one kid, Keegan, he helped me up and got me over to the bleachers. I think he does cross-country."

"Oh, I know him! He's kind of hot. All the girls in my grade love him." Wyatt beams in the back seat like she just might be one of those girls, and my stomach turns in knots thinking about her starting to get boy crazy. If she's anything like I was, then JoJo Siwa was right: karma really is a bitch.

I pull into the parking lot for Eye Care of Pine Grove and tell the kids to bring in homework while we wait in the lobby. They aren't allowed to have devices except for two hours before bed, and only once they finish their homework and complete their chores. At least this way, they'll get a jump start on it.

I approach the front desk and see the name plate for Lydia sitting in front of a woman around twenty-five with short brown hair, and a cute button nose.

"Hi, I have an appointment for my son, Sawyer Stewart?"

She beams up at me like I'm the reason the planets move around the sun.

"Of course, Ms. Stewart," she begins but I cut her off abruptly.

"It's Clark, not Stewart."

"Oh, I apologize, I just assumed you shared the same last name..." She trails off, obviously a little uncomfortable.

"No, it's fine, just wanted to clear it up."

People have been asking me for a year why I switched my name back to Clark so long after losing my husband; some even wonder why I changed it back at all. It has nothing to do with Preston and everything to do with the fact that I regretted taking his name the second I changed it. I always loved the alliteration of Quinn Clark. Each similar sound being made by a different letter? How cool is that? It's nerdy as hell, I know, but what can I say, I'm an English teacher to my core.

She hands me the paperwork I need to complete before Sawyer's exam on a clipboard with a pen that has a faux flower stem taped to it—the universal signal for "we don't want you to steal our pens, but we're making it seems like it's a stylistic choice to have fake flowers in the office." The thought makes me giggle—humans will do anything but be straightforward.

I go through the basic questions of Sawyer's name, age, birthday, etc., and he comes over to ask for homework help.

"I don't remember how to solve inequalities." He looks at me with hope, as if he hasn't just spoken the equivalent to Mandarin Chinese at me. He's in advanced math at school, and he's surpassed me in what I know. They lost me at fifth grade fractions, and I never looked back.

"Sorry my guy, you know math and I have never been friends."

Sawyer huffs a sigh, frustrated. "Can we call Aunt Dani? I forgot the next step."

"Of course, I'll send her a text now and see if she can help you when we get home. Sound good?"

Sawyer nods, then heads back over to his belongings. I swear to God, I'd be toast without Dani for homework help. I can handle all of the other subjects, but math? No chance.

I finally move on to the more arduous bits of medical history and insurance information. I'm almost done when a nurse in hot pink scrubs calls us back to the exam room. The kids take what feels like eons to collect their belongings; I've always been a quick mover, and I hate feeling like people are waiting on me—the nurse included. My parents are the type who believe being fifteen minutes early is on time, and being on time is fifteen minutes late. I try not to let it carry over to my kids, but if someone asked them how well I am doing on that front of parenthood, they'd probably recommend going to the grocery store with me to observe how fast I dart in and out of congested aisles and describe my stride as one that matches that of an Olympic speed walker.

"Make yourselves comfortable. Oh, you just sit in that chair there by the phoropter." But Sawyer stares at her like she's speaking in tongues.

"Sorry. By the machine," she amends. "It's what the doctor will use to check out your eyes."

Sawyer moves to sit where's she's indicated, leaving us all in our rightful places.

"Good," she says, "Dr. Thomas is finishing up with a patient and then he'll be right in!"

I linger only for a moment on the name of the doctor before the door closes, and a hush descends over the room. These are the moments I don't ever know how to occupy with the kids, because while I'm silly, they've never found my humor in dull moments all that fun. I decide to channel my inner goof ball anyway and grab a glove from the box. I walk myself into the corner of the room to hide it from the kids, even though I'm sure they know what I'm doing. Just as I finish blowing up the hand balloon, the door opens, and I turn around. The air gushes out of the glove as it flies around the room, but I don't even acknowledge it because I am glued to the floor, my heart hammering in my chest.

"Quinn?" a breathless, almost husky voice infiltrates every inch of my body.

I know that voice better than almost any other; the one that stole my heart and held the promise of every dream I had as a teenager. Suddenly, all the air is sucked out of the room, and I am transported twenty-two years into the past.

Chapter Two

Then, Seventh Grade

"Mom! What's the weather going to be like out there again?" I look at my bag, unsure if I've packed enough layers for the unpredictable weather of the Mojave Desert in November. Sometimes it's thirty degrees, sometimes it's eighty.

"Oh, Quinny, you're still packing! We're leaving in 10 minutes!" I can tell she's frazzled; she always is right before a trip, and it's probably partially my fault. If I'd pack sooner, I'd be able to help more.

"I'll be done faster if you just remind me of the weather..." I sing song.

"Right, it'll be chilly at night. Low thirties, but up to the sixties during the day. Now hurry up. You know how your dad gets right before we leave." She says this completely unaware of her own habits that only come out before a trip.

I toss in another Roxy hoodie, a beanie, and a second pair of knit gloves—my snow ones are buried somewhere downstairs, and I don't have time to hunt them down right now. I look around my room, trying to figure out what things I can bring to entertain me while everyone goes on rides, and decide on my poetry journal and a new book my friend recommended, *Twilight*. Apparently, they're turning it into a movie, and I always like to read the inspiration first—it makes me feel like I'm in on a secret. Finally, I grab my pink iPod mini and headphones, stuffing them into my pocket, and race down the stairs.

June and Liz have already claimed their spots in the RV: the couch for June, the recliner for Liz. That leaves me with the least comfortable seating option: the diner style booth. It's only four hours out to Dumont Dunes from our house in Pine Grove, but it feels like ages in an RV with limited air flow.

Dad pulls out of the driveway, and as we descend down the steep curved roads of the mountain with expert precision, I can't help but be impressed by his ability to maneuver the RV, even though the curves of the mountain are tight and he makes it look easy. Since I get motion sickness on the sharp turns, I keep my eyes trained out the front windshield so that I'm not barfing by the time we get off the mountain. It's one of the only perks to sitting at the table: I can't lay down and make it worse for myself. I wait to even cue up my music before Dad is done so I don't remove my eyes from the road for even one second. Finally, after what feels like an hour, but has really only been fifteen minutes, the curves of the road straighten out, and we enter the highway.

Pine Grove is a small town, with maybe eight thousand people max, settled in the San Bernardino Mountains of Southern California. My parents lived in various towns on the mountain since well before I was born, but they moved to Pine Grove when I was two and haven't left since. It's okay as far as towns go, we get a lot of snow days out from school, which is nice, but it takes at least forty minutes to get to the nearest big store, and it feels like everyone knows everyone which can be a blessing and curse.

I pull out my iPod and scroll to my song of the moment. A song called "Ocean Avenue" by this band called Yellowcard. It's really catchy, and I like their sound. That probably sounds like I'm cooler than I am, or at least think I am, but I know I'm not. June put a bunch of her music onto my iPod a few months ago because I kept asking her what was playing, and now I keep finding music that I really like.

After an hour of replaying the same song over and over, Dad pulls into the In-N-Out in Barstow, and we lumber out of the RV. My stomach always feels a little queasy after the trek down the mountain, but it's nothing a juicy cheeseburger can't fix. As we wait for Dad to come around, I notice the Thomases standing across the parking lot next to their own RV. Weird. I didn't know they were the camping type.

Bryan and Lianne have known Mom and Dad for years. Actually, Mom was friends with Lianne, and Dad was friends with Bryan, and they set my parents up back in the 80s. They've been family friends for ages, but they've never been camping with us. Walking behind the adults, matching June, Liz, and me behind our own parents, are their sons, Forest and Rivers.

Yes, those are their real names.

No, I've never asked why.

I know June has been friends with Forest for a few years, and that they hang out with the same people, but I don't think Rivers and I have ever spoken a word to each other. I mean sure, we go to the same school—we even have Spanish class together—but that doesn't mean we're friends. He's in eighth grade, and I'm just in seventh.

"Bryan, good to see ya," my dad's voice booms. He's pretty intimidating honestly, stocky, with jet black hair, and green eyes. He's owned a construction business for years, and you can tell by the shape and power of his body. But Bryan is unphased—he's a police officer with the Los Angeles Police

Department and has a good five inches on my dad. If my dad is scary, Bryan is downright terrifying. "How'd the rig do headed down the pass?"

"Oh, it was fine. Rivers said he got a little nauseous, but that's to be expected."

Rivers looks like he wants to be anywhere but standing in an In-N-Out parking lot while his dad talks about the strength of his stomach, and I have to agree with him.

He groans, then turns to look at me. "Hi, Quinn, sorry my dad is gross."

We've never talked before, but seeing as we're about to spend the next week camping together, I decide to offer him an olive branch and try to forge some type of friendship or things are about to get really weird, really quickly.

"If it makes you feel better, I almost barfed in the trash can on the way down," I joke.

He looks surprised, like he can't believe I've just spoken to him, but seems relieved. "Well good to know that we were both *almost* disgusting."

I laugh a little and then start walking towards the restaurant because we can just as easily talk in there while we eat as we can out here in the wind. Our parents follow behind us, and Forest and June follow behind them. I look around for Liz because she's only five and see her right behind Rivers and me, her face pink, looking down at her feet like she's embarrassed.

"You alright, Liz?"

She looks up at me like she is anything *but* alright and swallows. "Yep!" Her voice is pitched high, and it sounds like her throat is closing in on itself.

"Want me to take you to the bathroom?"

"Yes, please." She grabs my hand like it's a lifeline, and we start walking toward the restroom immediately when we walk through the door.

"Hang on, let's tell Mom and June what we want."

I linger next to Mom and Lianne while they talk in line, trying to be respectful, but needing to get a word in. Finally, they both pause, and I'm able to give her my order and tell her I'll be in the bathroom with Liz.

Liz may be only five, but she's one of my best friends. She's got a great sense of humor, and as the youngest child, she's grown up faster than she probably should have. She looks at her reflection in the mirror and her eyes are filled with tears. I stroke my hand down her long brown hair to put her at ease.

"What's wrong?"

"My stomach feels really weird."

I back up on instinct. While I love my sister, I am not willing to let her puke on me.

"It doesn't feel like I'm sick," she clarifies.

"Oh, well what's it feel like?"

"Like...well, okay. You know how when we go over the bumps on the road too fast and it makes your stomach feel weird?"

I know what she's talking about. There's a stretch of road on the way to our aunt's house that we call "the bump way" because Dad always takes them too fast so that we get to feel like we're on a rollercoaster.

"Yeah, I know that feeling. Why do you feel that right now?" I'm confused because we haven't been over any bumps, and there's nothing I can think of to make her stomach feel like it's in free fall.

"I just looked at Rivers, and that's what started happening. I think I'm in love with him."

I stifle a laugh because sure, Rivers is good looking, but he's eight years older than Liz.

"Got it. Sounds like you have a cruuushhhh."

I elongate the pronunciation and wiggle my eyebrows at her. In response, she punches me in the arm.

"Ouch!" I rub the spot where she landed her blow. "Listen, I love you, but Rivers probably hardly even knows you exist. You have a crush. No big deal."

We make our way out of the bathroom and find our seats. Thankfully for Liz, my mom has saved a seat next to her; not so thankfully for me, the only other open chair is right across from Rivers. I sigh, sitting down in the chair, and start to unwrap my burger.

"Sorry, I know I smell *awful*." Rivers take a giant bite of burger and smiles.

"Huh? You don't smell...?"

"Oh, then why did you sigh when you realized you had to sit with me?" He's called me out with a joke, when he could have been offended.

"Sorry, it's not you. I guess...I don't know. We just haven't really ever talked, you know? It feels like our parents are forcing us to be friends this week? Almost like a forced play date. Not that I don't want to be friends with you, I just..." My face flames in embarrassment. I'm definitely making this worse.

Rivers laughs and leans in conspiratorially. "I heard they're trying to get us married someday."

My eyes go as big as saucers because no one, especially not a boy, has ever spoken to me like this. I splutter, trying to find a response and settle on, "Yeah, if it doesn't workout with Forest and June, they have to have a back-up plan."

"Exactly, glad we're on the same page."

He backs up into his chair again, and I smile to myself. Rivers's sarcasm is fun. I don't think I've ever talked to anyone like this before.

When we finish eating, our families walk out to the parking lot in the direction of the RVs. I hear Forest laugh at something June said and think they actually do look kind of cute together. Maybe I'll ask June about it on the drive.

I wrap my arms around my middle. The wind is really picking up, and I left my sweater inside the RV.

Rivers senses my discomfort, and says, so only I can hear, "See you out there, Quinn." Then he starts sprinting to his RV and yells, "Dad! Open it up, it's freezing out here!"

I can't help but feel like he knew I would stay out there freezing until I died rather than interrupt my dad to unlock the RV; it makes me smile. I think Rivers could be my friend.

***

Three days later, our parents go for an "adults only" ride over the dunes. Bryan and Lianne have quads, but my parents take them in their sand rail, leaving us back at camp. Forest and June took Liz over to climb a dune, so it's just Rivers and me here. I'm sitting in my chair by the fire pit, listening to "Ocean Avenue" (again), and trying to write a poem, while Rivers hits golf balls into the endless desert in front of me. When I was in fifth grade I won a poetry competition for our school district, and after that my parents treated me to a new journal for every holiday and birthday that I'd fill up with whatever I could think of. After a few minutes of jotting down some words, I realize Rivers is staring at me.

"Quinnnnnnn. Quinn? Hello?"

I pull my headphones out of my ears, wincing as one of the ear-buds tugs on my earring. "Sorry, how long was I ignoring you?"

"Not long." He shrugs and sits down next to me. "What were you listening to?"

I throw my head back and sigh to the sky, dramatically. "Ugh. I cannot get this stupid song out of my head," I say, handing him my earbuds and queueing up the song again so he can hear.

Rivers nods his head to the beat, and smiles. I can tell he likes it, and that makes me feel...happy? Why?

"It's good! It kind of reminds me of Weezer a little bit?" He looks at me like I should know what or who Weezer is.

"What's a Weezer?"

"Oh, come on Quinn! You know Weezer. 'Island in the Sun'? You've probably heard it."

He takes my iPod and scrolls all the way to the W's, and of course thanks to June, Weezer is already on there. He hands it back to me so I can listen. My eyes go big because I recognize the song from a movie I really like but will never admit to—especially in front of Rivers Thomas of all people. As a thirteen-year-old girl, liking the movie *Aquamarine* is definitely embarrassing, but hey, what's a girl to do?

Keep silent about where I recognize the song from, that's what.

"Hey, do you recognize it? Your eyes went wide like you've been trying to find the song but haven't been able to."

"I do, but I don't want to tell you why I recognize it. It's kind of embarrassing." I feel really shy and awkward, biting my lower lip—a habit my dad has been trying to get me to break for ages.

"Quinn, I won't laugh at you. If we're gonna be friends then you need to know that I'll laugh at you for stupid stuff, but not for the stuff I can tell you actually care about."

What middle school boy talks like this? I don't even think the few girl-friends I have talk to me like this. I inhale, trying to build courage because Rivers actually seems genuine. "Promise you won't tell anyone?"

"Who would I tell Quinn? It's not like we run in the same circles. But to put you at ease," Rivers holds his hand up in the air, "I, Rivers Thomas, do solemnly swear that I will not share Quinn's secret Weezer confession, or any other confession she decides to tell me, with anyone, ever, unless she's going to hurt herself or something because that actually is what a good friend would do."

I laugh out loud, clutching my belly. Rivers keeps catching me by surprise. "Okay, okay. I recognize the song because it's on a movie I like that's definitely too young for me."

"Quinn. I like *Lord of the Rings*. You know how nerdy that is?"

"Yeah, but *Lord of the Rings* is popular, and there's blood and guts, and stuff."

"Fair point, okay." Rivers considers this for a second, and then says, "I watch *The Aristocats* weekly while I hold my cat. Does that match your level of embarrassment?"

It's sweet of him to try and put me at ease. "Fine, it's on a movie called *Aquamarine*. Which I also watch weekly..."

"Mermaids, right?" Rivers asks casually as if I haven't just offered him a piece of gossip that could destroy my very fragile middle school reputation.

"Yeah," I glance away from him. This is probably the most mortifying experience of my life.

"Who cares?" Rivers taps me on the shoulder so he can look me in the eye. "If I can watch talking cats, and movies with elves and Hobbits, why should it be embarrassing for you to watch something with mermaids?"

The sound of the sand rail coming back to camp reverberates off the RVs. Rivers stands up, putting his golf clubs back in the trailer, and comes out with his helmet, placing it on his head and buckling it under his chin. "Want to come on a ride?"

"Nah, I don't ride anything that doesn't have a seatbelt now." I've crashed on ATVs, been thrown off of them, and rolled down dunes. It's no longer something I'm interested in.

I walk back towards the RV to grab my book, not wanting to write poems anymore, but before I sit, Rivers yells over to me. "Quinn!"

I look back at him, my brow furrowed.

He brings his ATV over right next to me. "Your secret is safe with me."

"Thanks." I look down at the ground then back up at him with a challenge in my eyes. "Yours isn't!"

He laughs, and I smile as he speeds away.

Chapter Three

Now

Time stills.

My heart nearly goes into cardiac arrest.

My mouth is so dry I've lost the ability to speak.

"Mom?" Sawyer looks at me like I've lost my mind, and honestly, I can't blame him.

I'm standing here with my jaw agape, the balloon hand discarded on the floor, staring into the steel blue eyes of Rivers Thomas.

Holy. Shit.

"Yeah," I try (and fail) to compose myself, "sorry, bud, um..."

How do I introduce my kids to the man I was head over heels in love with but haven't seen since I was eighteen? Especially when he looks like this? His sandy hair is shorter on the sides but textured and longer on the top, and his residual tan from the summer makes him glow. Teen Rivers was hot, but adult Rivers is downright sexy.

Rivers senses the predicament I'm in, though his gaze seems to be assessing me as well. The subtle dip of my hips, my hair spilling over my shoulders. Thankfully, he swoops in and saves me before I say something stupid in front of the kids.

"Hey, I'm Dr. Thomas. I used to be really good friends with your mom."

My eyes dart to his and hold there. He and I both know that we were so much more than friends.

"Cool," Wyatt chimes in. "When did you guys meet?" She's looking at me expectantly since Rivers has just done the hard part for me.

"Uh, Mimi and Papa were really good friends with Dr. Thomas's parents, so when they wanted to do stuff, we would hang out, and then we started to just hang out on our own as we got older." I try to be cool about it, but my face must look like a fire engine.

"Oh, so you dated," Wyatt says it with such nonchalance; she truly doesn't know the bomb she's just dropped.

I cough into my fist trying to form words. Did we ever date? Technically, no? Though, that didn't stop most people from speculating given how frequently we showed affection.

"Not exactly," I finally utter, looking at Rivers. "We were just really close." My eyes move to the floor, unable to hold his stare for even a second longer. My answer feels more like a lie of omission than anything else. Wyatt shrugs her shoulders like she hasn't just opened the biggest can of worms.

"So, which one of you is Sawyer?" Rivers looks between my kids, smiling. His dimple is on display, and God if it doesn't damn near knock me over. I used to be obsessed with that dimple, and he knew it too. It's disarming to see it on him now with the way his eyes crinkle in the corners as he talks and under the five o'clock shadow playing along his jawline. Almost as if he knows the effect he has on me, Rivers turns his head away, so I no longer see it.

Sawyer timidly raises his hand and turns his face, so the redness of his eye is on display. Rivers laughs as he sits in the chair across from Sawyer, smiling. "Dang, that's a shiner if there ever was one. Can you tell me what happened?"

Sawyer launches into the story about his injury, how it was an accident at school, even expressing that it embarrassed him. Rivers sits there, his hands clasped loosely in his lap, taking it in.

As they talk, Wyatt peers up from the chair beside me, and I glance down at her. "Yes?" I draw out in a whisper through the clenched teeth of my smile.

"You're looking at the doctor weird," she says, which causes me to adjust my face. If my daughter can see how taken aback I am, there's no question Rivers will too.

"It's just been a long time since I've seen him is all."

Rivers took up the most formative years of my life; seeing him again feels surreal.

"Wow, that sounds like that kid has quite the spike on him!" Rivers is still talking to Sawyer about the injury. "Quinn, do you just want me to look him over?"

Hearing my name on his lips sends a shiver up my spine; his deeper voice ignites sparks in my heart, and I think, just for a moment, what it would sound like whispered in my ear.

Fuck.

These types of feelings and emotions have lain dormant for a long ass time, and I do not need them resurfacing right now in front of both my kids. *Get it together, woman.*

I put my hand to my neck to hide the blotchy blush I feel creeping up toward my face. "Shauna, the school nurse, mentioned that it might be good to get him looked at to make sure he didn't sustain any eye damage. I tried to get him in with his pediatrician, but they were booked until tomorrow, and I just wanted someone to look. Sorry, I know that probably sounds overbearing."

"Not at all," Rivers answers emphatically, like he knows I need reassurance. "Honestly, I'm glad you brought him in. Eye injuries are not something to take lightly."

I will never be able to understand how he's has always been able to calm the worry in me so effortlessly. It's like he has "Quinn-tuition."

"Let's do a routine eye exam just to rule anything serious out and go from there."

He starts taking Sawyer through procedures, asking him about his interests. Sawyer tells him about cross-country practice but that in the winter he wants to join the wrestling team. The admission surprises me. It's the first Sawyer has mentioned it.

"I didn't know you were interested in wrestling, Sawyer. That's great!" I say as Rivers shines a different light into his eye.

"Yeah, I love cross-country, Mom, I just still want to keep doing sports after the season is over."

I worry that Sawyer is trying to appease my love of the sport since running is something we usually do together, but I don't want him to be glued to a sport just because I like it.

"Hey, you can do whatever you want!" Rivers is still shining different lights in his eyes, but I want to make sure that he knows this. "Dr. Thomas here used to wrestle when we were kids."

"You did?!" Sawyer seems excited to talk to someone who understands the sport, and it kills me that I can't be the one to give that to him.

"Sure did," Rivers smiles at me. "I used to go to all your mom's cross-country meets, and she'd come to all my wrestling meets. She knows more than you think she does." He winks at me, and I feel the familiar swoop of butterflies low in my belly.

The memory of us going to each other's events makes me smile. Rivers always came prepared to my meets with as many snacks as he could think of—never knowing what mood I might be in after a race; and I used to show up to his matches with signs that said, *I'm just here to watch sweaty guys hug,* or Rivers's favorite, *Singlet and ready to minglet.*

"Cool! I didn't know that, Mom!" Sawyer seems genuinely happy, something that's been more difficult to come by the older he's gotten—especially with the move.

Rivers tosses his gloves into the garbage and turns to face me. Apart from looking more like a man, Rivers hasn't changed much. I can tell he's still active; even under his doctor coat, I can tell he frequents the gym. The button up shirt he has on, accentuating his Adam's apple, makes me bite my lip. God, he looks good.

"Quinn Clark! You stop biting that lip right now, or I'll make you drink apple cider vinegar!"

A laugh bubbles out of me; the impression of my dad trying to break my habit is so spot on. Rivers even has one hand on his belt buckle just like my dad used to.

He smiles, his eyes skating over my face taking me in. "Sawyer should be okay. I didn't see anything wrong with his eye. I'd ice it when you get home to help bring that swelling down, but if he's still complaining about it being blurry by Friday, bring him back in or get him in with the pediatrician."

"Thanks." I try to find out what to say next, but the words get stuck in my throat. I don't want this to be goodbye, but I also don't know how to continue. "Um, I'll see you..."

Before I can finish the sentence, Wyatt chimes in, sending me off-kilter. "Mom is trying to say she wants to see you again but doesn't know how to ask you politely. She might also be trying to spare me and Sawyer from it being awkward."

"Sawyer and me, young lady," I quip, the English teacher in me never far out of reach. "But...yes to all the other stuff she said."

I am *mortified*. I hide my face in my hands to escape the embarrassment. Almost instantly, Rivers gently pries my hands away, and each of his fingers sends tiny sparks over my skin, igniting me in warmth.

Rivers gives me a half smile. "I'll call you. I'll pull your number from Sawyer's file. It was good to see you, Quinny."

"Yeah, you too."

The kids and I make it back to the car, and Sawyer starts in on me first. "Mom, it doesn't really seem like you and Dr. Thomas were just friends..."

Wyatt chimes in next. "That's because they weren't, obviously. I think they might have loved each other." She wiggles her eyebrows, suggestively. Wyatt has always been better at understanding social cues than Sawyer. He's smart as a whip, but when it comes to social norms, subtlety, and body language, he's a bit clueless.

"We loved each other as *friends*," I emphasize, knowing I'm lying through my teeth. "But it was nice to see him."

"Says the lady who is as red as a tomato after the cute doctor touched her hand," Wyatt says, climbing into the car.

"But you still love Dad, right?" Sawyer's question stabs my heart with guilt.

I have to tread carefully here, talking so openly about another man in front of them. To them, Preston will always be the only man I can love, and I don't know how to broach that subject with them, if I even need to.

"Of course. Your dad will always be a huge part of my heart. Now, let's go home and get some dinner. I have the stuff to make a chicken pot pie, and then we can do family movie night?"

"Or..." The kids look conspiratorially at each other using their not-real twin telepathy, and I know without either of them saying a word what they're about to ask me. "We could get pizza from Roadhouse?"

I give in because one, it's the best fucking pizza known to man, and two, my head is so full of Rivers Thomas; I'd ruin any recipe I attempt to cook right now.

***

"How'd he look?" Dani nearly fell out of her chair when I told her I ran into Rivers today.

I probably could have handled the confession a bit better; I'm sure me charging at her like a bull and accosting her with the information right when she sat down at my kitchen table didn't help things, but it's too late now.

"He looked..." I trail off, remembering his hair, his eyes, his dimple, the way his touch felt on my skin, and how well he filled out his clothes. When we were kids, he was tall and lanky—until he joined wrestling junior year and filled out a bit. Still, even that had nothing on him now—and that was under his doctor's coat.

"Shit, you're down bad," Dani chuckles.

"I am not!" I say, swatting her with a kitchen towel. "I just wasn't expecting to see him. And to answer your question, he looked good. Older, but it suits him."

Dani rolls her eyes at me. She can tell I'm underplaying how my heart jolted to life at the sight of him, and how his voice alone made me dizzy. She's known me far too long to not know exactly the effect Rivers has on me.

"Keep telling yourself that, babe. Maybe eventually it'll come true." She smirks at me like she's already rolling the *"I told you so"* tape in her mind. "Sawyer! Bring me your math homework. Let's take a look before the pizza gets here," she bellows through the house.

He sits next to Dani, and I feel an immense sense of gratitude for my best friend. We met our first day of high school; Dani had just moved to Pine Grove and didn't know anyone.

After Preston died, Dani flew to Kansas City and stayed with me for a month, taking shifts with Sybil, my mom, June, and Liz so that I wouldn't be alone. She coordinated with her parents to watch her son, Will, while she was gone. She made sure the kids were fed and bathed, made room in my refrigerator for casseroles I'd never eat, and held me in my bed while I sobbed. She paid my bills, helped me submit the claim for his life insurance policy, and coordinated with my school district to get me a long-term sub for the rest of the school year. As an elementary educator, she even got my kids into homeschool so that she could keep them up to speed in the comfort of our own home, sparing them from kids looking at them like some exhibition on pain.

The doorbell rings with our pizza, and I collect it from the driver. It smells delectable, with crisp pepperoni and a sauce that has just enough spice in it to shine through with the cheese, then drizzled with hot honey that pools in the slices of meat. We've probably eaten it once a week since moving back—the kids are obsessed.

"Pizza here?" Wyatt bounds down the stairs and takes a deep inhale. "Ugh, hell yes! I'll go grab plates!"

"Wyatt! No swearing." She knows the rules, she's just pushing boundaries.

"It's hardly a swear mom, and you curse all the time."

"I'm an adult and know when it is and isn't appropriate to swear, young lady." I level a look at her with my eyebrow raised—a silent indication for *don't push your mother right now.*

"Are you also an adult who's going to say yes if the hot eye doctor asks you out?" She says it with so much sass, it scares me. She has her arms crossed over her chest, hip cocked out to the side.

Wyatt has always been a spitfire—I swear to God she came out of the womb screaming and didn't stop until she could walk. It was like she was telling the world, "Let me walk or hear me roar!", and we certainly did—hear her roar that is. Where Wyatt has always been compliant in school, puts forth her best effort in her passions, and has been, for the most part, obedient; she has also been, what her pre-school teacher deemed "really great at self-advocacy." I love her fierce independence, but damn I am not ready for her to channel that as a teenager.

"We'll see what I say *if* he calls me."

She furrows her eyebrows at me, not used to seeing me be less than self-assured. I remember feeling the same way about my parents; that they had all the answers to my problems.

"He's going to call, Mom, and for the record, I'll be okay with it if you say yes."

She says this as if it's not a big deal whatsoever if I start dating again. On the surface, I think she really doesn't view it as an issue. But underneath the prospect of me dating lies so many more complicated emotions and problems. Will the kids still feel safe to express their feelings about Preston's absence? Will they allow someone to integrate into our routine? Will they feel safe with that person? Will I feel safe to let that person close to them? And so many others.

"Alright, well thank you for your confidence, kiddo. Let's go eat."

And then I give one swish of my dish towel as she laughs down the hall.

***

After dinner, Sawyer, Wyatt, and Dani's son, Will, clean up while Dani and I set the TV up for a movie night. The kids decided on *Pirates of the Caribbean,* and I can't help but let my mind wander to Rivers being obsessed with both the movie and the ride at Disneyland. His bedroom even had a classic looking pirate ship miniature that we named *Ashes of Atlantis.*

"Where's your head, Quinn?" Dani is fluffs pillows and pulls out everyone's favorite blankets, while I try to find the movie on the right streaming app.

"Just thinking. Rivers loves this movie. Or at least, he did. Feels a little serendipitous that the kids would choose it tonight."

"Quinn, I hope you know that whether or not Rivers calls you, and whether or not Rivers asks you out, you're a great mom. You, taking an interest in dating again—"

I start to protest, because I am NOT dating again, I just ran into the man.

But Dani lifts her finger to shush me. "...does not negate how great of a mom you are, how much you love your kids, or how much you once loved Preston. There isn't a limit on how many people you get to love in life. There's always room for more."

I brush away a tear as the kids come bounding in. She gives my hand a squeeze then launches onto the couch.

"Dibs on the corner seat!" Sawyer shouts, through teeth clenched around at least five licorice sticks. Will tries to wrestle him out of the corner but gives up easily and plunks down next to Wyatt. Once Sawyer's mouth is free of the candy, he adds, "Mom, you should post a poll asking which character is the hottest. Elizabeth Swann, Will Turner, or Jack Sparrow."

Sawyer has always been a fan of collecting useless data points, just like me. Do you toss the laundry soap cup in with the wash or keep it out? Is Nirvana an alternative rock band or a classic rock band? The ideas are endless, but we've been doing it for so long, it's become customary.

"It's obviously Jack Sparrow, but I'll post it anyways," I tease, knowing all three kids will think that Jack Sparrow is most certainly *not* the hottest character.

"Elizabeth Swann," Will says, starting us off.

"Will Turner," Wyatt casts her vote.

"Will Turner," Sawyer agrees.

Dani and I look at each other, trying to determine if Sawyer is choosing this moment to open up about his sexual orientation, or if he's just being objective.

"Elizabeth is pretty, but Will Turner is in *Lord of the Rings,* and I can't overlook that. Who's your choice, Aunt Dani?"

Dani loops her arm around Sawyer and Wyatt like their second mom. "Nope, you'll have to see my vote on your mom's poll."

"That's not fair!" Wyatt argues. "We don't get to vote because we don't get to have social media!"

"That's the perk of adulthood, young grasshopper. Now watch the movie, so I can watch who I know is the real hottest character."

Chapter Four

Then, Seventh Grade

I hurry to put my autobiography into the English section of my binder, knowing that I only have about thirty seconds to corner Rivers before I make my way over to history in the upper building and he heads down to the gym for P.E. Since the desert, we've seen each other during passing period almost every day and have waved to each other every time, but this is the first time I'm trying to talk to him at school. Spanish class isn't really an option because we sit on opposite sides of the classroom, and I really need to ask him something.

I bolt down the stairs with my bag bouncing against my hip and spot him walking towards the gym. I run up to him, chest heaving from being out of breath, and only then do I realize he's standing with Trevor Samuels, who I know, but I've never talked to.

"Oh sorry, Trevor. I didn't see you."

"No worries, Quinn!" He looks between me and Rivers like he can't quite understand what I'm doing talking to either of them.

"Rivers, I was wondering if you could tell me your favorite Weezer song? I've listened to 'Island in the Sun' like a bajillion times, and I think I need something new."

His face lights up like he's honestly excited I like the song that much. "Hmm, I don't think I can give you a favorite, Quinn. I like them all too much."

"What about your favorite right now?" I hedge, hoping he gives me something to go on.

"That I can do. Listen to 'Pork and Beans'."

I splutter. What the hell? What kind of song is called "Pork and Beans"? "Are you serious?" I can't tell if he's messing with me, and I worry that Trevor standing here with us might be the reason Rivers wants to be cruel.

"That's a good one!" Trevor chimes into the conversation. "It has a funny name, but the song is actually pretty good."

"I have to get to class, but let me know if you like the song, Quinn! See ya!"

I stand there for a second taking in the conversation. A song being called "Pork and Beans" does not make me feel confident in Rivers's music taste anymore. But Trevor agreed with him, so maybe it actually is a good song? Someone shoves into my back, and I realize I only have two more minutes to get to class before the bell rings.

Sliding into my seat, I pull out my newest journal and write "Pork and Beans?" trying to remember the title for when I can get home.

***

That night I convince June to invite Rivers over, since Forest and a few of her other friends are coming to hang out. All it cost me was my dignity, pride, and trading June's job of stacking the firewood for my bathroom duty.

My parents go on a weekly date night every Friday, so it's going to just be us and June's friends here. June is extremely responsible, and my parents' golden child. She never messes up, follows the rules, and is trustworthy enough for my parents to deem it okay for them to go to dinner forty-five minutes away while she has four teenage boys over.

We also live sandwiched between two sheriff's deputies.

I brush a coat of mascara onto my eye lashes just as June walks into the bathroom. "That looks nice on you. Want some help with your hair?"

She taught me how to curl it a few months ago, but they still don't look as nice as the ones she does. "Yes, please."

"What are you and Rivers going to do tonight?" I can tell she is trying to figure out if I have a crush on him or something, but I don't mind it coming from her. June has always been more like a second mom to me than a sister. I feel safer when she's around, and she knows how to get me to open up without embarrassing me like Mom sometimes does.

"I don't know. I didn't really think it all the way through," I admit, biting my lip.

"Well, I think we're going to hang out on the trampoline and stuff for a while if you want to start out there with us. There aren't enough spots for you guys to play Rock Band, but you can watch us if you want?"

I nod my head feeling a little bit better now that June has approved us crashing their party. "Thanks, June."

"Do you have a crush on Rivers?" She asks it gently and casually as she sections off my hair.

"No," I admit. "He was just fun out at the desert, and we see each other at school. I just wanted to talk to him more. Well, more about a song, specifically."

"Oh, that's fun. Forest has good taste in music too. But Quinny, you know it's okay if you do have a crush on him right? He's a nice kid."

"I know, but I don't think I know him well enough to like him like that. At least not yet..." I trail off. "Do you like Forest like that?"

"Quinn!" She swats me lightly with the comb. "He's just a friend. I think he might like me, but I don't feel that way about him. He's more like a brother than anything else."

She runs her fingers through my curls and stands next to me, admiring her handiwork. Looking at us, you'd never be able to tell that we're sisters. I have short brown hair next to June's long blonde, and despite there being four years between us, she's two inches shorter than I am. "You look pretty, Sis," I tell her, and even though I know she isn't trying to impress Forest, I think she still likes to hear it.

Liz bounces into the bathroom with all the energy of a rabid hyena. "Can someone please cook me bagel bites? I'm starving!"

We trundle out of the bathroom, and get her fed. The boys are supposed to get here at eight o'clock, which is when Liz is supposed to go to bed. That way neither of us has to entertain her while they're over.

"I still don't understand why I can't come to the party," she mumbles through a mouthful of food.

"Sorry, cool people only," I answer.

"Aw, June gave you a pity invite? That's cute." She sticks out her bottom lip to really amplify her faux compassion. If there is one thing Liz is good at, it's sarcasm. She has to be in order to fit in with our family, I can't imagine what it would be like if she took offense easily.

"You're just sad yours got lost in the mail."

"Alright, that's enough." June puts an end to our banter. "Liz, clear your plate then go jump in the shower. Quinn will be in to read to you soon."

Liz asked me if I could read her to her at night instead of Mom, since I always do character voices. I wouldn't say it hurt Mom's feelings, but she wouldn't agree unless she was able to sit in and listen too. Right now, I'm reading Liz the first *Harry Potter* book.

"Quinn?" Liz's eyes droop as I finish up the chapter.

"Yeah?"

"Don't tell Rivers I have a crush on him."

I smile. She understands sarcasm and humor, but she's still learning what level of playful teasing is and isn't appropriate. "I won't. Night Lizzie."

Her eyes close just as the doorbell rings.

***

As I come down the stairs, I see Rivers standing slightly off to the side of the older boys. He looks unsure of himself, with his hands in the pockets of his jeans, his black Vans nervously tapping on the floor. He has on a navy-blue zipper hoodie that make his eyes look more blue than gray—there's a vulnerability in them I'm not used to. River's is always so sure of himself; seeing him like this makes him seem more human.

Forest leans in and gives June a hug, and Brandon and Jared both go in for a fist bump. It leaves Rivers and me unsure of how to greet each other. I hold one arm across my stomach and lift my other hand to curl my hair behind my ear.

"Hey," I say, giving Rivers a half smile. Seeing him while camping and at school was different than this; those times Rivers was there because other people told him he had to be. This time, I asked him to be here. The thought of him accepting my invitation when he could have declined unleashes a small flurry of butterflies in my stomach. I try to tell myself that Rivers probably just wanted to hang out with Forest, like I do with June, to quell my excitement, but it doesn't do me much good.

"Hey, Quinn," he gives me a half smile of his own, and the awkwardness of our older siblings watching us try (and fail) to interact is getting to me.

Thankfully, June sees me floundering and puts me out of my misery. "Let's go outside for a bit! Then when it starts to get colder, we can come back in."

I start to walk outside, shuffling behind Brandon, when Rivers grabs my arm. I turn, startled, and lookup to meet his eyes. "Aren't you going to be cold? It's like forty-five degrees outside." He eyes me up and down in my long sleeve t-shirt.

"Oh, right! Yeah, I'll go grab my coat. Meet you outside?"

"Nah, it's cool." He fusses with the zipper on his sweater. "I'll wait for you."

I race up the stairs and suddenly feel overwhelmed by my outerwear choices. I don't think I've ever contemplated which coat to put on just to go hang out in my own yard, but here I am. Rivers said it was forty-five degrees, which is colder than just a sweatshirt for me. I get cold all the time, but I also don't want to put on my snow jacket—that would be embarrassing. Ugh. Why do I even care?! I quickly grab a brown corduroy coat with white fur trim that my parents got me for Christmas, and head back down the stairs while I button it.

"Did you get lost on the way to your own room?" Rivers jokes as he comes back into my view.

"Nope, I was just hoping you'd take a hint and go back home." I elbow him lightly in the ribs so he knows I'm teasing.

Rivers brings his hand to his chest in mock offense. "Well, good to know where we stand then."

I laugh and walk across the small bridge my parents have in the yard that crosses over the stream that cuts our land in half. The older kids are bouncing on the trampoline, so I head over to the swing set and sit down, gripping the chains, and kicking my feet into the air. I expect Rivers to sit on the swing next to me, but instead he climbs up to the monkey bars behind me and sits on one of the beams that supports the bars, his feet dangling.

It's silent for a few seconds, and I don't know how to start talking to him, thinking I'll say the wrong thing, or that I'll make a fool of myself.

"Damn, Quinn. I can hear you overthinking from here." Rivers laughs.

"I'm not *over* thinking, I'm just...regular thinking."

"Uh huh, sure." He's quiet for a second. "I think it's cool that you invited me over tonight."

"You do?" He's putting me at ease, and I appreciate that he's always so honest.

"Yeah, I've kind of wanted to just get to know you more since camping, ya know?"

I do know. I'm not sure what it is about Rivers, but the few interactions we've had make me want to know everything about him. "Yeah, I know. Maybe we should play the question game? Then we can rapid fire ask each other stuff?"

"Okay! But we have to answer the question the other person asked *and* ask one of our own. That way neither of us can cop out by asking the same question."

I like that he's considered this too, because it's something I hate about conversations. It feels lazy to ask, 'what about you?', instead of coming up with a question each turn. I hop down from my swing and walk over to the monkey bars so that I can be next to him while we play the game.

Once I climb up, Rivers scoots over, and I extend my hand to him.

"Deal," I tell him.

His hand slips into mine, and I let out a little gasp. His hand is bigger than mine, but it's also so much warmer.

He brings his other hand to mine and rubs it between both of his, creating friction to warm it up. "Jesus, your fingers are like ice cubes."

"My parents say I have poor circulation, but don't think it's worth going to the doctor. Honestly, it probably wouldn't be so bad if I actually used my pockets."

"Give me your other hand," he demands.

I give it to him, but once he's done warming it up, he doesn't immediately let my hand go.

I'm not sure what he's thinking, and I want to save him from the embarrassment he's always saving me from, so I pull away and adjust how I'm sitting, using my hand to help regain my balance.

"What's your favorite candy bar?" I blurt out.

Rivers's head snaps up to look at me, startled that I've ignored the brief moment of us holding hands to get us back on track with the game. "Reese's is the only correct answer."

"First of all, that's an insult to Snickers, and I won't stand for that. *But* follow up question: the mini-Reese's cups or the full-size ones, because they are different, I don't care what anyone says."

"Okay, wait!" Rivers looks animated, like I've just breathed life into him. "I keep saying they are two different foods, and no one understands me!"

"Of course they're different! The mini ones are sad food, and the full-size ones are happy food!"

He looks at me like I've grown a third head. "No..." he begins slowly, "the mini ones are more chocolaty, and the full-size ones have more peanut butter. Same with the holiday shapes, those trees get me every year. But wait, what the hell is a happy food? Or a sad food?" His voice is laced with suspicion.

"It's pretty simple, there are foods you eat when you're sad, and foods you eat when you're happy."

I can tell he's trying his best to understand.

"Okay..." he hedges, "but you're eating peanut butter cups either way, so? How is one sad and one happy? I can see eating peanut butter cups being happy, and broccoli being sad, but not both types of the same food being in different categories."

"Ever seen *Pirates of the Caribbean?*" I start, and I can tell he's got whiplash from this conversation again.

"Yeah, it's one of my favorite movies."

"Great! You know the part when the guy says that the rules are more like general guidelines?"

He nods.

"That's the same thing for food. Mini peanut butter cups are sad because you can sit there with the whole bag and get lost in unwrapping them one by one until the bag is empty. Plus, chocolate is just kind of a sad food. The full-size ones you have to savor and enjoy because you're likely to only have two of them. You eat them when you can appreciate them."

He looks at me like he's solving a puzzle, but I think he's slightly amused. "I think that sort of make sense, but I will absolutely be tossing out random foods at you to see where they fall on your food spectrum."

I roll my eyes but smile all the same. "It's your turn to ask a question, and it cannot be about food."

"Ugh! But what if I wanted to know what your death row meal would be?!"

A laugh catches me by surprise. It tumbles out of me, loud and silly. I can't contain it, and I don't want to. Rivers makes me drop all my inhibitions, I don't ever feel like I need to hide myself with him. It's a nice change from how I feel at school most days.

"Okay," I amend. "You can't ask questions about if food is happy or sad. Other food questions are allowed."

"Great. What's your death row meal?"

"Easiest answer I'll ever give you. My mom's teriyaki flank steak with twice baked cheesy potatoes. A nice-cold Squirt soda, and to finish, a homemade chocolate chip cookie with extra-large chocolate chunks. Yours?"

"Sounds like you've thought about being on death row. Suspicious. My meal is also an easy answer," he starts. "A bag of mini peanut butter cups, because if I'm eating a death row meal, I'd be sad, and that's the only sad food I know about."

The older kids go quiet on the trampoline, which makes Rivers and I curious about what they're up to. We both jump down from the monkey bars and walk toward it, as everyone else shuffles around to make room for us.

I lay back on the trampoline and stare up at the stars, keeping my hands in my pockets, and everyone else does the same. The trees tower around us, but the sky is clear and dark, helping us easily spot Orion, the Big Dipper, and the Seven Sisters. It's peaceful, and the trampoline makes all of our bodies gravitate to the middle, keeping us warm.

Rivers is right next to me; he's so close I can feel his breath in my ear as he takes in the expansive sky. Forest tells June something about the zodiac constellations and when they're visible, but I'm not paying attention. I feel small and vulnerable like this, but not in an uncomfortable way.

I've always been a sky watcher, even as a little kid. My mom used to find me on the deck during the summer, just staring up, trying to find Venus or the moon. One time, in fourth grade, my teacher offered extra credit if our parents sent in a note saying that we watched a lunar eclipse. I made my mom drive me around trying to find the best viewing location, and then stood there, still as a board, mesmerized by the randomized alignment that allowed me to witness the moon turning crimson right before my eyes.

Around me, I'm vaguely aware of movement on the trampoline, but I'm so wrapped up in the stars and the sound of the crickets chirping, I barely notice. Eventually, my leg twitches, and it's not until I go to scratch my ankle that I realize Rivers and I are the only ones still out here.

"Where'd everyone go?" My head swivels around as if they might reappear.

"Inside to play Rock Band, but you looked really comfortable, and I didn't want to leave you out here alone."

I feel bad that I was so oblivious: he's been out here, sitting with me in silence the whole time.

"I'm sorry you were just sitting here...I just..." I tuck a piece of hair behind my ear to cover my embarrassment. "I get easily distracted by the sky." I sit up, wrapping my arms around myself. It's getting really cold, but I don't want to go in quite yet. It's kind of nice being out here with just Rivers for company.

He laughs, good naturedly. "That's okay, I've never been great with naming stars. Do you have a favorite constellation?"

"Yeah, it's the Seven Sisters," I say, pointing to a small cluster of stars.

After a minute, Rivers says, "Mine is Orion."

We take in the sky together for a while, finding planets and other constellations. "Hey," Rivers says as if he's just remembered something. "What did you think about 'Pork and Beans'?"

The safety of the darkness has me feeling braver than I would be during the day. "Honestly, when you and Trevor were talking about it, I thought you were joking. Almost like you were giving me a crap song as a joke or something."

"Shit, I'm sorry, Quinn. I didn't mean to make you feel that way. I really do love that song."

"No, I know. I knew you were being serious once I listened to it. I really like it."

"You do?"

"I do." Deciding in this moment that Rivers really is a person I can tell things to, I continue. "I like how it's a song about not caring what people think and that they used that title kind of ironically."

"Yeah! Because when you hear 'Pork and Beans' as a song name, you kind of already judge it because it's weird. And then you start to listen and realize what it's about and feel like crap for doing the exact thing the song doesn't want you to do."

"Exactly!" I laugh. I don't think I've ever had a friend I can be this honest with, it's nice. "Rivers, I..."

I hesitate to tell him how much fuller he's made my life by being my friend. I don't want it to be weird, but going from a person who has spent most of my life contentedly alone to a person who watches the stars with someone who makes me feel seen for the first time feels significant. He looks at me expectantly, no look of judgment on his face.

"I just want to say that I'm really thankful for you. I've sort of spent most of elementary school and the first part of this year alone, but with you, I...I guess you're the first person I've ever felt like I can talk to or laugh with outside of my family, and I'm...grateful."

"I'm your first friend, Quinn?" He sounds hurt for me.

"I've had people who I talk to in passing, but no one that I've ever really joked with or invited over."

"Why? You're not socially awkward; you're actually a lot of fun."

"I think I just don't like being the first one to say something? Like I'm afraid I'll put myself out there and people won't like me. It's easier to be alone than to be hurt, you know?"

He holds up his pinky finger to me. "Well, I promise to never leave you alone."

We latch pinkies when I hear footsteps walking towards us from the bridge and see the light catch June's blonde hair.

"Are you guys going to come in soon? You're gonna freeze to death!"

We laugh at her observation. She isn't wrong, but we make no move to go back inside. She moves closer to us so we can see her instead of just hear her.

"I'm serious, you need to come in. Our parents will kill me if you guys get frostbite or something."

We start to move when June pulls out her digital camera. "Hang on, stay there." She raises her camera and points it our direction. "Rivers put your arm around Quinn."

We look at each other, slightly unsure.

"Come on, it won't kill you. I just want a picture of you guys for my scrapbook. I'll title the photo 'The Long Haulers' since you stayed out here so long."

June is always taking pictures, and not just of herself like a lot of teenagers do. She takes pictures of Liz and me, Mom cooking dinner, and everything in between. I finally relax now that I know she wasn't implying anything. Finally, we laugh and scoot next to each other. Rivers puts his arm around me and leans his head toward mine. I do the same, putting my arm around his waist and lean into him, smiling while June snaps a few shots.

Once she's done, and walking back inside, Rivers and I put our shoes back on and start toward the bridge after her. "So, what is it, Quinn Clark?" I hear Rivers behind me.

"What's what, Rivers Thomas?" I make my voice sarcastic so he knows I'm rolling my eyes without him even seeing.

"'Pork and Beans'."

"That would be a song."

"Nope."

"What do you mean nope?" I turn to face him, and look up at his eyes, confused.

"I mean, it's not a song." He pauses for a beat, amping up the suspense. "It's a happy food."

I consider this statement and decide I agree with him, not that I'll tell him that. I want to hear his justification.

"What makes it a happy food?"

"Well apart from me thinking about pork burritos which are always happy because Mexican food can never be sad..."

I'm agreeing with him completely so far.

"I think it will always make me think of you now, and you make me happy too."

I blink down to the ground and bring my hand to the back of my neck, feeling exposed as the blush coats my skin. He puts things so plainly that it catches me off guard, but I also crave his honesty. I find the smallest amount of courage within myself.

"I think you may be getting the hang of this."

"I think so too." How does he match me beat for beat all the time?

He smiles, and it's the first time I notice he has a dimple. The butterflies in my stomach erupt, and I lose my will to contain them.

It's this moment that I realize I'm officially crushing on Rivers Thomas.

Shit.

Chapter Five

Now

"Mom, hurry up! We're going to be late!" Wyatt's voice carries through the house like she's been at a concert for the last two hours and isn't aware of her own volume.

"I know, I'm just grabbing earrings and I'll be ready!" She ambles into my room and lays back on my bed, acting as if we're three hours late to the Fall into Fall Festival that goes from four to eleven...it's three twenty-seven.

"Can I walk around with my friends when we get there? I'm old enough to do that, right?"

I try not to let my heart feel the sting of her pulling away little by little; I know it's good for her and Sawyer to cultivate greater independence—especially in this new town, but I'd be lying if I said it doesn't sting.

"Yeah, that's fine. Let's just walk the loop once together so we can scope out where things are when we need to meet up later, okay?"

She agrees and heads out to the car, only for Sawyer to come into the bathroom and watch me put my shoes on.

That's motherhood for you.

"Hey, bud. You ready to go?" It's been a week since the P.E. incident, and though the swelling has gone down a lot, the color of his bruise is still pretty nasty and greenish.

"Yeah..." He trails off, and I get the sense that he wants to say something but is trying to find the words. I find it's best to just give him time to sort out his feelings instead of probing him with questions like I do Wyatt. "Mom, would you really be okay if I went out for wrestling?"

His question catches me off guard; I've never inhibited them from going after what they want. Why has he been so funny about this? "Of course. Why did you think I wouldn't I be okay with that?"

"I don't know, it's just...kind of similar to jiu jitsu, and I didn't want to make you sad or remind you of Dad."

Understanding dawns; when Sawyer was younger, he got into jiu jitsu, and after Preston died, he stopped going. Not because I asked him to, he just said he didn't want to anymore. It's only now I realize that he stopped going because he thought it would be too painful for me, not for him.

Fuck.

"Sawyer, you listen to me right now." I gently place my hands on each side of his face and notice every freckle over his nose as I look into his green eyes that mirror my own. "It is not your job to protect my feelings. It is your job to live your life in the way that you want to, while being and doing the best you can. If you want to wrestle, wrestle. If you want to go back to jiu jitsu, I will sign you up on our way to the festival. But do not, for one minute, keep yourself from things you love because of me, got it?"

"Got it," he says, while the corner of his mouth curves upward.

I pull him into a hug, which he (shockingly) allows. "I love you."

"Love you too, Mom." He leaves the bathroom and walks out to the car where Wyatt is now honking the horn to get me to hurry up.

I grab my Kindle; June said she and her husband have plans tonight, which is sort of shocking given their estrangement the last few years, and Dani has to handle something with her asshole ex-husband, Brad. I've known him since middle school, but he latched onto Dani our junior year. Rivers hated him almost immediately. I'm sure I'll wander through the booths of this festival, but I want a book to escape into if the kids decide they want to be there late, and the Kindle gives me options.

The parking lot to the Goodman Brothers' grocery store is mostly full, but I find a spot, and we meander over to the festival. It's only the first week of September, but the town gets a little eager when it comes to a change in season. It looks like everyone has shown up. It's nice being back here like this. As a kid, I sort of hated how small Pine Grove made me feel—everyone knew everyone, and because of that, everyone knew your business. It's how my parents found out I was not at the movies with Dani when I was a junior and instead at my boyfriend, Justin's house; and how my parents found out that Rivers and I had skipped school once to go to the lake. Now though, it feels like having a community of people that want to support me; it's comforting.

"...and then maybe we can get a funnel cake before I go meet up with Marley and Addison?" I've missed at least ninety percent of whatever Wyatt just told me, but I nod along and allow her to lead the way.

We walk up to a carnival game where you hit moving inflated balloons with air soft pellets. My aim is notoriously bad, and Sawyer and Wyatt poke fun at my inability to hit the balloons as they destroy them with ease on either side of me.

"Mom, how are you this embarrassing?" Sawyer laughs so hard he has tears coming out of his eyes.

"Every hero has to have a weakness. Hand-eye coordination just so happens to be mine."

"Yeah, that and anything related to numbers," Wyatt chimes in, and I bump into her hip with my own.

"You two are talking a big game for a couple of kids who don't even know how to locate the laundry bin!" I take a deep breath and fire at a red balloon, popping it. I jump up and down and do a victory dance, mortifying my children further which fills me with glee. When I'm finally handed my prize, a six-inch creeper from Minecraft, the kids launch their much bigger prizes at me to carry as they walk toward the funnel cake truck. The smell of fried dough mixed with the sticky sweetness of the powdered sugar is intoxicating.

"Three funnel cakes with powdered sugar please," I tell the young woman working in the truck. None of us have ever liked the add-ons to funnel cake; Preston used to call us Puritans, which the kids didn't understand but I always thought was funny. He liked to heap on as many toppings as the plate would allow, and I'd tell him he might as well order a slice of pie before he'd steal some of the plain cake and joke that it was his palate cleanser.

The kids sit at one of the picnic tables facing the festival as I set their plates down.

"Mom, isn't that the eye-doctor?" Wyatt calls back to me.

I see Rivers making his way through the crowd of people toward the funnel cake truck, and once again my breath catches in my throat. He's wearing dark wash jeans and a Rolling Stones t-shirt, and I can't make out what it is completely, but it looks like he has a tattoo peeking out from under the sleeve. God, he's gorgeous. He's with a man I vaguely recognize who is a little shorter than he is, but I can't think of his name.

"Uh, hello? Earth to Mom? I said isn't that the eye-doctor?"

"Sorry, yeah, that's him."

"He didn't call you, did he?" She looks at me as if she's trying to decide if he did call and I kept it from her, or if he really didn't call me.

"He hasn't called; I would tell you if he had."

"Dick," she mumbles.

"Wyatt!"

"What? He is! He said he would call, and he didn't."

I'd be lying if I said I wasn't the tiniest bit disappointed, but it's only been a week, and he probably feels weird about calling too. It's not every day you run into your ex-best friend after not seeing them for what feels like a zillion years.

Just as I think we're going to put this to rest, Sawyer stands up and cups both hands around his mouth like an amplifier. "HEY! DR. THOMAS!"

Rivers turns to look over at us, and I feel my face go up in flames of embarrassment.

"Sawyer! What are you doing?" I seethe. Everyone warns you what it's like to have newborn babies. *"You'll be so tired,"* they say, or *"Yep, they keep you on your toes!"* but not one fucking person tells you that teenagers act like it's their goddamn mission to humble you whenever they see fit.

"I'm gonna call him out, obviously," Sawyer starts. "WHY DIDN'T YOU CALL MY MOM?"

"Sawyer. Sit. Down." I speak through gritted teeth; it looks like half the festival is looking in our direction. "He doesn't need to be called out! He's a grown man. He can decide if he wants to call me."

"Nuh uh," both of the kids reply.

"He said he would call you," Wyatt starts.

"So, we want to know why he lied," Sawyer follows up.

Rivers talks to the man he came with, then approaches the table and smiles at us, like being called out by name in front of the whole town for *not* calling me is just like any other Saturday around here. "Hey, Quinn. Sawyer, how's that eye?"

Sawyer crosses his arms, while Wyatt raises her eyebrow at him like he's the most unimpressive thing she's ever seen.

"Why didn't you call my mom?" Wyatt begins, attitude lacing every word.

"I went out of town last week for an optometry conference in Phoenix. Unfortunately, they didn't give me a plus one." Rivers smiles, like he knows they can't be mad at him for having a prior engagement out of town.

"Last I checked, phones work in Phoenix," Wyatt chirps.

Rivers's previous calm gives way to looking slightly panicked, which only serves to heighten my own embarrassment.

"A girl who doesn't mince words; I like it. I didn't call because I was scared your mom wouldn't answer the phone or would say no if I asked her out. Does that answer work for you?" He looks at Wyatt, and she nods. "Now, Sawyer, how's the eye?"

"It's alright," he starts, embarrassed by his display. "Sorry I yelled at you."

"No hard feelings, protecting your mom from terrible men used to be my job. I'm glad she has you guys now."

"Whoa, now, I did not need protecting from terrible men, thank you very much," I start.

"Tage, Benson, Justin, Trevor." He lists them out on his fingers as he smirks. "Do I really need to go on?"

"First of all, Tage and Benson were one date a piece; second, Trevor was not a terrible guy, we just worked better as friends, and you know that. And third, do I need to remind you about Katie?"

"Katie was nothing, and you know that. She was just jealous that you were everything she couldn't be." He's smooth, I'll give him that.

"*A-hem*." Wyatt clears her throat, looking back and forth between us, and Sawyer's eyebrows are nearly to his hairline. I almost forgot they were here.

"Any other questions?" Rivers looks at my kids like this conversation should clear up any confusion they've had over why he hasn't called.

Wyatt and Sawyer look between each other, communicating silently like they always have. I remember the first time I saw it happen. They were two and three, and it was pouring rain outside. I was making cookies, and it was too quiet—a tell-tale sign that something is amiss when it comes to toddlers. I looked around for them, and found them by the back door, looking at each other and locating their rain clothes so they could go splash. It was fascinating, but eventually they were ready to go and ran out to jump in the puddles. It's been their language of choice ever since. Eventually, they both nod and face our direction.

"What's mom's favorite movie of all time?" Sawyer asks him.

"*The Wedding Singer,*" Rivers answers automatically. "And she'll watch the airplane scene twice because that's her favorite love song."

"What's her favorite flower?" Wyatt fires off.

"Dahlias, but she will almost always answer roses because dahlias aren't always in season."

"What color roses?" Wyatt clarifies.

"Anything but yellow, because yellow roses are for sick grandmas—or so she says." He motions toward me.

The kids confer again, this time for longer, and I mouth *"I'm sorry"* to Rivers so he knows I didn't put them up to this.

As they deliberate, I think about his answers and justifications—they're all right of course. It's something I've always loved about him. He's never been interested in surface level responses. He wants the reason behind the answer, even in school. In math, he'd always ask what an equation was used for in practice; in music he'd pose theories about why a certain word was used over something else. My attraction to him always extended to more than his appearance; his mind carried equal hold over me.

"What's her favorite moon phase?" Sawyer says.

"And why," Wyatt follows up, incredulous; they think they have him with this question—it's written all over their smug faces.

Rivers laughs at this, and I hide a smile behind my hand. They don't know that Rivers was the only other person with me when I declared my favorite phase. They don't know that we were holding hands under a blanket when he asked. They don't know that the glance Rivers shoots in my direction or the cocksure lift of his brow tells me he's thinking about all the nights we spent under the stars just like I am. "The waning crescent because she thinks it looks like a smile, and the waxing crescent looks like a frown."

The kids look at each other, surprised like they didn't think he'd answer that correctly. Eventually, they've gathered all the intel they need to make a decision about Rivers's moral standing. "Okay, you passed. Anyone who knows the moon thing really gets her," Wyatt tells him.

Rivers chuckles to himself. "Well, I'm glad I passed, and I'm glad you know your mom that well. The moon question was a good one."

"Thanks." She smiles, tucking her hair behind her ear.

"We're going to go hang out with our friends now, but we'll meet you back here in a few hours, Mom?" Sawyer speaks for both of them.

"Oh, that's what you're doing? You're not even going to ask?"

"Please, we know you brought your book to read. Don't act like you're not itching for us to go away for awhile," Wyatt says.

Rivers laughs.

"Alright, alright. Go have fun, call me if you need me, and meet me back here in three hours." I hand them each some cash, and they scurry off, leaving me alone with Rivers.

"Sorry about that, I didn't know they were going to interrogate you...or yell at you for not calling me."

Rivers bats his hand through the air like it isn't a big deal that my kids just subjected him to an inquisition as he comes to sit down next to me. "It's fine, they're protective. It's sweet. And I'm sorry I didn't call, I planned on it, but I really was at a conference, and I really was, am, nervous."

"It's okay, I didn't expect anything."

"You should expect it from me; the only one holding me back from setting something up is me. And only because I don't want to fuck it up before it can go anywhere." He looks down to his hands, then casually shrugs his shoulders. "Besides, I like to keep you on your toes."

His shoulder bumps mine, and the contact makes me dizzy. "You okay?"

"Yeah, I just...I didn't expect to see you here. It's nice."

He rests his hand on my knee, a gesture so common between us in a past life it shouldn't make me jumpy. He's done this a thousand times, in a thousand places. It's familiar and foreign in tandem, and my feelings about it are equally convoluted. His palm is cool compared to my leg, but the weight of his hand and the stroke of his thumb feels like he's setting me on fire, and I never want it to stop. His hand skates higher up my thigh, and he must hear my breath hitch. He looks at me with a heat in his eyes I haven't borne witness to in years, and I want nothing more than to keep it there.

But then his phone rings, startling us apart.

"Sorry, Quinn, I have to take this." He stands up from the table, and I lean my head back toward the sky, trying to get myself under control. Rivers's voice is hushed but urgent; it sounds like something serious that I don't feel right eavesdropping on. Don't get me wrong, I love hearing other people's drama, but Rivers isn't a stranger, so it feels invasive. I get up from the table and walk toward the car to put the kids' prizes away, then snap a picture and send it to Sybil.

> The furries have escaped! img.png

> Sigh. I guess I'll have to get rid of all these litter boxes now.

I snort, thinking about how at least once a year a parent would start a rumor that the school was putting litter boxes in school bathrooms for students who identified as furries, and inevitably, all hell would break loose. They were never in the bathrooms, of course; parents just always leapt to conclusions like a jaguar on its prey.

Once I'm back in the festival, I wander aimlessly through the booths of games and people selling items for their small businesses. Things from homemade jewelry, to dreamcatchers, to cheese. I catch sight of a booth with rare books and bring a copy of *Little Women* to my nose, breathing in the smell of old, worn pages.

"Ah, some things never change," a deep voice says next to me.

I turn to look at the speaker and am momentarily stunned.

"Trevor?! Oh my God!" I throw my arms around him in a hug. He's massive, and handsome, and it feels like seeing a ghost. I haven't seen him since his parents got divorced my junior year and he moved from Pine Grove with his mom. "How are you? What are you up to these days?"

"I'm doing really well—I'm actually working in the film industry now."

"Just like you always wanted; that's great! Are you living up here again?"

"Yeah, I moved back two years ago. It's a bitch of a commute down to Hollywood, but at least my head is clear when I get home, and I live close enough to Rivers for us to still hang out." He rakes his hand through his messy brown hair. He always looked like a surfer to me, but it suits him now.

"How's your mom?" I didn't know until a few years after they spilt that his dad would beat the shit out of his mom. From what I understand, it happened for years, but when his dad hit his little sister, his mom finally called it quits.

"She's doing great—happy. She's remarried now, and volunteers at the battered women's shelter. How are you? I heard about your husband, I'm so sorry."

"I'm doing okay. The first two years were the worst, but I feel like I've gotten to a good place now. I just moved back here with my kids for a fresh start." Trevor and I tried the dating thing as teens a year or so after Rivers and I became friends, but it was always so platonic and almost felt more like we were siblings than we were a couple. I've missed him.

"I'm glad you're doing well. Have you seen Rivers since you moved back?"

"Yeah, last week. We ran into each other unexpectedly, and I actually just saw him about an hour ago. He was with some other tall guy?"

"Was he wearing a shirt with rubber ducks on it?!"

"I can honestly say I don't remember, but feel like that's something I should remember," I joke.

"That's Theo!" Trevor sounds delighted. "We were all supposed to meet up to try the new fall lagers the brewery came out with, plus I have to hunt down my mom's favorite pumpkin cheese."

"Well, don't let me stop you! I'll see you around?"

"Definitely," he agrees. "Let's meet up for a drink or something. I need to fill you in on my dating woes!"

We hug goodbye, and then I'm left to my thoughts as I wait around for my kids. It's so nostalgic being back here, surrounded by people I used to know but don't anymore, in settings I used to live vibrantly in, and somehow feel like a completely different person now. I wonder what younger me would think if she saw me sitting here in Pine Grove, widowed with two kids, at Fall into Fall, after flirting with Rivers freaking Thomas.

I sit down on a bench and pull my phone out, to text my mom. She and my dad are on a cruise to South America right now, but I wish they were here so I could sort through this with someone.

> Love you mom! Hope you're having fun.
> Call me when you're home. I need some
> Diane wisdom!

I pull out my Kindle, opening to the newest Fredrik Backman book, and let the noise of the festival swirl around me as I fall deeper and deeper into my novel. It's my favorite way to escape reality, immersing myself in worlds with fictional characters who help me heal and grow through their own adventures. In my line of work, getting students to fall in love with reading is arguably the most difficult part of my job. There are so many distractions with social media, video games, and streaming services, but every year I have at least one student who realizes the magic of a book and comes back for more. It makes it all worthwhile. Mostly.

After a few hours, I stand up to go meet the kids back at the funnel cake truck. Rivers is gone, but his answers to the questions the kids asked still make me blush. It takes a special kind of man to remember a woman's favorite flower—especially if he's only purchased them for her once, and nearly two decades have passed since the topic was discussed. Dani is going to lose it when I tell her about *that* conversation.

"Hey, Mom!" Wyatt and Sawyer walk up together, and I give them each a hug which they abruptly shake out of.

"Have fun?" I ask them.

"Yeah, we both had a bunch of friends here. I saw Keegan, too. He's so cute." Wyatt sing-songs like she's in love, and Sawyer rolls his eyes, not a fan of his sister crushing on his new friend.

We make it to the car and listen to "Cruel Summer" by Taylor Swift for Wyatt's pick and "Lose Yourself" by Eminem for Sawyer. I showed him the song on a run once because it's great for keeping the right cadence, and now he's fully immersed into rap music, which I'm trying to view through a lens of poetry and not expletives.

Parenting is a balancing act.

***

Later that evening, I go into Sawyer's room to say goodnight. He's got *Percy Jackson* out, and I wait for him to get to the end of his page. "Did you have fun tonight?"

"Yeah, I really like it here. Kansas City was too big to do any stuff like that."

"I agree, that's one of the perks of small towns." I smile.

"It's weird that Wyatt has a crush on Keegan." He looks down at his hands, like he's embarrassed to be talking about feelings with his mom.

"Why?"

"I don't know, he's my friend, and he's also kind of her friend? Isn't that weird to like your friends?"

I think about Rivers and I being two kids, two best friends, and never knowing how to broach the subject of our feelings with each other.

"I think it's only weird if they make it weird. Liking your friends is probably the smartest thing to do because you like who they are as a person before you find them attractive."

"Like you and Dr. Thomas!" Wyatt shouts from across the hall, and damn her for calling me out *again*. "Oh! I forgot!"

I hear her rummaging through the pile of dirty clothes in her basket.

"Did you like Dr. Thomas when you were young?" Sawyer looks at me with questions in his eyes that neither of us are ready to talk about.

"I did, but Dr. Thomas and I didn't handle things the best. We kind of always pretended our feelings weren't there."

Wyatt finally comes into Sawyer's room with a piece of paper in her hand, and Sawyer perks up. "Oh yeah!" he says. "I forgot about that too!"

Wyatt extends the paper to me. "Dr. Thomas gave this to us at the festival. He said he tried to find you, but he couldn't. He was also with some guy who said he knew you and to tell you that he found the cheese?"

That would be Trevor.

I gingerly take the note, trying to decipher if they've read its contents. His handwriting is messy, but still legible, and even though the message is short, I feel my cheeks heat, and the corners of my lips turn up.

Quinn,

   I hope you're not creeped out that I still know all your favorite things, but how could I ever forget? Sorry about the phone call.

Sawyer and Wyatt,

   I'm assuming you're reading this too because I was once a teenager and would have done the same thing. I hope you know I will definitely be calling your mom—thanks for calling me out in front of the whole town.

      P.S. A waning crescent does look like a happy face (:

Chapter Six

Now

A pples, check.

Bananas, check.

Whole wheat crackers, check.

My grocery list seems eternal as I walk through the aisles after work. I leave it on the fridge so the kids can add to it throughout the week, but sometimes I have to make some executive decisions. Case in point: I'm not buying gummy bears, gummy worms, peach rings, *and* fruit snacks, regardless of what they may want.

Sawyer and Wyatt would eat me out of house and home as toddlers, constantly asking for snacks in any given setting. It didn't matter if we went on a walk, went to the trampoline park, or were just driving in the car, the question was always the same: "Did you pack a snack?" Nowadays, they pack their own lunches and grab their own snacks when they're hungry, but it's still a ton of food. Sawyer would eat a whole bag of apples a day if I let him.

Once I check that everything on the list has made it into the cart, I start piling it all onto the conveyer belt. That's one thing about small towns—self-checkout is viewed as treason, so even though the last thing I want to do is make small talk with the cashier after wrangling middle schoolers all day, it's my only option.

"Oh, these grapes look delicious!" she starts.

"Yeah, coming into that season."

I pull out my phone to check my messages while I have a minute. There's a text from Wyatt about English homework and one from Dani about a new creative way she's imagined having her ex-husband castrated. To Dani, I write:

> I don't doubt that a beaver *could gnaw off his balls, but I'm pretty sure they're herbivores. Find a new method (;

Then I fire off a message to Wyatt:

> I can help you when I get home. Just checking out now. Are the chores done?

Finally, I pay the small fortune for my groceries and wheel my cart out to my car. I try to be intentional about where I put my eggs and bread, and as I am arranging, another text from Dani buzzes in.

> Ugh. Screw you for taking away my fun. What about an otter? They're carnivores right?!

I chuckle softly to myself. We've been joking about Brad's castration for more than ten years, and it never gets old. Ever since he cheated on Dani—thrice—he's been on our shit list.

Once I put my cart back into the cart return (because I am not a terrible person, despite the text messages I send to my best friend), I put the key in the ignition and...nothing happens. My car won't start. The more I think about it, the more I realize this is probably supposed to happen given I haven't replaced my battery since before Preston died. Quite frankly, the fact that it lasted five years of Kansas City winters is pretty remarkable.

I pull open my phone to call my dad but remember almost as swiftly that he's still on the cruise with Mom for three more days. I get out of the car and pop the hood, a silent plea to passersby, imploring them to *please help me jump my car* in a public setting, and start to locate the number to my insurance company should I need roadside assistance for the jump.

Going back to my trunk and rummaging through my groceries to get to my emergency kit, I locate my jumper cables and bring them around to the front. Hopefully whoever comes to help will know which cable goes where. I can't ever remember if red goes on the positive or negative charge. I'm ninety-two percent sure my dad taught me a rhyme to remember it once, yet here I am, still unsure.

I hear a cart wheeling behind me and turn around to find Rivers approaching. His face lights up with a smile, and I'd be lying if I said it didn't melt me on the spot. "Hey, Quinn! You need a jump?"

"Yeah, for now. I probably need a new battery, honestly; I haven't replaced it in at least five years."

"Oh, I can help you with that, too. Here, let me take a picture of what type of battery you have. We can walk across the street to Mike's, and I'll install it for you here."

"You really don't have to do that. If you give me the jump, I can just bring it into Mike." Mike's auto shop is slightly more than just across the street, it's probably a quarter of a mile from here, but he's the best mechanic around. Even off the mountain with all their fancy equipment, Mike could tell you what's wrong with your car just by listening to it.

"But then you'll have to pay Mike to do it when I can just install it for free. Really, it's not an inconvenience. It'll take fifteen minutes."

It'll take more than that with the walking.

I still don't protest; I want to spend time with him even if it's just a walk up to Mike's.

He unloads his groceries into his car and then starts walking toward Mike's shop, leaving me with nothing to do but follow him.

"I hope you don't have a bunch of frozen food in your car." I know I shouldn't feel embarrassed about my car battery, but I don't like inconveniencing people.

"Oh, just three gallons of ice cream, no big." He turns his smile at me, trying to put me at ease. "It's fine, Quinn. I'm serious. If I had stuff that wouldn't last, I would have just jumped your battery."

The weather is perfect today with a light breeze that sends the smell of the pine trees through the air. Rivers guides me toward the inside of the sidewalk by my lower back, the barest sliver of my skin is exposed to his touch. Despite the warm air, I get goosebumps.

"Good to see your reaction to that is still the same," Rivers's deep voice rumbles next to me.

"Some things never change," I answer.

"Yeah, they do. I'm just glad that's not one of them," he whispers in my ear as we walk into the shop, and it makes me wonder what other reactions my body would have to Rivers's touch.

To his kiss.

I'm getting ahead of myself, but I feel hungry for him.

Rivers talks to Mike in the shop and locates what I need. After I pay, Rivers hefts the battery onto his shoulder, and we make the walk back toward Goodman's.

"So, you just have all the tools you need in your car to change a battery?" I look at him skeptically.

"I just keep the basics in there, but yes." He breathes out a soft laugh. "I should have everything I need."

When we get back to my car, Rivers busies himself by loosening up the battery and getting the new one hooked up, while I admire his handiwork. His muscles are so defined, and I can see more of his tattoo. It looks like it might be something nautical, but I can't be sure from this angle.

"What's your tattoo of?" I ask, trying to make it seem like I'm more curious about the art and less about how he looks like he's been sculpted from stone.

Unfortunately, the arrogance of his stare tells me he sees right through me. "Maybe some day you'll find out," he says.

I can't stop my tongue from grazing my lip. Hearing Rivers be so openly flirtatious is fun and sexy, and dammit, I'm drooling over him.

Literally.

Rivers laughs at me, then gestures towards his tool kit. "Can you hand me the socket wrench?"

I bend down to pick it up, and mistake the distance, thinking he's further away than he actually is, when I hand it to him. Our hands brush by accident; leaving me to feel a shock of electricity so strong, I'd think it was from the battery if I didn't know better.

Rivers skates his thumb across the back of my hand as we look into each other's eyes. "I've missed you, Quinny."

I swallow as he turns my palm upward, entwining our fingers. It thrills and emboldens me, so I step closer to him. "I've missed you too," I say, moving closer to his body. "But you're slacking on the job," I whisper close to his jaw. Despite every instinct in my body begging me to stay this close to him and see where it gets me, I extract my hand from his, and take a small step back, a teasing smile playing on my lips.

"You're trouble, Quinn Clark. Pure trouble." He turns back toward the car and tightens the battery into place, then jumps into the driver's seat to start the engine. I feel the curve of my smile; it's been so long since I've had someone to banter with, let alone do all the stuff that I don't know how to do.

Rivers gets out of the car and closes my hood, then looks at his watch. "Damn. Twenty-six minutes, guess I underestimated this taking up such a huge chunk of my day." He bumps me with his shoulder.

I shrug my shoulders and say, "It's your three gallons of ice cream, not mine." We hold each other's eyes, our smirks matching. "Thank you, Rivers. You really didn't need to do all of this."

"I didn't want you to get home, and it not start again. Your parents are out of town, right?" Sometimes I forget that our parents are still friends despite everything that happened.

"Yeah, they come back in a few days. I would have called roadside assistance or asked my neighbor or something, but I'm glad it was you."

"Me too, it's nice seeing you around town like this—bumping into you unexpectedly. It feels like old times."

"We never bumped into each other; we were always joined at the hip!" I joke, but it's true. We weren't ever surprised to see the other because we were always just there, existing together as one entity. It was more of a surprise to be without the other person than it was to bump into them by accident.

"That's fair, but I stand by what I said. It's been really nice to see you back here." He leans against the hood of the car taking me in. I move next to him and lean my head on his shoulder. It feels like home. Rivers puts his arm around my shoulder, drawing lazy circles with his fingers on my shoulder that only serve to increase the pounding rhythm in my chest.

We stay like that for a minute before Rivers says, "I better take off. Trevor, Forest, and my friend Theo are supposed to come over. I'll see you around, Quinny." He squeezes me closer to him before he walks away.

"See you, Rivers."

As he drives away, I'm left feeling giddy, something I haven't felt in a long time. Maybe somehow, Rivers replaced two dead batteries today.

***

"God, Mom, what took you so long? We're starving over here!" Wyatt's attitude immediately greets me when I walk into my house, weighed down by all the grocery bags because I refuse to make two trips.

"Sorry! My car wouldn't start so I had to wait for someone to help me and then we just replaced the battery in the parking lot." I choose to omit the fact that Rivers and I talked for a few minutes more than was completely necessary.

"Who did you find in the parking lot of the grocery store to replace your battery? Isn't that like...way more than road-side assistance covers?" Sawyer enters the conversation, and of course, because he's Sawyer, knows the common ins and outs of roadside assistance.

"Uh, Dr. Thomas, actually. He was grocery shopping too and happened to be there."

"Wow, what a co-ink-a-dink," Wyatt says with a grin, and absolutely zero inflection.

"Yes, well, I asked him to jump it so I could come straight home, and he insisted that he replace it so that I didn't need a jump in the morning, and so I wasn't charged by the mechanic."

"Sounds like a gentleman." Wyatt's eyebrow now looks like someone has a fishing hook through it, it's arched so high, and I swear she sounds more like Dani than she does me at this point.

"It was very nice of him," I deadpan. "Now go get your dinner, it's in the car." The kids squeal with delight as they discover burgers from "The A" in the front seat—the best burgers in town since I was a kid. I had intended to make a grilled chicken salad tonight, but with the delay, I needed something quick.

Sawyer and Wyatt scarf down their food so voraciously, it startles me. As small children, they ate like birds and were basically vegetarians until Preston died; he'd be shocked to see them eating a quarter pound of beef each, now. I don't know what changed with their eating habits, but sometimes it feels like they realized that being picky was a waste of time if everything they knew could be over in an instant.

"Wyatt, what was your English question? I want to make sure I get to that before Aunt Dani comes over." She rummages through her backpack as I put the dishes into the dishwasher and emerges with a cluster of disorganized papers.

"I just don't understand the difference between a main idea and a theme. How are they not the same thing?" She lets out an exasperated breath as she sits back down in her seat.

It's a question I get often at the middle school, but with my own kids it's easier to explain because I know their interests. "Okay, let's pretend you're having a party. The main idea would be what type of party you're hosting. So, for example, it could be a movie party, a birthday party, a graduation party, an end of summer party."

"Okay..." she starts.

"But the theme is how that party is decorated. We might know it's a birthday party, that's the main idea, but the theme is how that party is presented. It helps us make meaning out of the party. Like when I turned thirty my birthday party was all black decorations. Why would I do that?"

"To show that you were sad about turning thirty?"

"Right! It was silly, but it helped my guests know how to interpret the party."

"Fine, but how does that work for books?"

"Let's use *Harry Potter* because we're both familiar with it, yeah?"

"Sure," she obliges.

"If I asked you what *Harry Potter* is about, what would you say?"

"Hmmm." I can tell she's thinking about the series as a whole and not just an individual book. "Probably, that it's about a kid who finds out he's a wizard and goes to a magic school and has to defeat a bad guy."

"Perfect, that's the main idea. But what does *Harry Potter* teach us? What do we learn about *ourselves* from the story?"

She looks at her hands, with her brow furrowed. We've talked about some of these things before, but Sawyer predominantly drove that conversation. I'm interested to hear what she comes up with on her own. "Probably that good can overcome evil, and that good friends are more important than popular ones. Oooh! Also, that we get to decide what we become."

I smile at her, proud that she's gleaned this much. We read the books religiously before bed, just like I used to do with Liz. Even still, the kids demand we watch every movie through the month of July in honor of Harry's birthday—some years we even attempt to recreate Hagrid's cake.

"Those are the themes, baby. What we learn for ourselves because the book keeps pointing them out to us—just like decorations at a party—is the theme, or what the author wants us to know."

"Okay, that helps. Mrs. Slater wants us to write down themes and main ideas for all of the stories we read this year, but I wasn't sure how to do it. Especially when we start *The Hunger Games* next week."

I give her a hug, thankful that there are still things she needs me for, when Dani and Will walk into my kitchen. Will is the same age as Sawyer, and even though they've known each other since they were small, all three kids have become close friends since moving home. Dani breathes heavily, carrying a stack of papers so thick it looks like she robbed Office Depot on Black Friday.

"Hey!" She smacks the papers down onto the table and the whole thing shakes beneath its weight. "Sorry, I needed to print all of these, but since I'm using them tomorrow, I need them stapled before class starts!"

This is one of a long list of reasons that I would not be cut out to teach elementary or intermediate school. Where I teach the same lesson four times a day, Dani has to teach at least a dozen different lessons once a day—it makes her planning way more intensive than mine.

I pull out my stapler and sit down, ready to help. "Dani, it's the first month of school. How do you have so much already?"

"Elementary school, babe. We're still making 'get to know me' posters and sharing all about our families."

Wyatt leaves the kitchen with Will and snacks in tow while we get to work assembling Dani's packets. There is not one single surface of my table that isn't covered by her shit. I snap a picture and send it to Sybil, laughing.

> Thank God we went into secondary and not elementary. img.jpg

Dani glances at me after I hit send. "Sybil?" she asks.

I first introduced Dani to Sybil when Dani and Will came out to visit during the summer. We left the kids with Preston and headed out to get drinks at a pub designed for showcasing women's sports and accomplishments. Little did I know they would hit it off and give me shit for the rest of my days. After Preston died though, Dani used Sybil to keep tabs on me when she wasn't there. I wouldn't have made it if they didn't stay in contact.

"Yeah, just sent her a picture of the whole deceased rainforest," I tease, pointing to the mass of paper.

"Yeah, yeah, you secondary teachers have it made," she says as she rolls her eyes.

Sybil responds with a GIF of a man worshiping exaggerat-edly. I show Dani, but all she does is scoff. I take in a breath, summoning the courage to tell her about my last two encoun-ters with Rivers. "So, guess who replaced my car battery and held my hand in the Goodman's parking lot today."

Dani abruptly stops stapling and looks up at me. "Quinn Clark, you better spill all the fucking tea right now, or I will call the man *myself* to get the details."

I laugh and go through the ordeal while Dani's jaw hangs agape looking at me. "So, you're telling me that he refused to just give you a jump because he was *worried*, had the tools in his car to replace it, AND you felt sparks from an accidental touch that made it to the second base of hand holding?!"

"That is...correct, yes, but there's also more."

"SPILL IT, QUINN!"

"I also saw him at the Fall into Fall a few days ago..."

"AND YOU'RE JUST NOW TELLING ME?"

"It's been busy! And you've been dealing with Brad!" We let out a faux barf in unison. Brad is an involuntary gag reflex trigger for both of us.

"Fuck Brad, bitch! Tell me about the festival! Starting with what you were wearing—I'm imagining him drooling over you in my head." This is one of my favorite parts about Dani—even in our mid-thirties she still hypes me up just like she did when we were young.

"I was just in straight leg jeans and black body suit, nothing fancy."

"You mean the black body suit that snatches your waist and makes your boobs look like you're a solid ten years younger?" Her eyebrow quirks.

My cheeks blush; Dani was with me when I bought the bodysuit, and she's not wrong, it looks great on me—especially when I'm tan. "That's the one. The kids were also there, and they asked him a bunch of questions trying to decide if he knew me well enough to talk to me."

"Shit, what'd they ask him?" She laughs as her stapler jams up. She yanks it open trying to get the deformed piece of metal out with her fingernail.

"Some basic stuff: favorite movie, favorite flower. But they did their silent communication thing and asked him about my favorite moon phase."

His answer, and maybe more importantly, the confidence with which he gave his answer, has made me swoon for days.

"And let me guess, he gave the perfect answer because he was the only one there when you decided that?"

I move over to my purse that's hanging by the door and root around for what I'm searching for. Finally, I procure the note that Rivers gave to my kids for her to read. "What am I going to do Dani? He still hasn't even called me; all of our meetings have just been chance encounters. He said that he was nervous to call, but I feel like I haven't given him a reason to be afraid."

"You mean besides the history you two have where you ran away from him the second he was finally honest?" I glare at her. "Look, maybe he doesn't want to seem desperate, maybe he really is nervous, or maybe he just needs time to figure it out. What I do know is he's giving you a lot of good signs, and Rivers has never wanted to hurt you, Quinn. I say if he doesn't call within the week, then the next time you see him, you ask for his number and show him that you're really interested."

I nod, her words a soothing balm over my fears. "Okay. Now, tell me what Brad fucked up this time."

"UGH! Well, you know how he promised Will that he would take him to Velocity Vortex as a birthday gift back in *JUNE*?"

"Do not tell me he backed out. DO NOT TELL ME HE BACKED OUT!" I slam my hands down on the table enraged, sending papers and packets flying.

Brad has been notoriously bad with Will's birthday from the start. The day he was born, he went to the bar like a jackass.

Actually, for the last twelve years since Dani left, he's managed to forget to call on Will's actual birthday—despite it being tattooed on his fucking forearm. He usually just calls in the general time frame, but never the day of.

"He backed out."

"What's his excuse this time?" He's made countless promises to Will for his birthday but has never made good on any of them. Will is a good kid, but like any kid, it sucks to have a dad that doesn't give a shit about you—and who shows it so obviously.

"He bought a new Camaro and had to use the money for a down payment."

"Sounds about right. I guess we're taking the kids to Velocity Vortex, then?" I will quite literally do anything for Will. He's practically a cousin to my kids at this point—even if it means enduring an amusement park during the hottest part of the year.

"Yeah, I guess we are."

Chapter Seven

Then, Eighth Grade

T wo months and six trampoline nights later, I can say with ease that Rivers Thomas is my best friend. No one understands me better than he does or makes me laugh as hard. Unfortunately, Rivers Thomas is also my first real crush, and I don't have a single clue how to deal with that.

My parents decide to spend the Fourth of July with the Thomases this year, and I'm honestly so excited. I have on a new pair of denim cut-offs and a red t-shirt with my white lace up Converse. It's the first time that I've been aware of how I look, wanting to look nice for someone else.

We climb into Dad's truck and head into town where we'll meet the Thomases for lunch at Big Rick's Barbeque truck—the greatest hot dog in maybe all of America. The Jamboree Day celebration is in full swing by the time we arrive for lunch, and parking is a nightmare. Dad parks on Pine Shade

Drive, a little less than a block from where Big Rick always parks the food truck, and the butterflies threatening to explode out of me over seeing Rivers increase with every step.

I see Lianne first and wave at her, signaling to both our families that we've connected. She pulls me into a hug then leans back with her hands on my shoulders to look at me. "Well, you look about as cute as a button, Quinny Girl!" And I feel my cheeks flush.

Rivers moves to stand next to me, with his hands in the pockets of his blue jeans. The white shirt he has on makes his tan complexion nearly glow. Bryan is half Hawaiian so both Forest and Rivers tan naturally during the summer. He looks good.

"Hey," he says. "I have a bone to pick with you."

I chance a glance is direction as we walk toward the food truck. "Oh yeah?"

"Yeah. I listened to the song you brought up, God what was it?"

"'The Sweet Escape'?" I ask.

"Yes. Quinn, someday, someone is going to torture someone by asking you to make a mixed CD for them." He bumps me with his elbow and I feel myself shiver down to my toes at the contact. I throw my head back in a laugh, masking the feelings I'm fighting against.

"I'm thinking that I can't trust you to suggest music, Quinny."

"Alright, alright. You can recommend music, but it's up to me to decide food groups. For example," I gesture to Big Rick's truck, "this is a happy food." Big Rick cross hatches the all-beef hot dogs, letting the edges get crisp over the open flame. The buns are always toasted so they have a nice char, and I don't know what Big Rick puts in his special sauce, but it's the perfect amount of spicy and sweet—almost like a cross between a barbeque sauce and ketchup?

"Of course it's a happy food! We only get it once a year!" We asked Rick why he only comes out for Jamboree Days because he could make a fortune opening a restaurant or investing more into the food truck to make it a full-time gig, but he said people only want hot dogs on the Fourth of July.

I think it's a load of crap.

Our dads find a table, but it's so cramped for all of us that Rivers and I are practically fused together down the entire length of our bodies. I can't say I hate it, but I swear he has to hear how hard my heart is thrumming in my chest.

Eventually, when we're all stuffed to the brim, we start walking toward the Thomases' house through the endless rows of booths and stalls.

"Quinn, check that dog out!" Rivers points to a poodle whose fur is colored to match the Fourth.

"Gross!" I joke. "It's a dog, not an accessory!"

"St. Patrick's Day! Easter! Halloween! The options are endless"

"To look super tacky? No thanks. I don't care if it costs two-hundred dollars every time you dye it—ugly is ugly."

"Oh, ye of little imagination." He bats his eyes and looks like he's performing.

"It's little faith, pal, and I can imagine doing it, I just can also imagine how ugly it would be." He shoves me a little bit, and the water I'm carrying spills down my front.

"Shit. Sorry Quinn."

"Rivers Thomas! Keep those words out of your mouth," Lianne bellows from somewhere behind us.

He and I laugh at each other, and I dump the excess water over his head. "Yeah, Rivers Thomas, keep those words out of your mouth!"

"Ooooh, I'm going to get you, Quinn Clark!"

I run through the crowd, knowing he's chasing after me but refuse to look back and lose speed. I try to bob and weave, but Rivers is fast and there're too many people for me to move as efficiently as he does. Eventually, he grabs me from behind, so his arms go over my shoulders and I grip his arms in a sort of reverse hug. "I don't have anything to douse you with right now Quinny, but you better watch your back."

He removes his arms, and I feel everywhere he isn't—it leaves me feeling empty somehow.

As we walk through the stalls toward the Thomas's house, Liz finds a stall selling mood jewelry. Even though I know the stones change based on temperature, the concept is still fun. I find a ring where the stone is the center of the sun and Liz settles on a turtle necklace. Rivers buys something too, but he has the stone in his grip so I can't see what it is.

When we get back to the Thomas's house, my dad and Bryan pull out cornhole in the front yard, then force Rivers and me onto their respective teams. Rivers throws first for their blue team and, of course, sinks it right through the hole.

"Nice job, Rivers. That's three points if we can keep Quinn from scoring." My dad snagged Rivers for his team and left poor Bryan with my bad aim. Bryan is intimidating to people who don't know him—he has to be with his profession—but underneath the tough and gruff, he's honestly a giant teddy bear. Rivers's next three bags are misses, and I can't tell if he does it on purpose because he knows I'm terrible at this, or if maybe he's as bad as I am.

"Alright, kiddo, take a deep breath and do your best." Bryan's voice is gentle, and I follow his instructions but over-shoot it, and my red bag falls off the back of the board. "It's okay, try again, you can do it." I throw again, but instead of overshooting, I undershoot it by at least two feet. Bryan seems unfazed though, so I pick up my next bag, and give it a little more than my second attempt. It lands on the board in a miracle of miracles, and I jump up and down in delight. Bryan roughs up my hair then gives me a high five before I pick up my fourth bag. I set my shoulders and take a deep breath like this is for the Olympic gold title of cornhole and not round one on the Fourth of July.

Extending my arm backward to get just the right swing on the bag, I look at Rivers, and his smirk devastates me. I smile back, release the bag, and it falls right through the hole—a perfect shot.

The score at the end of the game is seventeen to twenty-one, and I decide to apologize to Bryan since it was mostly him keeping us alive after my (semi) impressive first round. "No need to apologize, Quinn. It's a game! And you were a good teammate!"

"Thanks Bryan," I give him a side hug since he's like my second dad and walk back into the kitchen before heading out to the porch. Lianne is making a plate of snacks to take out with her as I wash my hands. I quickly grab the sliding glass door for her, noticing her trying to balance the plate, her drink, and the handle all at once.

"You're a lifesaver, Quinny. Be a doll and go grab the extra blankets in Rivers's room? The breeze is making it chilly out here now."

I race up the stairs to Rivers's room, spotting his ship, *Ashes of Atlantis,* on the dresser. The Thomas's house is older so their linen closet is inside of Rivers's room. He's sitting on his bed, fidgeting with something in his hands that I try to make out but can't quite place.

"Hey," I say as I walk in.

His eyes look up, startled, like he's been caught red-handed.

"What do you have there?" I ask him, pointing to the thing in his hands.

"I got these for us today." He opens his palm, and I realize it's the mood jewelry from earlier. Each bracelet has what looks like a goose on it, which feels like the most random animal imaginable.

"Geese?" I laugh.

"They're swans," he says. "They're one of the only animals that are friends for life."

He puts mine on my wrist, but even with it all the way tightened, it's too big. I loosen the strings, takeoff my shoe, and slip it over my ankle. The charm glows against the tan I have on my leg—it's pretty. "I haven't exchanged friendship bracelets since fourth grade." I'm joking but feel touched. I like that Rivers views me as a person he wants to keep around.

"Well technically, that's a friendship anklet now," he gestures toward my foot.

"Oh yeah, I was way off," I say, bumping his shoulder.

"Come on, Quinny." He pulls me to my feet and helps carry the blankets downstairs.

***

"Please Dad!" Rivers says as the sky starts to grow darker. We're trying to convince our parents to let us walk down to the bonfire on the lake to watch the fireworks, which is where most of the kids our age are.

Our parents all look at each other, trying to decide if we can be trusted to walk the quarter-mile down the road to the lake.

"We both have our cell phones," I say, trying to tip the scales in our favor.

Eventually, they agree to let us go over there, but we aren't allowed to walk back; my dad will come pick us up after the display since the Fourth of July always brings out crazy driving.

We're both so excited about the prospect of having some time alone and time without parents that we're almost out the door holding snacks and water before Lianne stops me. "Quinny, won't you be cold?"

Almost as soon as she says the words, Rivers runs up the stairs, then descends with his favorite blue zipper sweater extended to me and covers himself with a gray hoodie I've never seen before.

"You sure you don't want to wear your favorite?"

"I'm good, the zipper is probably easier for you to put on without messing up your hair or anything." He's always considering things I haven't thought about myself, and it's one of my favorite qualities about him—that he's observant.

"Thanks, I promise to treat it respectfully," I say in mock reverence while placing my arms through the sleeves and zip it up. I know Rivers is bigger than I am, but I guess I didn't notice how much bigger until I see that my fingers are covered by the sleeves, and the bottom of it hits the very top of my thighs. It smells like him and feels like he's hugging me. I like it.

We leave the house as the sky grows darker. Pine Grove isn't like the suburbs where neighborhoods have streetlights. We rely completely on the light that the sky offers us, which is exactly why, when Rivers looks over at me with a playful grin, like he can't believe we convinced our parents to let us wander out alone, I trip over a crack in the pavement and fall to the street.

"Shoot! Are you okay?" Rivers extends his hand to me and pulls me to my feet.

"Wow, that was embarrassing. I didn't see that at all!"

"It's because you were lost in my eyes." He says it wistfully and brings his hand to his heart, making me realize I'm still holding his other hand from when I fell. I'm suddenly aware of every nerve ending in my palm. I know Rivers notices it too, because his thumb skates gently over my own, and I swear to God I hear my heartbeat in my ears. Can he hear my heartbeat in my ears? Do I mention it? Do I ignore it? This is uncharted territory, and I am so disastrously lost. "Want to see how my parents hold hands? People think it's super weird." He's trying to calm my nerves without letting go of me, and I realize that this is the first time I've ever actually held hands with a boy on purpose. The night he warmed my hands up outside at my house was over too quickly, and now it feel like he's trying to extend it.

"Sure, but I feel like there's only two ways to actually hold hands?"

"Maybe if you're a loser, which you're not. Here, give me your pinky." He slots my pinky between his pointer and middle, and just like that, we fit together like Legos.

"That's surprisingly comfortable." I give his hand a squeeze, and he returns the gesture as we slip into silence. It's not awkward, I'm holding hands with my crush, sure, but I'm also holding hands with my best friend, and that removes any awkwardness I feel.

The bonfire is already ablaze when we walk across the street to reach the shore of the lake, still hand in hand when someone flings an arm over my shoulder, and I see the other is over Rivers. Trevor stands between the two of us smiling.

"Rivers and Quinn! Glad you guys were able to come!"

"Hey Trevor!" I give him a quick one arm hug because my phone is in my other hand, and Rivers seems tense when I stand back next to him.

"Quinn, how is training for cross-country going?" The thing I like about Trevor is that even though we just became friends, and only because Rivers is friends with both of us, he's never made me feel weird for crashing their duo. He's always made me feel like we're friends regardless of Rivers being around.

"It's pretty good?" It comes out like a question. This is my first time ever really doing a sport, and Trevor was on the cross-country team in seventh and eighth grade. "I like that I'm really only competing against myself." It's a vulnerable thing to say, but it's true. I've never been really competitive, so it's nice that I can choose to be the best all around, or just the best version of me without it impacting too much.

"Damn. I like that," he says. "Let me know if you ever want a partner. Those long runs can get boring after a while."

"I will. Thanks, Trevor."

Rivers stands with his hands in his pockets watching us go back and forth, like he isn't sure how to insert himself into the conversation. It makes me uneasy since he's always so easy to be around.

"Let's go find somewhere to buy drinks?" Rivers looks at me, seeking approval. I'm not thirsty, but I'm desperate to pull him out of whatever funk he's in.

"Sure." We start walking toward what looks like a tent. "Hey, have you ever used an iTunes card before?" It's a silly thing, but I swear I'm the only teenager that isn't keeping up with technology.

"Yeah, a few times." He turns to face me as we get in line. "Why? What do you want to buy?"

"I heard a song on the radio today and I can't stop thinking about it. I asked June if I should just download Limewire to my mom's computer but she basically said she'd kill me if I did that."

He laughs, and I assume it's because he knows why Limewire does not belong on my mom's computer. I don't know how it works, I just know it's how most people get music. "Yeah, don't do that or your mom will be buying a new computer. What's the song?"

"I honestly don't know. I think I'll know it when I hear it? But it's by a new girl named Taylor Swift and she sings about Tim McGraw."

"I'll look it up. Hopefully it's better than your last recommendation."

After a while, we're just enjoying the heat of the fire, talking, and laughing as the crowd whirls around us. I see girls from school walking around in groups, and adults my parents know eager to keep an eye on the kids. For the longest time, I've felt out of place in the world. I've never had a core group of friends, or someone to save me a seat in the crowd—not until Rivers at least. He gave me all of that.

"I don't like not seeing you every day," Rivers whispers it in my ear so no one else can hear him. "Texting you isn't the same as seeing you."

"I know. It'll be so much better when you're able to drive. Hey, did you hear our parents booked our spring break trip for the year?"

"No, where are we going?" He crosses his fingers and begins to mutter, "Please say the beach, please say the beach."

"Yosemite," I crush his dreams in one word.

"The hell? Like John Muir Yosemite?" His response is not dissimilar to my own when my parents broke the news.

"The very same," I confirm. "At least we'll have each other? And my mom said June and Forest are both coming."

"I don't need anyone else, Quinn." I feel Rivers put his hand in mine again and I'm filled with a longing for him that I'm scared we'll never fulfill. "Just you."

Our hands stay connected in secret the rest of the night. We don't want anyone to see, but we also don't want to acknowledge it ourselves. We hold onto each other when we sit down in the sand, underneath the peak of my legs, and we find each other when a group of us play hide and seek.

Where he goes, I go.

Where his hand is, mine is.

And when he skates his thumb back and forth across my skin, I see stars. I have to squash this. I don't want to.

When the first fireworks go off, my body flinches. I've never liked really loud noises like this. Rationally, I know we're far away from where they're being lit, but the noise is still unnerving. Rivers scoots closer to me on instinct. "Is it the noise that bothers you?" he starts.

"Yeah, just overwhelms me a little."

"Here." He extends his headphone ear bud to me, and I put it in, wondering what he's queued up. Teitur's "One and Only" comes on, and I'm momentarily stunned. I told him about this song months ago, and how it always makes me think of fireworks because of *Aquamarine*. "You said you wanted to have her water tower moment." His mouth quirks in a small smile that makes me burrow into his protective side.

That night, when I crawl into my bed, I sleep in Rivers's sweatshirt, tracing patterns on my palm as if the magic that seeps out of him has been left on my skin.

***

Three weeks after the Fourth of July, June's final box is packed up for her move to Vermont, ready to be shipped off. She leaves in three days, and even though I know I'll be okay, it feels like I'm on the edge of everything changing beyond my control.

"You know you can still call me, Quinny. Anytime you want!" she says, pulling me into a hug.

"I know, but you'll be busy doing stuff. How long is your cosmetology program again?" June has always loved doing hair; it's a good fit for her.

"Like two years? But I think I can do it faster if I stay longer at the school to get practical hours."

"So, you'll be gone at least two years?"

"Well, I'll come home to visit for holidays and stuff, but yeah. I'm not planning on staying out there, I just want a change for a little while. See what it's really like to be on my own." We've been over this, but I still don't understand why she chose Vermont of all places. She could move to L.A. like Forest and still have to figure everything out for herself.

I sniffle into a tissue, and she pulls me into a hug. "It's not forever, Quinn."

"I know, but who am I supposed to talk to about stuff?"

"What stuff? You hardly talk to me about stuff as it is!" She laughs. She isn't wrong, but ever since Rivers and I started hanging out, it feels like I'm on the cusp of having things to share.

"Like how Rivers and I held hands walking to the lake a few weeks ago!" I blurt it out before I realize what I've done. I was trying not to make it a huge deal, but I haven't stopped thinking about it, and how much I want it to happen again. He hasn't even brushed elbows with me since that night, and I don't know what to make of it.

June's eyebrows rise, and I can tell I've surprised her with my confession. "You what? Why didn't you tell me? Are you guys like together?"

"No?" It comes out like a question because I don't know what we are, and I don't know how to figure it out, and for crying out loud, I don't know how to navigate any of this without her.

"Quinn! Why didn't you say anything?!"

I fall forward dramatically onto my crossed arms.

"Okay, do you want to be together?" she asks.

I want to be with Rivers which I know sounds silly because I'm only thirteen, but I can't help it. "I do, but I don't know if *he* does." I lie down on her bed and cover my eyes with my arm, groaning in exasperation.

"Okay, chill. Have you asked him about it?"

"Yeah, sure June. Because that's how we communicate at the middle school. Very transparent with all of our feelings to each other." My tone is so sarcastic, it would make Adam Sandler jealous.

She must realize what she's asked of me; she sits down on her bed and rests her hand on my calf. "Okay, that's fair. What if you write him a note? Just tell him how you feel about him and see what he does."

"You think that could work?"

"It seems more on brand for middle school, if that's what you're asking. But if I could have it my way, I'd just have you ask him the next time you see him."

Talking to him about it face-to-face is out of the question. I can talk to Rivers about most things, but this feels too big and leaves me too vulnerable to risk it. "If I write him a note, could you get it to him?"

"Yeah, we're stopping by there on our way out of town so I can say goodbye to them." She means Forest, but she won't admit that to herself.

Later that night, I sit down at my desk and stare at the piece of paper in front of me. I want to be honest with him, but not too honest—I don't want to scare him.

Rivers,

This isn't the normal way of talking for us, but it's the only way I know how to do this without freaking myself out. I'm really glad our parents forced us to go camping because it gave me a best friend I didn't know I was missing. You're so easy to be around and you never make me feel like I'm too much or not enough. I guess what I'm trying to say is that...I like you Rivers, and not just as a friend. I don't know if you feel the same way, sometimes it feels like you might. But I felt like if I didn't tell you I would miss out on something really special. If you don't feel the same way, it's okay. I still want to be friends. I just...wanted you to know.
--Quinn. P.S. June showed me a band I think you'd like. Look up Reel Big Fish.

The morning she leaves, tears pour out of my eyes that I have no control over—I'm going to miss her so much it hurts. She waves and holds up the sign for "I love you" as she and my parents pull out of the driveway headed for the airport.

Fifteen minutes later, my phone buzzes with a text from her.

I love you, Quinny! Your letter has been delivered ;] Let me know what happens!

But nothing ever happens. Rivers doesn't talk to me again for weeks.

Chapter Eight

Then, Eighth Grade

Two weeks after June leaves, I haven't heard a word from Rivers. Not knowing what he's thinking forces me to channel my anxiety into something else that's more productive. I'm training like crazy for cross -country now, which is how, half-way around the lake one morning in late July, I bump into Trevor, who is doing the same thing.

"Hey, Quinn!" he says, out of breath.

I pull my headphones out of my ears to talk to him. "Hey, Trevor. How far into the trail are you?"

"Only about half way, you?"

"Same," I say. "Want to finish it out together? I'll probably be slower than you so if you don't want to that's fine."

Trevor appraises me for a second before he agrees. "Yeah, but let's go at your pace. It'll help increase my endurance."

We run in tandem, only a few stints peppered with conversation about our running shoes or playlists we listen to that help us stay focused. It's nice having someone here with me; I usually do this alone.

The Goodman's parking lot comes into view, which is where my mom picks me up every morning.

"Damn Quinn! You're fast! I thought when you said you'd be slower that I would run a little more casually, but you're almost on pace with me!" Trevor says, out of breath.

I agree to meet him the next morning to run the whole three miles together, which turns into us going to get smoothies afterward, and then Trevor inviting me to watch a movie at his house.

"You're spending a lot of time with Trevor," Mom observes after three weeks of Trevor and I running together every day.

"Yeah, he's a good friend," I say.

"Did something happen with you and Rivers?" she asks. "Lianne says he's been a little distant since Forest left for college."

I try to decide how much to tell her. Mom has never made me feel bad for being honest, she's never made me uncomfortable, but I still wish it was June I was telling this to and not her.

"I wrote him a note confessing my feelings for him and I haven't heard from him since," I say through my quivering lip.

Mom pulls me flush against her in a hug. "I'm sorry, baby. Boys this age..." She breathes out a heavy sigh. "Even the good ones act like real dummies sometimes."

"I just want my friend back, Mom."

"I'm sure he'll come around sweetie. Just give him some time."

The rest of summer passes in a blur of runs, smoothies, binge listening to Taylor Swift songs, and longing for the one person who knows me better than anyone else. By October, Trevor and I are so close to dating that his friends have started calling me his girlfriend, but Rivers only talks to me when our families are around, and because of that, I've never felt more alone.

***

Eighth grade is the worst.

I have no friends here. My boyfriend is at the high school, and most of the time it doesn't even feel like he's my boyfriend. Rivers barely speaks to me. And to make matters worse, I finally started my period. At school. While I was wearing *light colored jeans.*

By the time spring break comes around, I'm beyond ready. Being this isolated at school is starting to take its toll on me. I'm such a loner, I've been eating with the school librarian, Mrs. Corinth, for months, and no one has even noticed that I'm not there.

Trevor and I have been together since the beginning of October, and it's April now. Six months isn't bad for a middle school relationship, but considering we rarely speak to each other, haven't held hands, or hugged since the bonfire, do we even have a relationship?

It's just so weird talking to him without Rivers there. It feels like I got into this relationship because it was convenient, not because it mattered to me. All I want is the distance between Rivers and me to be fixed, and I don't know how to. Which honestly says a lot about my feelings towards Trevor, or lack thereof, I guess.

We're driving up to Yosemite in the RV now with the Thomases trailing behind us in theirs. I'm in the middle of making a playlist to listen to while we bike around, trying to keep the songs peppy even though I feel shitty. I'm not sick, just emotionally spent. Right after I add "Last Night" by Motion City Soundtrack to my playlist, my phone buzzes with a text.

> Trevor: Quinn? Are you going to talk to
> me at all over break?

Shoot. It's almost one thirty in the afternoon and I haven't even said hello to him today—the worst part is I didn't even realize it because I was so caught up thinking about spending a week with Rivers and how weird it's going to be. I don't respond to him, trying to give myself time to think when it dawns on me that June is sitting a few feet away from me.

"June? Can you come back here?" I call up to her where she sits on the couch.

She moves back to sit next to me at the table and glances at my laptop. "Motion City Soundtrack is great! Look at you growing without me."

"Honestly, I'm not. Rivers showed them to me; along with practically everyone else I like."

"That's not true, you showed me that Taylor Swift girl and I've been obsessed ever since." When June came home from school for Christmas we found her CD at Target and loaded all the songs onto my iTunes—we did have to scrounge Limewire for "I'd Lie" though. I don't understand why it didn't make the final cut; it's my favorite song.

"Fair."

"So...what'd you need me for?" I almost forgot I called her back here to talk about Trevor—there he goes slipping my mind again. God, I'm the worst.

"Oh, right. Um, how do you breakup with someone but...nicely?" I figure that's what I need to do here; I have only platonic feelings for him.

June pulls her head back to look at me; she's confused. "Who the hell are you breaking up with? Since when did you get a boyfriend?"

It occurs to me now that because Trevor and I have done virtually nothing that would signify us as being in a relationship apart from the night we watched a movie at his house, I haven't even told my sister—my closest confidant—that we started dating. "Trevor Samuels? We started dating in October."

"OCTOBER? What the hell, Quinn?!" She lightly smacks my arm.

"I forgot to tell you, okay? Honestly, that should tell you everything you need to know about how boring the entire thing has been. We haven't even held hands!"

"Isn't Trevor one of Rivers's best friends?"

"Yeah, probably explains why he's said what feels like nine words to me the last six months." I hunch over the table, crossing my arms and lay my head down.

"Damn. Okay, so you want to break up with Trevor...why?"

"I don't like him like that at all, June. We got close training for cross-country, and we sort of jumped into it, but that was it. I haven't felt anything but friendly about him this whole time. He just texted me." I show her the screen and try to hide my embarrassment.

"Okay." She takes my phone in her hand and looks up towards the sky like she's seeking inspiration. Finally, she starts typing something out, and my anxiety begins to ebb. "How 'bout this?"

> Trevor i think ur really nice but i think we r better as friends. im sorry if this hurts u but i think its 4 the best

I take a look at what she wrote and fix the grammar: I can't let it stand as is. Finally, I summon the courage and press send. Trevor's text comes back almost immediately.

> I get it. I hope we can stay friends.

Relief hits me instantly, knowing that I don't have to pretend anymore and that he still wants to be friends with me; the only sadness I feel is that I let it go on for as long as I did. I text him back so that he knows that I want his friendship.

> I'd like that. Sorry Trevor.

My phone chimes again, and I assume that it's Trevor, but to my surprise I see that Rivers has texted me; my first from him in months.

> You broke up with Trevor?

I look at June who has her eyebrows raised at me, but decide there are some things my sister is privy to and others she is decidedly not. This falls into the latter category. She stands up when I turn my screen away from her. "Thanks, June." She walks back to her chair while I text him back; Trevor must have told Rivers right away.

I try and brainstorm what to text to Rivers. Is it insensitive of me to ask if Trevor is okay? Is it weirder to not acknowledge it at all? I decide to go with my gut. Trevor's friendship is important to me and I want to make sure he's not angry or hurt.

> Is Trevor okay?

He's alright. I think he knew it was coming for a while.

What makes you say that?

Well as he says it, you've never even flirted with him...

I guess I wasn't feeling it.

So why'd you date him?

He went after what he wanted...

...good to know. What are you doing? My parents keep trying to talk to me and Forest. It's driving us both nuts.

Making a playlist to bike forty five miles a day. Just added Motion City Soundtrack

No Reel Big Fish?

This is the only acknowledgement Rivers has made to the letter I wrote him.

> Relax, Quinn. I can feel you thinking through the phone. Add the song "Coffee Shop Soundtrack" by All Time Low. You'll love it.

> Hopefully June has it in my library!

It's too late to get the song if it's not already on my iPod. I scroll through my library crossing my fingers that it's in here and pray that whatever geniuses walk the Earth will find away for us to get internet wherever we are someday. I've never heard of the band, let alone the song, but I know it'll be my new favorite song in a matter of seconds if it's something Rivers suggests. By the grace of God, I have it.

I'm hooked immediately.

> WELL?! You have me on pins and needles here, Quinn!

> I have it.

> AND?!

> And I like it. A lot. You're way too good at this.

> (: See you up there, Quinny.

***

When we start approaching Yosemite Valley, June, Liz, and I have our jaws firmly on the floor. We live in the mountains, but never in my life have I seen anything more beautiful than this. The Merced River gushes, and the wildflowers are fully in bloom. I feel like I'm driving through a postcard. Out every window of the RV is a new sight that leaves me speechless. I know we gave Mom and Dad crap for choosing Yosemite of all places to take us on spring break, but holy hell. This is incredible.

We go through a tunnel that blocks our view for a few minutes and when we emerge on the other side, I think I might pass out. Peaks of granite jut towards the sky, and we're encompassed by the tallest pine trees I've ever seen. The water carves a path between the pillars of rock and out the front window, the double Yosemite Falls bursts. The drive through the valley feels slow and fast all at once and I am still astounded by what I'm seeing. I pull out my phone to text Rivers, needing to know if he's having the same out of body experience that I am.

> Are you seeing this?!

Holy. Shit.

***

When we finally get our campsites set up, Mom and Lianne immediately jump into cooking dinner. June, Liz, and Forest sit around the campfire, but I'm itchy to do something after sitting in the RV for so long, and I realize that what I really want to do is talk to my best friend.

I approach him while he's layering another sweater over himself—it's spring, but it's still cold here in the valley. "Hey, wanna bike over to that bridge we saw coming in?" He looks up at me with questions in his eyes.

"Yeah," he decides. "I'll convince our dads since yours likes me more than he likes you." He says it with his classic Rivers sarcasm that makes me feel like we'll get back to how we were.

"...just be safe, alright? Don't get close to the water; it's faster than you think. Stay up on the bridge." Bryan gives us this instruction, knowing we're two young teenagers—we're obviously going to get closer to the water.

I pedal lazily toward the bridge. It's not far, maybe a quarter of a mile from the campsite but far enough away that Rivers and I can have some privacy without our parents being suspicious.

Rivers gets there first, and we park our bikes in tandem. The water is loud, but not as deafening as it would be if we were near a waterfall. And the smell in the air is like breathing in a pine-scented candle. I'm sort of obsessed with this place.

The bridge itself is made of stone barriers that form chest high walls and are at least two feet thick. We each peer over the edge to take in the churning water below, and Bryan is right: the water looked deceitfully calm as we were driving, but this close, I can tell it's moving quickly.

Rivers climbs on top of the wall to dangle his feet over the edge, and I do the same. It's practically begging for us to sit here. We settle next to each other, not talking, though our hands rest between us. If I moved an inch, we'd touch.

"So, how's Freshman year been?" I don't know where else to start, but I've missed so much of this year with him that the most logical place feels like the beginning.

"It's been shit, Quinn. I haven't had my best friend at school or at home; and I've been plagued with trying to figure out if you and Trevor have kissed or not. How's eighth grade been?"

I bark out a laugh over his honesty. "It's fucking sucked." It's my first time ever saying the f word aloud to him, and he turns to me surprised. "I also haven't had my best friend at school or at home; I've been trying to figure out how to avoid having Trevor touch me for six months; and I ate lunch with the school librarian every day."

"I don't know how to do this with you, Quinn."

"Do what?" I ask him. That question could go at least seven different ways and have twice as many answers.

"This. I don't know how to be your friend and battle the constant need to want to touch you and be around you. I don't know how to be your friend and be okay with you dating people—especially people that I like and am friends with too."

"Well, I'm not dating anyone now, and honestly, it's been hard not being able to be close to you the last few months. I don't know how to do this either, but I know I can't do that again." And it's true. The last few months have been hell, I don't know how this friendship is going to look moving forward, but I'll fight to make sure we don't go back to whatever that was.

"I don't want to put rules up for you because it seems unfair, but can you at least warn me if you plan on dating anymore of my friends?"

"I won't date your friends again, that is something I can agree to as long as you extend me the same courtesy?"

"I wouldn't consider it anyways, but you don't have any friends for me to be interested in so..."

"Rivers! That's mean."

"No, that's honest. Why is that, Quinn? Don't you want friends?"

"First of all, I have friends." It's a complete lie; we both know it. "Second, the only person I actually want to hang out with goes to a different school if you'll recall?"

"God, next year is going to be so much better." I could not agree with him more; we're finally going to be at the same campus again and I feel so much lighter when I think about it. This year has been heavy. Between June leaving and this wedge between Rivers and me, I haven't felt like myself since last July.

"It really is! What foreign language do you want to take?" We're a year apart, so our core classes are going to be different, but we can try to line up our electives, and we talked about doing our language together last year.

"You pick: Spanish, French, or American Sign Language?" he asks.

"Honestly, Spanish sucks. I'm always terrible at the accent, and French only sounds good if you're from France. I say let's do Sign."

"I was hoping you'd pick that! When do you guys choose classes for next year?"

"Right after we get back from break, you?"

"Same, so we'll choose ASL 1. What other elective are you taking?" I've thought about this extensively, but I just don't know what to choose. I'm interested in a bunch of things but don't feel ready to commit to any of them.

"I don't know. I wish there was a class I could just read books in."

"You mean, English?" he quips.

"No, I mean like a book club. I don't want to analyze it, I just want to read it. I'll figure it out though. At least there'll be a chance for us to have Sign Language together."

Rivers holds out his hand to me like he always does. "What do you think this means?"

I clasp onto his hand. It feels like a second chance, and in some respects it is. It's felt like ages since someone has touched me, and I don't want to let go.

"I think it means we're friends again?"

"We always were, I just didn't know how to do that. Do you still have your friendship anklet?"

I pull up my pant leg to show him. "I never take it off. It's the only part of you I've had this year." I look down at our hands, avoiding his eye. I can let my guard down with him but only to a point.

"Quinn, you'll always have me. I know that last summer was weird, and everything with Trevor got weird, but I pulled away because I don't know how to be like this with you when you're with someone else. It's me trying to protect myself from getting hurt."

"I get it, but we have to figure it out because I can't do another year like this, and I need to be free to date people I want to date, Rivers."

"We'll figure it out. For right now, we're both single and we do know how to do this, so let's just enjoy the week." Our hands rest on his knee, I lean my head onto his shoulder, and despite being twenty feet in the air with our legs dangling over a freezing cold river, it's the most secure I've felt in months.

***

Rivers and I have returned to the bridge nearly every night when we get back to camp while our parents cook dinner. It's been nice laughing and being close with him again. I didn't know how starved for him I've been until I got him back and finally felt full. I'm trying to be honest with myself, in that, I know I'm still completely infatuated with him. Those feelings didn't go away, and being around him like this again makes me remember why I fell so hard to begin with. I don't want to lose him, but I don't want to kid myself into thinking that this is more than it is; this is how Rivers does *just friends*.

Forest and June are talking to both sets of parents and glancing at Rivers and me sitting on top of a rock the size of trailer. "What do you think they're talking about?" I nudge him in the shoulder.

"I don't know, but it looks like it involves us."

"Rivers! Quinn! Come down here!" my dad yells for us. We find our way down the rock without slipping and make our way over to the adults.

"You guys want to go hike to the bottom of the upper Yosemite Falls?" We had talked about going up there, but with Liz, it wasn't feasible; she's still too small.

"Today?" I ask, because it's already almost eleven thirty and we still haven't had lunch. That hike is supposed to be like six hours long.

"Yeah, we'll eat lunch and you older kids can head over there," Lianne tells us.

We race back to the RVs to scarf down some food and pack a backpack with snacks and water. As we're prepping our pack, my dad and Bryan lecture us about safety. While the beauty of Yosemite has gotten to each of us, two days ago in the gift shop my mom found a book titled *Death in Yosemite* that we all joked about at first, but once we opened it we saw that most of the deaths that have happened here were accidental and not people necessarily being intentionally reckless.

"Don't lean over the edge to get a better view," my dad starts.

"Don't lose sight of the trail. If you get off course sit down and call for help," Bryan follows up.

"Don't flip your kayak upside down while white water rafting—especially when you're close to a waterfall and see a moose!" Lianne yells it to lighten the mood, a call back to the book. Even so, we take what they say seriously. Yosemite averages twelve to eighteen deaths a year; we don't need to be part of that statistic.

Once we bike the three miles to the trail head, Forest and June remind us of the rules, and we come up with a plan to take turns carrying the backpack. It's another steep incline (like everything else here), and we need to preserve energy. The first two hours we feel fine; the trail is mostly dirt, and it's steep but at least it's in the shade. By hour three, we start to focus more on what's in front of us than the company around us. And by hour four, we're asking nearly everyone we pass how much further till the base of the upper fall. As we approach it, signaled only by the sound of twenty-four hundred gallons of water a second rushing over the side of a mountain, the trail becomes less made of compacted dirt and instead gives way to rocky terrain that's slick with water.

Eventually, the slippery rock curves around the mountain and the "trail" is about three feet wide with a sheer drop on one side. It's so steep that the only visible ground is at least three hundred feet below. Forest and June go first, showing us where to step and how. My anxiety spikes when it's my turn, and as I take my first step, my shoes slide on the rock, putting me off balance. Before I even know what's going on, Rivers's hands are on my hips, holding me steady. I feel my heartbeat in my ears, but he pulls me back against him. It's just us on this side of the curve as Forest and June wait for us around the bend. His hands are around my waist, and his breath is in my ear, and the feel of our breathing being so in sync is making my head spin.

"You are not allowed to fall of the side of a mountain, Quinn," he whispers against my ear.

"It's my shoes; they made me slip! I can't keep going, Rivers. I need to turn back."

"Absolutely not, you're going to do this, and I'll be right behind you. Let's just breathe through it."

He helps me steady my breath and I muster the courage to try again. "Forest!" Rivers yells over the din of the water.

"Yeah?"

"Quinn is headed your way, I'm holding her hand from back here, put yours out so she can grab it as she rounds the corner!"

I move my feet slowly, carefully placing my feet on areas of stone that are more textured than others. I clutch Rivers's hand, and then grab for Forest's with my other. It's only a few steps, but when I finally round the corner, I'm greeted with the most incredible view I've ever seen. I see why June and Forest weren't concerned with Rivers and I taking our time on that last corner—they were busy looking at this.

Ahead of me, the water falls in a surge of power that looks like a piece of white fabric blowing in the wind. Beneath it, the pool of water swirls into thousands of eddies that aren't visible from the bottom of the falls. It's...breathtaking.

"Holy shit," Rivers comes up behind me and rests his chin on my shoulder.

"So...this is great," June says, "but I'm fucking starving. Where are the snacks?" We all let out a laugh as she takes the backpack from Rivers and starts rifling around in it to pull out beef jerky, water, Snickers bars, and an apple for each of us. It's without question the best meal I've ever had up to this moment, and I think the same goes for everyone else too.

"That last bend was terrifying," Forest says as he takes a massive bite out of his apple.

"So sketchy," I agree. Rivers and I tell Forest and June what happened when I crossed the first time. My heart rate is still elevated thinking about having to do it again.

"On the way back, let's do the hand chain again. June and Quinn, you guys will go in the middle, Rivers and I will go first and last." Both June and I are about to protest, but Forest continues, "If you guys fall off the side of this mountain, your dad will haul mine and Rivers's asses up here to throw us off the cliff himself."

We sit overlooking the water for thirty minutes while we rest and eat. It's nice to joke like this with the four of us again; it feels like last summer on the trampoline. Once our legs are rested and our bellies are full, Forest finally makes us pack up and start our descent down the mountain. I thought we would make better time coming down, but it's so steep we have to go slow so it doesn't turn into a slide.

Our legs feel like Jell-O by the time we make it to our bikes, and the trek back to camp feels like a unique brand of torture. We've collectively decided to omit the part where I almost slipped to my death as we tell our parents about the hike. Their faces look like they regret letting us go up there alone as it is. I'm still shaken from earlier, and because he can read my mind, I get a text from Rivers a moment later.

Bridge?

We tell our parents we're headed to the bridge and sit through Bryan's spiel about not getting too close...again, then finally, it's quiet.

"You okay, Quinny?" I'm not sure why I feel like everything is too much, but I appreciate, especially right now, that he's always been able to read me like a book.

"I don't know? Everything just felt too loud."

"Are you okay after the mountain? When you slipped, I felt my stomach in my throat."

"Believe me, I did too. Thanks for holding onto me." I turn to face him with tears in my eyes; I didn't realize how shaken up I was until I was firmly back on the ground. Rivers pulls me into a hug, and I break down crying into his neck. He alternates between rubbing small circles on my back and lays a soothing hand over my hair; it's the safest I've felt all day.

"You're a really good hugger, Rivers Thomas." I mumble into his neck.

"Only for you, Quinn Clark."

"I'm serious, Rivers. Did you go to hug school or something? I've never been hugged this well in my *life*." My body perfectly curves into his, and his arms apply the perfect amount of pressure.

His laugh surrounds me, and it feels like magic to be this enveloped by it. "No, I did not attend hug school. But I'm glad to know I can add it to my list of special skills."

"Top of the list if I'm being honest." We're overlooking the water, but since we've been on our feet all day and my teeth are starting to chatter, I pull away from the hug and start to head toward my bike.

"Quinn." He moves toward me again, pulling me into another hug, and whispering into my ear like a confession. "When I said I was only a good hugger for you, I meant that...um..." I can feel him trying to find his words, and since the hug is as comfortable as the one before, I don't mind waiting. "I meant that sometimes it feels like I was made to hold you like this."

I swallow, unsure of what to say, and opt for silence.

"And even if we're only friends," Rivers continues, "I will hug you like this whenever you let me, because it makes me feel like I can breathe."

With that, Rivers pulls away, hops on his bike, and pedals back to camp. Leaving me stunned, speechless, and swooning.

Friends my ass.

Chapter Nine

Now

My phone starts buzzing as the last student leaves my room. It's a California number I don't recognize, but since the recent move, I'm inclined to answer. It could be any number of the companies and services I've set up in the last month and a half.

"Hello?" I answer, gazing over a grammar worksheet on compound sentences that I know I'm going to have to spend more time on. These scores are awful. The assignment is supposed to be a review, but students are notorious for brain dumping everything they've learned in previous years.

"Quinn?" Rivers's voice greets me on the other end of the line. I haven't talked to him since he helped me change my battery last week.

"Hey, what's up?"

"Does Pine Grove Middle School still release early on Fridays?" There's a hint of mischief in his voice that makes me smile as much as it piques my curiosity.

"It does…and why is an optometrist such as yourself familiar with the bell schedule of a middle school, you weirdo?" Sarcasm drips from every word, which Rivers has always been able to detect from me.

"Well for starters, a buddy of mine just started working there, and he told me about the bell schedule. But, I was also calling because my last three patients of the day canceled, and I wanted to see if you wanted to join me for a walk?" I can tell he's nervous, he always speeds up his speech at the end of his sentences when he's building up the courage to say something.

"I actually have to stay for my contracted time, and I'm sort of drowning in terrible middle school grammar worksheets that have to be graded…" He breathes out a sigh, disappointment echoing through the line until it's almost palpable.

"…But," I add on, "I'll be free in an hour if you want to meet me at the lake. We can walk the loop?"

"That would be great! What about your kids, are they good to be home alone for a while?"

A smile curves on my lips that he can't see; I love that he's concerned for their well-being.

"Yeah, they'll be good. Sawyer has cross-country practice after school and then he's going to June's house; and Wyatt has art club till four, then I think she was going to a friend's house to work on a project, so I should be free till six."

"Perfect, I'll see you in a bit then?"

"See you in a bit."

We hang up the phone, and I grade and record the work from today's classes. With each passing stroke of my pen, my heartbeat increases. I try to keep myself in line but feel the warmth of a blush tinging my cheeks thinking about meeting Rivers. This isn't a date, right?

It's just two old friends catching up, I tell myself.

Apparently, I did not move back to California, but instead to the land of delusion.

Oh, God, does Rivers think it's a date? By the time I've made it out of the school parking lot, I'm nearing cardiac arrest and decide to call Dani because what the *hell* am I supposed to do? She answers on the second ring.

"Hey, what's up?" I can tell she's also driving because there's a slight echo reverberating in my car—the elementary school gets out earlier, so she must be close to home.

"So, um, remember how I told you I ran into Rivers a few days ago?"

"Yes..." she answers, a note of suspicion lacing her voice.

"Well, he just called me to ask if I wanted to go on a walk with him, and I sort of said yes? And now I—" My speech is cut off thanks to Dani squealing like a piglet who just came in first place at the county fair and gets the trough all to herself.

"Ahhhhh! Oh, *hell* yes. I swear to God, I've been rooting for you two for like twenty fucking YEARS. Are you gonna jump his bones?"

"Dani!" I shout. "I am NOT jumping his bones; we are going for a walk!"

"Yeah, and then you'll go to dinner, and eventually give everyone who has known you two forever the ending we all expected."

My eyes well up with tears for more reasons than I can count. She must notice the shift in my mood because she says what she always does when I'm in a crisis: "Tell me the biggest thing first."

"Guilt, Dani. So much freaking guilt. What would Preston say?"

"That he wants you to be happy, Quinn. It's been five years; he wouldn't want you to be alone forever. And of all the guys to ask you out, Rivers is kind of the best case-scenario. That man has loved you since you were thirteen."

"He did a long time ago, that doesn't mean he does now."

"Maybe not, but it doesn't mean he couldn't eventually. What's the next big thing?"

I sigh, knowing what she's going to say before I even ask it. "Is it a date?"

Her guffaw into the phone tells me all I need to know.

This is a date, and I'm no longer a teenager able to pretend we are just friends or explain away the butterflies threatening to explode in my chest.

"The next big thing?" she asks me, and I can tell she's rolling her eyes over my lunacy.

"What do I wear?"

***

When I get home to look through my clothes at Dani's request, I'm immediately greeted by the last family picture we took before Preston died. We had taken the kids on a cruise to the Bahamas for spring break, and we look so blissfully happy. I'm tan, glowing in love, the kids anchoring us on each side. Preston's goofy smile looks back at me, and the deep, familiar ache in my chest resurfaces. There was no way for us to know that just eleven days after it was taken, he'd be gone. It's one of the few pictures I still have up in the house; not because I don't want to see him, I want the kids to remember their dad and all the joy he brought us—but I also don't want to be reminded of him and the loss we suffered every time I step into a room.

That constant reminder was one of the biggest driving factors of our move. We lived in the house without Preston for five full years before I finally decided to leave Kansas City and move back home to Pine Grove; it felt like the kids and I were stuck in a limbo of his memory that we couldn't escape.

My parents had encouraged me to come home much sooner, but I think to an extent the kids and I needed the time and space to be able to grieve before we cut ties and started fresh somewhere else. I think if we had left too soon, the new place would feel too empty without Preston as opposed to a new beginning that we all needed in our own unique way. It also felt like a natural time to start fresh now that Sawyer and Wyatt both started middle school this year with the way Pine Grove structures their school district—by having grades six through eight in the same building. Doing it this way gave them the chance to make new friends at the same time as all their peers, be in the same building as me, and have each other if all else fails.

A glance at the clock tells me I need to kick my ass into gear and decide on an outfit. I need to meet Rivers in twenty minutes and it's a ten-minute drive over to the lake. Lake of the Pines is small, all things considered, but the three-mile trail around its bank has been one of my favorite runs since I was a kid. It was the first place I learned about Stinging Nettle, where my sixth-grade teacher trusted us to make rafts for her to float on out of two-liter bottles and duct tape, and where I'd tell my parents I was going to run before I'd stop at Rivers's house and ask for water at the half-way point. His mom would always tell me to be careful and tell her when I got back safely to my car, just like my own mom would. I think after I ruined everything with Rivers, losing Lianne was one of the biggest heartbreaks I'd endured up to that point. Rivers's family was like my own, and I'd lost them all.

I settle on black leggings that accentuate my long legs, and a rust-colored cropped tank with a square neck that I've always liked the placement of for my collar bones. I wear my favorite running shoes for comfort and have my signature Chiefs hat that Preston always loved to help block out the sun. Despite moving back to California, I can't let go of my Kansas City patriotism regarding sports—even if it is painful to watch all these years later without him.

I swipe on an extra layer of deodorant, then jump back in my car and head towards the lake and the center of town. As I drive, Taylor Swift's "'Tis the Damn Season" plays through the speakers, and the words hammer in my chest like a drum. I allow the melody to fill the car, knowing I am about to go on a date with the man whose heart I singlehandedly obliterated eighteen years ago; leaving behind the man who singlehand-edly obliterated mine with his death in my rearview mirror.

***

Refusing to be a hypocrite who always harps on my stu-dents when they're tardy, I get to the lake five minutes before three—enough time to see that my make up has sort of melted off my face in the mid-September heat, and my hair needs a highlight; I'll have to call June to get an appointment soon.

Rivers's luxury silver Lexus pulls into the parking lot, mak-ing my Toyota Four Runner look like even more of a mom car than it already is. God, he looks good. Gray joggers that hug his thighs in all the right places, and a white Nike top accentuating his chest and arms. His tattoo peeks out just a bit from his sleeve, making his tan arms look even tanner. His facial hair has grown out a bit since last week, leaving him with the perfect amount of scruff. I feel butterflies swoop low in my belly and try to calm my nerves.

"Hey!" He turns around to find my voice and then opens his arms for a hug. When we were kids, we used to joke that nobody hugged better than us—and to a degree, I think we were right. We always knew exactly where our arms needed to be on the other's body and exactly how much pressure to apply to the squeeze. Stepping into his arms, I realize we haven't lost that particular talent; this hug is perfect.

"Hey, Quinny," Rivers's low timbre whispers the old en-dearment against my ear, and I can't help but take in his scent with a shiver. It's new to me; spicy with a hint of citrus, in direct opposition to his axe body spray and general teenage boy sweat from twenty years ago.

God, he smells incredible, his voice is sexy as hell, and the feeling of his body against mine? I don't ever want to pull away from him. It feels like he's my docking station, and I don't know how I've lived without him all this time.

We separate from our hug, and Rivers starts walking us east, toward the middle school. "How was your day?" He looks at me like he genuinely wants to know how it feels wrangling eighth graders for a living. It's like herding cats, in case you were wondering.

"Oh, you know. Dramatic. Kids at that age have a lot of big feelings."

Rivers glances over at me with a smirk. "Like confessing their undying love to someone in a letter, and then jumping into a loveless relationship a few weeks later because the recip*ient* doesn't recip*rocate*?"

"Wow, okay. No holding back, I see." I playfully punch his arm—it feels like hitting stone. "In my defense, I had it on good authority that you liked me too and thought I was doing you a favor by telling you first."

"Uh, huh. Sure. And what about the immediate loveless relationship?" He quirks his eyebrow up.

He knows he's got me there, and I can't help appreciating how easy it is to fall back into this banter with him. Rivers has always been good at dishing out as much shit as me, but it's rarely, if ever, been more fun with anyone but him.

I decide to answer him transparently though, because even if nothing more than friendship comes from this reconnection, I don't want to get tangled in the web of crappy communication with him anymore. "Honestly, I took it back because you didn't talk to me for two weeks after I confessed, and I thought if I told you I was over it, I'd get my best friend back."

He tosses his arm around my shoulder, its weight a comfort and a distraction. My mind can't stop wandering into territory that should be firmly off limits right now. "You never lost me, Quinn. Even when you didn't have me, you did." It's the nicest thing he can say to me right now given everything I put him through.

"Hey, I meant to ask you. Who is your friend that just started at the middle school? Do I know them?" When he brought it up on the phone, I was too distracted by the second part of his answer to ask about it.

"Oh, maybe? His name is Theo Webber. He teaches history," Rivers says as we start the first incline of the trail.

"Oh, the guy from the festival! Is he from PG?"

"Yeah, that was him! Did you see his duck shirt? He was my college roommate, but he grew up in Temecula. His sister just moved up to Pine Grove a few years ago. I just convinced him to move out here in May. He's kind of been through it the last few years. Apart from Theo, my other friends all left."

It's weird being disconnected from him like this. He doesn't know Sybil, I don't know Theo. We used to be so ingrained in every part of the other's life.

"You and Trevor are still friends though."

"Yeah. Bonded over the shared heartbreak at the hand of Quinn Clark," he jokes by bumping into my arm. Logically, I know I broke Rivers's heart all those years ago, I've just never heard him say it.

"Best Weezer song right now?" I quickly change the subject to the game we used to play, willing to be vulnerable, but not quite enough to completely tread through all the shit I know we eventually have to talk about. "And don't say 'Island in the Sun'. You and I both know that's a copout."

"I'll allow you to deflect the hard stuff for now, Quinny, but don't think I'm not on to you. Best Weezer song right now is 'Pink Triangle'; the beat is stuck in my head."

I smile up at him. "Pink Triangle" is on an album we never listened to together. It was there the whole time; it just wasn't one that we had in our rotation, we usually listened to the *Blue* and *Green* albums the most, mixed with a few from their *Make Believe* record. The record that "Pink Triangle" is on sat there, quietly, patiently, waiting for its turn. The thought of this being the first time Rivers has ever given me this song as an answer makes me smile, thinking of it as a fresh start for us, but still connected to our roots.

I pull out my phone and put the song on, dancing as we walk just like I would at fifteen to whatever song Rivers had just deemed the best song of the round. I see the moment his thirty-seven-year-old self breaks away as he brings a closed fist to his mouth like a faux microphone to sing the words and laugh at how nothing and everything has changed all at once.

He quirks an eyebrow at me, and I know without him saying anything he wants to do our dance routine right here on this dusty trail as cars whiz by us. I turn to face him completely and extend my arms willing him to lead. He takes my hands, and a jolt of electricity ignites in my palms, right where he touches. We pull apart, then allow our opposite shoulders to touch, then pull apart and do the other side. I separate one hand from him, and he twirls me out to his left, then I spin in towards him, so my back is to his front. Clutching his other hand, he twirls me out to his right, I twirl again, and spin back into him, and his other arm snakes around my waist. I turn my head to the side to face him and he's so close I can feel his breath on my skin. His eyes dip to my lips, and I'm equally as fascinated by his. How the bottom one sits like a pillow, and how his cupid's bow has always been more pronounced. Our eyes meet, and the heat I see in his must match what he sees in mine. There's not a chance he can't read exactly what I'm thinking right now, but sensing I'm not ready to acknowledge the growing tension between us just yet, he lets me go, and we walk again, singing the words to the song.

When it ends, we both grin at each other. I throw my head back and laugh; it's the lightest I've felt in five years, and I immediately play the memory of a moment ago back in my mind, wanting to relive feeling so unencumbered, so free. Rivers shakes his head to himself, almost self-conscious that we just performed a dance for the whole damn town.

"Who knew 'Pink Triangle' brought out the dancing queen in you?"

"Oh please," I tell him as I roll my eyes, "you know that we can't play the Weezer game without it ending in that stupid dance."

"Ah, and here I was thinking you wanted to play the game as an excuse to let me touch you."

My mouth opens a little bit, surprised by his candor. This straightforwardness is a new element to our old dynamic, and it must make my brain misfire a bit because, before I can stop the words from coming out, I turn to Rivers and ask, "Is this a date?" I feel myself blush but trudge on. "Because I think it's a date, and that sort of terrifies me, but I didn't know if you thought it was, or if we were just catching up, and..." I trail off.

Wow, Quinn, way to stay cool.

I try to take in a few deep breaths, but my heart pounds in my ears.

Rivers eyes at me with a quizzical look in his eye, his head turned slightly to one side, considering me. The light makes his tan skin glow, and I'm suddenly feeling very insecure. "Do you want it to be a date, Quinn?" His voice is like a mixture of syrup and whiskey; warm and smooth.

Shit.

"I don't know? I called Dani earlier because I was kind of freaking out, and then I started thinking about Preston and feeling guilty about being excited to go out with you, and I just...you're the first date I've been on since...everything." My breathing starts to come out in shallow puffs, and I'm talking so fast that I hardly register the tears stinging my eyes.

Rivers wraps his arms around me and counts in my ear, just like we used to do when I had a panic attack. He'd count, and I'd take deep breaths every time the number ended in five and exhale every time it ended in zero. He caught this attack so fast in me this time, I didn't even realize I was starting to spiral.

"What are five things you see, Quinn?"

He's doing my favorite grounding exercise with me, and the fact that he's remembered that this is something I need fills my chest like a balloon is expanding inside.

"The ripples on the lake, the pine needles on the trees, a bird feather on the ground, two squirrels humping behind that stump" Rivers snorts out a laugh as I say the last thing I see, "and you."

"Good, honey. Now four things you can touch."

I back away from him, placing my hand on my phone in the pocket of my leggings, never breaking eye-contact with Rivers. "My phone, my leggings," I bring my hand to my hat, as my third item, "and you."

"That's it, keep breathing. Three things you hear."

"The birds singing, my heart beating my ears, and you."

"Two things you can smell?"

I walk into his arms again, laying my head on his chest. "The pine needles," I lift my nose upward into the column at his throat, inhaling him, "and you."

Rivers swallows. "Good, now one thing you can taste, Quinn."

I gently brush my lips to his neck, opening my mouth ever so slightly to touch the tip of my tongue to him, and give the hollow of his collarbone the most imperceptible suck.

Rivers is so still, like he'll combust if either of us moves. A groan escapes him, "Fuck," he whispers.

"You," I murmur. It's the first time my lips have ever touched him in any capacity, and I feel him everywhere. It feels familiar and foreign, but right. Like this is where I need to be, even though it scares the shit out of me because he's oxygen and I can't get enough air. It makes me wonder how Rivers would taste if I kissed his mouth, and what it would feel like to have his grip in my hair as he pulled me deeper to him. Rivers's breathing is shallow, like mine. He looks down at me, considering. I move my mouth up toward his while his eyes search mine. Neither of us moving; neither of us can. We're frozen here, by time, by grief, just breathing in tandem, trying to build up the courage to commit to something more.

A car horn honks, jolting us apart. I glance down, disappointed that I didn't seize the moment when it was right in front of me, and start walking. "Thank you for that, my anxiety has been better for a long time, but the last couple of years it's sort of come on with a vengeance. Kind of overprotective with the kids now that it's just me. And this, with you, it's just...a lot."

"I understand. You've been through hell. It makes sense your anxiety is on edge." His voice trails off, and I can tell he's at war with himself. "Can I tell you something, Quinny?"

"Of course."

"I've never seriously dated anyone, and being here with you kind of freaks me out too. Why do you think it took me so long to call you?"

"What? No way. I'm sure Trevor has to tell girls to leave you alone all the time."

"Nope. I mean I've had a few girlfriends here or there, but none of them lasted more than a couple months. I've never been with anyone seriously."

"Why?" I'm scared of what his answer is going to be.

"Honestly, I didn't really have a heart to give to anyone. When you left, you sort of took mine with you, and I knew I'd never be able to give it to another person because you were it for me, you always have been."

His words exhilarate and terrify me in equal measure, but I don't want to interrupt him. I think he knows I need him to be the one whose heart is exposed right now even though it's so unfair of me to ask him to.

"When you walked into my office, I felt like I could breathe again, like I hadn't been fully living for the last twenty years, and my heart just came back in like it had never left. So, to answer your question from before, Quinn, I hope it's a date because I've wanted to date you since I was thirteen years old, but if you need more time to grieve or figure out how to exist in this world without Preston, I can give that to you. If you need me to be a friend to you right now, who grounds you through an anxiety attack, I can be that. But please, Quinny, please, let me be here for you, because I fucking miss you, and I think if my heart walks away from me again, it'll damn near kill me."

I stare at him, genuinely surprised by his declaration. After all this time, it shocks me that he never moved on from what we had. I look at my watch to see how much more time I have before I need to be home and see it's only four thirty.

I inhale a shaky breath, knowing I am drawing a line in the sand I can't take back. Everything is about to change irrevocably. Rivers is offering his friendship, but I want more than that; I want to let him consume me, and I want to be brave enough to let him this time. I'm going to have to talk to my kids, talk to my parents, make amends with Rivers's whole family, and somehow find a way to make peace about how Preston would feel.

Taking Rivers's hand in mine just like we used to do when we'd walk nearly anywhere, with my pinky finger between his pointer and middle, I look up into his eyes. "Want to go get dinner?" I smile.

"That depends," he says, seriously.

"On what?" I ask, nervous.

"Burgers or tacos?"

Chapter Ten

Now

"**O**rder for Livers?"

A snort bursts out of me as the man in the taco truck butchers Rivers's name, and he glowers at me with fabricated indignation. His name is unique, and he's always gotten questioning looks for it, but this one might take the cake. He gets up from the wooden picnic bench that's set up in the parking lot of the baseball fields and walks to pick up our food. Throughout the week, one food truck takes the "spotlight" spot, and then on Friday at the Food Truck Roundup, a new spotlight is chosen for the week. This week is Rosa Maria's which is the absolute best Mexican food to ever grace the Earth. They've been around forever in a brick-and-mortar location at the base of the mountain, but the food truck is recent, and one of the best things they've ever done for business. Nothing is better than Rosie's.

Rivers returns and sets down my deep-fried tacos with braised beef, a mango salsa, and habanero queso with chips.

"Everything look alright?" He starts to unwrap a burrito the size of a newborn baby.

"Are you kidding? I think I'm in heaven! I haven't had Rosie's in years; I completely forgot about it. And to be eating it with a man named Livers?" I scoff and roll my eyes, like my luck could not get any better. "A dream come true."

Rivers's eyes sparkle with mischief as he looks across the table at me. "I'm glad. Though, I think between the two of us, me eating a meal with a woman named Quinn might actually be the dream come true."

My cheeks flush pink, and it's not from the queso; Rivers has become a smooth talker in adulthood—not that he wasn't when we were kids, but he has a quiet confidence now that makes his words feel intoxicating.

I bring my hand to my neck to hide my blush and take a bite of my taco. It's so fucking good, I don't realize that grease is dripping down my hand until it reaches my wrist; I must look like an animal. Hastily, I grab a few napkins and start to wipe up the mess on my hands, and the corners of my lips. "God, sorry I'm disgusting!"

He laughs good naturedly. "Need I remind you of the donut incident circa 2006?"

"Oh my God, please don't ever remind me of the donut incident." He's referring to the time we found our selves at a party hosted by his mom, and as teams we had to eat a jelly filled donut as fast as we could.

While it was tied to a string.

And we couldn't use our hands.

He and I were on a team, our parents knew better by then to try and separate us, and where he ate his donut with relative ease, I had jelly all over my face, neck, and shirt.

"All I'm saying is, I've seen you be disgusting before; glad I got to witness it again."

I toss my napkin at him but also view this as an opening to ask about his mom; I've missed her. "Speaking of the donut incident..."

"We should have that trademarked," he interjects, but he realizes what he's done and clears his throat. "Sorry, you were going to say something."

"We could totally have that trademarked." I don't want him to think I'm upset; honestly, I want him to keep laughing and teasing and falling further and further into his orbit. "But I was actually curious how Lianne is doing. Both your parents, really."

When Preston died, I got a flower delivery from the Thomases, a pretty arrangement of pink tulips, with a simple card that read, *"Hugs, Love, Bryan and Lianne."* I remember appreciating the gesture at the time, but I haven't talked to them.

"They're good. My dad retired ten years ago, and now he and my mom are always traveling around in their R.V. They still have the house though. They say they need the room for Forest's kids. They miss you; when my mom heard you moved back, I think she was hoping you'd reach out."

"Okay, hold on. There's a lot to unpack there. First, they still have *the* house? Second, how many kids does Forest have? Third, your mom was hoping that I'd reach out?" I try to digest everything he's just told me. I would sell my soul to step foot into the Thomas's house again, that house raised me as much my own parents' did; it was basically my second home. But more importantly, Lianne wants to reconnect? Tears prick my eyes, feeling relief that I haven't burned my bridge with her beyond repair.

Imitating my speech, Rivers begins holding up fingers. "One, yes, they still have *the* house. They haven't even moved my pirate ship—I swear it's like fucking time warp in there. Second, Forest and Ashley have three kids, two boys, one girl, and yes, my parents spoil her as much as you might imagine. She's the only girl they've ever had to dote on! And third, she talks about you all the time, Quinn. If you called her to meet you for ice cream right now, she wouldn't even hesitate."

"I guess I kind of just figured I ruined that relationship...my mom stopped giving me updates on them shortly after...after everything..." I trail off. Rivers knows what I'm talking about as much as he knows that Lianne tried to help me all those years ago.

"Quinn. Come on. If you and I are able to sit down on what I am absolutely counting as our first actual date, then my mom, the great Lovely Lianne, has no hard feelings. She's always just wanted both of us to be happy."

"Okay." I accept it as truth. Rivers has always made me feel like what he says is what he means. It's always been his actions that have felt inconsistent to me. "How's your burrito on a scale of mediocre to incredible?" I ask, instead of digging deeper.

He lets out a soft laugh as he drizzles more salsa Verde over his food.

"Love the subjectivity of that scale, but I raise you one better: It's *fucking* incredible," he mumbles through his bite, and I love that we haven't lost the easiness between us.

How many times in life do we find a person who understands us so completely? Who matches our rhythm and accepts our mess? Rivers is handsome, there's no getting around it, with his easy mannerisms and comfortable swagger, I feel myself falling just as fast as I did back then, but before I ever saw him as something more, he was my friend, my best friend. I think Emily Bronte was onto something when she spoke of souls being made of the same material; it's always described Rivers and me. Nothing has ever felt forced; it's just been easy.

"Ah, fucking incredible, the best of all the incredibles," I joke.

"I'd argue that the best of all the Incredibles is Elasti-Girl, but you always were more of a Dash lover if I recall," he mocks.

"Rivers Thomas! Is that a dig at me running away eighteen years ago?!"

"Yeah, but only a little bit." He knocks his shoulder to mine, and we settle into an easy quiet as we eat our food.

The lake looks gorgeous as the sun sets behind the hill, painting the water in varying shades of orange, pink, and yellow while the trees are silhouetted. I pull out my phone to snap a picture so I can show Wyatt later. She's been loving painting sunsets lately, and I think this is one she'd find challenge and joy in.

"Still a sky watcher, I see?" Rivers pulls me from my thoughts.

"Yeah, but now I have a kid who loves it too. Wyatt is all about sunsets and sunrises right now; well, painting them, I should say."

I stand up from the bench and move toward the water, it's too pretty to have so much dirt obstructing my view. Rivers sits down on the dirt and pulls me down to him so I'm sitting between his legs, while his arms circle my waist. I feel weightless; like if he let me go, I'd drift toward the clouds, and all I want is to be tethered to him.

"Tell me about them; your kids, I mean. It's weird to not know that part of you."

I lean my head back against his chest and consider his question. I understand what he's saying. I've always felt like people are chameleons, adjusting their personalities to fit their environment. There are versions of me that even the people closest to me won't ever know. My parents won't ever know Ms. Clark, the teacher, and my students will never know Quinn, the daughter. We occupy space based on the company we share. And Rivers is right; he doesn't know Quinn the Mom, or Quinn the Widow; it's foreign.

"It is weird, isn't it? Not knowing?" Rivers tightens his hold on me. "Wyatt is confident and kind. She's a good friend, but she doesn't let people walk all over her, which I admire. She's intuitive with people's feelings, but struggles to communicate her own." I look up at the cloud for a second. "Hmm what else? She loves art, and she says she loves gymnastics, but she's never stuck with it long enough to progress more than a cart-wheel? So that feels like it could be debatable.

"Sawyer is reasonable, but emotionally unattached. He views the world pragmatically and doesn't ever really let feelings ruffle him. Like a kid at school said this thing he was working on was dumb, and Sawyer just shrugged it off because it only mattered that Sawyer cared about it. He's protective of Wyatt, but I think to some extent he also gets jealous of her ability to let people in freely. He cares a lot about being healthy, and I think if he was given like...three hours to look at all the world's research on cancer, he'd find a cure."

"They sound like they complement each other well," he says.

"They do. They've been through a lot, but I think they're starting to find themselves again."

"How did they take everything, with Preston? I'm sure that was probably brutal."

"Oh God, that was the worst day of my life for so many reasons. They told me over the phone that I needed to get to the hospital as quickly as I could because they weren't sure how long Preston would last. But I couldn't imagine not giving my kids the closure of saying goodbye to their dad, so I stopped at the school to pick them up first.

"I think they thought that we were taking them somewhere fun because sometimes Preston would do that; like buy tickets to a Chiefs game on a whim, or get them out early to go to the Aquarium? But when they saw me crying in the front office, they knew something was wrong."

Rivers takes my hand in his, gently reminding me that I'm safe.

"I remember looking in the rearview mirror on the way over to the school and thinking *I'm about to destroy their entire world.* And I did, in the snap of a finger. Sawyer asked what was wrong, and I had to tell them that Preston had been shot at work, and we were going to the hospital to say goodbye.

I hadn't even called either of our parents because I was so focused on making sure they got that closure."

I dab my eyes with my hand. "I'm sorry. I've been through that day so many times, but I always get hung up on how quickly I dismantled everything they thought they knew. Mom guilt at its finest."

"I don't want you to feel like you have to tell me anything you're not ready for," Rivers says against my ear. "I'm here for you regardless of if or when you decide you want to share. It's just that I know the Quinn of twenty years ago, but I want to know the Quinn of right now, even if she's covered in scars. Your past doesn't scare me; it makes me hurt for you and your kids, but I'm not afraid to step into that pain with you if you need it."

In this moment, I don't see Rivers as the guy I'm on a date with, but Rivers the best friend I used to tell all my scariest, ugliest parts to.

"I appreciate that. I don't think I'm able to share more right now other than you should know that every day my kids and I wake up, I think it's a miracle that we're all still here."

Rivers skates his thumb back and forth across the top of my hand. I pull my hand back and wipe the back of it to my eyes, but I feel the absence of his hand almost instantly and reach for him again.

"Quinn, don't discredit everything you've done for your kids."

I start to interrupt him; I didn't do everything alone. I had Dani, Sybil, my sisters, my mom, Preston's parents, years of therapists for the kids and myself.

"Hold on, let me finish." He raises his hand up, knowing I'm about to protest. "You had a lot of help and support in the beginning during that first year, I know that. But for the last four years? It's just been you. I mean, damn. Your kids are well-adjusted, they're involved, they talk to you, they have interests, and they sound happy. I'd say that's a miracle, but it's one that you fought for."

It is without question the kindest thing anyone has ever said to me. My biggest worry as a single parent has been the happiness of my kids; I've never wanted them to feel different and have tried so hard to foster their mental well-being—sometimes at the expense of my own.

I let out a sigh, not of relief exactly, but of being able to confide in someone about the past who didn't live through it with me. It makes me feel like I've healed, at least to some degree, and that I'm getting stronger.

"Thank you." I look down at our arms tangled together and relish in the sight of it. Seeing his strong arms roped with muscles and veins encircling mine like they're his to protect is euphoric.

"You're welcome. But Quinn..." Rivers's voice is low, and his hot breath on my ear makes me needy for him. It takes all my restraint not to turn and face him and see what he'd do if I touched my lips to his. "You broke the cardinal rule..."

At this, I do turn to see him, and the furrow of my brow must make the confusion on my face crystal clear.

"You cried *sad tears* over Mexican food!"

I throw my head back against him in a laugh. "Wow, I'm the WORST! Next date we'll have to eat Pop Tarts and Reese's minis while we *joke!*"

"Next date, huh?" He looks at me, and I see the whisper of teenage Rivers poking through, but the gleam in his eye is new.

"I mean, unless I've cried too many times, and you want to run for the hills. That would be understandable."

"Wouldn't dream of it. I've waited far too long for this to run away over a few tears."

"Great, then you bring the Pop Tarts and I'll bring the Reese's."

"Deal, and while we're at it, bring me a list of your current favorite songs," he says, squeezing me tighter.

"Why?"

"I just need to see if your music taste is shit now that I haven't been giving you suggestions."

I bring my hand to my chest in mock horror. "Oh, ye of little faith!" I laugh again at how quick he is on his feet.

"So, is it a date?"

"It's a date." I grin and then sink back into his embrace like it's the only place I belong.

Chapter Eleven

Now

My parents are finally home from their cruise, and we're all eager to see their photos and hear about the trip. They got home ten days ago, but things have been so busy that this is the first time all of us can get together. Mom talked to me briefly about their shore excursions, but I've made her keep most of the details to herself.

They downsized their house once I moved out; they didn't need a big house when it was just them and Liz. Despite it not being where I grew up, it still feels like home when all of us are here. Between me and my kids, Liz, June, her husband and kids, and my parents, the small house feels too cramped, but it's comforting. The kids are outside on the lawn while we wait for lunch to finish. I've been trying to decide if I should tell my family that Rivers and I have reconnected, but I don't even know how to begin to broach that subject. And is it too early to broach? We've been on one date.

One *really* good date that I haven't stopped thinking about. My heart knows that this is more; Rivers has always been more.

"When is lunch going to be ready?" My oldest nephew, Brecken, calls from the front door.

"It's ready now!" I tell him. "Bring everyone inside!"

We all sit in our usual seats and start prepping plates. We've made a feast of corn on the cob, barbeque chicken, vegetable medley, and watermelon. When we set a menu, we try to divide the work up so the meal isn't falling to one person, and I'm so thankful my parents made us all learn to cook as kids. I'm trying to teach mine the same lesson, but it sucks having to teach all these lessons alone. Mom and Dad said they'd tell us about their trip after lunch when the kids don't have to hear about every detail, so it's mostly small-talk until I hear Sawyer share about getting his black eye at school.

"...Yeah, and then Mom took him to the eye doctor, and we met her old boyfriend." Wyatt relays the tale to June's kids as she stuffs her face with chicken. Everyone turns to look at me just as I choke on a corn kernel.

"Justin became an *eye* doctor? Wasn't he like...a complete idiot? Please tell me you kicked him in the family jewels, Quinn?" My dad is horrified at the prospect of Justin re-entering my life: a more than fair response.

"Wyatt, he was *not* my old boyfriend," I say through a clenched smile, "and Justin did not become an eye doctor, Dad. Last I heard, he does something in finance in some big city."

"Who's Justin, mom?" Sawyer asks, and I shake my head indicating that this is not the time, place, nor company to discuss Justin.

"I'm texting Aunt Dani about him, now," Wyatt chimes in, and I swear my head is about to explode. Dani is even worse than my family when discussing my sordid history of terrible dating partners.

"Oh, does she mean Trevor?" My mom is playing the guessing game now, and everyone is looking at me. "Wait, no. You said he wasn't a boyfriend, so it couldn't have been Trevor." Mom starts mumbling names trying to figure out who it could be.

"No," Wyatt shouts, "his name was Dr. Thomas."

And that's when the table goes silent.

Liz, June, my parents, hell, even June's husband who hasn't looked at me in almost five years is staring at me with bug eyes. "And then we saw him at Fall into Fall, and a few days later, he helped Mom change her car battery in the parking lot of Goodman's, and they went out went to dinner on Friday."

Finally, I hide my face in my hands. I am so unprepared to deal with this.

"Kids," June is trying to remain calm, but her voice is clipped. "Why don't you take your plates outside? It's nice out."

When Sawyer finally files out the front door and closes it behind him, all eyes are on me, and I have no idea how to break the tension. After a few seconds, like a scene from a movie, they start throwing questions at me simultaneously.

"Did you know it was him when you booked the appointment?"

"Was he mad at you?"

"Did you kiss?"

"How was the first date?"

"God, I knew I always liked him; having the tools to change a car battery with him just like Bryan and I have always told you guys to do? He's great." That's from my dad, naturally.

They fall quiet again, and my mom reaches for my hand. "How are you feeling about all this, Quinny?" With her question, the rest of the family seems to realize that while Rivers and I reconnecting is a huge deal, I've been a widow for the last five years, and that makes everything so much more complicated. It's not like I'm just dating someone new; it's that I'm potentially dating someone *at all*.

"I feel...heavy?" A tear makes its way down my cheek as I continue. "I've enjoyed every moment I've had with Rivers so far, but in the back of my mind, there's a voice telling me I should feel guilty. Preston was the love of my life, and I feel like if I keep going with this, it will be like some type of betrayal."

"Quinn," my dad grabs my other hand. "You and Preston loved each other very much, and what you lost is immeasurable. But Preston also wanted you and the kids to be happy, and not just happy—because I know you're going to say you're happy on your own—but fulfilled. He wanted you to live your big, beautiful life, and he wouldn't want his memory to get in the way of you doing that."

"What are you thinking?" Mom asks.

"I think I want to give Rivers and me a try. I feel like we owe it to ourselves after all this time to really try and see if we work, but I also have my kids to think about and whether they'll feel like I'm betraying their dad for this man they don't know, and I'm thinking about people's judgement and Preston's family, and if five years is enough time before I start looking to the future for something new."

My voice wobbles and comes out fast, and the tears pour out of my eyes because I don't know how to *do* this. They don't give you a manual in the hospital when you decide to pull your husband from life support titled, *Moving On: A How-To Guide at Finding Love Again.* They don't even give you one on navigating grief.

"There isn't a timeline, Quinn," June begins. "Only you get to decide what feels right for you. Preston's family wants you to be happy too, and I bet they'd tell you that if you called them. And maybe more than that, your kids deserve to see their mom happy, they deserve to have someone else in their life that loves them..."

"And," Liz cuts in, "You could do a hell of a lot worse than Rivers Thomas for you and your kids, Quinn. I will never forget how he included me when we were young, and how thoughtful he was towards you. I used to make up stories in my head that I'd find someone who loved me like that."

"But, if you don't feel ready to give your heart to someone else, that's okay too," Dad says, gently grasping my hand.

I think about everything they're telling me and see the truth in it. They're looking at me, waiting for me to speak, and I appreciate that they're holding space for my silence. Each of these people loves me. Deeply. They carried me through my darkest years and never wavered.

"I think...I think *I'm* ready to explore what else is out there for my heart, but the judgement from other people makes me hesitate to actually try. And if I'm being honest, reconciling with Lianne and Bryan terrifies me. I hurt them all so badly."

"Sick Dani on the haters," Liz starts. "She'll bury their bodies and go to jail like it's a party if it means you get to be happy."

"God she's terrifying," my dad agrees. "How that woman teaches fifth graders I'll never know."

Mom glares at Dad, like *this isn't the right time to talk about how scary our daughter's best friend is*, but presses on. "We're here to support you however you need, Quinny girl. But if you're scared that *we'll* judge you for going after the man we've all loved since you were kids? Then you don't know us at all. And if you think for a second that Lianne and Bryan won't celebrate this, then you don't know *them* at all either. You're not responsible for what other people think or feel, sweetie."

I stand to give them each a hug, feeling marginally lighter knowing that they support me. They're the easy ones though; I think my next few conversations are going to be a lot more difficult.

***

The car ride with my kids almost feels like torture. I don't think any of us really knows what to do or say. I don't want them to feel blindsided, but I also don't want them to feel like they need to tiptoe around the subject either.

"What's on our calendar this week?" It's the best icebreaker I can come up with, but it helps us all know what's going on with each other and stay organized.

"I have art club after school Tuesday and Friday," Wyatt starts. "We were asked by the Rotary Club to do something for forest fire prevention."

"Okay, pick up is at four o'clock, right?"

"Yeah, but Banks and I might go to Aunt June's after, depending on our math homework."

Banks is June's youngest child, and he helps Wyatt with her math, while she helps him with English. It's a good trade-off. Sawyer will sometimes join their study group when they get stuck, but he's in the advanced classes and a year ahead, so he's less familiar with their course work.

"Got it, you guys can use our house too if you ever need it." They've been using June's house a lot, and I don't want to overexert my sister more than she already is. Where my life is chaotic because my husband is no longer here, June's is chaotic because her husband doesn't do anything. He has a great job, but he hasn't been a partner to her in a long time—I hate it; he never used to be this way. "Sawyer, what do you have?"

"I have an away meet for cross-country on Tuesday, and the parent meeting for wrestling is Thursday night. Is it still okay with you if I sign up for that?"

"Of course! I'll try to make it to the meet, too."

"No, don't worry about it, by the time you get there my event will be over. Besides, I think Papa said he'd come to it."

Thank God for my parents. Preston's absence has made being at all the things for both kids a challenge, and I've never wanted them to not see someone that loves them in the crowd. I need to make sure and tell my dad thank you.

"What's on your calendar, Mom?" Wyatt asks.

"Nothing crazy. I think I'll prep for a ten-mile run on Saturday, but otherwise I'm pretty open."

"Will you see Dr. Thomas this week?" Sawyer meets my eyes in the review mirror.

"I'm not sure. We haven't planned anything." I pause, mustering the words to leave my mouth. "Would you be okay if I did?"

"Obviously!" Wyatt sounds exasperated that I'm even asking, but my question is primarily for Sawyer. He's the one that hasn't seemed as enthusiastic, which I understand, but I also need to make sure he's okay before I proceed any further with Rivers.

"What would that mean for us and for Dad if you started dating again?" Sawyer has always been my analyst. He wants as much information as he can get before he decides anything

"Well, for me, it would mean that I might fall in love again. That doesn't mean I'll ever stop loving or thinking about your dad. It just means that I get to find love again with someone new. And for you, it can mean whatever you want it to mean. It can mean that you have a new person in your life that loves you and supports you; it can mean that you keep your distance until you get more comfortable; it can mean both of those things at the same time. The only thing I will say is that you can't be mean. If you want me to wait, I will wait until you feel more comfortable, but if you agree that this is okay, you have to come to me if those feelings change. You can feel however you want, and you can be honest with me about those feelings, but you can't take those feelings out on Rivers or me."

"Were you in love with Dr. Thomas when you were young?"

His question surprises me, but I choose to answer honestly. "Yes, I think that Rivers—Dr. Thomas—was probably my first love."

"His name is Rivers?!" Wyatt can't contain herself over his unique name.

"Yes, and his brother's name is Forest."

Her eyes go wide. "I wish you gave us cool names!"

"But he wasn't your boyfriend?" Sawyer aims to get the conversation back on track.

"He wasn't. We never actually dated. We were best friends who flirted and acted like we were dating but never did. We never kissed; never said I love you. We never even went to a dance together."

"Can I take some time to think about it, Mom? I'm sorry. I just...I want to make sure I'm really okay with this."

"Of course. Take as long as you need, bud. That goes for you too, Wyatt."

She nods, and it's the first time I see her taking this seriously. Moving forward with this has the potential to irreversibly change things for our family.

I pull into the garage, and the kids go to their rooms to decompress, leaving me to take care of some mindless tasks around the house: breakfast dishes, vacuuming, and a small load of laundry. It's taken me a while to get to a place where the house runs smoothly on my own. When I first started therapy, I remember crying to my therapist at the time that I couldn't get everything done that I needed to do. The house was falling apart without Preston. How was I supposed to work, play with my kids, be responsible for all the meals, and manage all the housework? I went from partners with my husband to a single mom overnight, and I didn't know how to cope or keep us functioning.

"Choose what you can let go of, choose what you can outsource, and handle the rest," was her advice, and I've been following it ever since. We eat out twice a week and eat with my parents once, I have a house cleaner come every other week, and the loft in my house has a door on it so I don't have to see the mess. Maybe it's not a perfect system, but it works for us.

I knock before I enter Sawyer's room with his clothes. "Hey, can we talk?"

He takes the clothes from me and starts putting them away. "Sure."

"I want you to take your time thinking about me dating again, but I really want to make sure you know a few things, okay? First, I want you to know that I will always love your dad and that no one could ever replace him. I will always love him, and no one will ever fill that hole. My heart might expand to love someone new, but it's not replacing the man we lost or the love that we had, okay?"

"Okay," he nods, and sits on his bed looking at the floor.

"Second, I don't want you to make this decision because you think it will make me happy. I want you to really think about if you're ready to handle this without feeling guilty or worried that I will be upset; it's not your job to protect me. Remember what I said about wrestling? It is not your job to protect me or my feelings. Got it?"

He nods again, and I tilt my head to look down into his eyes that mirror my own. "I love you, Sawyer."

I put my arm around his shoulder, the closest to a hug I'll get from him.

"I love you too, Mom."

Closing the door behind me, I head into the living room to pull out my book. This is the only time I've had to read this week, and I need to unwind from it all, not that a Backman book is particularly relaxing, though. Usually, I'd draw a bath and light some candles, but I'm too exhausted from everything to even do that. My eyes start to droop with every word, and before I know it, I've fallen asleep.

When I wake up, I'm so groggy that I know I need a coffee if I'm going to make it through the rest of this day. I check my phone and see that I slept for an hour and missed a text message from Rivers.

How's your weekend been?

Ha. If only he knew the can of worms my daughter just unloaded at my parents' house. Actually, there's nothing stop-

ping me from sharing, and he should know in case he sees any
of them.

> Well, Wyatt decided to share with my en-
> tire family that we went to dinner on Fri-
> day…

I think it'll be a bit before he responds since his first text
came through more than forty minutes ago, but it's almost
immediate.

> Shit, how'd they take it?

> Pretty good, honestly. They're all sup-
> portive.

> So does this mean I can ask you on an-
> other date…like tomorrow? (:

> We could probably do something, but I
> told the kids that I'd give them space to
> figure out if they're really okay with this.
> I'm sorry, I just need to be so protective
> and careful with them and just want to
> be honest with you.

My phone starts ringing with an incoming call from him,
he's always been this way. Texting just isn't his style.

"Didn't want to text about this, huh?" I answer with sarcasm lacing my voice.

"Quinn, I need to make something extremely clear to you."
He's not kidding around. He's full of urgency that catches me
off guard. "You do not need to apologize to me for protecting
your kids, giving them space to manage their emotions, or
letting them take as long as they need. I cannot imagine having
to weigh the pros and cons of my parents dating again as a
teenager; let alone after that parent has been widowed for five
years. Tell them to take all the time they need, seriously."

"Tha—" he cuts me off before I can finish thanking him for
his generosity.

"For that matter, *you* take however long you need. If you're
not ready, I meant it when I said I can just be here as a friend
for you, as long as you don't cut me out."

I consider his offer for a moment. I think if it was anyone
else, I may not feel as ready to hand my heart over so easily,
but this is Rivers, and he's known me to my core for almost as
long as I've known myself. "Actually, I don't think I need more
time..." I say, trailing off. "I think if you're willing to give me
another chance, and my kids are okay, then I'd like to try this
with you."

"Then I'll wait as long as you need me to, Quinny."

***

When the call ends, I tell my kids that I'm driving to Parchment and Grounds, the local coffee and book shop to get the
caffeine I need, lest I crash and burn by five in the afternoon.
It's one of my favorite places in all of Pine Grove, despite it
being a newer addition to the town. It has ivy growing up the
walls, and there's a row of old typewriters always queued up
along a far edge for people to type out poems that strangers
read in weekly poetry slams. Dani and I came a few weeks ago,
and we were both crying by the end.

The door opens for me, allowing a group of teenagers to
exit, along with the sound of a Gracie Abrams song I vaguely

recognize but don't know the words to, and a laugh I'd know anywhere.

I *love* that laugh.

I spot her with arms full of boxes, presumably full of pastries, and feel the urge to move toward her. She's aged a lot, naturally. Her hair has more gray in it than the sandy blonde I'm used to, but it's her.

Lianne.

She's looking through the tables and bookcases, and I realize that she's trying to find the best way to get to the parking lot with her stuff. There's got to be at least three boxes of goodies and her giant Mary Poppins style bag to contend with, and I figure this is as good an opportunity as any.

I try to remember what Rivers said about how his parents would greet me if they saw me when we were at the taco truck. It fuels me to call out her name. "Lianne!" My voice carries across the twenty feet between us, and she finally makes eye contact with me.

"Quinn?!" I hustle over to her, so she doesn't have to walk with all her stuff to me. Without missing a beat, she sets the boxes down, throwing her arms around me like we haven't lost almost two decades. "How are you, my girl?! I heard you moved back but didn't want to overwhelm you!"

"I'm doing really well. What's with all the boxes?" Her stack is sitting on one of the few café tables, and the barista glowers at us; this table is prime real estate here in the busy shop.

"I volunteered to bring baked goods to the senior center last week and got lazy. I'm just going to drop them off. Want to come?" She starts to heft the boxes up, but I stay her hand and take them myself. I want to say yes, but I can't. Not yet.

"Actually, I have to get home to my kids, but let me help you get these to your car."

She laughs quietly to herself as we walk out to the parking lot. "I almost said *'Thanks kiddo'* but you're not a kid anymore, huh? It's crazy how fast time flies."

"It really is, Wyatt is the same age I was when our families started hanging out all the time."

"Wow, that feels like yesterday." We make it to her car, an orange Subaru of all things, but I guess she's always sort of marched to her own drummer, and I'm glad to see that hasn't changed.

"It does. I don't know how you guys did it. It always seemed like you guys had all the answers, and I still feel like I don't know anything at all."

She loads the boxes into the front seat and turns to face me, her hand over her eyes to shield the sun. "That's parenthood for you," she shrugs.

It feels like a natural end to the conversation, but I don't want to walk away without knowing I'll see her again.

As if sensing my thoughts, Lianne says, "What are you doing this week, hun? Let's grab a tea!" She's never been a coffee drinker; tea was always her go- to.

"I'm actually a teacher at the middle school, and my afternoons are pretty packed this week. Maybe next week?"

"Of course, I think I remember your mom saying you were working there! Just come by the house, we'll do tea on the porch." She pulls me in for a hug, and she smells like she always has, lemongrass and teakwood. It transports me to Laguna Beach where we camped once, and she sat on a blanket and watched the tide come in with me when everyone else went back to the fire. "It's good to see you, Quinny."

"You, too."

And then she's gone.

I'm emotionally drained on my drive home. Today has been nothing like I imagined. If someone had told me this morning that in the span of three hours, my family would know that I went on a date with my childhood best friend, I would ask my kids' permission to continue to date said best friend, then on top of all that, bump into his *mother* and schedule a tea party, I'd say they were crazy. But here I am.

I catch sight of the barest hint of changing color on the maple trees as I drive by, reminding me that life comes in seasons and cycles—that the beauty of these colors will be lost, and new ones will replace them in a few months, and that's okay.

Nothing about my life is turning out the way I thought it would. I never intended on being a widowed single mom at the age of thirty-one; I never thought I'd move back to Pine Grove; and I sure as hell never thought I'd get to drink tea with Lianne Thomas on her porch again. It's a strange kind of dissonance to mourn the life I had and be thankful for the one I'm building.

And maybe that's okay too.

Chapter Twelve

Then, Freshman Year

My alarm goes off at five-thirty in the morning, and I groggily walk across my room to turn it off. I go into the bathroom and begin applying my make-up, and straighten my hair, paying close attention to the dramatic swoop of my side bangs. It's my first day of high school, and I'm terrified.

I pull on a pair of dark wash skinny jeans and a pink v-neck t-shirt, throw a gray vest over it, and pull out my trusty Chuck Taylors. I'm still extremely angry that I did not get ASL with Rivers. He has it first period, and I'm stuck in fourth.

Mom takes a picture of me and Liz before I head out for school, and Dad takes me to the bus stop. I won't get to start driving till next year which sucks, but Rivers said he'd start driving me once it was legal. I'm bummed I won't see him; we don't even have the same lunch.

The bus ride takes thirty minutes because the road along the mountain's edge is treacherous, but it gives me time to steady my breathing before I walk into school. I know where all my classes are because June walked me around before she headed back out to Vermont. I'm probably the only freshman who does.

I exit the bus and make my way to the front entrance. There are *so* many kids that my nervous system is immediately thrown into overdrive. I start to walk to my art class, trying to remember the route I took with June, and as I do, I notice a group of older boys watching me. Because I'm tall, June has always complained that people think I'm older than her, and to be fair, my body does look more developed. I'm not curvy, necessarily, but my boobs have been bigger than hers for a while. I smile at the boys; it doesn't bother me that they are looking. Considering I have no friends besides Rivers here, it makes me feel seen at the very least. Until one of them approaches and I'm...stunned?

He's huge.

And hot.

"Hey, I'm Cody. Cody Ponds," he extends a hand to me.

"Quinn," I start, "Quinn Clark," I shake his hand.

"Clark...are you June Clark's sister?" Hearing June's name calms my nerves.

"Yeah, June's my older sister."

"I didn't know June had siblings. Are you a freshman or a sophomore?" he asks.

"I'm a freshman, so it's my first day."

"Oh, nice! Can I help show you where to go so you don't get lost?"

He's really nice, and it puts me at ease. I don't want to keep being a loner, so even though I know where to go, I might as well take him up on his offer.

"Oh," I laugh unsure of myself, "That would be great, thanks."

"Of course! Where's your first class? Do you have any classes with friends?"

"Um, first period, I have art with Mr. Morrison. But honestly, I don't really have friends?" I say self-deprecatingly. "My one friend is a sophomore, and we didn't get our foreign language together."

"Damn, good luck with Morrison. He's kind of a psycho."

We walk toward the art room, and Cody points out where stuff is. "The whole school is divided into wings for each subject—English, math, science, electives, and then the 'Hello Hallway' for foreign languages. Here, let me give you my number in case you get lost."

I hand him my phone, and he texts himself from it so he has my number too.

"Thanks, you didn't have to take me all the way here."

"It's literally my job to take underclassmen around; I'm student body president!"

"Wow, so you're telling me the first person I meet in high school is the most popular person around?" I joke.

"And you're telling me that the only freshman I walk to class is the little sister of June Clark? We should call the news crew."

"Oh yeah, those are the stories they want to hear all about."

We laugh as the bell rings. I don't want him to leave, it's been nice. I gesture my thumb over my shoulder toward the art room. "I'm going to head in, but it was nice meeting you, Cody Ponds." I give him a small wave signaling my goodbye.

"You too, Quinn! And seriously, if you need anything, text me. I'm happy to help you!"

He turns to leave, but when I turn around, Rivers is standing behind me with his mouth agape. "Quinn, was that Cody Ponds?!"

"Uh, yes. Why?"

"Oh, I don't know, he's only captain of the football team, student body president, and the star of the baseball team! Why was he talking to you?"

Yeesh. Cody was likeable, so I can see why he'd be student body president, but it's not like I knew that. "I don't know, Rivers? Maybe he thought I was hot?!" I say it in a way that suggests Cody absolutely did *not* find me hot, but Rivers isn't fast on the uptake.

"WHAT?" Rivers is beside himself.

"My God, would you chill out?! He offered to walk me to class. It's not a big deal; he probably does that for a lot of people."

"I don't think he does, Quinn. I've been here for a year, and I think he's nice, but he's not 'walk-a-freshman-girl-to-class nice.'"

Rivers seems genuinely puzzled by Cody's actions, but the bell rings for passing period, and I know he has to get to sign language. "I'll find you after school and we can talk?"

"He said it's part of his duties for student government, but yes, we can talk more after school."

He gives me a quick hug and then starts walking to his class, leaving me alone. I try to remind myself that my goal for this year is to make some friends, and I while I know it's ridiculous to think that Cody is my friend, I feel like for the first time in a long time, I might have hope.

When I walk into the art classroom, I notice a girl with dark red hair and glasses sitting at a table. I don't recognize her, but she looks young, like me. I wish I was good at starting conversations, but I've never been the type to reach out first. I don't mind a conversation once it starts, I just don't want to be the one to start it. I sit in the chair across from her, and she looks up at me in surprise.

"Hey, I'm Dani."

"Quinn," I say. "Nice to meet you."

She plows forward with a joke, and I like her instantly. "Are we supposed to shake hands or something?"

I laugh, "God, no!"

Dani tucks some hair behind her ear, then pulls out a pencil from her bag. "Good, you passed your first test of not being a weirdo. Who were the hot guys you were talking to out there?"

"Do you mean one hot guy?" I ask, assuming she means Cody.

"No, I mean two hot guys," she says, enunciating the 's'. "You were talking to one for a minute who was like a giant wall of muscle, and then another who was standing behind you at first? He was smaller than the first guy, but still pretty hot."

I've never truly considered Rivers as being hot before; handsome, maybe. To me, though, my attraction toward him has always been more about the way he makes me feel. It's startling to realize I'm also objectively attracted to...him.

Finally, I answer. "Cody Ponds was the first guy. I just met him this morning by accident. The second is Rivers Thomas. He's my best friend."

"Yeah, I'm sticking with you if those are the kinds of people you attract."

I stifle a laugh to myself; she has no idea how few people tend to be around me at any given moment.

"So what grade are you in?" I ask her.

"I'm a freshman, I just moved here from Rancho Cucamonga."

"Oh, nice! I'm a freshman too. What classes do you have?"

We compare schedules and determine that we have this class, second period biology, lunch (thank God), and P.E. fifth period. Most of our core classes are the same, but we have them at different times—at least we'll know someone though.

"What's your phone number? That way we can text each other for homework help or whatever!"

I cannot believe this. Two phone numbers in one day? I give her my number, and type my name in.

"What's your last name?" I ask her.

"Baratelli—my parents are Italian. Hey, do you know where biology is? I'm so lost, a counselor had to walk me here this morning. Maybe we can walk to second period together?"

I agree to walk with her; she's funny and easy to be around, and hey, at least this way I'll know someone in there too. Class starts, and we hear Mr. Morrison drone on about how if he sees a cell phone, he'll smash it with a brick, his late work policy, and how much he hates teaching high school. It's inspiring, really. Maybe someday when he's grown up, he'll figure out what he wants to be.

The bell rings, and Dani clings to my side.

"Holy shit, he was awful. Why do people teach if they hate kids?!" she says.

"I don't know, but I think he needs a career change."

We're moving slowly through the herd of people headed to their classes, but it's technically a twenty-minute free period right now. We're allowed to go wherever we want, but since it's our first day, we figure it's best to just go sit in the biology room for now.

My phone buzzes, and I assume it's mom or June checking to see how things are going, but it's Cody.

Hey Quinn! How was art? Did Mr. Morrison throw you out of class yet?

I show the text to Dani and start typing back, laughing. I'm glad he gave me the warning about Morrison, or I'd be scared out of my wits right now.

"You know, texting and walking is like drinking and driving."

"No, it isn't," I argue. "I do it all the time."

"Mark my words. You'll see."

And, like some kind of wizard, Dani has predicted my fate. I don't even see the set of four steps before I'm falling down them, phone still in hand, message half-typed in response to Cody. Dani and I are both laughing so hard I can hardly breathe, and it takes her at least three minutes to collect herself before she can help me stand up.

"Are you okay?" she has tears in her eyes from laughing so hard, and I know without question I just found a new best friend.

"I'm fine. No more texting and walking for me!" We laugh again, as we find our way to biology. The teacher, Mr. White, tells us it's open seating, but once we find a seat that's it for the year. And just as we sit down, an announcement is made over the loudspeaker.

"Quinn Clark, please come to the counseling office. Quinn Clark, please come to the counseling office."

"That's you, right?" Dani looks at me.

"Yeah, but I don't know why they want to see me."

I approach Mr. White and let him know that I was just called to the counseling office. He gives me a syllabus to get signed for my homework, and thankfully, despite his domineering posture, he's nice enough to tell me how to get to the counseling office.

I don't know much about the counseling office apart from the fact that they are responsible for making and adjusting schedules, and I think they can help students figure out what they want to do with their lives. But I didn't request a schedule change, mostly because I knew it wouldn't go through. They don't adjust schedules just so you can have one class with a friend.

"Hi, Quinn, I'm Ms. Northrop. Please have a seat." She's probably around my parents' age with blonde curly hair. She was June's counselor, and I know my mom likes her, but this is the first time I've ever talked to her.

"Hi." I don't know what else she wants me to say.

"How is your day going so far?" It feels like she wants me to open up, but I really don't have anything I need to do here, and I don't know her well enough to feel like she's someone I can confide in.

"It's fine, but I've got to be honest, Ms. Northrop, I don't know why I'm in here."

"Well, I have some big news to share, and if you agree, it's going to end up changing your schedule quite a bit."

"Okay?"

"Your class voted you class president last year, Quinn. And part of being class president, means you need to be in student government—which is only offered fourth period."

"Hold on, my classmates did what? But I didn't run for class president."

"I know that, and it's why I'm giving you a choice. You don't have to assume the responsibilities if you don't want to. But if you choose to, it means you're the representative for your class: you help plan and organize assemblies, help plan school dances, and approve fundraisers for clubs. It's a great way to make some friends."

My ears perk up at that.

"To do this though, you'd have to take ASL first period instead of fourth, and take leadership fourth period in place of art."

So, I would lose one class with Dani and gain one class with Rivers. "Would I be the only freshman in student government?"

"Yes, but it's a great group of kids in there, and I'm sure they would support you. No one else in your class was voted in for student government."

I didn't vote at all because I didn't care, but it's weird that my class voted for me. I don't even talk to most of them.

"Can you tell me how many people voted for me, Ms. Northrop?"

"Sure!" She looks down at a sheet of paper. "It looks like you got one hundred and eighty-nine votes."

"And who got the next highest amount?"

"Well, that's what's weird, there aren't votes for anyone else." She's quiet for a beat while I sit on her words. "Do you want to do this, Quinn? I need to know quickly."

I have no idea what's happening, but I know that assuming the responsibility of class president gets me what I want. "Sure."

***

I get lost on my way to the student government room since this wasn't something June showed me. I thought about texting Cody, but it felt needy. The bell rings before I get to class, so I'm left wandering until I can sort it out. A teacher helps point me in the right direction, but when I walk in, the room is quiet, and everyone looks at me.

"Quinn?" Cody stands up and walks toward me.

"Uh, yeah. I just got moved into this class." Embarrassingly, tears prick my eyes. All of these kids are older than me, and I'm the only person I know apart from maybe two sophomores I've never spoken to.

"Hey, hey." Cody rubs his hands up and down my arms trying to comfort me; I appreciate his easy nature. "What's going on?"

"I think my classmates voted me to be class president as a joke. I don't have any friends, and I think they are trying to humiliate me. I told the counselor I would do this because she said I might make friends. And I need friends, Cody." It should be weird that I'm telling this guy everything, but it isn't. He feels like a big brother somehow.

I see him swallow and nod his head. "Everyone, this is Quinn. She's the freshman class president, and all of you are going to be nice to her or you'll hear from me."

"Cody, don't make threats." The voice comes from a female teacher in the corner.

"Sure, Mrs. D," he says, but everyone in the room seems to take Cody's threat seriously anyways. The chairs are arranged in a giant circle, and I don't know where to sit, but Cody pulls another chair up next to him and makes room for me.

The next fifty minutes pass in a blur. People introduce themselves and share what they do for student government, and they tell me how they can help when it comes time for me to complete my commitments. I'm so thankful for all of them, but especially Cody.

He offers to walk me to fifth period, P.E. and I let him; walking with Cody is like walking with a protective shield. Everyone is friendly, but I feel less fragile. "Listen, Quinn. I'm going to find out what jackass freshmen decided to vote you in without you knowing and when I do, they're going to be ruined."

"It's fine, kids are mean. Honestly, I think it's for the best, your friends seem nice."

People are staring at us walking together, and while Cody is objectively attractive, his personality really does feel brotherly toward me. "They are nice, when people are nice. But I'm not dropping this. Just know that I have your back. And speaking of people having your back, are you friends with Forest Thomas's little brother? Rivers, I think?"

"Yeah, he's basically my only actual friend, why?"

"Keep him around. I knew Forest when I was a sophomore, and if Rivers is anything like his brother, then he's a good kid. Text me tomorrow when you get to school and I'll tell you what I find out today. See you around."

He leaves me at the entrance of the gym, and I notice Dani and a group of other girls gaping at me. "Yeah, so you're gonna need to tell me everything that happened when you left second period, like right now."

She's as surprised as I am, but I think the biggest shock of the story for her was the part where Cody basically threatened a group of thirty-five students if they weren't nice to me.

The rest of the day passes quickly, and I barely register what's happening during lunch and my last two classes. This whole day has felt so unreal, that I'm basically functioning in a daze as I walk to the busses. What did Cody mean when he said he'd tell me what he found out? What is he going to do? I haven't even been able to tell Rivers that I'll be in first period with him now, and after one day of walking with Cody to class, older students are waving at me like they know who I am. What the hell?

As I wait in line for my bus, I see Rivers running through the crowd to try and reach me. "Quinn! Quinn!"

I lift my arm up and wave to show that I see him and start to move in his direction. "Hey, guess what!"

"I don't know. I just heard that Cody Ponds is asking about you from like thirty different people, trying to find out how you became freshman class president? Why didn't you tell me you campaigned?!"

I see the hurt in his eyes thinking I would keep this from him.

"Rivers, I didn't run. My class voted me in as a joke, but I accepted the role from the counselor today so that I could have ASL with you first period."

"We get to have first period together now!?"

I nod and give him a hug.

"Wait," I hear him say in my ear. "What the fuck do you mean you were voted in as a joke?"

"I mean that's the conclusion I came to. I didn't run for this, and I have no friends—the only thing that makes sense is my class voted me in to be funny and hurtful."

He steps away from me and looks down into my eyes. He's gotten a lot taller this year. I'm tall, especially for a freshman girl at five foot ten, but Rivers has at least three inches on me now. "Did you save Cody's number in your phone?" His question takes me by surprise.

"Yeah, why?"

"Let me see it." I hand him my phone, and he adds Cody's number to his own.

"What are you doing?"

"Just let me handle it." He pulls me in for another hug, and the tension of my day melts away ever so slightly. "I'll text you when I get home. See you in sign tomorrow, Quinn."

***

The next day is just as strange. There's a seat open right behind Rivers in ASL which feels too good to be true, and during our free period, Dani demands that she get to meet Rivers in person. He texted me to tell me that he's in the quad, so we make our way out there, but what I see makes my head spin.

Cody, Rivers, Trevor, and at least ten other guys stand in a group talking. Dani and I approach tentatively, not wanting to disrupt their testosterone fest, but when they ignore us, she makes them notice we're here.

"Listen up," Dani's voice is a little shaky, but loud. "I don't know what you're all doing, but this bitch," she gestures to me, "is the only person who talked to me yesterday, so if you're plotting the demise of whoever tried to hurt her, I want in."

Rivers looks at me with confusion, startled by her only knowing me one day and being willing to have my back so casually.

Rivers makes sense in wanting to defend me, maybe even Cody in the way a brother might. But I just met Dani yesterday, I broke up with Trevor months ago, and these other guys are here because what Cody says, goes. I appreciate their loyalty, but not necessarily on behalf of me; they don't know me well enough.

"Right," Cody looks just as confused, "can you try to question a few freshmen girls about it? Then let us know what you find out?"

Dani looks stunned by Cody's attention to her, but she nods in agreement. Cody dismisses the group and gives me a side hug as he leaves, which I notice makes Rivers's jaw clench.

Dani and I approach Rivers and Trevor as the upper classmen walk away. "Rivers, Trevor, this is Dani. I met her in art yesterday."

Trevor gives a quick nod as a hello, but Rivers just looks at her.

"Rivers?" I ask.

"Yeah, it's just...how can someone so scary be so small?"

Dani is at least a foot shorter than I am, but I can't argue with him. She'd be terrifying if I didn't know her.

Dani huffs a laugh like she gets this all the time. "Just take this as a public service announcement that you may have known her longer, but she's my best friend now, too."

Rivers is willing to play along with her, so he loops his arm around my shoulder, which makes Trevor look away, and says, "I'll allow it, but only because I know Quinn's allegiance is to me."

They bicker back and forth which leaves Trevor and me watching their nonsense. We've seen each other a few times since I broke up with him, but we haven't talked. "What are you doing here?"

"Just because we don't talk much anymore doesn't mean I want people to be mean to you, Quinn. I'd still like to be friends like we talked about, but I don't know if that's weird for you."

"No, but whatever we've been doing is weird. I feel like we've been avoiding each other."

"Maybe a little, but let's try harder. Especially now that we go to school together again." He seems a little sad, and I wonder if it's because he liked me more than I liked him.

"You can have her at school," I hear Rivers say. "But I get her on weekends and holidays." They're arguing about me like it's some type of custody battle. I like it.

"Or, she can decide for herself, thank you very much."

I give Rivers a hug and whisper, "Thank you for always taking care of me," in his ear.

"We have to get to biology now." Dani turns around and sticks her tongue out at Rivers as we walk away, and somehow, despite whatever is happening with the freshman class, I feel like everything is going to be okay. Mostly.

Chapter Thirteen

Then, Freshman Year

"No, you need it to be a 'p' handshape, not a 'k' hand-shape," I tell Rivers as we go through our ASL words for the week. He keeps messing up the sign for "people" by pointing his fingers out in the form of the letter k, instead of down, like the letter p. "P is for people, think of it like that or something." I grab his hands to correct his form.

"Hey that's a good trick," a guy two tables away tells me. "What other tricks do you have?" He's handsome, with sandy brown hair and blue eyes and by the looks of his t-shirt, he hits the gym—at least for his arms.

"The sign for story looks like you're pulling something out of a source to lengthen the ideas?"

He looks down at his hands and signs it to himself. "Hey you're right. What's your name?"

I decide to keep him on his toes and spell the letters in sign language for him: Q-U-I-N-N.

He squints his eyes at me in a challenge. *NICE ME-MEET-YOU Q-U-I-N-N. MY NAME J-U-S-T-I-N,* he signs. The best part about being in sign language the last few weeks has been how quickly we can use the language. I took two years of Spanish in middle school and still can't say anything besides *me gusta queso.*

Mrs. O'Connor, the sign teacher, taps her hand on the board to get our attention, then waves her hand at us. She told us at the start of the year that Deaf people feel vibrations and use their eyes to get each other's attention, and she will do the same in her classroom. She starts explaining our grammar lesson which focuses on the 'topic, comment' structure.

"For example, in sign, you wouldn't say 'I LIKE COOK-IES,'" which she signs as she speaks, "you would say, 'COOK-IES, I LIKE.'"

Our grammar lessons last week talked about ASL sentences being written in all capital letters, which is called Gloss. She also told us that on our tests, we would be marked down if our sentences weren't written in the correct format, so I've been trying to take everything she says seriously. It's interesting being in a foreign language that still represents English in so many ways but has its own grammar rules.

"Open your books to page fourteen and practice the sentences with a partner. Then we'll take turns presenting those sentences in front of the class."

Rivers turns back to face me so we can start practicing, when Justin cuts in. "Hey, can I practice with you, Quinn? This guy gets to practice with you every time," he says, pointing to Rivers.

"Yeah, probably because I'm her best friend so I'm who she's going to practice with."

I understand Rivers's frustration, but I'm not his to claim. I've really liked getting to know other people this school year, in large part due to Cody, but still.

"I'm going to keep practicing with Rivers, but maybe we can practice next time?"

Justin nods his head and turns to his partner, a girl I recognize from middle school but not well. I think her name is Sophie.

Rivers and I practice our sentences in silence; he's irritated by the exchange with Justin, but I don't know why. I don't even know him. "Are you mad at me?" I ask him on our way out the door.

"No, why would I be mad at you?"

"You can hardly look at me. I didn't practice with Justin, I stayed with you."

"I just know that he's an asshole. I don't like the way he looked at you, and I don't like that he's trying to get to know you. He treats people like shit—he always has." Understanding clicks in my brain. He's nervous that I'll get close to Justin and that Justin will get close enough to hurt me.

"Rivers, I don't even know him; you saw him introduce himself to me. There's nothing to worry about."

***

As I'm walking out of my English class at the end of the day, I think about how much my life has changed just a few weeks. When I first got to high school, I was friends with one person, and thought that was fine. It feels like my whole world has opened up since being here, and even though it's been a bit unorthodox, it's been a good change. I didn't realize how much the loneliness was affecting me.

Startling me from my contemplative mood, someone shoves into my shoulder, and I pull out my headphones.

It's Justin from ASL.

"*HOW YOU?*" he signs.

I chuckle; he's really committed to the bit. "Good, how was your day?" I say back.

"It's been fine. I saw that you have Mrs. Lafferty for English? What else do you have?"

I run through my classes with him.

"Hey, we both have biology with Mr. White!" He says it excitedly, and I'm surprised; I haven't seen him in there. "Not the same hour," he clarifies.

"Right, got it." I feel dumb, and also disappointed? I hear Rivers's voice saying he's an asshole in the back of my mind, but Justin is charming and friendly.

"It looks like you're taking a few sophomore classes? Am I...in the presence of a genius?"

"No, but I didn't see the point of repeating Life Science and Algebra as a freshman, so I just took the next class I could."

Rivers did the same thing, which is helpful for me because he's just as smart as I am and can help me if I get stuck. Dani is doing the same thing though, so we can study together.

"Smart," he smirks. "Well, in that case, maybe you can help me when I get stuck." He pulls out his phone. I assume he's texting someone, but when he hands it to me, I realize he's asking me for my phone number. I hesitate, but decide that Justin asking for help is harmless and type it in. Besides, helping Justin out is the least I can do given how much people have been there for me. "Thanks, maybe I'll see you around?"

"Yeah, maybe. See you later." I smile to myself as I walk to the bus but try to keep it in line in case I see Rivers. If I tell him my smile has anything to do with Justin, he'll blow a fuse.

Dani has started riding the bus with me so she can go to her equestrian lessons after school, which are coincidentally, right by my house. It's been fun having her around. I like that she doesn't let people treat her badly. I like that she only knew me a day and came to my defense. She's on the bus before I am, so I sit down next to her. She hardly registers that I'm here; it's unlike her. "Dani?"

"Sorry, I just...sorry." She looks uncomfortable, like she's seen a ghost.

I know we've only known each other for a few weeks, but we connected so easily, and I haven't seen her like this before. "Dani, what's wrong?"

"Nothing. How was your day?"

I tell her the basics of my day, highlighting sign language in particular and how weird it was with Justin and then Rivers being adamant that I shouldn't engage with him at all.

"You can't honestly be surprised by Rivers, Quinn."

"I mean I know that he's protective, it was just weird how quickly it happened."

"It's really not that weird when you consider the fact that Rivers is completely in love with you, but what do I know?" Her words cause me to start. In *love* with me? There's no way. After Yosemite, Rivers and I have been totally platonic. I don't even think Dani has seen us hold hands.

"He's not in love with me! He's my best friend, Dani. That's it."

"Actually, I'm your best friend," she stands up from her seat to get off at her bus stop which is just one stop before mine, "and he's in love with you." And then she marches off the bus with a flick of her hair, leaving me momentarily stunned.

Rivers and I have been over this: we're friends. We always will be, because one of us is always too stubborn to feel our feelings all the way. At my stop, my phone buzzes with a text from an unknown number.

HELLO, Q-U-I-N-N =]

I save his name as J-U-S-T-I-N to be funny. In the back of my mind though, I'm scared that this is going to backfire. Will Rivers see it? Why does it matter? And what does Dani mean that Rivers is in love with me? Sometimes I still feel flickers of those feelings for him—especially when it's just us—but does he? We've gotten close to talking about our feelings a few times, like in Yosemite, but I think we're both too afraid by the prospect of losing each other to talk about it openly. I hate it, but I'm not willing to risk it either.

***

Cody pulls me away from the bus the instant I step off the next morning. His grip is strong, and people move out of the way for us. It feels like they can tell that today isn't the day to cross him. I don't know why he's so agitated. Finally, he pulls me into a quiet corner of a hallway that only has one math class in it, and before I register it, he's pulled me into a hug.

Cody has never hugged me before.

"Cody, if you don't tell me what's going on right now, I swear to God, we will not be friends anymore." I feel him inhale around me; it puts me on edge.

"We figured out how you got voted into being class president. It's fucked up, Quinn."

I pull away from his hug, nodding that I understand, but he pulls me back to him again. It makes me think he doesn't want to look me in the eye when he tells me how this all happened. I assumed from the beginning that I was voted in as a joke; however, Cody's response makes me feel like maybe it's worse than I imagined. "Just tell me."

"They..." He inhales again, "God, they voted for the 'biggest loser' of your grade."

Tears prick my eyes. I knew that it was something malicious, but I didn't expect this level of cruelty. I don't know most of my class, sure, but I've never been mean to them. And now I have to act as their representative for something that has real consequences. The tears begin to fall as Cody holds me to his chest. "Which one of you found out?"

"It was Dani, actually. She overheard some girls talking about it, and then she told Rivers." That explains why she was acting so weird on the bus yesterday. "I guess he and Trevor jumped a few kids last night and pulled the rest of truth out of them. He was so furious when he called me last night, I thought he was going to explode."

Rivers and Dani knew? And they didn't tell me? That doesn't seem like them. Rivers especially has always been honest with me.

"Why didn't he tell me?"

"Ask him yourself," Cody pulls away.

Turning around, I see Rivers. His knuckles look scabbed over, and his lip is split, but he crushes me into a hug so firm I feel like I might break in half.

"Why didn't you tell me, Rivers? And why the hell did you fight over it? Your parents are going to kill me when they find out that all this," I gesture both of my hands to his bruises and cuts, "was for me."

"I didn't want to make your pain about me, and my emotions were too strong last night to be able to do that. That's why I didn't tell you. And when I told my dad where I was going, *and* why, he just told me not to be stupid." He still hasn't let me go.

Cody's head hangs low, like he's thinking of how to fix this problem but can't quite figure out the formula. But I'm too stunned to speak. Rivers told his parents, and Bryan didn't stop him. Rivers physically harmed himself and someone else over me?

"You told your dad?" My heartrate spikes: I don't want my parents finding out.

"No, I told him that someone was mean to you, and I don't like when people are mean to you, Quinn. He won't tell your parents. I downplayed how bad it was."

"Yeah, well fuck you too!" I hear Dani before I see her. Her dark red hair swooshes around the corner, her glasses perched on her nose. I'm more curious about if she really found out about this from eavesdropping or through more sinister methods.

"Damn girl, who pissed you off this morning?" Cody jokes.

I pull away from Rivers, taking them all in. "More importantly, how did all of you know that this little powwow was taking place?" They look at each other one by one, a silent confession that they talked about how to handle this.

As if on cue, Trevor materializes with a few of Cody's friends.

I'm officially humiliated.

"'K, what's the plan, Cody?" the biggest guy asks. I recognize him from student government, but I don't know his name.

"I vote we alphabetize the freshmen class and beat them up one by one," Rivers announces. It's not the calm voice that always acts like a balm to my worries. It's laced with menace and sounds intimidating.

"You tie 'em up, I'll do the torturing," Dani adds with glee.

Cody's face is horrified. He may be the ruler of the school, three years older, and a hundred and fifty pounds heavier than her, but she's scarier than all these guys put together. I love it.

"No. Here's what's going to happen. Quinn, you and I are going to go to homecoming together; people know we're friendly, but the dance should cement that I'm protective of you and not to mess with you. If anyone asks, no we are not dating, we *are* friends, though, and people should take that seriously." The dance isn't until the end of October, but asking me to go with him this early will definitely turn heads.

Rivers doesn't look mad, but he doesn't look pleased by this plan either; maybe Dani was right about his feelings.

"Yeah, yeah, sure. We get it: you're the coolest mother fucker that's ever lived," Dani rolls her eyes as she talks, "but how does this help her long term—like when you graduate in eight months? *And,* how does this get revenge on the freshman class for doing this to her?"

"It helps get her the clout she needs so that in eight months when they're gone, everyone already thinks she's cool." Rivers's voice is low, but he sees the truth of Cody's plan as well as I do. High school is all about image. What your peers think becomes the truth, even if the truth was something else before. By using Cody as my buy-in to the 'cool club,' people will forget that I was once a loser and only see me as someone that Cody thinks is good enough to hang out with.

"Cody, I can't ask you to give up your senior homecoming to take some freshman kid with you who needs a social makeover," I protest.

"You're not asking me, Quinn. I'm telling you that this is what's happening."

I look around the group, taking in all the people here that have stepped up to help me. I can't say my feelings aren't deeply hurt by the cruel joke my class pulled; they are, but I also don't want to stoop to their level either. If anything, this experience has taught me the importance of kindness and how just a few people, like the ones standing around me, can change everything.

"If I agree," I level them each a look, "then all of you have to promise you will not retaliate against any freshmen." I glance down at Rivers's knuckles, to his lip, and finally to his eyes. "I want people to get to know me and like me for me, not because they're scared, which includes being nice and giving grace to people who deserve it."

Rivers's nod is almost imperceptible, but it's there; a shrunken agreement that he won't beat someone senseless for being an asshole.

Then Cody drops a bomb that leaves me throwing my head to the ceiling in frustration. "Great. So, Quinn, when can I introduce myself to your parents, so they know who's taking you to the dance?"

***

"Absolutely not." My dad shakes his head so hard I think it's going to pop off and roll away.

I told my parents that I got asked to homecoming, and they were fine about it until I told them that it was Cody...or I guess until I told them that Cody was a senior. I understand their hesitation. They don't know Cody, they don't know how well Cody has treated me since the first day of school, and they certainly don't know that I've been dealing with a social catastrophe the last few weeks.

"Please? Rivers will be there too, and he knows Cody. Actually, June does too, why not just call her? We're just going as friends, I don't even like him like that."

This piques my parents' interest.

"If you're going as friends, why not go with Rivers?" Mom asks.

"More importantly, just because you don't like him doesn't mean he doesn't like you." My dad is still full of suspicion. I can't blame him. There are exactly zero justifiable reasons for Cody Ponds to ask me of all people to homecoming.

"Dad, I swear to you he views me like a little sister. And I'm not going with Rivers because he didn't ask; Cody did. Besides, it's not just us. We're going as a group."

My parents are still unconvinced, as they should be. I am keeping a pretty massive secret from them, but I can't tell them everything that's happened. It'll humiliate me more than I already have been and make them worry, which I don't need on top of everything else right now.

The sound of the line ringing through the speaker of Dad's phone reverberates through the room as we wait for June to pick up, and I hope that Cody's reputation as a sophomore was as outstanding as it is right now; otherwise this whole plan is going up in smoke.

"Hey, Dad!" June's voice sounds bright and bubbly.

"Hey, June Bug! How's it going out there?" Dad asks.

"It's good, what's up?"

"Well," Mom starts, "your sister got asked to homecoming by a boy."

"What?! Quinn, that's awesome! Who asked you? Rivers?"

Dad looks at me like I'm the biggest moron for not going with Rivers to the dance, but again, *he didn't ask me!*

"No, actually," I have to take a deep breath before I drop this bomb. June is going to freak out. "Cody Ponds."

"WHAT?! Like senior, student body president, captain of every team he's ever been on, Cody Ponds?"

"The very same, yes. But we really are just friends! He helped me get around my first few days of school and introduced me to everyone in student government, and I want to go with him AS A FRIEND," I look at my parents, "but Mom and Dad think it's weird that he'd ask me and think he's a creep for going with a freshman. Can you *please* talk some sense into them?"

June is quiet for a few moments, processing all that information and I realize I've made a terrible mistake. "Why are you in student government?" is all she says.

"I unknowingly got elected as freshmen class president," I confess.

Mom drops her drink on the kitchen floor, my dad stares at me like I've sprouted a third head (fair), and Liz has finally poked her head into the kitchen at this news.

"But you're kind of a loser?" Liz says.

"Yes, thank you for that analysis," I say. "But ever since I've been talking to Cody at school, I'm not as much of a loser, which is actually sort of nice."

I hear June breathing over the phone. I think she knows that something isn't totally right with my story, and I'm certain I will have to give her every single detail later, but thankfully she doesn't push it with my parents here.

"Listen guys, Cody Ponds is probably the nicest person apart from Rivers I could think of to ask Quinn to a dance. He's never been a weirdo or a creep, and if he's telling her he's her friend, he's being honest. The fact that he's shown her around and introduced her to people alone says a lot about his character."

"The age difference is my biggest concern," Mom says.

"He said he'd like to meet you both before the dance so you can get to know him *as my friend,*" I enunciate, "so that you're more comfortable with it. He really does feel like a brother."

The interrogation finally ends with them saying they'll have an answer to me in a few days, and I slip into my room, slumping over on my bed with my head in my hands. Right on cue, June's text pings in my hand.

> Spill. Now.

> My class voted me in as a joke. "The Biggest Loser." Cody and Rivers are taking care of it in their own ways.

> So Cody is helping you repair your reputation.

> Yeah, pretty much.

> I'll work on Mom and Dad. Sorry I couldn't be there for you, Quinny.

After two days of serious deliberation, I'm finally told that I can go with Cody on the following conditions:
1. My parents have to meet him
2. Rivers *and* Dani ride in the same car as us
3. I have to be home by eleven o'clock

I groan internally that my parents are making Rivers and Dani babysit me, but agree to the terms so that we can move forward with Cody's plan.

I just hope it works.

Chapter Fourteen

Then, Freshman Year

October goes by at the speed of light. Rivers and I see each other in ASL every day, Justin tries to talk to me as often as he sees me, and Cody has singlehandedly taken me from contented wallflower to someone alluring that everyone wants to know. I don't think he fully considered how making me popular would expose me to people that are less than upstanding.

He learned that the hard way four weeks ago when this senior named Max asked for my phone number and called dibs on taking me to the winter formal. I declined, of course. Max asking me felt creepy, like he saw me as a prize to pass around the school, where Cody has always been brotherly—especially after meeting my parents. He brought his parents with him, which surprised me, but they got along well. His dad is the

Pine Grove fire chief which my dad appreciated, and his mom teaches special needs kids at one of the elementary schools.

June's endorsement also didn't hurt. She told me later that she never talked to Cody at school, but she knew of him and knew that he was a good guy. He eats lunch in the special needs class most days as part of the school's Friendship Club, which tries to foster community between special education students and the rest of the student body.

The day they came over, my dad asked Cody what his intentions were with me, like some 1970s sitcom, but Cody's answer was perfect: "To shield her from anyone who tries to take advantage of her innocence." It was just brotherly enough to firmly solidify us as friends. After that, my parents were almost disappointed by the age gap between us; Cody is a catch—just not the catch for me.

I think Rivers has mostly gotten over Cody taking the driver's seat in the "protect Quinn" car, but sometimes I catch him watching Cody like he's trying to parse out his jealousy. I don't understand him.

Liz helps me put my dress on, a black and silver knee-length ensemble, and I pin a black flower in my hair. June tried to guide me on how to do my hair over Skype last night since she works today. It looks okay, I think. Cody said he'll match me so we'll be coordinated in our photos.

When I come down the stairs, Cody's giant frame leans against the wall by the door in black pants, a silver shirt, and a black tie.

I guffaw.

"Where did you find a silver shirt?" My voice is borderline teasing, but I can't help it. He said he'd match but I didn't think he meant like this.

"My mom found it somewhere. I was just as shocked as you. Let's talk about your dress though! It looks great, Quinn." He's so genuine and gentle tonight, a direct juxtaposition of who he was on the football field last night. He led Pine Grove to victory, but the Cody on the field as the quarterback, and screaming profanities to the opposition, compared to the Cody in a silver shirt standing in my parents' foyer are like two separate humans.

We take our pictures and pose in all the ways my mom tells us to, but each one is as platonic as the last. At last, Rivers arrives with Lianne and Bryan, along with Dani and her parents. Rivers agreed easily to the terms my parents offered. Dani said it would be weird if he was just third wheeling with Cody and me, which is how she ended upon my parents' list of demands. I don't think that Rivers liked that terminology very much, and if his facial expression is any indication, he's still not thrilled about the matching outfit I share with Cody.

The music is so loud when we arrive, we can hear it from the parking lot. Student Government has worked for months on preparing for this dance, and I'm excited to see how it all came together. The theme this year is "sports" which is about the worst theme for a dance I've ever heard of. Cody wanted to do an "Alice in Wonderland" theme, but the student body voted on this, and unfortunately, we are a representative democracy.

There's blown up sporting equipment for decorations with at least two hundred helium balloons under the steel structure that covers the dance floor. Teachers hover near the concession stand, making sure no one spikes anything, and even though the theme is objectively terrible, the atmosphere is electric.

The moment we walk in, people stare. Everyone is trying to congratulate Cody on his big win, but he keeps me close to his side. "Have you met Quinn?" he says to a few people, and it's only after him nearly hiding me from others that I understand he's trying to shield me from people he doesn't want me talking to. Rivers and Dani follow behind us, bickering of course, probably about the importance of balloons as a party decoration or something else equally as stupid.

At last, we reach the dance floor where we find Trevor, along with some of Cody's other friends that helped with the class president debacle. The DJ plays the best songs, making it easy for us to let loose. It's a sweaty heap of people in here, but I've never felt so free. When Weezer's "Island in the Sun" comes on, I sprint to Rivers so that we can dance this one out together. I don't know where the routine comes from, but before I know it, he and I are in a rhythm, and there's a circle of people watching us. He spins and twirls me, cages me to his body, and I'm laughing so hard by the end of the song my stomach hurts.

"New rule!" I yell to Rivers as we make our final pass.

"What?" he says as I spin out to his right.

"We have to do this exact routine every time we hear a Weezer song!"

Rivers laughs while nodding his head. "Deal, but we also have to establish our new best Weezer song before we dance." I extend my pinky to him as the crowd around us breaks into applause over our display. He grips my pinky on his own and pulls me into a hug; we're sweaty but don't seem to care. Just content to be here, two best friends, lost in our own world.

The next song that plays is a slow one I don't recognize, but the melody is pretty. Someone taps on my shoulder from behind me, and Rivers stiffens in my periphery.

"Want to dance, Quinn?" Justin holds out his hand to me. "I can't promise that I can spin you around as good as Rivers, here, but I can try."

I hesitate. I know that this is the last thing Rivers wants me to do, but he'll be right here. It's not like Justin is going to attack me in the middle of the dance floor. I feel like I owe it to Justin for being brave enough to ask, so, after a moment, I place my hand in his. "Sure," I say. "Let's dance." dani stands next to him

Justin guides me to a spot with a bit more room, and as I glance around, I see Rivers shooting daggers in our direction with his eyes, while Dani stands next to him, her jaw so far open it looks like it has a broken hinge.

I'm definitely going to have to answer to her when we get to my house tonight.

"What's the deal with Thomas?" He nods toward Rivers as his hands rest loosely on my lower back—maybe just a touch too low if I'm being honest.

"He's a little protective," I say with a laugh.

"Are you guys like together or something? I swear I heard you were single, but if not, I can leave you alone."

How do I even begin to explain what Rivers and I are? I decide it's not worth it, especially with Justin of all people. "We aren't together. We've been friends for a few years, and he just gets a little weird when other guys show an interest. Actually, when anyone shows an interest." I laugh nervously. It took him nearly all of September to trust that Dani wasn't clout chasing, and even still he grills her any chance he can.

Justin is quiet for a while after that, like he's contemplating what a protective friendship looks like when it's between two people who could theoretically be more. There are a few moments of small-talk throughout the dance. I learn that he's on the golf team of all things, that he has an older brother and younger sister, and that he thinks *Avatar* is the best movie ever made, but mostly the conversation is quiet and surface level.

When the end of the song comes, he leans close to me and whispers, "You look stunning, Quinn. I hope you know that." Then he kisses my cheek and goes back to find his friends, leaving me unsure of what to do. It wasn't unpleasant, but it wasn't expected either.

Does Justin... like me? I haven't felt that way about him before, but after that cheek kiss, I'm reconsidering if my feelings are fully platonic. Thankfully, Dani appears at my side in an instant, and I have someone to work through all of that with.

"So," she starts, "what the fuck was that about?" Her lack of a filter never ceases to amaze.

"I...I don't know. We chat on our way to the busses after school most days, but I didn't know that he had any interest. He doesn't know anything about me."

"Do *you* have interest? Cause he looked like he wanted to eat you..." she trails off. "That's bad by the way."

I laugh as she and I make our way to the concession table in search of water. "I don't know Justin enough to have an interest in him. I think he's hot, but that's not interest, is it?"

She stands there, thoughtful for a beat. "I think it could be the start of interest? Attraction is a pretty natural first step, ya know?"

It makes sense. But I wouldn't say I'm even remotely close to saying I have a crush on Justin. Maybe if I learn more about him? But even still, I don't know if I even want to learn more about him. Rivers seemed pretty adamant that Justin was a no go for prospective dating partners.

Dani and I make our way back to the dance floor in search of our friends, as the bass from the songs permeates through our shoes. I throw my hands up in the air to "Yeah!" by Usher, and "Sexy Back" by Justin Timberlake. I've tried to find Rivers for the last fifteen minutes, but it seems like he disappeared after my dance with Justin, and I decide I can't worry about him right now.

The dancing quiets the thoughts in my brain begging me to think about them, but they can wait for later. For right now, I just want to enjoy my friends. Cody is doing the sprinkler, and Dani and I come up with a new dance move called "the toaster" where we bend in half, arms tucked in, then pop up like toast. It makes everyone laugh, and we can't stop coming up with stupid moves like "the waitress" or "the shoe shiner."

Eventually, a slow song comes on, so I turn to face Cody, expecting him to dance with me for the first time tonight. But instead of him holding my waist or taking my hand like all the other guys are, he leans in and whispers, "Quinn, if I dance with you, I think Rivers's head will explode—especially after your little dance with Justin. Give him a break and dance with him."

"Why is everyone so convinced of Rivers's feelings but him? He and I have talked about whatever we are, and it's clear we're just friends," I tell Cody.

"If that's what you need to believe, fine, but I'm not slow dancing with you when he's looking at me like he wants to rip me apart and feed me to the wolves." Cody lets out a low chuckle like I should know all the ins and outs of Rivers's emotions, but I don't.

Exasperated, I huff out a sigh and turn to face him. His eyes light up when I step closer to him, and I don't even ask if he wants to dance before I put my arms around his neck and force him into a slow sway while I glare at him with defiance.

"Sure, Quinn, I'd love to dance," he says, mockingly.

"Why are you staring at any boy who comes within four feet of me like you want to murder them?" My smile is so fake it could be on a Barbie.

Rivers leans his head close to me. His lips brush my ear, my heart races, and every inch of skin where his fingers press into my back tingles. "Because I do—especially Justin."

I pull back to look at him, confused. "Why? The rule in Yosemite was that I couldn't date your friends, but here I am, not dating anyone, and you're still being possessive."

"Jesus, Quinn. Look at you! You're the most beautiful girl in the room tonight, and you don't even know it. You look like you stepped out of a fucking magazine in that dress, and everyone can see it but you. But the worst part is that I know what you look like with dirt on your nose, and sweat in your hair, and you're still the most beautiful thing I've ever seen. So, forgive me for not wanting all of these fake people looking at you like they know anything about you. They see you because Cody made them see you, which I understand was the point, but I see you because you're the goddamn sun."

Blinking in surprise, I furrow my brow at him. It's the closest he's ever come to being fully honest with his feelings. I move closer toward him, bringing the tips of my fingers to his chest, unsure of what to make of his declaration. Something like hope flares in me, thinking that maybe, just maybe, he's finally ready to acknowledge what we've been ignoring the last two years.

"Rivers..."

He runs his fingers through his hair, a sign of frustration, as he takes a step back. "Just do me a favor, Quinny. I know I asked you to please not date any of my friends, but what I really need is for you to make sure that whoever you choose to date is someone who likes you for you, and not because you're the newest commodity. Can you do that for me?"

He shatters me in an instant, any hope I had for us dashed. He still doesn't want me, he just wants to make sure that whoever does is worth my time—like a good friend would.

"Yeah," I choke out, willing myself to hold back the tears forming in my eyes.

Dani must sense something off in my body language. She pulls me away from him, takes me to the bathroom, and lets me cry on her for the rest of the dance as I tell her every detail of mine and Rivers's friendship: from the first camping trip, to the letter I gave him, to every line we walked but didn't cross in Yosemite.

She doesn't interrupt, doesn't ask questions. She just listens to me pour my heart out until Cody finally texts me to tell me that Rivers got a ride with Trevor, and he can take Dani and me back to my house.

"Are you okay?" Cody's voice breaks the silence on the drive home. "I saw you leave for the bathroom in the middle of your dance with Rivers. What happened?"

Dani tells him the basics—Rivers's comment about me being the sun, and then his abrupt request of me. She leaves out the part where I felt like maybe we'd finally moved into a place where we told each other how we felt and break our walls down, but I think Cody is smart enough to read between the lines.

At my house, I get out of the passenger seat, and Cody meets me at the front of his car with his arms open, pulling me into a hug. "It's going to be okay, Quinn. I've only known you for two months, but already I know that you're not someone I want to lose. If Rivers has had you for two years, I can only imagine how scared he is of losing you by fucking things up with dating."

"Thanks, Cody," I mumble.

As I fall asleep, I think of how ironic it is that I confessed my feelings to Rivers, leaving me broken. Now, he's finally reciprocated, and I'm still here.

Broken.

Chapter Fifteen

Now

On Wednesday morning, the kids and I are exhausted. Wyatt's art club is heading up the forest fire prevention campaign for the Rotary Club this year which means their designs will be seen around the mountain, and potentially the state if they go far enough. It's actually pretty great that they extended the job to the middle school; usually they keep big projects like this for high school students. My dad told me that Sawyer hit a new PR for his mile time—six minutes and twenty-one seconds! I'm so proud of him. He and I have been working so hard this last summer to adjust to the altitude of living here with grueling runs around the lake and conditioning him to push through the reduced oxygen. Needless to say, we're all spent.

It's Wyatt's day to decide the music. She's chosen something soft for this morning, which is nice. Most days she chooses something really peppy, but this is pretty and relaxing. I glance at the screen in my car so I can add the song to my library;

it's called "Déjà Vu" by ROM COM, and I might be obsessed with it.

"This is pretty, Wyatt," I say, but she doesn't hear me. "Wyatt?"

She turns to look at me, and I repeat myself. "I said this song is pretty."

"Thanks, I found it a few days ago. Hey, I wanted to talk to you about Dr. Thomas."

She sounds like she's just remembered, and I chance a glance at Sawyer. I don't want him to be persuaded by her either.

"Okay, want to talk about it tonight? I'd like to give your brother some space to think on his own."

"No, we already talked about it together, Mom."

Sawyer looks at me in the mirror; I can't get a read on him, but I appreciate that he and Wyatt talked about it together. It's not as long as I expected them to take—it's only been two days, but I guess I don't know exactly what they're going to say.

"Okay, well let's talk about it then." I take a deep breath, schooling my features so that my response stays neutral. I don't want to seem too excited or too disappointed by their answers. I can't let my feelings get in the way of their boundaries.

"We haven't really decided anything," Sawyer continues. "I don't think either of us can really make a decision about it until we get to know him better. So far, we've only seen him at random places, but we want to know what it's like to spend time with him before we say it's okay or not."

It's a fair request, and one I know I have to honor. I nod while I formulate a response to them. I'm glad they've considered the implications of this decision beyond just saying they want me to be happy, or that it doesn't matter. It does matter. This could change things for all of us. I love that they are emotionally mature enough to realize this, but I also hate that they've had to grow up so quickly—too quickly.

"Alright, I'll try to coordinate something, but it probably won't be for a few weeks. I told Aunt Dani that we'd go to

Velocity Vortex with her and Will this weekend, and our week-days are always too crazy."

We pull into the parking lot of the school and start to un-load. I park in the back lot so that I'm closer to my classroom, but since I'm on the upper floor, it doesn't really matter—I have a walk no matter where I park. The kids come to my class-room with me every morning before they go find their friends; they aren't supposed to, but no one has ever stopped them. Sometimes they sit at the desks before they go or straighten my bookshelf, sometimes they stay the whole time and leave at the bell. Today, Wyatt left after getting a snack from my cupboard, but Sawyer is still here.

"Remember you're helping cook dinner tonight," I tell him as the bell rings. I've been having them choose a meal to learn to cook, and once a week they help see it through to the end. It gives me some one-on-one time with each of them, and they learn an important life skill.

"Yep, I remember. I chose Greek chicken bowls." He comes over to give me a hug before I open the door to let students come in. "When do you see Dr. Thomas again?"

"Um. I don't actually know, now that you ask." I let out a laugh. "We talked about maybe doing something small when I talked to him on Sunday."

"Well, it's your turn to call him now, since he called you." He raps his knuckles on the desk in front of him, the picture of hesitation. "Love you, Mom," he finally says, then turns, and walks out my door.

I pull out my phone and text Rivers. I don't have time for more than a few minutes this week with the kids' schedules.

> **Lunch plans today?**

I'm having my students explore common themes and ideas in *The Outsiders* before we really get started. I want them to think about the issues that each of the boys grapples with in the novel and how they overcome them, if at all. I put them into small group rotations, having them explore concepts like identity and belonging, the cycle of violence, and friendship. They answer questions together, then we'll discuss the ideas as a class before we jump into reading. As they enter the second rotation, my watch dings with an incoming text message.

> Sure! I'll bring lunch. Meet me at the overlook?

His suggestion is perfect. It's only a few minutes' drive to get there, leaving us with most of my forty-minute lunch break.

> Perfect (:

I move through my lesson first period, but every minute feels like it takes forever. I want to see him, and I want to see what he thinks of my kids' proposal. After three more classes fielding questions of *"What does 'identity' mean?"* (oh my god), and four thousand iterations of *"can I go to the bathroom?"* at the worst possible moment, the bell rings for lunch, and I bolt to my car.

The overlook is empty when I get there. It sits above the lake, taking in sweeping panoramic views of the water and the town. It's funny; when I was young, I used to think that Pine Grove was suffocating me, but now, I see how picturesque it is. The barricade reminds me of the walls that lined the bridge in Yosemite all those years ago—tall enough to keep you in, low enough to see over, and made of the same rocky material.

My phone pings with a message from Sybil, and I let out a cackle.

Is there a politically correct way to tell a parent that their child is acting like a dumbass?

The correct answer: Johnny is such a fun student to have in class, and I've seen great improvement from him this year. Recently, he's been having a difficult time not talking while I'm talking, and today it was so bad that the entire class was struggling to stay focused because of it. I know he's better than this, and wanted to make you aware.

What I want to say: If I was given one free pass a year to tell a student to please SHUT UP, I'd use it on your kid. PLEASE tell them to stop talking so I can do my job!

I tuck my phone away as the sound of a car engine rumbles behind me. Rivers steps out in gray chinos, a white button-down shirt with the sleeves rolled up to expose his forearms, and brown leather shoes.

Quite frankly, he looks like a figment of my imagination.

He never mentioned what he was grabbing us for lunch, so when he pulls out a paper bag that has the old Big Rick's logo on the front, I nearly pass out. I haven't had these in years, and I don't even know how to process that Big Rick's can be purchased outside of July 4th now.

I eagerly grab the bag. "Explain!"

"Big Rick may or may not owe me a favor." He shrugs like he hasn't just brought my favorite meal of all time to our impromptu lunch.

I sigh. "Man, I thought I'd be able to buy it somewhere. I want to show my kids, but we weren't here for Jamboree Days this year."

We start walking over to one of the few benches the overlook offers. "Stick with me, and you can. Big Rick owes me a standing favor—as in, if I give him a few hours' notice, he can have food ready."

I start unwrapping my hot dog, feeling stupid for being emotional over a wiener, but this really is such a good surprise.

"Before you start, I brought more toppings in case your order has changed over the years." He unloads pickles, onions, banana peppers, and what looks like sauerkraut.

It's extremely thoughtful of Rivers to assume my taste has changed over the years, to be aware that I'm not the same person I was to him before, and be willing to accept those changes without confining me to my past. I grab a dill pickle spear and a bit of the onion, thankful for the options.

"Thank you," I say as I pile them onto my food. Rivers has even brought an extra little container of Big Rick's famous sauce, "This might be the best meal I've had in twenty years. Why does Rick owe you indefinite hot dogs, and where do I sign up?" I joke.

"I only aim to please," he says as he takes a bite. "And I actually pulled his daughter out of her car after she rolled it a few years ago."

"Seriously?"

"Yeah, it was out there on the eighteen, just past Strawberry Peak. She just took that big turn too fast, and I was right behind her. I didn't want another car to hit her on the blind turn."

I think about my own kids learning to drive on these same treacherous roads where I learned to drive, and how thankful

I'd be to someone like Rivers for pulling them to safety. As a kid, I was always attracted to Rivers's ability to *see* people even at his young age, and to never be the person to let someone else take action. He always stepped in or stepped up. Knowing that he still does this as an adult is sublimely attractive.

When I take my first bite, I'm transported back in time to every memory I've had with this same meal. The time that Liz almost choked because she laughed too hard. The time that I dropped my hot dog on the ground and Rivers stood in line with me for thirty-five minutes so I could get a new one while everyone else went to the lake. The time that I tried the special sauce for the first time and thought I might drift away to heaven because I'd never tasted anything so delicious. Every 4th of July until the year I turned eighteen had been spent eating this meal, with this man, in this town.

It only takes us a few minutes to finish our food; we practically inhale it. I stand up to collect our garbage and place the crumpled-up napkins and foil wrappings into the bin by the edge of the overlook.

The sky is cloudless, a blue so stunning it looks like someone painted it instead of just occurring naturally on its own. It heightens the beauty of everything around me, and I'm left wondering for the second time today how I could have ever wanted to leave this place.

Rivers comes up behind me and curls his arms around my waist, pulling me against him. I can't help but shiver. My breath comes out in shallow spurts; I can't think straight with his proximity to my body, his breath in my ear, and the need to taste him.

"You ever think we'd be back here together, Quinn?"

"I didn't think I'd be back in Pine Grove at all, let alone with you!"

He laughs into my neck, and my body ignites.

"...But I'm glad I am."

He squeezes me tighter, just like he used to, and it feels so easy to fall into him like this. Like I'm fifteen and there isn't anywhere else I'm supposed to be but right here, like this, with his arms holding me against him.

"How has your week been?" he asks.

"Pretty good, things are busy right now with the kids, and Dani needs me to go to Velocity Vortex this weekend for Will's birthday because Brad dipped out again."

It takes a supreme amount of effort not to barf at the mention of Brad.

"I always hated that asshole," Rivers grumbles.

I'm glad to know that his disdain of Brad is still alive and well in him too.

"That'll be fun though!"

"It'll be good for the kids, but Dani and I get motion sickness now so the kids will be doing everything on their own." At the mention of my kids, I remember in part, the reason I asked him to lunch. "Hey, I just remembered why I invited you on this lunch outing!"

His arms squeeze around me tighter, and I'm captivated by him. His smell, his warmth, how easy it is for him to hold me like this. "You mean it wasn't because you needed an eye exam?" He turns me to face him, looping his arms low against my waist, then looks into my eyes trying to decipher the condition of my corneas.

"Actually, it was because I had a *That's So Raven* style vision and knew you'd find a way to bring me a Big Rick's hot dog," I deadpan.

"God, I always knew you were psychic!" He throws his head back like he can't believe he forgot some fundamental part of me, but as he does, I'm mesmerized by the long column of his throat.

When he swallows, I see his Adam's Apple bob, and this close to him, his pulse beats steadily beneath his skin. I move back into him, his hands resting on my hips, and put my lips just over his pulse point so I can feel it beating.

"My kids have a request of you before they commit to an answer." My voice comes out as a whisper against his skin, the gravity of this moment settling in around us.

"Oh." His chest rises and falls against mine with an unsteady breath and his muscles tighten as he braces for what I'm about to tell him, like his happiness depends on what they said.

"They asked to get to know you more before they decide..."

He pulls back to look me in the eyes as my mouth curves up in a smile. "Seriously?"

The hope in his eyes and in his voice knocks something loose in my chest.

"Seriously."

He nods his head. "Okay, well, when are you guys free? I'll move whatever I need to move to make it work." It's considerate of him to offer. Rivers is an adult with adult responsibilities. Making schedules align is tough, but I appreciate that he sees I have three schedules to manage, not just one.

"Well, we're full the rest of this week, and then we have Velocity Vortex this weekend, so maybe next week sometime? I have to ask the kids what they have, but that's probably the soonest."

"Sure. I'm supposed to have dinner with my parents and Forest one day next week, and Trevor, Theo, and I were supposed to do a poker night, but they haven't set a day yet so let me tell them to keep it tentative until I know, okay?"

The mention of his family reminds me that I haven't told him I saw his mom, or that she asked me to have tea with her. I've been delaying it; Lianne didn't give me any indication that she harbored negative feelings toward me when I saw her, and if my parents are to be believed, she doesn't, but it doesn't erase the guilt of what I did, or what I said to her. "Speaking of your mom, I ran into her on Sunday. I forgot to tell you."

"How was that?" Now standing to the side of me, he takes my hand in his like he can sense my trepidation and knows that this is a sure-fire way to calm me; he's right. Every graze of his thumb lights tiny fires along my skin, until I'm covered in goosebumps and thinking about all the ways his thumb could move along other parts of my body.

"It was good. I told her I'd come for a tea party." I don't want him to know that the idea of sitting down with Lianne when we both have time terrifies me.

"You two and your tea parties." He rolls his eyes.

Rivers was never a tea guy. He liked coffee for a while, but really, he survived primarily on Mountain Dew when we were younger. "Are you still obsessed with Mountain Dew?"

He laughs, caught off-guard by the sudden shift, and it's like hearing the ocean for the first time—invigorating and life-altering. "Probably as obsessed as you are with Taylor Swift."

"So still the number one supporter of the brand? Got it."

We joke back and forth for a while about the merits of my music taste, about fad diets, and multi-level marketing schemes before my alarm rings, reminding me that I still have two classes and forty students to get through today. Before I get back into my car, he pulls me to him, his hands on each side of my face. We both know he can't kiss me; we both want him to. I bite my lip, trying to muster enough self-control to get through the next two minutes with him looking at me like he could devour me in seconds, wishing we had the time and permission for him to do what we're both aching for. His thumb tugs my lip from my teeth, and skates across it as his gaze bores into mine. "You are not allowed to do that in front of me again, Quinn." His voice is low, and rough.

"Why not?" I tease.

"Because the next time you do, I'm biting that lip myself until I hear you beg for me to stop."

He leaves me with a kiss on my temple and my heart hammering a thousand beats a minute.

Chapter Sixteen

Now

Dani and Will stay the night at my house Friday night so that we can leave for Velocity Vortex early Saturday morning. It's only a two-hour drive, but leaving at seven in the morning with three teenagers felt like a dice roll we weren't willing to take in order to avoid traffic.

The temperature in Valencia is supposed to reach eighty-five today, so I've decided to wear a pair of denim shorts that hit me mid-thigh and a basic white t-shirt to help keep me cool. My legs are still tanned from summer, and running has kept me toned. At thirty-six with two kids, I realize my body isn't what it used to be, but I'm proud of what it can still do.

Dani meets me in the kitchen with coffee and appraises my outfit with a glance up and down and a slow whistle. She doesn't say anything. She's never been a big shorts girl—but I'm still technically following my mom's rule from when I was twelve. Shorts and a t-shirt, or a tank with long pants. I think this will keep me cooler, and I won't complain about catching a bit more sun before the weather turns.

The kids talk in the backseat, but ultimately all fall asleep after thirty minutes in the car while Dani and I plug into an audiobook about faeries that we refuse to let them know we listen to; they give us crap for almost everything we do, we don't need to add a shadow daddy to the list too.

When we're thirty minutes away from the park, Dani pauses the audiobook. "I forgot to ask you, have you noticed Will and Wyatt being a little touchier with each other than normal?"

I look at her confused. "What? No."

"I'm not saying they have a crush on each other, I've just noticed that they've been a little... hmmm ...friendlier than normal?"

"I haven't noticed, but I'll be paying attention today."

Groggily from the back seat, I hear Sawyer's voice. "What are we paying attention to today, Mom?"

Thankfully Will and Wyatt are still asleep, but I need to come up with an answer for Sawyer before he catches on.

"To see if I'm limping," Dani says with a straight face. "I think I pulled something in my workout two days ago."

Sawyer's face is full of confusion; I can't blame him—why would I be watching Dani's limp—even so, he seems to believe us.

The parking lot isn't too full when we arrive; I'm sure it will get worse as the day goes on, but for now the kids should have a pretty easy time getting on the rides they want to go on. We approach the ticket counter to get the teacher discount that isn't available online while the kids stand off to the side kicking a rock back and forth between them. Will and Wyatt are standing closer than necessary, but I haven't seen them even brush shoulders since we got out of the car. The shrill ring of Dani's phone cuts through the air right before it's our turn at the counter.

"You take your call, I'll grab the tickets, and you can pay me back me later," I tell her.

She steps away as I'm called for my turn, where I have to present two forms of I.D. just to get the discount on my tickets, one of which had to be my school issued badge. As I tuck my money into my bag, I walk toward the kids and tear each ticket on the perforated line. Dani stands with her hand over her eyes looking toward the parking lot as if she's searching for someone. My mind instantly thinks that Brad decided to show up for the first time in a decade. Moving on instinct toward Will so that he doesn't see him until Dani is ready to explain what's going on, I turn him away and try to shield him from the impending doom that is his deadbeat dad.

"Mom, turn around," Sawyer says.

I try to look at him to communicate silently like he and Wyatt always do, but then I see Wyatt and Will looking at me with smiles on their faces too. "What's going on?" I ask.

"We may have asked Aunt Dani for a favor..." Wyatt says.

I turn around to find none other than Rivers Thomas, standing four feet away from me, wearing sand-colored shorts, a blue polo that hugs his sculpted arms, and brown lace-up sneakers. I see the swirls of black ink stretching across his bicep and have to physically restrain myself from pulling his sleeve up and seeing what it is he has tattooed there and how much of his skin it covers. I never thought he'd be the type to get tattoos, especially one so big, and discovering this part of him has my fingers itching to explore him.

"Hope it's okay that your kids invited me?" he asks sheepishly.

I whirl around to my kids, my brain moving a mile a minute trying to understand how all of this happened.

"We wanted to get to know him," Sawyer whispers.

"So, we asked Aunt Dani to see if she could invite him to come." Wyatt shrugs as if this is the most casual request she's ever made, then starts walking toward Will and the entrance of the park.

This feels different than the other times I've seen him with my kids; bigger somehow. The other times were accidental; they saw him for a few minutes before they went on their way to something else. But this? This is us spending an entire day at an amusement park together where they might argue, or misbehave, or get motion sickness. This is...big.

Dani sidles up next to me, a feat considering our height difference. "Please don't be mad. The kids told me that they asked you to set something up with him but felt like you might put it off, then came up with the idea of inviting him here as a surprise for you."

I bump into her arm to knock her off balance. "I'm not mad, but I am surprised."

"What surprises you?" She knows that I have a minimum of fourteen thousand thoughts in my head right now.

"That the kids asked you to do it, that he agreed to spend his day here, seeing him. All of it really."

Rivers points to a fountain ahead of us and gets in line with the kids before shouting, "Three, two, one!" and they all bolt away like bats out of hell, racing toward the water. Sawyer gets there first, unsurprisingly, followed by Rivers, Will, and finally Wyatt. The kids are instantly calling for a re-match and to his credit, he obliges.

Repeatedly.

Until they're all out of breath and in search of water, which Rivers pays the astronomical price to get.

Once they chug their waters, the kids point to the reason for this adventure: Skyrend, an insanely fast coaster where they strap passengers in face down as it hurtles them through corkscrews, pretzel loops, zero-g rolls, and more, all while staring at the ground.

The sight of it alone makes me want to barf.

Dani helps guide the kids toward the attraction as Rivers falls into step with me. He's sweating after performing amusement park style suicides with a group of teenagers, but I can still smell his cologne teasing me. He takes my hand in his like he's done more times than I could begin to count, our fingers falling into their designated places as we walk. "You haven't said much since I showed up. Do you want me to leave?"

"No! I'm still just processing that my kids asked Dani to set this up and that they all hid it from me! I'm glad you're here. It means you get to go on all the rides with the kids so I don't throw up over all these strangers." I motion my arm outward toward the crowd, and a guy passing by looks at me in disgust.

Fair.

Rivers lets out a laugh. "It would be my honor to save these fine pedestrians from the partially digested contents of your stomach, Quinny." He places his hand on his heart, and I snort.

"The partially digested contents of my stomach?! That is the grossest sentence I've ever heard!" I bend over to catch my breath from laughing so hard—his quick wittedness never ceases to impress.

We look at each other, still holding hands, and he gives mine a squeeze. "I could get drunk on the sound of you laughing like that, you know."

"Better find a designated driver for the way home then," I say with a smirk.

Dani turns around to face us, noticing our hands linked together. I bite my lip, unable to hide my blush. Before I register it, Rivers has pulled me between two buildings and pressed me against the wall.

"What are you doing?" I say, looking between his eyes.

"I warned you about the lip, Quinn," he says, as his breath skates across the length of my jaw.

My hands find his, my breathing coming out in shallow spurts. I pull away from him, locking my eyes with him in a challenge as I bite my lower lip one more time.

"Quinn," his voice is hushed, "I know I can't kiss you right now, but staying away from you feels like torture."

"Why can't you kiss me?" I answer in barely a whisper.

He swallows, like it's physically paining him to restrain himself. "Your kids. They haven't given us permission..."

"What if I give you permission?"

"Do you?" He moves closer to me; we're less than a breath apart.

I kiss his jaw, then the corner of his mouth. "I," I start, then brush my lips against his, in a hint of a kiss, so gentle that someone passing by might think we bumped into one another. I let my lips linger as I say they final word, "do."

He crushes his lips to mine, fireworks explode on every inch he touches. His hand moves to my jaw then tugs on my hair as his tongue swirls against mine in a dance. He bites my bottom lip, tilting my head back to deepen the kiss, while my hands clutch his shirt. He groans into my mouth, and I'm so consumed by this moment I'm scared I'll wake up and it'll all be a dream.

Rivers pulls away slowly, our breathing shallow and heady. "Holy shit," he breathes.

"Holy shit," I echo, taking in the blush in his cheeks and how my fingers have mussed his hair. We've been playing this game for so long, tip toeing around the inevitable, but if I'd known that Rivers would kiss me like his life depended on it, like we were each other's air, I would have let him do it ages ago.

I pepper him with a few more soft pecks, and he pulls my mouth deeper against his with one more swipe of his tongue. I press my body closer to his and feel the firm line of him straining against his shorts. "You're torturing me, Quinn," his voice comes out as a whisper.

"I'm torturing myself," I answer back.

He leaves one more chaste kiss on my lips, before he takes my hand again and steers us toward the ride where the kids are so engrossed with their conversation, they don't even notice Rivers silently letting go of my hand as if to say, *I want to respect what they need.*

"Who's going to sit alone?" Wyatt asks the boys as Rivers and I approach. "We can take turns throughout the day, but what are we doing for this one?"

"Whoa, whoa, whoa," Rivers cuts in. "No one is sitting alone; I'm riding these rides with you guys. So, I guess the real question is who has to sit with me," he says it self-deprecating-ly, like sitting with him is worse than riding alone.

All three kids stare up at him in shock. Dani might be a little surprised too, but I'm not. Rivers has always been a roller coaster junkie; we both were, actually. It wasn't until I had Sawyer that I started to get motion sickness.

"You're going to ride with us?" Sawyer sounds impressed.

"Absolutely, I am!" Rivers pretends to be offended that the kids would even consider him *not* going on these rides.

"I'll sit with you first, Dr. Thomas," Sawyer offers.

"Okay hold on," Rivers begins. "Before we start this day out, I need you to start calling me Rivers. We're well past being so formal."

The kids look to me, unsure of how to proceed. We've al-ways talked about the importance of giving adults respect with what we call them—especially using proper titles. My parents still get after me for not using a "sir" or "ma'am" when talking to anyone; especially their friends, and it's been important to me that my kids do the same. I see far too many students in my line of work think that they run the show, or that they can get away with being disrespectful, and I refuse to let my own kids be part of the problem. This is different though; they've never been in a situation like this before.

"Guys, do you remember when we were first learning about the Civil Rights movement, Native American communities, and transgender people?" They nod, confused looks on their faces as to why I'm bringing this up right now. "What have I always told you about what we call each of those communities? Why do we use 'people of color' or 'indigenous people' or a preferred name?"

I see the moment the light goes on in Sawyer's mind. "We use the names people ask us to use."

"Right," I smile.

Sawyer looks back up at Rivers, who has a good eight inches of height on him still, and says, "I'll ride with you, Rivers."

"Sweet!" Rivers pumps his fist into the air, then extends his hand out to Sawyer, offering what can only be described as the beginning of a bro high five.

Instead of taking it, however, Sawyer grips Rivers's hand and tells him to dab, or maybe dap, him up? I can't be sure with the youths of today. It takes a bit of explaining on the part of the kids, but eventually Rivers figures it out, and the kids take turns doing some type of grip with their hands all the way into the line, leaving Dani and I to ourselves.

"And this is why I teach fifth grade," she monotones.

I snicker as we walk toward the bench by the exit of the ride where they'll come out. "I'd take whatever the hell that was over crying kids," I sing-song, knowing it's the least favorite part of Dani's job.

"Thanks for asking him to come, Dani," I say, once we've been on the bench for a few minutes. "I wouldn't have thought this would be the right setting, but I think letting the kids get to know him away from me is smart."

"You're welcome. How are you feeling about everything now that you've spent some time with him?"

"Pretty good, I think. I still have a lot of reservations, but I'm trying to be open to the idea of something new." I pause for a beat, considering everything I'm trying to navigate. "I'm also trying to be honest with myself and with everyone around me. I don't want anyone getting hurt, me included." We watch the coasters whiz above us, taking in the screams of glee and terror from the passengers.

My phone vibrates with a text from Rivers attached to a picture. They're in a line of four, with Rivers at the far end, Sawyer in between him and Wyatt, then Will at the opposite end. They're all smiling, though, traces of fear linger in Wyatt's eyes. She's a daredevil once she gets started with whatever it is, but the lead-up usually makes her jumpy. I aim the screen towards Dani so she can see, but she pulls my phone towards herself before I register what's happening.

"Are you seeing this?!" She practically shouts even though I'm six inches away from her face, and she wiggles the phone in front of my eyes like I should be shocked by what I find there.

"Yes...why are you freaki—" I stop immediately when I realize what she sees. It's hardly visible, and the angle could be playing tricks on our eyes, but if we're seeing it right, Wyatt and Will's hands are clasped together, their fingers entwined.

We look at each other as if to confirm our suspicions, then, with all the exuberance of thirteen-year-old girls, start jumping up and down, squealing, and hugging one another. It must be an image, watching two thirty-six-year-old women behave like children in public, but I can't find it in me to care.

"What do you think it means?" Dani asks me.

"I really don't know. She told me just a few days ago that she was excited to see Keegan somewhere!"

"Well, you better find out! You know Will isn't going to tell me shit!"

Less than thirty seconds later, our attention shifts to the exit of the ride where the kids are laughing and jumping, and Rivers encourages all of them like he's their ringleader.

"Fun?" I ask them.

"Mom that was *awesome*," Wyatt says. "We want to go again. Is that okay?"

"Will, is that okay with you? We're here to celebrate your birthday," Rivers asks him.

I love that he remembers that this day is important for Will. That he knows how shitty Brad is and that we recognize the reason we're here at all is because Will asked to be here.

Will agrees to go on Skyrend one more time, changing up the seating arrangement that puts Rivers in the middle because all the kids want to be around him (swoon), then we'll make our way over to the Drop of Doom, which doesn't sound sketchy at all.

They have the same response as the first time they came out, jumping around ecstatically in laughter as if they've just won a million dollars each.

When Rivers links arms with both of my kids, and instructs
Will to link up with Wyatt, so they can form a can-can line
complete with high kicks as they walk toward the next ride, it
feels more like having four kids to watch here instead of three.

I fucking love it.

Rivers's easy nature makes the day so much more fun than
it would have been without him, and I think that's why I've
always loved being in his presence: it's never a bad time without
him, but everything is amplified when he's around. Life seems
fuller, more colorful, and appears brighter just by having him
be part of it.

The cycle repeats with every ride of the day: they go on as a
group and come off laughing to meet Dani and me. We decide
to stop at the Twisted Taco for lunch, ordering more food than
we know what to do with.

The heat starts to get to all of us, but no one is ready to
leave after only being here half the day. Dani suggests the River
Rapids ride that she and I can go on with everyone, and to my
surprise, the kids seem genuinely excited that we get to go with
them on something.

We sit down in a circular tube with a handle in the middle
for all of us to grab. The kids have conveniently positioned
us so that I sit with Rivers on my left and Dani on my right,
insisting that they don't want us to be able to communicate
what's happening behind us. It feels like they just want to see
us sit together though, as if we're back in middle school and
our friends are coordinating our arrangement.

At the first drop, a deluge of water spills over the raft and
onto Rivers and me, mostly missing Dani, but she's definitely
more damp than she was before the ride started. It sends the
kids into fits of giggles watching us shake off the water and
brace for the next blast from the raging rapids beneath us.

After the second drop, I curl my body towards Rivers in an
attempt to get less water on me, but his arm around me does
little to shield the torrent of droplets. We are all soaked to the
bone when we step off the ride, and I thank my past self for

wearing a nude-colored bra today instead of something more colorful. The water slides down my arms and legs, glistening in the sun, and makes me feel sticky in the way these types of rides always do.

The kids run ahead, leaving us alone to process how doused in water we are.

"Holy shit that was fun," Rivers says as the kids walk toward an ice cream cart.

"Fun. Freezing. They're hardly synonyms," I joke.

"I'm going to feed that kid so many fucking vegetables this week," Dani seethes, her teeth chattering. She took the brunt of the water after that first drop, but she can't complain about it being hot anymore.

"Make sure one night is cauliflower rice," I tell her, knowing it's Will's least favorite. "And make sure you tell him it's from me."

Rivers laughs at us; I don't mind the water—it really was a cool reprieve from the heat. Dani might not be kidding about torturing Will with vegetables, though, and since I love my adoptive nephew slash potential future life partner of my daughter, I decide to at least rescue him for one night.

"Actually, do you and Will want to come watch the Chiefs-Patriots game Monday night? We could do dinner?" I hesitate a moment before I ask Rivers to join, too. Inviting him to our house seems like a big step, but the kids asked to be able to spend time with him. "Rivers, do you want to come too?"

He kisses me so softly on the lips, if I wasn't soaking wet, I'd think I was dreaming, drifting closer and closer into the pull of his orbit until I'm nothing but stardust. His blue gray eyes look between my own as if trying to decipher my innermost thoughts. "Yeah, Quinn," he finally says. "I'd love to."

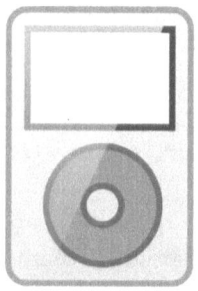

Chapter Seventeen

Then, Freshman Year

By Thanksgiving in the desert, Rivers and I are back to normal as if nothing happened at homecoming.

Like he didn't ask me to be choosy with who I date.

Like he didn't tell me he wanted to murder anyone who gets near me.

Like he didn't tell me I was the sun.

It was weird at first, stilted. I knew what he said, but we still wouldn't acknowledge it, and he wouldn't admit that he came that close to being fully transparent with his emotions, but at least he didn't make it too weird. After a few weeks though we snap back into our usual banter, forgetting everything we did and didn't say.

The Monday following Thanksgiving break, June flies back to Vermont. It's lucky she does, too, because that night a giant snowstorm moves in with a vengeance, leaving the ground covered in a blanket of white so deep, the schools have no alternative but to cancel Tuesday morning for the safety of the buses.

For us, though, it means the only way we know how to spend a snow day: Ever Wild Park. Both my dad and Rivers's dad are masters at driving through terrible road conditions, so by seven-thirty in the morning, we're on our way down the mountain headed towards Anaheim.

"Should we take the ninety-one, or the two-ten to the fifty-seven, Diane?" Dad asks my mom as we reach the bottom of the mountain.

"The two-ten. You know the ninety-one has traffic no matter what time of day it is," she says.

After an hour and a half or so, I'm listening to the song "Just Let Go" by Mae (another Rivers suggestion) when my parents' voices finally cut through the noise of my headphones. "Quinn!"

I pull out my earbud and hit pause on the song. "Yeah?"

"Can you text Rivers and see where they are? Tell him we're about to be at the fifty-seven, ninety-one interchange," my dad says.

I do as Dad instructs and wait for Rivers's response.

> My dad says we're almost right behind you. We just passed Cal State Fullerton

I relay the message to my parents, thankful we won't have to wait long to meet up with the Thomases. Liz brought her portable DVD player, so she's been watching *Kim Possible* since we got off the mountain. She'll be with Rivers and me for most of the day—our parents usually just wander around the park since we have season passes and they've been on everything. They'll take Liz on some stuff though, like when Rivers and I want to do the bigger rides since she's still too small to go on most of them.

We meet the Thomases at the trams; Lianne has on her turquoise visor she always wears, blue capri pants, and a floral top that makes her look like she's more ready to walk along the beach than here—she must have been freezing in Pine Grove this morning. Bryan pulls Liz and me into hugs. He calls us the daughters he never had.

We talk about whether we think we'll get another snow day tomorrow as we wait for the trams, but eventually we're on our way, and without any of us saying anything, we set off for Forgotten Current—an almost pitch black boat ride about mermaids turned sirens that lure sailors to their doom. It's cheesy as hell, but fun. We come here so often we all know the order of things: get a RapidRider Pass for Skeleton Crossing, go to Forgotten Current, ride House of Horrors, go back to Skeleton Crossing, then head over to the hand-dipped corn dog stand. After that, it's up in the air.

The smell of chlorine in the air is strong when we enter Forgotten Current; some people think it's overpowering, but I've always liked it in some twisted way. My mom tells the park ranger (how Ever Wild refers to their employees) we have seven people in our group, and they give us three rows in the boat: my parents take the first one with Liz, Bryan and Lianne are in the middle, and Rivers and I are in the back, alone.

The ride moves us forward, and we're sent into near complete blackness as we bob along through the water. There's a figurine of an old man playing a banjo to the left, and a restaurant you need reservations for to the right. As we approach the first drop of the ride, the animatronic sailor head above us repeats the mantra, *"There's no turning back now."*

After much anticipation, the boat flies down the first big plunge, but instead of being startled by a splash of water that hits my thigh, I'm startled by Rivers's arm resting over my shoulder, pulling me closer to him. I chance a look at him, we've been on good terms, but far less touchy since homecoming. "I feel like I might combust if I don't have part of me touching you, Quinn. Is this okay?" he whispers against my ear.

I lean up to meet him, my body turning towards his, "Yes." I've also felt the absence of his touch these last few weeks, and I've hated it. The desert was fine this year, and we had fun. But we didn't hold hands; we didn't even hug. I've missed it, missed him.

The ride passes—we spot the jewels and gems that someone tried to steal from the park once, along with the dress that belonged to an actress who loved the ride. Rivers removes his arm from my shoulder so that our parents don't see, and the loss of it feels like a tooth that's been pulled. Like that cavity is supposed to have something there so your tongue keeps searching for it but only feels its absence.

House of Horrors and Skeleton Crossing are no different. Rivers holds my hand during House of Horrors and rests his hand on my thigh during Skeleton Crossing. I should have known him to be a traitor though, because the second the skeletons start their bow and arrow fight, he starts tickling my leg, making me squirm and hold his hand in an effort to escape.

We eat lunch early, around eleven, because even though the park isn't too busy, it is starting to fill up more, and we don't want to be left without a place to sit and eat our corn dogs.

"Can we go to Railway Roadsters?" Liz asks when we finish eating. It's one of the bigger rides that she can go on that my parents can't do with their motion sickness. Rivers and I tell the adults we'll take her to Railway Roadsters, then to Space Cadets, since the concentric circles are what make my parents sick, and that we'll meet them at Galactic Blasters.

In line for Railway Roadsters, we play games like "I Spy" and make up narratives for the people around us, like "that guy is here with his mistress, but the lady that looks mean is his wife and he doesn't know she's here, spying."

Eventually, when we get close enough to see where they give us lanes, Liz pulls me down to her. "Quinn, I'm feeling a little nervous."

"It's alright, Liz. You've ridden on this one before and you had the best time!" She scoots closer to me, and I put my arm around her shoulder. She's seven now, but sometimes I forget that seven is still little.

Rivers gets on his knees right in front of her, and takes her small hands in his. "Hey, we'll put you right in between us so you're nice and snug, okay?"

She gives a quick nod of her head.

"I won't let anything happen to you, Liz," he promises, and my heart swells over his kindness.

As promised, Liz sits in between the two of us with her hands firmly placed on the lap bar in front of her as we plunge into the dark. Rivers and I toss our hands in the air at the same time, squealing with delight as we make our way up the first big incline. He clasps my hand, and the butterflies in my stomach are only in small part due to the drop of the roller coaster.

***

Once we drop Liz off with my parents for the Ferris wheel, we're torn between where to go next. We could go ride bigger rides without her. We could go walk through the Ever Wild Mercantile.

"You decide, Quinn. I'll go wherever you want," Rivers says as we walk away from our parents.

What I really want is go back to Forgotten Current and sit in the dark with Rivers while I hold his hand. It's like we both are desperate to touch; starved for it.

I rock back and forth on my heels, the picture of indecision.

"Let's go back to Current," I whisper.

The side of Rivers's mouth twitches in a half-smile before he slips his hand into mine and pulls me toward the ride.

The parks are so quiet today that we walk right back onto the ride, and before we're even out of the light, I'm plastered to his side, begging to feel him. He has one arm around my shoulder, holding me against him, while the other holds my hand resting in my lap.

I can't hear the ride. I can't hear his breathing. All I hear is my heartbeat in my ears, threatening to explode out of me over this contact. Rivers calms every fear I have, every worry. It's like he knows that he's the thing that makes me feel the most alive, and I never want it to end.

"You're thinking too loud," he murmurs against my temple.

"Tell me what I'm thinking about then," I joke.

"Well, you're thinking that this ride was better before they put the palm trees in it," he starts. "And you're thinking that people who eat at the Siren Song are pretentious assholes."

I laugh out loud at that.

"You're so close, but no," I answer as we round the corner before the second drop.

"Then tell me what I'm missing, Quinny, because not knowing what you're thinking is kind of scaring the shit out of me."

I burrow closer into his chest just as he squeezes my hand, prompting me to go on.

"I'm thinking that you're the best part of my day, Rivers, and I don't like how it feels when you aren't touching me." It's the bravest I've been with him in ages.

Rivers swallows and plays with my fingers before he says, "The feeling is mutual."

***

After three hours of us hopping between Forgotten Current, Skeleton Crossing, and House of Horrors to cloak ourselves in the cover of darkness, my dad calls to tell us to meet them by Galactic Blasters for one last ride before we go home for the night. I think, briefly, as we approach our parents that Rivers is going to let go of my hand, but he doesn't. I know our parents see it, and I know mine are going to ask me about it on the drive home but for right now, I don't care. This is where my hand belongs.

Since we're all planning on having school tomorrow (my parents have been told the snow is melting pretty quickly), our parents don't let us stay for the fireworks and parade. It's okay, we've seen it before, but I think it would feel like magic to watch the show with Rivers tonight. He's been different today; we've been different today. I hope it means what I think it means.

Like clockwork, the moment we're back on the fifty-seven-freeway heading home, Dad immediately starts questioning me about Rivers and why we were holding hands.

"I don't know, Dad. We just were."

"Do you like him?" my mom asks. Liz sits next to me with a shit-eating grin; she lives for the drama—other people's drama that is. Honestly, I can't disagree with her. Knowing about other people's business is a hobby we have in common.

"Trust me, me liking Rivers is not the issue here," I say. I put my headphones in, teenager code for *'leave me the hell alone now,'* and rest my head against the window as "Trouble Sleeping" by The Perishers comes on.

***

The sound of my phone buzzing next to my head pulls me from my sleep. It's still dark outside, so I know it's not time to wake up yet, and it's only then that I register that someone is calling me.

Groggily, I answer the phone. "Hello?"

Rivers's whispered voice greets me on the other end. "Quinn?"

A glance at the clock pulls me from my delirium entirely. "Rivers, why the hell are you calling me at two in the morning?"

"No major reason," he says casually, as if it's midday and we're eating lunch. "just that my hand hurts."

I laugh. "And that's the purpose for this call?" I let out a yawn.

"Sort of." He's tired too; his voice is slow and scratchy.

"Well then what's the purpose of you calling and waking me up?"

"I miss you."

"Rivers, you saw me five hours ago."

"Yeah, and now I fucking miss you. My hand hurts because yours isn't here. It feels..." he trails off, "empty."

I try to lighten the mood. "What an observation, Einstein. Your hand is, in fact, empty."

"You know what I mean, Quinn. I feel like you're supposed to be here, and you aren't here, and now I can't sleep because the only thing that would make me feel like half of me isn't missing, is you."

"Oh," is all I can manage.

"So yeah," he says. "I miss you."

I'm silent for a few minutes. These late-night confessions feel more like drunken ones—they're safe to admit here in the dark but come morning we'll pretend they didn't happen just like we always do.

"I miss you, too."

***

Cody's plan worked like a charm, so by the time spring break of freshman year rolls around, I'm fielding more requests to hang out than I know what to do with. I've been dates—one with a guy named Tage and another with one named Benson—but I felt like I was hanging out with Cody both times because everything was so platonic. It also doesn't help that the only person I want to go on dates with is the one person I feel like I can't tell that to.

Mom and Dad decide to skip Yosemite for spring break this year, instead opting to rent a house on the Colorado River in Arizona. Bryan and Lianne can't come until Wednesday because Bryan has to work, so Rivers comes early with us. The best part about my friendship with Rivers is that my parents were the ones to force it to happen so they can't give us too much shit for wanting to be around each other.

What's even better? That Rivers has been around the family for so long, he knows how to dish it back when they do.

Ever since that trip to Ever Wild, Rivers and I have definitely been more affectionate than usual; we're practically joined at the hip. I don't like being apart from him, and it seems like the feeling is mutual, because Rivers has to be touching me if we're in the same room.

Tuesday evening, after dinner and a full day of swimming, Dad suggests we go get ice cream from the local shop, Sprinkles and Scoops. Somehow, Rivers ends up in the middle seat between Liz and I despite him being the biggest out of all three of us. He finds this the most opportune time to rest his hand on the middle of my thigh; every time I try to move it off, he starts to tickle me, but I can't scream or squeal because Dad is driving. It's torturous. I pull out my phone to text him. While my parents are oblivious to our physicality, they aren't deaf.

> Do you mind?

> Nope, it's quite nice actually. Do you?

> Nope (:

He turns to look at me after my last text and shoots me a rueful grin that has so much left unspoken I don't even know where to start.

We pull into the parking lot and Rivers helps me out of the car; I mean it when I say he will find any excuse to be close to me. Rivers orders a peanut butter and chocolate flavor that looks delicious, but I've always liked fruity desserts more than chocolatey ones, so I order a sour rainbow sherbet and add gummy bears to it like I have to every sherbet I've ever ordered—it's just better this way.

Mom and Dad sit at a table next to us and Liz, and ask about if Rivers has heard what time his parents will be leaving tomorrow to get here, if we want to go to the lake or stay by the pool, and what classes Rivers and I will take next year. There's two ASL 2 classes, but from the sound of it, both of us have schedules that mean we'll have to take it third period because sixth period won't work. In the middle of this conversation, the song, "Beverly Hills" by Weezer comes on, and Rivers and I hop to our feet, dancing the routine we came up with at homecoming before they even sing about the *"automobile"* being *"a piece of crap."* My parents and Liz watch us twirling around this little ice cream parlor, the sticky sweetness of waffle cones scenting the air, until the song ends, and the patrons give a perfunctory applause as we take each other in. Rivers's eyes glance to my lips, then he leans in and whispers, "You have ice cream on your lip."

He steps away but doesn't break eye contact, so I do the only thing I can: swipe my tongue gently across my lip, probably too slowly, but there's a hunger in his gaze that wasn't there before.

Game on.

The drive back to the rental consists of Liz begging Rivers and me to watch *Transformers* with her, which we readily agree to but tell her we have to look at the stars first. They're brighter in the desert, and we want to catch fifteen shooting stars before we head in for the movie.

We lay on the edge of the pool, staring up at the night sky answering Liz's questions, and locating the ones we don't want to miss. Rivers and I lie down, side-by-side while Liz sits up, leaning back and using her hands to rest.

"Do you think aliens are real?" she asks after we've pointed out all the constellations we can identify without a map. Orion for him, the Seven Sisters for me.

"For sure," Rivers says.

I turn my head to face him. "Really?" I don't know why it surprises me; it's not like we've ever talked about our extraterrestrial theories.

"Yeah! All that open space? I think it would be crazy not to believe there are other life forms out there. I don't know if I believe that they look like people or like little green things with big heads, but I definitely think there's intelligent life out there somewhere."

"Maybe they're looking up at us right now too, asking the same question," Liz says.

"Yeah, maybe," Rivers agrees. "Maybe we should all do something that shows them what being a human is all about."

I close my eyes and think about what it means to be a human. Is it our ability to use logic and reason? Is it our capacity for love? For hate?

Liz stands up and twirls in a circle with her arms extended to the sky. "What are you doing?" I ask.

"I think being a human means you try to be happy!" she shouts, still twirling and dancing hoping the aliens see her.

"What do you think it means to be a human, Quinn?" Rivers whispers next to me as Liz's shrieks carry around the pool deck.

"Hmm, I think Liz is right about chasing happiness, but I also think that it's about finding someone to share that happiness with."

"Me too," he says as he links his hand with mine, as if to say *I'm chasing happiness with you,* just as the fifteenth shooting star dances across the sky. Maybe the aliens like what they see; I know I do.

***

My parents are tired and want to go to bed, or at least relax in their bed, so it leaves us kids in the living room unattended for the rest of the night. Rivers and I sit next to each other, and I feign being cold in an effort to get closer to him; he can't stand to see me uncomfortable, so I take advantage because the truth is, I crave his touch as much as he craves mine.

Halfway through the movie, Liz falls asleep, so I carry her into the room we share, then make my way back out to Rivers. I sit down next to him, until he pulls me down onto him so my legs are stretched out on the couch and my head lays in his lap, as I take in every detail of his face. The movie is turned down low, and the whole world falls away.

I find his hand and rest it on my stomach where my shirt has ridden up. Our skin is warm from sun exposure today, but it feels electric. His breathing is shallow, like my own, as he inches closer, leaning down toward me so our noses are close to touching, considering our position.

No one could look at these circumstances and say we're just friends. Friends don't find any excuse to touch. They don't stargaze and hold hands like the other person is what keeps them alive. Friends don't make up dance routines to one specific band and perform it out of obligation to each other in the middle of an ice cream shop. They don't call you the sun and live every moment of every day like you are.

But then I think about two years ago, when I told him I liked him, and how he didn't speak to me until after I'd broken up with Trevor, and how losing him now would feel like dying. I think about how crushed I felt after Homecoming, and how no matter what Dani said, I would never be able to unhear Rivers calling me the most beautiful thing he'd ever seen and then shutting me out in the same breath. The fear of losing him is insurmountable.

As if sensing my hesitation, Rivers pulls away from me creating what feels like a chasm between us.

I sit up and stand in front of him while he looks at me in what can only be described as painful confusion. "We can't do this Rivers." I look to the floor.

"Do what?" His voice cracks, and there's a pain there I know I placed.

"I can't do this. I can't lose you, or risk losing you."

Rivers nods his head in understanding. "Let's talk about this tomorrow, Quinn. It's late, we're emotional."

I agree and walk to my bed, bracing for tomorrow. But it doesn't matter; we never speak of it again, paralyzed by our fear.

***

On the last day of school, I can't stop the tears from forming in my eyes. It's been such a whirlwind of a year, but ninety percent of the good experiences have come because Cody took me under his wing. I don't know what I'm going to do without him next year. He's assured me we'll stay friends because he's going to the local community college while he goes through the fire academy, just like his dad did, but I can't be convinced.

"Jesus, Quinn, you can't do this to me. You know I hate seeing you cry," he says on the way to student government.

"I'm not doing it on purpose! I just don't know what I'm going to do without you next year. Who am I going to sit with in here?!"

"The juniors who also love you, the sophomores who think you're hilarious, or I don't know, the people in your own grade who voted you to be the president again, but because they think you're awesome now because they got to see how cool you actually are?"

God that feels like a lifetime ago. I can't believe how I started this year. Back in April, Cody convinced me to run for class president again. He thought it would be important for me to take control of my own social life and show people that how they treated me was wrong and give them a chance to try again. To my surprise, I got it; along with my vice president, Sophie, from ASL, and my secretary, Jaclyn. I don't know either of them well, but I'm excited. I begged Dani to run for treasurer, but she gave me a *'hell no'* that could be heard around the world.

"Fine, have an answer for everything why don't you?" I joke.

Cody laughs good-naturedly. "I'm just saying that things will be okay, Quinn. You were scared last year too, and look how everything worked out?"

Student government is mostly a bunch of tearful goodbyes from the seniors, and before I know it, I'm walking to the bus for my last day of freshman year.

Cody promised that he'd come by my house before graduation so we could get a picture together since he only got so many tickets to the actual ceremony, but it feels heavy waiting for him, knowing that this really is the end of our current arrangement.

The only good news is that June is home for the first time since Thanksgiving and gets to be here for three full weeks before going back to Vermont. She only has a few months left of her program, so it'll be interesting to see if she stays out there or moves home for good.

"He's not dying, Quinn. You'll still see him around." She's trying to comfort me; I've been mopey all day. "Did you like him or something?"

I laugh because I cannot even imagine Cody being anything other than friend. "No! He just...kind of transformed my life, and it'll be weird at school without him." His car pulls into the driveway and he steps out with his royal blue graduation gown on. My dad shakes his hand in congratulations, and I step into a hug, falling apart the moment he squeezes me.

"Geez, Quinn, I know we're all surprised I've made it to graduation, but you don't have to cry about it!" He laughs, and the sound rumbles through his chest.

"It's nothing short of a miracle," I sniff. When we pull away, I realize I haven't formally introduced Cody to June. I know they went to high school together for a couple of years, but I don't think they really talked. "Cody, this is my sister, June. June, this is Cody."

"Thanks for taking care of this rascal for me!" June tries to tousle my hair, but I step back in time.

"He's here to take a picture with me, June. Don't ruin my hair!"

"What's it matter if your make-up is already smeared from you being a big baby?" Liz calls out.

I swear this family hates me sometimes.

Cody laughs again, then walks toward the lawn for our picture. June adjusts us so the light is angled correctly and snaps a few shots on her digital camera. I give Cody one last hug and wish him the best for the ceremony. We'll still have the summer to meet up, but outside of school, Cody and I don't see much of each other as it is. I think the lack of proximity will only increase that, and I hate feeling like everything is about to change again.

My whole family lines up in the driveway to wave him off, his big goofy grin on full display as he drives away. Before I turn inside, June leans over and stage whispers, "Props to you for staying platonic with him, he grew up to be *fine!*"

***

That night, the Thomases come over to taste test my new lemon bar recipe, and it's the first time Forest, June, Rivers, and I have all hung out since Yosemite more than a year ago. Forest is able to come home a lot easier since he's going to UC Santa Barbara, but June being on the east coast makes it hard for their schedules to line up. I can't imagine being so far from Rivers through college. We haven't talked about our plans, but I know we need to soon. He's going to be a junior this year which means it's starting to get real for him; he even has to take the ACT in a few months.

All of our parents gush over my lemon bars, and I tell Lianne I'll bring them to our next tea party on her back deck.

"You're like a grandmother, Quinn, I swear," Rivers laughs as he takes a bite of lemon bar, then abruptly starts coughing by inhaling the powdered sugar. Rookie.

"At least I know how to breathe!" I say, running off toward the trampoline.

Right as I gain my footing on the trampoline, Rivers tackles me down with his arms around me like we're spooning. He starts to tickle me, and I shriek. It took two weeks after spring break for us to figure out how to be comfortable with each other again, and now it feels like we're inching closer to the inevitable moment one of us decides to add boundaries again. The lines are constantly blurred between us; we never know what we are.

We finally lay back on the trampoline listening to the small stream in the yard, our parents' laughter on the deck, and Forest trying to show June how to play the guitar. "Rivers?" I ask.

"Yeah?"

"Do you know what you want to do after high school?"

He looks over at me, skepticism furrowing his brow. "A little, why?"

"Just with Cody graduating, and June and Forest hardly ever seeing each other, it's got me thinking if we'll still be friends and where we'll be, ya know?"

He's quiet for a few minutes. The sun sinks in the sky, but the moon starts to come to life along with the sounds of night: cricket songs and frogs along the water.

"I want to be a scientist, or maybe some type of doctor?" he eventually whispers. "I've never told anyone that."

"Why not? It's not like you want to be bird therapist," I joke. "Those are pretty normal jobs."

"I don't know, I guess it feels like maybe it's too ambitious for someone like me." His vulnerability is surprising. Rivers is one of the most confident people I know; I didn't know he was having doubts about himself.

"Someone like you?" I ask.

"Yeah, average, you know?"

"Rivers, you are not average." It comes out of my mouth immediately. Like hearing him say that he thinks he's average is a personal attack on me. "You're smart and funny and kind. I'd be miserable without you. I can't think of anything that wasn't made better just by you being there with me."

"Thanks, Quinn," he says.

"You're welcome. You're gonna be a kick ass scientist doctor and I'll make Dani fight anyone who says otherwise." He laughs at this. We never say we'll fight off anyone for each other, we always say she'll do it, and honestly, she probably would. It's why we never tell her names; she'll use them.

"Just promise we'll still be friends, Rivers?" I add. "I don't want to end up like June and Forest only seeing each other once a year."

He holds out his pinky. "That's the easiest thing I'll ever promise, and Quinn?"

"Yeah?" I say, clutching his pinky while I watch the clouds turn various shades of cotton candy.

"I'm moving your lemon bars to the top of the happy food pile."

***

The summer passes just as quickly as the last one with Jamboree Days, Rivers doing weight training so he can join the wrestling team, and me, conditioning for cross-country. At the end of school last year, I asked the student government teacher, Mrs. D, if we could coordinate with the school to have select students at readiness days to walk incoming freshmen and other new students around the building like Cody did for me on my first day. I wanted to find a way to pay it forward beyond just keeping my eyes open for kids who seemed lost. The elected reps and Mrs. D liked the idea so much that we had to cap the number of volunteers to five per grade. That way some students could hand out schedules, some could take emergency cards and make sure they were filled out right, a few students would showcase some of the clubs and extracurriculars the school offers, and the rest of us could give walking tours. Next year, I think I'd like to try and get club representatives to set up in the commons so they can talk about their own clubs and recruit members.

Mom makes me drive to the school while she sits in the passenger seat to give me driving practice, but I still make it there by eight o'clock. Mrs. D shows all of us how to verify that the emergency cards are filled out correctly, making sure that the box below allergies is initialed by each guardian because it's small, then reminds us that we are representing the school to new students and their families, and that we should be on our best behavior.

I organized the shifts and stations everyone will be at so that no one gets stuck doing the same thing all day, but tell everyone that if they find someone willing to trade with them, I don't mind. I find the two other girls who were elected in with me this year, Jaclyn and Sophie, and talk to them about their summers. We've spent some time together, but I want to make sure we really work as a team to make this a good year for our class.

In my mind, that starts with me showing them the ropes and helping them get used to this type of class like Cody did for me. Just as we're about to move to our designated places in preparation for when people start arriving at nine, the door opens up and none other but Justin Parks from ASL swaggers in at least three inches taller from last year, with a cocky grin, and seventeen new muscles that make my mouth water.

"What'd I miss?"

Chapter Eighteen

Now

Monday morning, I text Lianne to let her know I'll stop by after school for tea. Sawyer has cross-country practice, and Wyatt is going to Dani's house with Will before they come over for the game. I know myself well enough that if I delay meeting up with her much longer, I'll find excuse after excuse not to do it at all.

"Hey, Mom," Wyatt says from the back seat of the car.

"Hey, Wy," I respond.

She rolls her eyes with every drop of attitude in her body.

"What's up?"

"I...I made my decision about you dating Rivers."

This feels just like last Monday, but instead of requesting to get to know him, she's already decided.

"Oh," I inhale. "Okay, what did you decide?"

"I really like him, Mom. He was a lot of fun at Velocity Vortex, and he didn't have to be. When we asked Aunt Dani to invite him, we kind of thought that he would want to be around you most of the day, but I really like that he spent most of his time with us."

"Yeah, he's never been one to turn down a rollercoaster," I share. It shouldn't have been a surprise to me, his ease with my kids. Our countless trips to Ever Wild with Liz when she was little should have been enough evidence of his character.

"Well, I'm glad you liked being around him. Thank you for your blessing, baby," I tell Wyatt.

"Is it bad that I want to be around him? I don't know if heaven is real, but I keep thinking about Dad and if I'm hurting his feelings by telling you to go for it."

Tears prick my waterline. "I'm going to tell you something Aunt Dani told me, okay?"

Wyatt nods.

"She said that there isn't a limit on how many people we get to love in life, or how many people we let love us. Don't think of Rivers as a replacement, and more of an expansion."

She's quiet for a minute, letting the words sink in. "If I think about Rivers as someone who gets to love me *too* and not *instead of* someone else, I think that helps."

"Good. And you can always be honest with your feelings, sweetie. I know all of this is so new to us. Sawyer, have you made a decision? It's okay if you haven't. I'm just curious."

"No, not yet," he sounds shy. "I want to see how it goes tonight...but I also want to make sure that I'm allowed to talk about Dad whenever I want. I'm scared that if I say yes, I'll have to filter what I can and can't talk about around Rivers, and I don't think I can do that."

He's quiet for a beat. "I also want to know how much he wants to be part of our lives. I think it would hurt really bad to get close to him and then him decide we aren't enough for him or something."

His maturity astounds me. I realize that both he and Wyatt have had to grow up a lot faster than most other kids their age given all that they've been through, but even so. Wanting to work through this with Rivers like he's part of the team is a big deal, and the fact that Sawyer wants to be able to talk about the heavy things with him tells me he's really taking this seriously.

"I think that's really grown up of you, and I think that all the reasons you're hesitating are normal."

"I want you to be happy, Mom," he says. "But I also want to make sure that we don't get hurt again."

That response breaks me; these kids have been through hardships they never should have faced, and I hate that Sawyer has been burned badly enough to have to be so cautious.

After my kids give me hugs on the way out of my classroom, I feel hopeful for what's ahead of me. Tea with Lianne will be difficult, but the game tonight should be fun, and I'm excited for the lesson I have planned with my students today. We're doing a character analysis of the three Curtis brothers in *The Outsiders*, and I think they'll enjoy it. Today is going to be a good day, I know it.

By second period, I'm convinced I jinxed myself: what in the hell is wrong with today?

First period, I saw one of my students had written about her dad hitting her in her free-write journal. I pulled her out of the room to ask her about it, and she confirmed to me that her dad hit her Saturday afternoon.

Then I opened up my email to a notification that Marjorie Winthrop, the parent who was unhappy with my policies, requested a meeting with the principal and myself to discuss our emails.

This is what I mean when I say that parents are the hardest part of being a teacher. You have parents who request to meet with the principal over you asking kids to be punctual in their assignments, parents who view their children as possessions, parents who are absentee and don't care one way or another about the well-being of their child's education, and the select few who view you as someone on their team.

The killer part is that every child deserves the last group, and not enough of them have it.

My lunch today will be spent filing a report with Child Welfare Services on behalf of a thirteen-year-old girl whose dad cares more about alcohol than her. I've only had to fill out two of these in my thirteen years of teaching, but it's gut-wrenching every time. I feel so helpless knowing that this is all I can do for her.

To make matters worse, my second period class thinks that this activity gives them license to act like savages, so I have to pull out my stern teacher voice, give them a replacement characterization worksheet instead of this collaborative activity I spent way too much time planning and prepping for, all while keeping some semblance of professionalism.

My principal gave me the option to meet with him and Marjorie Winthrop during my planning period or at the end of the school day, and I agreed to use my planning period. I have plans with Lianne, but I also don't want to extend this bullshit longer than necessary, so at ten-thirty, I make my way to the front office, bracing for the worst.

I emailed copies of my syllabus and the correspondence I've already had with Marjorie to my principal before the meeting so that he knew what to expect, but I bring hard copies with me as well for easy reference. I also bring copies of Dalton's work with me so that Marjorie can see how well he's performing and that everything he's submitted has been on time.

My principal seems like a nice guy, and I've heard from the staff that they like him, but this is my first meeting with him where we've had a disgruntled parent, and all I can hope for is that he has my back.

"Mrs. Winthrop," he starts, "would you like to explain the reasons you requested this meeting?"

"Of course." Her feigned benevolence already grates on my ears. "I just worry that Dalton will get burned out too quickly, and that his mental health will deteriorate with the pressure of turning everything in right on time! Can we not show these kids some grace?!"

The principal looks at me to respond. "I understand these concerns, Mrs. Winthrop; however, students will never learn to be responsible or manage a deadline if we don't start setting those expectations. The high school's policy is similar to my own, and I want to prepare my students for that next year."

"It just feels like you're asking them to be perfect little grown-ups right now when they're only thirteen! And doesn't this violate some sort of district policy?" She huffs. "You can't go against what they say."

She thinks she's trapped me.

I know better.

My principal takes her question. "No, there are no district policies regarding late assignments. Those are up to each individual teacher, so Ms. Clark has done nothing wrong."

"I would also like to point out that Dalton is an excellent student," I say as I begin pulling out his assignments. "He's helpful to his peers, and gets his work done in the time provided in class. I very rarely assign homework because I don't think kids need one more thing to do when they get home, so most of my assignments are designed to be finished within the class period. Dalton has finished every assignment on time so far, with no issues."

She's quiet for a minute as she takes in his work. "What's our compromise?" she finally asks.

And forgive me, but what the fuck?

"I want to make sure that he's given a second chance at least once if he messes up the deadline."

Geez.

By the end of the meeting, I've finally offered one late homework pass per semester for up to ten days. If the students use it, they won't have a penalty for that one assignment; if they don't use it, they can get five points of extra credit (what I'm certain Dalton will be getting).

***

The Thomas's house looks like it's been preserved in time, down to the flowerbeds. Nothing has changed. Not the pale gray siding, not the dark teal front door and shutters, not the pavers that line the walkway, nor the door on the second story that leads to a small balcony Forest almost fell from when he was a toddler. Nostalgia hits me like waves as I take it all in, so that by the time I've finally registered everything about the exterior, I'm knee deep in sand. I can only imagine what it's going to be like inside.

Lianne greets me at the front door with a kiss on each cheek. And just like the outside, everything here has remained untouched. It feels like coming home. I take in the spaces and moments I've had in this house.

This kitchen where I helped prep food for countless barbeques. The den that sits above the living room where Rivers and I would hide out as he drew patterns on my skin with his fingers while I read books. The bathroom that Lianne decorated in lighthouses to bridge the gap between Rivers's pirate bedroom and the rest of the house. The porch where I'd drink a glass of water before heading back out on my run.

All of it, frozen perfectly in time, like I never left.

"Quinny?" Lianne stands in front of me now.

"Sorry, I got distracted taking it all in."

"That's okay. Do you still like the fruity teas, or have you moved onto other things?"

When I was younger, I always wanted something with raspberries; I'm less picky now, but Lianne always has the best selection, so I'm interested to see what flavors she has.

"I do still like the fruity ones, yes. Surprise me with your favorite!"

"You bet. Would you mind pulling out the teacups? They're in the same place as always."

She works on selecting bags and setting out the honey jar for me. She's never cared for honey in her tea, but Bryan does, so they keep it on hand. I open the cupboard and reach for Lianne's favorite teacup—a delicate piece from Italy that she picked up just outside of Milan. It's creamy white, with purple honeysuckles painted around the lip, and the handle matches the paint using petals to form a flower.

I let out a small gasp when I see my favorite cup tucked into the furthest corner of the cupboard. Lianne found it for me at a flea market when she first learned I liked tea too. The exterior of it is the lightest shade of blue with a gold rim and gold handle, but inside is what makes the cup so special. It's a white background with various painted flowers outlined in black, but at the top of the cup the shading of the flowers is black and white, and as they move down, they gradually become filled with color. Like with every sip, you get closer to being rewarded with a rainbow of blooms.

We take our tea to the back deck and sit down in Lianne's favorite Adirondak chairs while the sun warms our skin.

"I went on a date with Rivers," I blurt out.

Lianne smiles as she takes a sip. "You think your mom didn't tell me the day she found out?"

I laugh. "Lianne..."

She knows I'm about to apologize and cuts in before I can.

"No ma'am. You were a kid, Quinn. I shouldn't have pushed so hard, and you had every right and reason to be afraid. I've only ever wanted for you to be happy, and I'm so sorry that things have been so hard for you as an adult. I can't imagine what you've lived through. But you will not apologize for behaving like an eighteen-year-old when you were eighteen."

"Can I at least apologize for not treating you with the love and respect you deserved from me? You and Bryan were nothing short of second parents to me, and I owe you at least that much. I'm sorry."

"You're forgiven; you were forgiven a long time ago. Now tell me, how was this date?" She holds out her hand to me and it feels just like old times.

"It was..." I smile to myself. "It was really good. It felt like no time passed at all, but I'm also trying to figure out...everything."

"I'm sure. You have a lot more to consider now than when you were a teenager." Lianne has always been this way, and I've missed it. She's intuitive and genuine. She doesn't push or prod.

"I do. It's not just me anymore, you know? I have my kids to think about. My family, Preston's family, and of course, you guys. I can't expect everyone to just be okay with it."

She sits up to put her tea on the table between us and perches on the edge of her chair so she's able to face me easier. I let her take both of my hands in hers and know that she's going to make me cry—I can feel it.

"Quinn. If you dare lump Bryan and I into the group of people whose feelings you need to consider, then I have taught you nothing. We loved you when you were a kid, and we love you now—whether or not that includes our son. I mean it when I say we just want you to be happy again; no one deserves it more than you."

Tears well in my eyes at her generosity and grace. When I left, she and Bryan were here, picking up the pieces of Rivers's shattered heart, and I can't undo that. I can't undo his pain or take back what I said. And I can't process how she's able to be so forgiving; as a mother myself, if someone had left my kid's heart in shambles then asked for forgiveness years later, I'd still probably call Dani to help me *fix the problem*' and sit in jail, content.

As I pull out of Lianne's driveway, a big green pickup idles behind me, waiting to pull in. It's Bryan. I don't register what I'm doing until I'm halfway across the street, walking toward his truck, seeking a hug.

He's so big, I can barely wrap my arms around him completely.

"Quinny girl!" He's so delighted to see me. Not a hint of malice or meanness; just Bryan with his tan skin and gentle eyes. "Lianne told me you'd set up tea. It's so good to see you!"

"You too," I answer.

"Rivers treat you well on that date?"

"He did." I blush instinctively.

"Well, you tell me if he gets his head stuck in his ass again. Lianne likes to let the boys figure stuff out for themselves, but I'm not letting that boy lose you again."

I don't even need to ask for Bryan's forgiveness. I can tell he's already given it to me. "I will," I say with a laugh. "I have to go pick up my son, but it was nice to see you."

"You too, sweetie."

***

After I pick up Sawyer from practice, Dani meets us with Will and Wyatt at my house, only it's not just her car there when I pull up. It's also Rivers, my parents, both my sisters, and my two nephews; June's husband is notably absent...again.

"Sawyer, did you guys invite everyone else over for the game?" I can't imagine how they found out, but whatever, it's not like this day can get any worse.

"I think Wyatt and Will told Banks," he says casually.

It's just like my family to do this, too. We aren't the type of family to need an invitation, we never have been, but seriously? The first time Rivers is coming to my house, and my parents are here too? No one thought of calling me?

Rivers and my dad shake hands as Dani comes scuttling over to my car. "What the fuck, Quinn? You've always liked to stir the pot, but you could've warned me what I'd be walking into!"

"I didn't know!" I seethe. "Sawyer just told me that Wyatt and Will told Banks, and word must've traveled."

"What do you need from me? First big thing?"

"Well, my day was total shit because parents are the worst," I start.

"So real, they're the reason I'd quit the job. What happened?"

"Impromptu meeting with my principal and a disgruntled parent, CWS report, middle schoolers who fucked around and found out, and to top it all off, I just had tea with Lianne."

Dani's eyes are wide in horror. We've had bad days, but this day has been awful, followed by heavy, followed by what I'm currently feeling: four thousand shades of overwhelm.

"Fuck. Okay, I'll try to entertain your parents for a bit so you can catch up with Rivers, then I'll corner June and Liz and try to enlist them to keep your parents mostly occupied."

I hug her. How did I get so lucky?

"We're not hugging friends, babe. Love you, but this isn't us."

She walks toward my parents, and I swear my dad shrinks a little with every step she takes toward him; she's a legend.

Rivers finally catches my eye, then excuses himself from my parents, and moves toward me. I let him pull me into his arms and breathe a sigh of relief. This is the most peace I've felt all day, and what I've been looking forward to since Marjorie Winthrop. Now I have literally everyone around me and feel like I can't sink into him the way I want to.

"I've got to say, Quinn, you really know how to scare a man half to death. I didn't know I'd be spending the evening with your family." He laughs, but I feel guilty. He only agreed to dinner with me, my kids, and Dani.

"I'm so sorry, I didn't know they were coming. Wyatt told my nephew, and I think everyone took it as an open invitation. You can leave if you want to."

He pulls back to look at me. "Do you want me to leave?"

"No," I say. "But I also don't want you to feel like you need to stay now that this isn't what we agreed to."

"Then I'm staying. I agreed to have dinner with you, Dani, and the kids, and as far as I can tell, that's still happening."

The party finally moves inside, and true to her word, Dani situates my parents in the den with drinks and the remote. She makes sure Liz and June know to keep them in there until dinner, while she and Rivers are in the kitchen with me making food. The kids are sitting on the porch, filming some skit for Brecken's TikTok—I'm not even going to stop them. At least they're occupied.

We move seamlessly throughout the kitchen prepping pan-fried chicken, roasted green beans and peppers, and rice pilaf, but it isn't until I'm at my counter chopping veggies that I realize I'm still wearing the clothes I taught in, and I'm uncomfortable. The high neck of my blouse is itchy, the waist band of the hard pants digs into my stomach, and the hardware of my sandals rubs against my pinky toe.

"I'm going to go change," I tell them. "I'll be right back."

I sit in my room for at least five minutes debating what to put on. If I go full grunge like I normally do after work, I'll never hear the end of it from my mom, but if I change into jeans, it defeats the purpose of me changing at all. Eventually I put on a pair of black biker shorts and my favorite Chris Jones jersey; we are here for a game after all. I put a claw clip in my hair to get it out of my face and then make my way back to the kitchen, but Dani and Rivers's stop me short before I cross the threshold.

"Dani?" It almost sounds like he's whispering.

"Yeah?"

"I need you to tell me what happened to Preston. All I know is that he was shot, but I feel like I can't fully understand what Quinn and the kids went through unless I know all the ugly parts of it."

I hear her take in a breath, and I feel myself freeze. "Fine. But I'm only going to tell you this story because I do not want any of them to have to re-live it. Deal?"

"Okay," he says.

I come around the corner, appreciative that they were both willing to spare my feelings. It's my story to tell though. "Actually," I start, and they both look up at me. "Dani, would you give us a few minutes so I can tell him?"

She nods as she leaves the kitchen. I sit down at the table across from Rivers.

"I didn't want you to have to talk about it..." he says.

"I know. I appreciate that, but I also don't want there to be anything that we don't talk about. And if my kids are going to come around to this, then I need to lead by example and be willing to talk about Preston with you."

Rivers nods his head, waiting patiently for me to continue.

"I had just gotten home from work and was getting some things done before I needed to pick up the kids. Preston normally got off work at three, but sometimes, on days when there was a lot going on, he'd stay later to help out, and since we had just come home from vacation, he'd told me earlier in the day that he'd be staying late."

I remember this day so vividly, if I close my eyes the whole thing would play out like a movie. I can remember the adrenaline, the fear, the guttural sob I released when I answered the phone; all of it.

"My phone rang, and a police officer told me that Preston had been shot at work trying to stop an active shooter. Basically, they thought they had the shooter, and then a second gunman came out of nowhere from behind Preston and got him from the side—right through his head. They told me I needed to get to the hospital as quickly as possible, followed almost immediately by the hospital chaplain saying the same thing."

"You told me you stopped to pick the kids up from school first, I remember," Rivers says.

"I did, but there's more to it than that. I left the car running and sprinted into the office to grab the kids because the school wouldn't let them walk down to the office until I was physically in the building to pick them up."

I remember screaming at the secretary on the way over there that my husband had been shot and begging them to please have the kids meet me, but I kept being told that it was a security issue.

"I told the kids to run to the car with tears pouring out of my eyes and wouldn't say a word until they were buckled in their seats. The chaplain couldn't tell me any details about Preston's condition, couldn't say where he'd been shot, or how many times. All he told me was that he was in critical condition and I needed to get there. Fast.

"I had to tell the kids that I didn't know what was going on and had to process everything that was happening in front of them. I had no time to mask it, no time to explain what it meant. I couldn't even hug them when I told them that they were going to the hospital to see their dad, probably for the last time, because I was white knuckling the steering wheel."

I hang my head in my hands, catching my breath.

"Not being able to hold them to me while their hearts broke was one of the biggest cruelties I've ever experienced."

"God," Rivers says. "Quinn, if you need to stop, you can stop." He holds out his hand toward me, an anchor in the storm of grief I'm too familiar with.

"When we got to the hospital, the nurse took us to a quiet room to wait for the chaplain. There aren't words to describe it other than it being the most impersonal room to receive the most personal news in. There wasn't even a lamp. We were only there for two minutes before the chaplain showed up and walked us back to a different quiet room next to the main waiting room in the ICU. He held my hand and asked me if I'd like the child life specialist to be called to help explain things to the kids. I didn't even know that was someone's job; explaining how and why your dad was there and that he'd never talk to you again, never hear you laugh, or see you grow. That you'd never get to ride bikes with him again or sing him happy birthday."

I grab a tissue to blow my nose, the tears skating paths down my cheeks.

"After that, the trauma surgeon walked in with the neurosurgeon, and explained what was going on. Basically, Preston..." I inhale, preparing to utter the words I've dreaded saying more than any others the last five years. Rivers pulls me to my feet and sets me on his lap, looping his arms around me like he knows I need to be held to get through the rest.

"Basically, Preston had been shot through both sides of his brain, which meant that there was nothing they could do. Sawyer calls it by its formal name, a transhemispheric gunshot wound. He memorized the words because he didn't want Preston's death to be dumbed down for anyone."

"I understand," Rivers says. "If it's ever brought up in front of him, I'll make sure to call it and everything else by its real name." His generosity feels like a warm blanket. Being willing to hear me grieve over a man I love, a man who isn't him, can't be easy.

"When he got to the trauma bay, they did their routine tests, and he was completely unresponsive. No talking, no eye movement, nothing. They were thorough and checked for other injuries, but it was only ten or so minutes before they had him in a CT scan because he had brain matter coming out of his skull."

"I'm so sorry, Quinny, but I have a question." Rivers sounds pained as he interrupts, but he pulls me closer to him. "I thought that if a person was shot in the head that they die instantly? I'm sorry, I don't want that to sound insensitive, but I'm not understanding how he was still alive?"

"I had asked the same thing," I say, reassuring him. "They said if someone is shot in one lobe or just one part of their brain, there's a chance they could make it depending on the track of the bullet. But if they're shot through both hemispheres, they always die; it can be instant or take a few days. Preston lasted an hour and twenty-four minutes.

"The neurosurgeon told me that Preston's condition was a non-survivable injury, and that surgery wouldn't change or improve his outcome. And I just couldn't believe it. How could this man who protected me and the kids around the clock vanish so suddenly, you know?"

Rivers brushes a tear from my cheek with his thumb, handing me a tissue. He's being so gentle with my heart, it's like a balm.

"I asked to see his CT scan to get a better understanding of what they were saying, and Rivers, I swear to God, you've never seen anything so horrendous. That bullet carved an entirely new path through him; you could see the fractured part of his skull where it came out, and all the blood flooding his brain.

"The child life specialist got there next, and I don't think I could have done it without her. She came and sat with the kids while the surgeons walked me back to his hospital room. I felt like I could hardly see him because he was covered by so many tubes, wires, and bandages. He had two tubes coming out of his mouth, one was an endotracheal tube, or breathing tube. Just so you know the names if Sawyer ever brings them up. And the other was called an OG tube to decompress his stomach so that the air being pumped into him wasn't inflating it along with his lungs. He had wires to monitor his heart, IVs in both arms, and then two lines coming from his groin. A central line to get him meds quickly, and an arterial line so they could monitor his blood pressure with every beat. His head was wrapped in this pressure dressing to keep his brain from spilling out of his skull, and the tubes coming from his mouth were strapped to his face. I literally didn't even recognize him. The most bizarre part though, was seeing how normal his vital signs were. His blood pressure was stable, his heart rate was fine, he had good oxygen. It's weird seeing someone be so stable while they have a hole through their brain. To make matters worse, the hospital policy said that kids under the age of twelve weren't allowed into the ICU, and even if they were there could only be two visitors in his room at a time.

"So, I walked up to the charge nurse, and begged her to let us all go see him together, but she kept saying no, and that protocol only permitted two people at a time. But then, her phone got a notification, and I saw her screensaver that looked almost identical to mine. It was a picture of her, two kids, and a man on the beach somewhere, just like the one I had taken a few days before on our cruise.

"I asked if it was a picture of her family. When the nurse said yes, I held up my own phone with our picture and asked, *'Which one of your kids would you choose to let say goodbye to their dad if you had only minutes?'* She let both kids in after that, but the child specialist explained what they'd see so they were less afraid."

Despite this being the worst day of my life, I'm always thankful that the kids know that I fought for both of them to be able to say goodbye, and that they were able to see the nurse's humanity by extending us compassion when she could have said no.

"The child specialist told the kids that their dad wouldn't look like himself, and that he'd have a lot of tubes and wires coming out of him. She told them to be gentle with him when we gave him hugs. I remember Wyatt giving him the softest kiss on his cheek, like she thought that her kiss would break him. The nurse told us to tell him anything we wanted him to know. Sawyer just begged for him to be okay again. I remember hearing him say, *'But it's Tuesday, Dad. We have jiu jitsu tonight. Please don't leave us. Who will practice the Americana with me now?'*"

Rivers's eyes shine with tears. "I'm so sorry, Quinn. I would give anything for you to have him back. For the kids to have him back."

It's quiet for a second before I keep going. "We each said our goodbyes, which was hard for the kids because they could see that his heart was still beating, but almost immediately after Wyatt finished telling him that he was the best client when they played beauty salon, Preston's blood pressure skyrocketed, and his heart rate almost bottomed out. They say it's called herniation, but it really just means his brain collapsed in on itself from pressure and fell through his spinal cord.

"After that, they did something called an apnea test to declare him brain dead, which he was, and someone from the organ donation organization came to speak with us because I was adamant that I wanted his death to end in life. I wanted to leave with Preston's parents after we did the paperwork, but the kids were beside themselves, not understanding that it was machines keeping him alive, keeping his vital signs stable; nothing else."

"So, we compromised. I made them leave, but promised that we could come back to watch his honor walk the next day, and said we could pick a song to play while they wheeled him into his surgery. I wanted them to choose something slow, but they always listened to "Toxicity" by System of a Down with him, so that's what they chose. I don't think the nurses liked it."

We both laugh. I remember trying to persuade them to choose something more appropriate, but at the end of the day, this would be their last memory with their father—who was I to rob them of the little control they had?

"The surgery to procure his organs was two hours, and we stayed there in the quiet room for the whole thing," I conclude. "Preston saved eight lives with his organs and helped a few dozen more with his tissues. My parents took a red eye to be there with us, and my sisters and Dani came for the funeral, then took turns for the next few months after."

He doesn't say anything, just holds me to him like he knows there's nothing he can say. I think there's power in that; holding someone's sadness for them, holding them in silence without trying to fix or change it.

"Quinn?" he whispers.

"Yeah?" I say on a shaky exhale.

"There's nothing I can say to you to make this feel better, I know that. But I want you to know that your past doesn't scare or intimidate me. Preston was a good man, and I don't ever want you to feel like he needs to be erased or hidden to keep me around."

He kisses me gently on the head, and I breathe out a sigh of contentment. "Thank you," I murmur. I leave him with the faintest of kisses on his neck before checking on the meal.

Dinner goes by without a hitch—it feels like my family was told to be on their best behavior, and honestly, Dani probably warned them. The Chiefs win the game by the skin of their teeth, Dani recoils at my celebration, and Rivers is confused why neither of us is rooting for a team based in California. It's light, and fun compared to everything that's gone on today, but I feel like my head is going to explode by the time my parents (finally) leave.

Rivers doesn't linger once they go; I think he can sense that I need some time to decompress, but before he leaves, he scoops me into a hug, leans into my ear, and says, "I'll text you tomorrow," before gently brushing his lips to mine.

Chapter Nineteen

Now

The next day during my lunch, a knock comes on my classroom door. I move my papers to stand and cross the front of the room to open it, thinking it might be another member of the eighth-grade team, but it's Sawyer.

"What are you doing here, dude? Aren't you supposed to be in history?"

"We're doing a scavenger hunt. I just wanted to see if you could ask Rivers if he can help me with math tonight? He told me he could while we were at Velocity Vortex, but I need some help."

"Did you already ask Aunt Dani?" I ask.

"I asked Will if they were busy tonight, and he said that he had lacrosse tryouts. I just figured she'd be there too."

I remember her mentioning that to me. Lacrosse isn't a school sport, but there's a local club team that's gained popularity. "Alright, I'll text Rivers. Now get back to class!"

I move to hug him, but he shakes his head, and mumbles, "Not where people could see, Mom!"

That evening, as I wash the dishes, Rivers and Sawyer sit at the kitchen table, looking over his math homework. "I get that you use the order of operations still, I just don't understand what they're used for," Sawyer says.

"What do you mean what they're used for?" Rivers asks, confused.

"Like I get that the quadradic equation helps calculate the height of something being thrown, but I don't see what polynomials would be used for."

"Oh! You need to understand how it works in the real world. I'm the same way!" Rivers sounds excited, connecting with Sawyer over math.

"It helps me visualize it easier, yeah. My dad always used to explain how different math was used in the real world, and I think it helped me get better at it."

I glance over at them, curious to see how this conversation is going to play out. It's the first time Sawyer has brought Preston up to Rivers.

"That makes sense. What else did you like to do with your dad?" Rivers asks.

"We loved to practice jiu jitsu together. He always made the best fake volcanoes for us to explode, and he gave the best bounces on the trampoline. Mostly, I just miss talking to him."

I remember hearing them in Sawyer's room when it was Preston's turn to put him to bed. Sawyer would fire off a million questions a minute, and Preston would take them in stride, giving an answer to each and every one. I remember one time in particular hearing Sawyer ask how babies were made, and Preston didn't even hesitate. He just told him about how sperm would swim to an egg, and that satisfied Sawyer's curiosity. Preston never shied away from giving an age-appropriate answer; I think it's why Sawyer always felt so comfortable asking him anything.

"I've always loved wrestling and talking to my dad too. My dad and your grandpa taught me almost everything I know.

What do you think you'd ask your dad if you could talk to him one more time?"

I've always wondered about this, but I've never been brave enough to ask him.

"Polynomials," Sawyer jokes, and it makes all of us laugh.

"They're kind of awful, huh? I may not be your dad, but if you're okay with it, I can answer your question?"

Sawyer nods his head in agreement.

"Polynomials are mostly used to predict curves, and that can be for real objects or for data. You can use them to calculate the curve of an airplane wing, or what type of curve you need for computer graphics. Some people might even use them for understanding or predicting the stock market. It's math, but in a lot of cases, it can also be scientific."

I step away into the living room to check on how Wyatt is handling her own homework, and when I come back, the boys are working through problems. I could leave right now, but I want to hear them, so I plug into headphones but don't turn any music on as a I wipe off the counters.

"Rivers?" I hear Sawyer say.

"Yeah?"

"I know what I'd ask my dad." His voice is either hushed or muffled by my headphones.

"What would it be?"

In my periphery, I see that Rivers has turned his body to face Sawyer head on.

"I'd ask him if it's okay that I've found another person I like talking to..."

I try to tamper down the swell of emotion in my chest. It's so fucking unfair that Sawyer has to grapple with these feelings at all, but I know if there's one person equipped to help him with it, it's Rivers Thomas.

"You know, Sawyer, I never knew your dad. I wish I'd gotten the chance to get to know him, but from what I've heard from you, and your mom, and Dani, he seemed like he was a really good man."

"He was," Sawyer's voice breaks on the past tense.

"And I think that because he was, it tells me that he'd want you to be happy. I also think he'd want you to make sure that whoever you decide to talk to understands that they are not a replacement for the dad that you lost. They can be part of your world without trying to be someone they aren't."

Rivers looks at me, like this is just as much for my benefit as it is Sawyer's.

Sawyer nods his head in agreement. "Can I tell you something I haven't ever told anyone?"

"You can tell me anything, Sawyer."

"Sometimes I think..." Sawyer's voice is low, quiet. "I think if it weren't for Aunt Dani, Mom wouldn't be here. I think Aunt Dani saved her all those years ago."

The sting of tears pricks my eyes. I love my kids more than life, but after Preston was gone, I lost the will to live. If Dani hadn't shown up when June left, my kids may have very well lost both parents instead of one, and it breaks me to know that Sawyer has been harboring this for as long as he has.

"I think you save her every day, Sawyer. You and Wyatt are the bravest kids I've ever known." The chairs move with a screech, and I turn to find Rivers standing to hold Sawyer to his chest. "Thank you for trusting me with that. I hope you know you can talk about your dad with me any time, and that I will never try to replace him, okay?"

"Okay," Sawyer whispers. He collects his things and moves toward the hallway. "Thanks for your help, and for...everything else."

I step into Rivers's arms and lay my head against the firm planes of his chest, lulled by the sound of his beating heart. Being held like this, tethered to him, keeps my racing thoughts at bay. "Thank you for that," I whisper.

I feel his arms flex around me in a squeeze, as he kisses the top of my head. It makes me shiver despite the warmth. "All I've ever wanted is to be what you need, Quinn; that extends to your kids too."

I tilt my chin up to meet him, to taste the lime on his tongue from the beer he drank earlier and feel the heat of his breath against me. His tongue meets mine, slow and searching. I bring my hand to his hair and groan into his kiss. His hand moves to the sliver of skin exposed from my t-shirt and inches slowly upward toward the lace of my bralette.

The kiss becomes more urgent as Rivers backs me against the refrigerator and presses into me. He kisses behind my ear and down along my jaw while his hand falls to cup the curve of my ass. I stifle a moan and bring my hand to the front of his jeans, feeling the firmness of him pressing against me. His teeth tug against my lip as his thumb grazes over my nipple through my shirt. I'm moments from unbuttoning his jeans just as Wyatt yells for me from the den.

Rivers and I break apart, a flush building on my chest, my lips swollen from his kiss.

"We can't do this right now," I say, chest heaving. Wanting nothing more than to pick up right where we left off and see how much shallower he can make my breath.

"I know," he says. "I know."

"I want to," I tell him.

"I do too, but I want to do it right. And that means your kids have to be okay with it."

He pulls me to him, then kisses me one more time before walking to the front door and says, "Goodnight, Quinny."

***

As I'm finding shoes in my room four days later, Sawyer appears in my bathroom door, looking disheveled from sleep. I've always tried to be up and ready before the kids wake up so that I can facilitate their breakfast and do last minute things while they're getting ready.

"Hey, dude. Sleep good?" He walks over and leans into my shoulder for a hug. He's already so big, I can't believe one day it'll be me leaning on him.

"Yeah," he mumbles through a yawn. "I think you should date Rivers, Mom."

I run my hand up and down his arm, begging for time to slow down and freeze him just like this. "Why do you say that?" I'm pretty sure I know his answer, but I want to hear it from him.

"I like that he can be both funny and serious. I like that he knew what each moment called for and that he didn't try to back away or hide from all the ugly stuff. He really was fun at Velocity Vortex, but talking about dad with him a few days ago felt...good? Like even though he didn't get it because he wasn't there, he was still trying to make sure I felt heard."

I can't say I'm stunned by Sawyer's observation. Rivers has always been good at seeing what people need.

Sawyer sucks in breath. "If you're going to date—which I think you deserve to do—it should be with someone like him."

I squeeze his shoulder to me, and whisper, "Thank you."

"Yeah, yeah." He pulls away from me—he is still a teenage boy. "What's for breakfast?"

We move into the kitchen where Wyatt sits at the table, eating a bowl of Crunch Berries. She's curled her hair and mascara coats her lashes, causing Sawyer and I to look at each other in confusion.

"You look nice. Is it picture day?" I ask her.

"No, Keegan is studying with me, Will, and Banks after school today." She says it so flippantly, like she has no clue I've been knocked off my axis. I thought she and Will were getting closer.

"Oh, okay. Whose house are you studying at?" I need to know if I'm asking Dani or June to keep an eye on things and tell me everything they hear.

"Aunt Dani's. Aunt June told Banks that he and Brecken needed to get out of the house for the afternoon. Sawyer, do you want to come too? Keegan is helping us with math, and it works out because if we all get stuck, at least Aunt Dani is there."

"Sure," he says. "Maybe I could catch a ride with Keegan since we both have practice today."

Watching them make plans without asking me is other-worldly. They seem so grown, but they can't drive. They make arrangements with other adults without me knowing. I'm not comfortable with Sawyer riding with someone I don't know though. "Who is taking Keegan to Aunt Dani's? I don't want you riding in a car with someone I've never met."

"His uncle! You know him. He's the new history teacher at the school," she says.

My mind tries to place him in memories of the new teacher orientation we would have both attended, but then I realize that Rivers mentioned his old college roommate was the new history teacher.

"Do you mean Mr. Webber?" His face comes to me now. He's handsome. Tall with blonde hair, and a pretty good sense of humor if I'm thinking of the right guy.

"That's him, yeah!"

"Did you know he and Rivers used to be roommates in college?" I ask.

"No way? What are the odds?!" Sawyer says. Then he grabs a piece of paper, most likely trying to calculate the odds.

"Well, I'll talk to him today about taking you to Dani's, Sawyer. I'll get a message to you at school about if that works or not."

My phone rings with a call from Rivers as we walk toward my classroom before the bell. The kids must silently decide to give me privacy, because they lean in and give me a hug before going to find their friends. I answer just before I know it's about to go to voicemail.

"Hey," I say.

"Hey, is your lunch always at twelve twenty?"

"Twelve ten, why?"

"I don't have a patient between twelve and one, so I was going to see if you might like to grab a tea at Parchment and Grounds with me? I hear they also make panini's and wraps."

Butterflies surge in my chest. When I texted Dani while walking out the door to the car this morning that Sawyer had given me his blessing, she responded with an eggplant emoji, but she isn't necessarily wrong. With Sawyer's permission, this is the first time that I don't need to hide behind an excuse or someone else's feelings, and it makes me excited.

"That sounds great. I'll see you there."

***

Rivers steps out of his car when I pull in front of the coffee shop. I didn't know they made wraps or paninis here, but it's needed. This town has thrived on fried food for way too long to not have healthier options. I looked at the menu while my students were working on vocabulary so that I didn't have to waste time when I got here. He gives me a quick hug and a chaste kiss on the cheek, then opens the door and puts his hand on my lower back as we step in. I haven't seen him since we almost undressed each other in my kitchen, and the simplest touches feel like electric charges wherever his hand meets my skin.

"How's your day going?" he asks.

"It's good. Better than a few days ago, thank God. How's yours?"

"Better now." He shoots a smile at me, and it feels like I'm in a hot air balloon, floating up and up, higher and higher—lighter than air. "What do you want? I can order for us if you want to go grab a table."

I start to protest, but he levels me a look that tells me he's not arguing about it, and honestly, I need to pee so it's probably best if he orders anyways.

"The chicken pesto wrap, please." I kiss his cheek and make my way to the bathroom.

On my way back out to the lobby, I see Rivers talking with the woman behind the counter. I've been gone for only two or three minutes, but it should have been plenty of time for him to order. She's cute, and vaguely familiar, with short blonde hair, tan skin, and sun-spotted freckles across her nose. Her hand covers Rivers, and I feel a surge of jealousy pass through me before he pulls his hand away.

That hand isn't hers to touch.

I don't know if it's mine to touch either, but that's neither here nor there.

As I approach the counter, it dawns on me that I know this woman. It's Katie, Rivers's prom date from high school.

"Quinn, you remember Katie?" Something in the tone of his voice tells me he's trying to put me at ease.

"I do. Nice to see you, Katie."

"She was just telling me how she opened up Parchment and Grounds to try and make the perfect place for...what was it that you said?" He turns his attention back to her.

"The perfect place for booklovers to be solitary without feeling anti-social," she says through a chuckle.

A laugh bubbles out of me. "That's exactly how I feel when I read on my couch! I actually really love it here."

"Thanks. It was good to see you guys," she says.

I'm sure she means it was good to see Rivers. After what I pulled in high school, it was clear she's never cared for me, but maybe that's part of getting older. The petty shit we cared about as kids is lost to time, and eventually, we find ourselves eating in the establishment owned by someone who used to hate us but now shares similar interests.

Or maybe she was just trying to not be a bitch in front of Rivers.

We find a table close to the wall of ivy, and I'm stunned by how flavorful the wrap is. "This is delicious!" I mumble through a bite.

"Do you think she spit in your food?" Rivers asks.

"Rivers!"

"I'm kidding. She didn't touch your food, but you may want to watch out if you ever come back without me." He shovels another bite of his panini into his mouth. This man, I swear.

"Both kids gave me their blessing," I say after a few beats. Rivers's eyes go wide, but I grip his hand before he can say anything. "That is, if you're still interested."

His mouth twitches in a half smile before he speaks. "I don't know...I'll have to *really* think about it."

***

When I get home from school for the day, I change into a pair of oversized sweatpants and a sports bra with the knowledge that eventually, I'll grab a hoodie, but as I'm doing a few chores, I need to stay cool. I pick up the mess in the living room from the night before, load the dishwasher, then wipe off the counters. I vacuum the floors to get all of the crumbs, start laundry, and make my bed.

It's been so long since I've had an evening to myself with nowhere to be, and no one to chauffer. Dani told me that she would bring the kids home around seven but then messaged me again fifteen minutes ago and said they'd be back around nine instead. I thought three hours alone would be blissful, but five? It feels like dream.

I sit down to pull up *The Wedding Singer* on my T.V. After my kids asked Rivers about it at the festival, I've wanted to watch it but haven't had the time, or the kids have refused to watch it with me (again). I don't know why it's my comfort movie. It's not an Oscar worthy production by any means, but

Adam Sandler's singing has always done it for me—even with the mullet. The opening sequence plays, and Sandler's gravelly voice echoes through my speakers. I should get up and cook dinner, but why would I when Boy George is about to come on and sing his favorite song twice in a row?

My doorbell rings.

Of course I'll still be interrupted when my kids aren't even here. It's probably my dad asking to come look at my leaky faucets or change the oil in my car. I love my dad. He's trying so hard to be here for me, but I just want one evening! I toss a loose button up blouse on so I'm not just standing in a bra to greet my dad, but when I open the door, I'm met with the smell of my favorite pasta and the chest of Rivers Thomas clutching boxes of take out and a bottle of wine.

"Hey?" I say, puzzled.

He takes in my confusion. "Dani didn't tell you I was coming, did she?"

She's always been such a meddler. My phone buzzes right on cue, and I show Rivers the text.

> Did your present get there? (;

He shakes his head, and I let him inside as we walk toward the kitchen. "What'd she say to you?" I ask.

"She called me and asked if I had plans because she knew you were home alone and would probably be eating popcorn for dinner, so she said she'd call you to tell you I was on the way with real food. Glad to see she's still diabolical."

"You should hear about all the unique ways she wants to castrate Brad," I joke.

Rivers snorts a laugh then sets the food and wine down on my table. "Do you still like cacio e pepe?"

I look down at my feet, blushing. How many things about a person can we remember after not being around them for so long? How long until we let those little idiosyncrasies evaporate from our brains and disappear into the universe, never to be remembered?

"I do, especially from..."

"Cellini's," Rivers finishes. It's from a restaurant owned by an Italian man who moved here in the eighties and has taught all his kids the family business.

I move to the cupboard and grab two wine glasses as Rivers opens the bottle of Sauvignon Blanc. It's one of my favorites, but he wouldn't know that—we never drank together. It does pair nicely with the white sauce of the pasta though, so I can't be *too* impressed.

He moves around me, plating up our food and taking it to the table for us. It's easy and comfortable; it feels like something I could get used to, and that scares me. What if I lose him again? What if I lose him at all? What if Lianne is lying about forgiving me and she's just trying to be nice because she knows what I've been through?

Rivers notices me spiraling. "What are you thinking, Quinn?"

"Did I tell you I met with your mom a few days ago, before dinner?"

"No, but she did. How was it?"

"It was...good." I let out a sigh.

"Wow, I feel like I was there," he jokes.

"I don't know, Rivers. How can she just forgive me like that? After what I did to you? What I said to her? I just can't wrap my mind around that. And then a few days ago, with everything that happened, and all I unloaded on you, I just..." I lean my head back in frustration.

"You just what?"

"I just I feel like I've only made your life harder since coming back into it."

"Did I tell you that?" he asks. "Did I ever say that you've made my life harder?"

"No, but you didn't ask... for all of this." I wave my hand in the air.

"Quinn, I'm going to ask you something and I need you to be honest with me, okay?" He puts his fork down, and crosses one long leg over the other, resting his hands in his lap. "Do you *want* to date me? Do you want something more with us than just friends? Because I will be whoever you need me to be, but I want to know what you want. Not what you think I want."

I brace myself for the honesty I haven't been able to give him since the letter I wrote him more than twenty years ago. "I want to date you. I want to go on dates with you, and be affectionate with you, and finally give ourselves the chance to live unburdened by our fears. I am also scared to death that everyone is going to judge me, my kids, and your parents, and my deceased husband will hate me for wanting to pursue this, and I feel like it's not fair of me to ask you to deal with all of my baggage when you could go and spend your life with someone like Katie who doesn't have any!"

He's quiet for a second, and I think he's going to ask me to give him some time to really think about all of this too, but he doesn't. Instead, he asks, "Do you have a suitcase?"

The abrupt shift in conversation startles me. It's not what I was expecting him to say at all. "Yes, why?"

"Can you go grab one? I need to do something."

I go into the spare room to get the suitcase down. There's a few I can choose from, he didn't specify what he wants, but eventually I settle on one that's small and red. I wheel it back into the kitchen and see Rivers has cleared the table and wiped it off, standing with a pad of sticky notes he must have found in my junk drawer with a pen. He puts them down before he comes over to me, lifting the suitcase up and placing it on the table. He unzips it and lays it open, like it's ready to be packed.

Before I know it, he's pulled me into a hug that leaves me breathless. He's warm, and it feels nice to held like this. Like he's scared of losing me, and thankful he hasn't in equal measure. "So, I bet you're wondering why I made you go get a suitcase and then lay it on your table?" Since we're hugging his voice sounds low and mumbled.

"I can't say I'm not curious," I agree.

Finally letting go of me, he picks up the sticky notes from the table with the pen, and extends them toward me. "You told me that you didn't think it was fair of you to ask me to deal with all your baggage. So, I want you to write down everything you view about yourself that you consider baggage, and why, on a post-it and put it in the suitcase."

"I thought I was the English teacher, Rivers?" I quip.

He laughs.

"Why am I doing this?"

"Can you just do it?" he presses. "I promise I'll explain when you're done." I start writing things down, but he stops me. "One post-it for each thing, Quinn. I don't want a list; I want a pile."

So, I do. I write everything down on a pile of sticky notes at my kitchen table in my sweatpants while Rivers watches me.

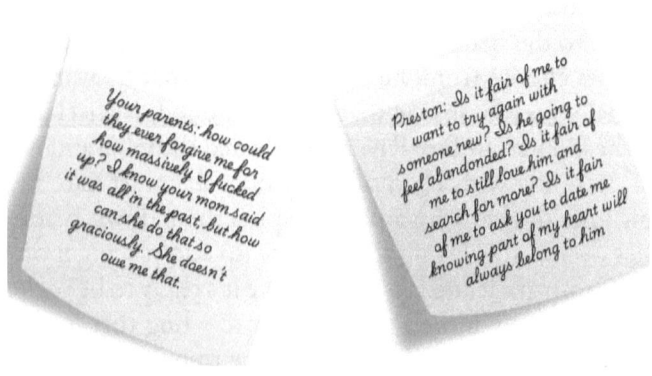

Your parents: how could they ever forgive me for how massively I fucked up? I know your mom said it was all in the past, but how can she do that so graciously. She doesn't owe me that.

Preston: Is it fair of me to want to try again with someone new? Is he going to feel abandonded? Is it fair of me to still love him and search for more? Is it fair of me to ask you to date me knowing part of my heart will always belong to him

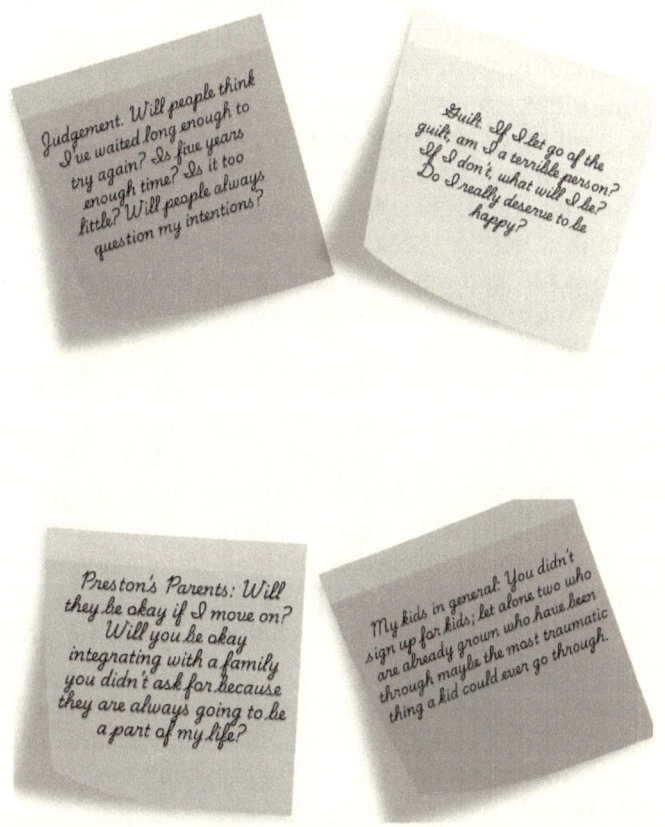

Judgement. Will people think I've waited long enough to try again? Is five years enough time? Is it too little? Will people always question my intentions?

Guilt. If I let go of the guilt, am I a terrible person? If I don't, what will I be? Do I really deserve to be happy?

Preston's Parents: Will they be okay if I move on? Will you be okay integrating with a family you didn't ask for because they are always going to be a part of my life?

My kids in general: You didn't sign up for kids; let alone two who are already grown who have been through maybe the most traumatic thing a kid could ever go through.

It feels good to write everything down like this, to see it all laid out before me. It doesn't make it any more manageable, but at least I can organize my thoughts. I place them, one-by-one, on the lining of the suitcase, taking it all in at once, then I look at him. I've done my part; it's his turn to explain what the hell is going on.

"Okay, now what?"

He leans over the suitcase and zips it, then pulls it off the table, smiling at me, and starts wheeling it towards the front door. "Rivers?" I call, but he doesn't stop, so I chase after him onto the porch.

He turns to face me head on causing me to bump into him so hard that when I start to sway off balance, he steadies me with his hands. We're so close there's hardly an inch between us, and I look up into his eyes—eyes that I've known for so long, I don't even remember not knowing them— and take in all the contours of his handsome face. Strong jaw, perfect nose, that fucking dimple. He places his hand on my jaw and grazes his thumb across my cheek.

"This is me, carrying your baggage, Quinn. And I'll do it over and over and over, for as long as you need me to if it means I get to stay in your life."

"You didn't even read what I wrote." I glance toward the suitcase. We're so close that my words fall onto his lips.

"Because I don't need to. I tried to date Katie after high school, Quinn, and it didn't work because she wasn't you, and I don't give a shit what baggage you have. If it's yours, I'm carrying it. You don't need to do it all alone anymore, and I refuse to let anyone else help you carry it but me. I'll be your own personal bellhop for fuck's sake, but let me carry it, Quinn. Got it?"

We hold each other's gaze as his words settle around us. This is without question the most romantic thing that anyone has ever said or done for me. "Got it." I bite my lip and see the heat flash in Rivers's eyes.

"Thank you for this," I gesture to the suitcase. "Who knew sticky notes held so much power?"

A laugh rumbles in his throat, and he cages me against the door with his arms. "You should see what I can do with an index card," he jokes. We're quiet for a moment; my eyes dip to his lips.

"What do you want, Quinn?" he asks.

We're standing on the threshold of my house, a line in the sand. A decision that can't be undone. If we go back inside, that's it. We're sleeping together, because there is no way I'll be able to control myself anymore. I already feel like I might combust if I don't touch him right now. If we say goodnight here, I go back in alone and we figure out our next move.

But I don't want to figure anything else out, this is what I want. I want him. I wanted him when I was sixteen in my parents' house and fighting the inexorable truth we both knew but would never admit. And I want him right now at thirty-six, finally willing to acknowledge what I've always known.

"You," I answer, my chest heaving from the admission. "I want you."

I pull him inside to the living room, and kiss him slowly. Like I have all night, and I guess, thanks to Dani, I do. I kiss the spot on his collarbone I tasted on our walk, and the dimple that's always felt like a gift. I move my hands under his dark gray sweatshirt to the firm planes of his stomach, rewarded with the perfect ridges of his abdomen, and pull it over his head revealing his sculpted frame. I discover the tattoo he's been hiding, which is a tragedy because the swirls of inky black only serve to accentuate the muscles in his arms and shoulders. I see now that it's an image of a pirate ship, *his* pirate ship, *Ashes of Atlantis,* on a turbulent ocean.

He rests his hand on my waist, making me shudder and my skin ignite against his touch as he pulls me flush against him, his thumb capturing my chin to look at him before he kisses me so slowly like he's savoring every moment. From the pressure I feel against my hips, I can tell he wants me, too.

"I'm yours, Quinn," he whispers. "I always have been."

I remove the shirt I have on, leaving me in a sports bra that leaves very little to the imagination; my nipples are so on edge with his touch, they'll probably slice through the fabric hell bent on keeping them contained.

"And I want whatever you're willing to give me." I pull my bra off, flinging it into the abyss, watching him take in the stiff peaks of my chest.

"God, you're perfect." He takes my nipple in his mouth, and swirls his tongue like it was made for this exact purpose, then plants kisses along my collarbone and stomach on the way down to his knees, and I'm too stunned to speak.

"Take whatever you want, just please don't stop touching me," I whisper as my fingers push through his hair. The grin he shoots me has a wicked gleam in it that pulses right through me. He pulls my sweats down, leaving my green lace briefs exposed to only his breath.

"Can I kiss you here?" he asks, pressing the palm of his hand against my core, and I let out a gasp. He leaves the smallest kisses and bites along my upper thigh and if they're any indication of what's to come, I'll be finished in seconds.

"Yeah," I let out.

My voice is hoarse, like it doesn't know how to breathe and speak in tandem anymore.

"Lay back, honey," he says as he pulls me down on the couch, so I'm splayed before him. He pulls my underwear off and over my feet, exposing me to his breath. Rivers moves his mouth between my legs and sucks, then ever so gently skates his teeth along the most sensitive part of me.

I throw my head back in pleasure, needing this, needing him. He hooks his arms through my legs so they're resting on his sculpted shoulders, his tongue swirling languidly, building my orgasm so effortlessly it's almost painful.

"You taste so fucking good," he whispers, and with the merciless licking and sucking of his tongue, I'd almost believe he's starved for me.

The coil in my belly winds tighter and tighter with every stroke, and then Rivers plunges two fingers into me, making me see stars. My back arches off the couch, pleasure cresting within me. Rivers keeps his other arm low across my belly, preventing me from escaping. "Come for me, Quinny," he says through laps of his tongue.

"Rivers!" I scream, so close to the edge, I'm about to burst.

"That's it," he coaxes. "Be a good girl and come on my fingers so I can taste you there later."

He wraps his whole mouth around me and sucks until the coil within me snaps, my orgasm radiating through every part of my body until I'm shaking on the couch, and coating Rivers's fingers just like he asked me to. He kisses between my legs, then pulls his fingers out of me, sucking them clean as he looks me in the eye.

Fuck, that was hot.

He stands up, but I'm too pent up to let him go anywhere. I sit up, gripping his hips and pulling down the joggers he wears that are clearly uncomfortable if the tent his dick has created is any indication.

"Quinn, you cannot look at me like that, and expect me to be honorable here." He swallows around his arousal.

"Who said I wanted you to be honorable?" I respond. "What if I want to be really, really, dishonorable?"

Heat flashes in his eyes, and I swear I see his dick twitch. "Do you have a condom?" he asks.

Fuck.

"No," I sigh. "I'm assuming you don't either?"

"No," he says on a chuckle. Contrary to what you might think, I really was just bringing you dinner because Dani told me to."

As if summoned by the gods, both mine and Rivers's phones chime with a text, which can only mean one thing: Dani.

> Shit! I almost forgot! Condoms are on the top shelf of your pantry, Quinn. En-joy the trip to pound town you two (; Be safe!

"I'm gonna kill her, then bring her back to life and thank her for having the foresight to buy us condoms," I joke as I make my way into the kitchen to get to the pantry.

When I grab them and turn around to make my way back to the living room, Rivers stops me. "Are you sure about this? I don't want to rush you," he says.

"I don't feel rushed," I answer honestly. "I feel like this is exactly where I'm supposed to be in my life right now."

I kiss him again, so he knows I'm serious. He takes hold of my bare hips, kissing me as he gently pushes us down the hall toward my bedroom. I turn on the lamp—giving the room a warm glow—and walk into Rivers's arms. His hands clasp together against my lower back, while mine curl in between us. "Rivers?"

"Mhm?"

"I don't want to rush you, either," I say.

He moves away from me, then cups his hand along my jaw looking back and forth between my eyes. "I've waited more than twenty years to hold you, Quinn. I think I've done my time." He kisses the side of my temple, then brings his hand up to my breast, rolling my nipple between his fingers as I moan into his mouth with another searing kiss.

I lightly push him onto the bed, crawling over him to straddle his hips. His gaze never leaves me, like he's trying to memorize this moment, cementing it in his mind. I take him in my hand, stroking the length and applying a hint more pressure at his tip.

"Fuck, Quinn." His voice is low and raspy.

I've never seen this side of him.

"You are fulfilling every fantasy I've ever had."

I laugh and roll the condom over him, raising to my knees so I can take him. I move slowly, savoring every inch as he fills me, then start to rock my hips, making his breath hitch.

It's slow, but my second orgasm builds with every motion of my hips as Rivers palms my breasts, then rests his hands on each side of my ass. Our gazes are locked on one another until my legs are shaking. In one swift motion, he flips me onto my back and takes in the sight of me beneath him. My hair fanned out, my chest colored in a blush he's painted me with, and heaving with a need to be closer, so much closer to him.

"You are the most beautiful thing I've ever seen," he says as he raises my leg to his shoulder and slides into me, deeper. He leans over me, kissing me behind my ear, and pinning my arms in place above my head.

The angle takes my breath away each time he pumps into me, spinning me tighter and tighter until I think I'll snap. "Rivers, please," I beg.

"Please, what?" he says moving torturously slow now.

"Please make me come."

He lets out a breathy laugh. "I thought you'd never ask," he says with a wicked grin, then moves his mouth to the inside of the thigh still resting on his shoulder and bites as he slams into me.

I scream, euphoria chasing through my veins in the perfect mix of pain and pleasure as Rivers's body shudders and he collapses onto me. I turn my head to kiss him, running my fingers along the swirls of ink, our breaths slowing.

He rolls off me to dispose of the condom, then comes back to my room with cookies that June left yesterday as I clean myself up. "Chocolate chip or double chocolate chunk?"

"That feels like choosing a favorite child," I say, searching for something to wear.

He hands me the hoodie he was wearing earlier and breaks each cookie in half as I pull it over my head. It barely covers my ass, but it's cozy and smells like him. After putting on a pair of underwear, Rivers and I move out to the couch to watch *The Wedding Singer*. He pulls me against him, my head on his chest with his arm holding me in place like I'm not permitted to leave.

We laugh through the scene where the wedding guests sing "Love Stinks" after Adam Sandler's character is left heartbroken on his wedding day and discuss the ethics of he and Drew Barrymore practicing her wedding day kiss. When Billy Idol starts talking into the airplane microphone, announcing San-

dler's song that always turns me to goo, Rivers stands pulling
me up to dance with him in the glow of the T.V. light, softly
singing the words in my ear like a promise that he's always
wanted to be held to. It's not our normal dance routine. It's
slow and steady. His hands grip my hips, and I loop mine
around his neck before I kiss the words off his tongue and smile
against his mouth.

We clean up the kitchen together, playing our favorite Weezer songs through the speakers, and pausing to dance or rem-
inisce about certain memories associated with each one. The
dishes dried and put away, the floor clean, and still with an
hour before Dani brings the kids home, we make a playlist of
all the songs we collected from each other in our youth.

I put on "I Will Follow You Into the Dark" by Death Cab
for Cutie as I turn back to the stove to make a mug of tea,
when Rivers comes up behind me, looping his arms around
my middle. I turn to face him, planting small kisses on his
lips when he tangles his tongue with mine again, igniting my
core and causing me to whimper and follow him back to my
bedroom again—the tea forgotten on the stove.

After we finish, I lay on his chest sated and comfortable, our
legs tangled together in my rumpled covers. "When do I get to
see you again, Quinny?" he whispers into my ear.

"Tomorrow?" I hedge. I don't want to be without him;
knowing he has to go home tonight already makes me miss
him.

"Tomorrow it is," he says before kissing my temple.

Lights illuminate my bedroom window, and Rivers and I
spring off the bed to find pants. I grab biker shorts that go
to my mid-thigh so even though the kids will know this is his
sweater, they'll at least know I have pants on.

He kisses me deeply one more time before the kids burst into
the front door in a riotous swirl of chaos.

"I'm just saying triangles don't have vibes, Wyatt! They're
triangles!" Sawyer sounds exasperated.

"And I'm just saying that an isosceles triangle will *always* be red to me!" she argues.

"Mom!" Sawyer yells, like I'm not standing fifteen feet away. "Oh," he rears back, taking in the sight of Rivers standing in our living room.

Wyatt rounds the corner, her eyes also going wide.

"How was your study group?" I ask.

"How was your evening *alone*?" Wyatt retorts.

Rivers coughs into his fist before I answer, "Less lonely than expected."

"Can someone explain isosceles triangles always being red? Because for some reason that works in here?" Rivers points to his head.

"Wyatt thinks that the different types of triangles each have a specific color in people's minds, but they're just triangles."

"Equilateral triangles are blue," Rivers says, and both kids' jaws open like a cartoon.

"Sounds like a question for the polls!" I chime in and pull out my phone to get it set up, walking further into the living room with Rivers following behind me.

He moves closer to the door to put his shoes on, while the kids continue their friendly bickering as they eat leftover cookies. He turns to give me a hug.

"Want your sweater back?" I move to take it off.

"No, I've always loved seeing you in my clothes, Quinny. You keep it." He leaves me with one chaste kiss on the lips that leaves my body craving more of his touch before he walks to the driveway toward his car with my suitcase wheeling behind him.

I'm so completely screwed.

Before Rivers is even fully buckled in his car, Dani hoofs it to my front door with a wicked gleam in her eye, and Sybil cued up on Facetime on her phone. "Spill, bitch. And don't leave out a single detail."

Chapter Twenty

Now

"I think my crush on Rivers Thomas is back, because what do you *mean* he made you put all your baggage into a suitcase and then wheeled it to his car?! Swoon." Liz shakes her head as it falls back onto the other chair in June's salon.

"What'd you guys do after that?" June asks, sectioning off another piece of my hair and applying the bleach into the foil.

I look down at the floor and try to tamper down the smile trying to escape. The flush in my cheeks gives me away though.

"Bow chicka wow wow," Liz chimes from her chair, her body writhing in a suggestive dance.

I shoot a hair tie at her to get her to shut up, but she just keeps teasing.

June swats at my hand to get me to sit still, tugging on another piece of my hair. "How was that?" she asks, pointedly.

"Yeah, Quinn. How was that?" Liz sing-songs.

"Fuck off," I joke as I throw up the middle finger.

June holds my gaze in the mirror, like she can see straight to the center of my soul. "How do you feel?"

Liz turns serious too, waiting for my answer and giving me the space to find it.

"I feel cautiously optimistic," I start.

"Not about the relationship, you donut!" Liz shouts. "The *sex!* How do you feel about that?!"

It's June's turn to smack her now. "I did *not* mean about the sex, I meant how do you feel overall. Cautiously optimistic is better than a few weeks ago where you felt guilty; what's still making you hesitate?"

"I don't feel hesitant. I'm just scared I'm going to ruin it all again and lose him a second time," I admit. Now that I have him back in my life, the prospect of him not being in it terrifies me. I'm not without guilt still, but I think it's less about grappling with how Preston would feel, and more about if I deserve to be happy again. I know I don't deserve to stay in a permanent state of sadness, but my brain is at war with itself, trying to decide if I actually should get to have this. "I'm also trying to believe everyone in my life that Preston would want me to be happy and not let the voices in my head make me doubt that."

June nods her head, sectioning out another portion of my hair. "Look, I get you being scared to lose him a second time, but you were also kids the last time you were anything at all. You're communicative adults now. You've both been pretty honest with each other, and I think it's safe to say that's going well for you."

"Bow chicka wow wow," Liz mutters under her breath and we all laugh.

"It's going well. I always wanted to talk to him like this when we were kids, but, we were kids, and being honest was scary. It feels nice to just have him tell me what he's thinking."

It's quiet for a minute. June has Brandi Carlile playing in the background as she continues painting bleach onto my hair,

Liz is scrolls through her phone, and I'm thinking of Rivers twirling me in the light of the T.V. to my favorite movie.

"The sex was also pretty great," I finally say.

"I knew it," Liz bellows.

I take my phone out to snap a picture and send it to Mom. She always likes seeing when we're all together like this. I asked if she wanted to come to the salon too, but she and Dad were going on an 'appetizer adventure,' whatever that is, so she couldn't make it. I type in Rivers's name, then attach the picture with a quick text.

> Wish you were here (; img.jpg

But before I can stop the message from going through, I realize I accidentally chose Preston's mom's name: Rita, instead of Rivers.

"Shit, oh shit!" I say, panicking. I try to stand up from the chair to pace, but June shoves me back into the seat.

"What's wrong?" She puts the bleach down on her tray.

"I just sent the picture of us to Rita!"

"Okay, so? I mean, yeah you look a little insane with the foil, but I don't think it's worth swearing over?" Liz rolls her eyes, legitimately thinking that my appearance is the issue.

"No! I also wrote 'wish you were here' with a winky face because I thought I was sending it to Rivers!"

They both fall silent. "You haven't told them?" June's voice is tentative, like she doesn't want to make me feel bad.

Honestly, I wasn't trying to hide it from them. We just haven't talked since Rivers and I reconnected, and I'm always so busy at the start of the school year. Rita knows I'll reach out to her when things die down. For the last four years, Rita didn't talk to me at all the entire months of September and October. She knew I was drowning in establishing my classes and needed to get into the groove of the school year again, and this fifth year hasn't been any different. I would have called her sometime this month to touch base or she would have, which is why this unprompted text message from me roughly three weeks early is so out of the ordinary and will absolutely cause her to ask questions.

I groan through the final foils June places, knowing I'm going to have to deal with the inevitable but choose to push it out of my mind until after my appointment. I'm not calling them with my sisters here.

"How are things going with you, June?" I decide to turn the conversation to her so I can have some breathing room. It feels like she and her husband are going through something I can't name. "I feel like I never see…"

She cuts me off before I can finish.

"Nope, we're not talking about me and my imploding marriage right now."

Liz and I look at each other. June has always been stubborn; she's always tried to stay strong and have a stiff upper lip. She's also always been terrified of confronting or talking about her feelings with anyone, so I choose not to push it.

I take a drink of my water, trying to figure out what to say next, but Liz breaks the silence for me.

"I got asked to send a picture of *'where I shit from'* by a guy holding a fish on a dating app three nights ago," she offers to diffuse the tension.

The sip of water in my mouth sprays over the entirety of June's salon mirror as I let out a cackle.

I may have to tell my deceased husband's parents that I'm dating again, but at least I don't have strange men asking for pictures of my asshole.

***

My favorite bench by the water is empty when I approach it. I pull out my phone, thinking of what to say and how to say it. Rita never responded to my text message, so I don't know exactly what I'm walking into here, but I know that they deserve the truth regardless.

I hit the icon for FaceTime with Rita—the closest I'll get to an in-person discussion with them. She answers on the fourth ring, while Gary, Preston's dad, sits next to her. They're in their living room; I can tell from the wall of windows that back up to their twelve acres of land. The sun looks lower in the sky there since they're two hours ahead of California.

"Hey there, Quinn!" Gary says.

"Hey guys," I respond with a smile. My voice is subdued. I don't even know if she read my accidental message.

"Where are the kids?" Rita asks, looking across my screen as if they'll magically appear.

"They're at home. I just got my hair done, and they didn't want to come sit at June's salon." It's the easiest way I can think of broaching this subject. If I can determine if she saw it or not, I'll have a better understanding of how to proceed.

"Yeah, I got your picture," Rita says. "I assumed that wasn't for me?"

Fuck.

I suck in a breath bracing for what I have to tell her. "No...it was for...it was for a man I'm seeing."

"I didn't realize..." she trails off. There's a hint of hurt in her voice that makes me feel ashamed.

"Rita..."

"How long have you been seeing him?" she asks. Gary's arm moves around her shoulder to comfort her.

"We've been on a couple of dates. I made sure the kids were okay with it. They invited him to the amusement park without me knowing last week. Sawyer gave his official blessing a couple of days ago."

"And how did you meet?" Gary is trying to be conversational, but there're tears in Rita's eyes. They sting.

"He was my best friend when I was a teenager," I grit out.

This is so painful; it's exactly what I was afraid of. I don't want to hurt them anymore than they've already endured. It feels like I'm rubbing salt in a wound that will never heal for them.

"Listen, I have to get home and start dinner, but I'll have the kids call you soon, okay?" I swipe a tear from my eye, the guilt feeling insurmountable.

"Quinn," Rita says.

"We'll talk soon. Love you guys," I say before I hang up.

I hang my head in my hands when the call ends. I know I can't base my life choices on other people's expectations or feelings. Logically, I know that. But my heart aches for them. It must feel like I've moved on or replaced their son with someone new. Someone they don't know has a real chance at forming relationships and having experiences with their grandchildren that Preston will never see, like walking Wyatt down the aisle and going to sporting events with Sawyer as adults. It's bittersweet thinking about the prospect of what will never be and what could be at the same time.

***

For dinner, it's just the kids and me. They asked me to invite Rivers over, which I did, but he's eating with his parents and Forest tonight. I still have yet to see Forest since moving home, but from what Rivers says, he and his wife are really busy with their jobs and wrangling their kids to different soccer tournaments.

Since I cooked dinner, it's up to the kids to clean it up. Watching them wash and dry brings back memories of Liz and me working together when June moved out, the same routine, like a dance every night.

"Do you guys want to do something when you're done?" I ask them from the table. "We could watch a movie or play a game?" I try to do something with them every night, so they get quality family time every day. I see too many students with parents who let them fend for themselves once they reach middle school and it shows. Kids need attention—no matter their age.

"Could we go for a bike ride, then get ice cream?" Wyatt suggests.

We can't bike to the ice cream shop since it's over by the lake and it would take us at least an hour to get there on bikes with the incline fluctuation, but I like the idea of riding with them then driving for ice cream.

Ten minutes later, we have our helmets on, cycling toward my old childhood home. The kids have seen it since we moved here, but they were so busy taking everything else in about their new town, I don't know how much they remembered.

It looks just like it used to, the windows covering the majority of the walls to bring in the light; the stream still trickling in the yard.

"Mom," Wyatt pulls me from my thoughts. "Which room was yours?"

"That one, there." I point to the one toward the back of the house on the second floor that overlooks the stream. "The middle floor had most of the bedrooms."

"Did Dad ever see this house? "Sawyer asks.

"He saw it, but he never went inside. Your grandparents moved to the house they're in now right after I moved out. They didn't need all the space once it was just Liz and them."

Sawyer is quiet for moment, pensive. "Can you tell us about a time with Rivers in this house?"

It occurs to me that there are very few places the kids have been that don't hold memories of their father, this being one of them. I laugh, thinking about all the stories I could tell them. "How about the night I decided that the waning crescent was my favorite moon phase?"

"That happened here?" Wyatt asks, peering throughout the yard and house like she's trying to capture the memory herself.

"Mhm," I answer. "You see the smaller roof right outside my bedroom window, there?"

I point to the additional small structure my dad added when I was a kid; he turned it into a movie room for us, but we only used it as a family.

"Rivers and I used to sneak out there while our parents were in the living room, which is those windows over there." I point to the set of windows that are catty-corner from the back bedroom, then laugh thinking about all the times they'd catch us and yell that we were reckless. We park our bikes along the side of the road, so I put an arm around each kid as we look at the house. They're quiet, waiting for me to continue.

"One night, we crawled out there as quietly as we could; your Aunt Liz was so mad we wouldn't let her come." They laugh at that. "But it was really cold, so Rivers crawled back into my room to get a blanket for our legs. We laid back against the roof, and I don't know what it was about that night, but the stars looked extra bright. Maybe it was the cold, or maybe it was just really clear because the moon was really small; either way, we could see everything. Rivers always loved to find Orion first, and I was always searching for—"

"The Seven Sisters," the kids say in unison.

"Yes," I answer, rubbing both their heads. "And that night, the Seven Sisters were more visible than usual, so Rivers was really able to see their magic. I remember him turning to me and saying, *'at least your taste in constellations is better than your taste in boys.'*"

The kids laugh, hearing about me being a stupid teenager.

"How embarrassing that an actual teenage boy had to tell you your taste in boys sucked, Mom," Sawyer jokes.

"So embarrassing," I agree.

Wyatt's impatience gets the best of her here. She huffs a breath at us and says, "Keep going with the story, please."

"Sorry," I start. "So, we were looking at the stars and Rivers asked me *'Quinny, what's your favorite moon phase?'* I didn't know how to answer him because I didn't know all the names of the phases," I say with a chuckle. "But I pointed to the sky, and said, *'whatever phase we're in right now is my favorite. It feels like the moon is smiling at me,'* and Rivers turned his head toward me on the roof and told me it was the waning crescent, but that the waxing crescent would look the same just reversed. I didn't agree, though. The moon was smiling at me, but I also liked that that it was the moon where I was warm, on a roof with my best friend, and it felt like the moon made the stars brighter just for us."

"I wonder if Rivers still likes Orion," Sawyer muses.

Preston was never a sky-watcher. He'd pull over for me to snap a picture of a great sunset or buy the special solar eclipse glasses when we'd needed them, but the kids have never had a man in their life care about the sky like we do.

"Let's ask him." I pull out my phone and dial his number, then put him on speaker phone.

"Hey, Quinny," his voice rumbles through the phone. It's intoxicating.

"Hey, I have the kids here with me. Sawyer wanted to ask you something."

"Sure, what's up?"

"Is Orion still your favorite constellation?" He sounds shy, almost, embarrassed, but he's still curious enough to want to push past the feeling.

"Where are you guys?" Rivers asks.

"My parents' old house. We're looking at our star roof," I answer.

"Hmm, lots of good memories up there." I can tell by his voice that he's reminiscing. "Orion is still my favorite, but I don't think your mom knows why."

My ears perk up. This is something I've never asked him before, and the prospect of learning new things about him—especially when they relate to things I already know—excites me.

"You have me on pins and needles, sir," I joke.

"I find Orion first because, once I do, I know just where to search to find the Seven Sisters."

I swallow a lump in my throat and smile like a fool the whole bike ride home.

***

At the ice cream shop, the kids order their flavors first then turn toward the small table that overlooks the water. In a few months, we'll start to get snow, and it will look completely different. I pay in cash, then feel my phone buzzing in my pocket as I walk toward the kids. I assume it's Rivers calling to make sure we made it back from our bike ride safely, since I forgot to text him.

But it's not Rivers.

It's Rita.

"Hello?" I'm nervous to talk to her again. I need more time to process everything that happened with her. I also know I can't delay talking to her, it'll only make it worse.

"Hey, sweetie," she sounds miserable. "I need to apologize for how I spoke to you earlier."

"Rita, really, it's okay. It's not fair of me to ask you guys to be okay with me dating. I'm sorry I was so insensitive."

"Quinn, we're happy for you," she says. "I shouldn't have made you feel guilty. You are allowed to find love again, and I want you to know we support you in that. I knew it would happen someday, I just always viewed someday as a hypothetical, and that's not fair of me."

Tears sting my eyes: for what they've endured, for how it impacts them. Every day, I wake up and recognize that my life isn't the same as it was five years ago. When Preston died, he left a hole in my life that made me feel like no matter which way I turned, I could walk off a ledge.

Over time, that hole became less sizable; that's not to say I don't miss him every day, because I do, it's just that I've learned to live without his big, beautiful persona. But if I had lost one of the kids? I just don't know how a person recovers from that, and that's what Preston's parents have had to live with.

Parents aren't supposed to bury their children.

Rita's voice brings me back to the conversation. "And we want you to know, that we really believe you have Preston's blessing too. He'd hate for you to live your life stuck in his memory."

"You know that I will always love Preston, right? He made my world spin, Rita."

I hear her sniffle through the line. It makes me wonder if she'll ever be able to talk about him without crying or if it will always be this way. I've been through five years of extensive therapy, and it's helped me get to a place where when I think of Preston, I think of putting mentos in a bottle of coke on our first date because neither of us had ever tried it. I think of him holding my legs during childbirth and putting Sawyer on my chest. I think about him teaching Wyatt to ride a bike and catching her before she fell into the grass. I think of him dancing with me on the cruise a few days before he died, and how he told me he was so happy that I was the one he chose. I wonder if Rita and Gary think about all the firsts he ever took, and cry, thinking of all the firsts they know he'll never have.

"I know you will, sweetie," she answers. "Go live your life, Quinn. You only get one."

We end the call, and I stand there looking at the lake on the brink of a change when the season turns. I didn't realize how much Preston's family accepting this meant to me until just now. I've been so worried about the kids and Lianne, I hadn't really thought about how much their approval and maybe, more importantly, their opinion on Preston's wishes, would make me feel this relieved.

I loved.

I lost.

But maybe I can love again. Maybe I'll get hurt, maybe I won't, maybe I'll see that regardless of what happens with Rivers, I had the courage to try again.

Maybe that's what matters.

Chapter Twenty-One

Then, Sophomore Year

T he start of my sophomore year isn't as eventful as the year before in terms of being a social pariah to my peers, but it is complicated. After Justin burst into the readiness day event (which was a smashing success, I might add. The principal requested we do it again next year!), we got to talking about our summers and our interests and now it's November and...he asked me to be his girlfriend.

I don't know how to tell Rivers; I think he's seen us flirting around school, and I'm certain that word has probably traveled to him by now since I delayed giving Justin an answer until tomorrow. Dani made me swear that I would tell Rivers before I give my answer, and I think it's a smart move. The last thing I want to do is hurt him. He and Bryan are coming over today to help my dad get something ready for us to go camping. I figured that now is as good a chance as any to tell him the truth.

Justin isn't any of the things that Rivers claimed he was. He's a little bit shy, has a wicked sense of humor, and is really easy to talk to. I told him about the situation from last year with student government, and how I miss June, and now Cody, and he just sat with me, asking questions that showed me he was listening and that he cared about my feelings. He did ask about Rivers and me; I think he's trying to understand our friendship, but he didn't seem bothered by it. In fact, all he said was, "As long as you don't kiss him, I don't really care that your best friend is a guy," which is great because I don't want to give up Rivers, and we don't kiss.

"Rivers..." I start the moment he pulls into the driveway and we're out of earshot from our dads.

"No. Save it, Quinn. You can do whatever you want to do with your life; it just sucks you didn't tell me." I can see his throat bobbing like he's trying to fight the words that want to spill out of him.

"I didn't say yes," I manage.

He eyes me, like at this point it's more semantics than anything else, and I guess he's probably right. Justin wouldn't ask me to be his girlfriend if he didn't think I'd say yes. "Did you say no?" he asks, knowing I can't argue.

"No, because I wanted to talk to you first."

"Why Quinn? Why does it matter if you say yes before or after you talk to me? I was clear about my feelings regarding Justin a fucking year ago in sign language when he slithered like a snake into our conversation and convinced you that he needed help studying when he's always been an 'A' student."

"I don't want you to hate me, Rivers. And I'm scared you will if I pursue this."

"I could never hate you Quinn, but I can't lie and say that I'll be happy for you either. I'm sorry, I just know how he is with people, and how he's treated girls in the past."

He's said this a few times before and it *always* frustrates me. "You say that, but you've never given me an example! How has he treated girls in the past? Because right now, he talks to me like we're best friends, and listens to me, and makes me laugh, and I just don't see this side of him you claim to know."

"Ask him about Marissa Jackson, Quinn. I feel like that's all you need to know." Rivers pulls me into a side hug, then leaves me alone in the kitchen, annoyed and frustrated.

Feeling like I need the counsel of someone older and wiser, but not quite ready to hear everything June has to say, I pull out my phone to text Cody.

> Do you know anything about Justin Parks?

He responds almost immediately.

> I know of him, yeah.

> Care to share with the class?

> He's smart, funny. A little bit of a tool. I heard a rumor about him a year or so ago, but don't know if it was true or not.

> He asked me to be his girlfriend…What was the rumor?

> Did you say yes? It was basically that he showed his girlfriend's nudes to his friends.

Not yet. Was it Marissa?

Yep, I have her number if you want to call her.

I choose, instead, to call Justin and ask him what happened with Marissa wanting to know if there's weight to the claims, and wanting to hear his voice when he's confronted about it. It doesn't seem like the Justin I know. If he did do it, then I understand completely why Rivers wouldn't like him, and it would deter me from pursuing Justin completely. But I can't operate my life based on a rumor that may or may not be true.

Justin picks up on the third ring. "Quinn, you have an answer for me?" I can almost feel him smirking at me through the phone.

"No, I was actually going to ask you about Marissa Jackson."

He's quiet for a beat. "Where'd you hear about that?" His voice is like ice; it doesn't sound like him at all.

"Just a friend," I say.

"An older student?" he asks, probably assuming Rivers.

"Yeah."

Justin sighs through the line. "Someone who isn't a friend started that rumor because he was pissed off that I wouldn't let him cheat off of my test."

I exhale a sigh of relief; I really didn't want Justin to be a bad guy.

"Okay, I'll have an answer for you tomorrow," I tell him.

"I'm sure you will. Night, Quinn."

Before bed, I text Rivers.

I'm going to say yes.

And I can't stop you.

***

On Monday morning, I walk into school, moving toward the biology room where Justin hangs out with the golf team. I spot him in a t-shirt and jeans talking to a group of guys I recognize but don't know super well. I suck in a breath to build my courage, then tap him on the shoulder.

When he turns around, he pulls me into a hug that's clunky and weird because of our backpacks but still feels right.

"How was your night, gorgeous?" he asks, pulling away from me.

"Pretty good. Just hung out. But I also have an answer for you." I smile up at him as I grip the straps of my backpack.

We turn to walk out of biology toward my first class: Honors English. Justin takes hold of my hand, immediately generating whispers and pointed glances from classmates.

"Oh, yeah? What's your answer?" Justin's voice sounds confident and sexy. He smiles like he knows what he's going to hear, and to be fair, he does.

"Yes," I say, blushing.

He twirls me to face him, placing his hands on my hips.

"'Bout fucking time, Quinn." He moves one hand to my jaw and pulls my lips to meet him.

It's my first kiss, chaste and sweet, and I let out a sigh of bliss. Justin laughs. I feel him smile against my lips before he slides his tongue gently between my parted lips to meet my own. He pulls away, and for the first time since he held my hand, I take in my surroundings. People look at us and give Justin high-fives in congratulations. But it's the one tall person in a blue sweater that's walking away down the Hello Hallway that makes my smile slip.

Dani moves forward from the crowd to greet me, clocking my sudden discomfort. "What's wrong? That kiss was hot!"

Justin turns around to smile at her; thinking that she was complimenting him. I shake my head to tell her that this probably isn't the place to discuss it.

He puts his hand on the small of my back to guide me through the crowd as we start walking toward class again.

The whole way there, Dani talks about the boy she likes from another town who she never gets to see, but after kissing Justin, I realize something. When I called him last night, he didn't deny that he shared Marissa's photos, he just said his friend started a rumor. I turn to face him, and the words burst out of me before I have the chance to fully process them. "Did you show people Marissa's photos?"

Dani's eyes move between us, assessing.

Justin huffs out a laugh as he takes me in. "What? I told you last night what happened."

I nod to myself, considering his words. It feels like he could have just as easily said that he had a hand in it or not, but he's being evasive again.

Dani looks between us, concern etching her brow. "Justin, I'm going to walk Quinn the rest of the way to English. You can go." Her dismissal of him is nothing short of iconic, but I mostly appreciate that she can tell I need a little space.

"She's my girlfriend, Dani. I'll walk her there."

"I have to talk to her about my period. You want to stay for that, be my guest; it's *really* bloody this time." Her smooth delivery makes Justin lose the color in his face. He kisses me on the cheek before he leaves, walking in the opposite direction toward math.

"What's going on, Quinn? You've been pining after him for months and now that you have him, you're acting weird," Dani starts.

"I know, I just hate knowing that Rivers is mad at me," I tell her as we finish walking.

"Hold on. Rivers is what has you messed up? I swear you two make life so much more complicated than it needs to be," she sounds exasperated. "He's never liked Justin, Quinn. This shouldn't be news to you."

"No, I know. It just sucks. I want my best friend to like my boyfriend."

"Fifty-three percent of us do! Minus the period thing, he was being a baby there." She tosses her thumb over her shoulder to signal that she's referring to Justin.

"Fifty-three percent?"

"I'm more your best friend than Rivers is. You can admit it, I won't tell him." We giggle as we walk into English waiting for the bell to ring.

Right before class starts, my phone buzzes.

> Ur tits look hot in that shirt today. U should wear it more often.

And so, my list of red flags begins to grow.

***

Justin and I last from November to February before he breaks up with me through a text message. I've been feeling a lot more pressure from him to be physically intimate, but I'm just not ready for that. He hasn't hurt me apart from the text that called me a prude and said that the reason I wouldn't put out was because I wanted to *"put Rivers in"* (gross) after Justin witnessed Rivers sitting with me while I was crying a few days ago.

I'm bracing myself for impact before I tell Dani, Trevor, and Rivers about Justin's mode of breaking up with me—and his reason—as we drive toward the Brew Crew Café for hot chocolates since it's so cold.

We sit down at the table we all like by the window, waiting for our drinks to be called. I love Lianne's tea, don't get me wrong, but there's nothing better than a cup of hot chocolate on a cold day. Dani gets black coffee like a psychopath, and Trevor? He gets something that has a sucker sticking out of the top.

"So, you guys know how Justin broke up with me?"

I figure the best way to go about this is the Band-Aid method: quick, but not painless. Everyone at school knows Justin ended it, they just don't know how...or why.

"Bleh," Dani says after a sip of coffee.

"Is it gross? I'll go get you something else," I offer.

"No, you said Justin's name. That's just my automatic response to that," she says, taking another swig.

"What'd he say, Quinn?" Rivers asks. He grips his tea with both hands. He looks stoic, like he's trying to not let his emotions slip through the mask he wears, but his hands give him away.

"He...texted me actually."

"Oh, for fuck's sake," Trevor growls.

"You're joking." Rivers is so unimpressed that his face hasn't moved apart from one eyebrow lifting upward.

"Nope," is all I can manage.

"Did he say why?" Dani asks.

"He did, but I can't read it out loud. I think I'll die of embarrassment." I tilt my phone toward Dani so she can look at it and verbalize to the guys what I can't do myself.

"Well, I hope Justin has a good day today, since it's the last one he's ever going to see!" Dani yells, standing up from the table. "Rivers, drive me to Justin, and don't forget the shovel!"

Trevor tosses his hands up, wondering why he doesn't get to see the message. Thankfully, Dani summarizes it. "He called her a prude for not putting out. Now, can we please go get that shovel?"

Rivers moves over to my chair, getting on his knees and looking up into my eyes. "What do you need, Quinny?"

"To cry? I don't know. I know it sounds dumb, but I was really looking forward to Valentine's Day. I bought these chocolate molds that looked like golf balls so I could make him homemade truffles. It's silly. I just wanted to make someone feel special and have them do the same."

"Do you honestly want to spend it with him, Quinn? I mean is being alone on Valentine's Day really worse than spending it with Justin Parks?" Trevor chimes in from behind Rivers.

"I don't; I just wanted one day to be romanced and feel special, as lame as that sounds."

"You won't be alone." Rivers's voice brings me back to looking at him. "You're spending it with me, and it'll be the best fucking Valentine's Day you'll ever have."

***

It's the worst Valentine's Day ever.

The blizzard hit on Friday night, which means no Rivers, and Mom and Dad have left me with a huge list of chores to complete instead of letting me just read on my bed. So far, I've cleaned the bathrooms, brought firewood into the house, and cleaned the stove top. I kind of look like a train wreck in my sweats and topknot, and I'm fairly certain the thing I smell is me. I didn't tell Mom and Dad about Justin; I feel like they wouldn't view him as a loss, so I choose not to argue about my chores punctuated by tears of teenage heartbreak.

I start dusting the loft just outside my parents' bedroom, then move my way down the stairs, wiping between the slats of the banister polls. When I reach the end, I move around the stairs back toward the dining room and bump into a person I don't expect to see: Rivers.

My headphones come out of my ears immediately. "What are you doing here?" I throw my arms around him in a hug, then realize my error. "Oh, God, I probably stink. Sorry!"

"You're fine," he says with a laugh. "Happy Valentine's Day, Quinny."

"Rivers how did you get here? The roads are awful!"

He runs his fingers through his hair in maybe the only sign of embarrassment I've ever seen him show. "I may have begged my dad to drive me here so I could spend Valentine's Day with you like I promised." He lets out a small grimace, unsure of himself.

I put the rag and dusting spray down on the dining room table, then pull him into another hug. I don't know what I did in life to deserve Rivers Thomas as a best friend. I do know I am so incredibly lucky.

"How long do you get to stay?"

"Your dad said he'd take me home when we were ready. How many more chores do you have?"

"I have to dust this main level, then I'll be done."

"Then get me a rag, Quinny."

***

An hour later, Rivers and I start to set up for baking. As I set the butter in a bowl to soften, he tells me he'll be back in a little while. I get my dry ingredients set aside and mixed, put the vanilla into my wet mix, and am just about to crack my final egg when Rivers comes back holding a bouquet of the most stunning flowers in varying shades of red, orange, and pink, and a small gift bag. "Rivers what is all this?"

"I promised you the best Valentine's Day of your life, you didn't think that came without gifts, did you?" He smirks.

"I didn't get you anything!" My heart hammers in my chest. No one has ever brought me flowers, let alone ones that are this big, this stunning. "What are these?" I ask.

"You didn't need to, Quinny." As he sets the flowers in a vase, he says, "They're called dahlias. You can't usually get them unless they're in season, but I think they probably preserve them somehow for Valentine's Day." He extends the gift bag to me, and I take it with greedy fingers. I can't seem to think of what he'd put in here besides my favorite candy or something.

"These are my new favorite flower," I say as I take out the tissue paper to the gift bag. I'm too stunned to speak. Rivers has hand sewn a stuffed animal out of fabric and batting. It's an owl, about the size of a piece of paper. Made from red velvet for the wings and a black and white patterned fabric for the body, it matches my room perfectly.

About a year ago, I saw a small stuffed animal I thought was cute but felt too old to buy something so childish. The fact that Rivers remembered overwhelms me with affection for him. His attention to the small things, the little extra details that show a person that they matter, has always been remarkable. I love how clearly he sees me. I love how nothing is too small in his mind when it comes to me or the things I care about. I love that in the two days since he decided we were valentines, he went to the store and made me my own stuffed owl because he cares so damn much.

It's infuriating how easy he makes it to love him.

He pulls me flush against him into another perfect Rivers and Quinn hug that no one could ever replicate. "Let's finish these cookies, and I'll get the movie set up."

"Rivers..." My voice trails off, still paralyzed with appreciation for him. He turns to face me, a smirk on his face like he knows that he has me wrapped around his finger but also that I can't verbalize what he means to me.

"I know, Quinny. You're welcome." He leaves me in the kitchen to mix up the cookies. He won't tell me what we're doing next, but if it's anything like what we've done so far, I know that he's going to pull out all the stops.

As I'm rinsing the dishes, Rivers comes up behind me and wraps his arms around my middle in a sort of reverse hug. We've never touched like this; it feels more intimate than our normal hugs. "Are you ready for your last surprise?" he says against my ear.

"Depends," I say. "Do we get to bring cookies?"

"Obviously. Why do you think I had us bake them?" he scoffs.

Once the cookies are plated up, Rivers takes them from my hands, along with my new stuffed creature, and guides me downstairs toward the family room. There's a faint glow coming from the archway that looks inviting. Before we get too close, Rivers stops me.

"Quinn, before we go in, I need to tell you something..."

I wonder, just for a second, just one fleeting moment if he's going to ask me to try and be something real with him again. After experiencing Justin, I think I'd be ready to give Rivers the chance. "I'm the reason you had to do chores all morning," he confesses.

"What?" That's not what I expected him to say at all.

"I called your parents to see if they could distract you this morning." We move toward the arch of the family room again, the warm glow of the light drawing us in.

"Okay, but why would I need a distraction?"

"So they could set up all of this." He walks me into the family room, leaving me speechless. There are no words for what he's done, and I know in my bones that no one will ever give me a Valentine's Day like this again. Fairy lights hang from the ceiling in swoops beneath swaths of white sheets that create a canopy and then fall to the side of the room like a tent. There are at least a hundred glow- in- the- dark stars hanging from fishing line, and inside the fabricated tent are piles of pillows and blankets. Rivers has enlisted my parents to make us a fort. It's beautiful and romantic and so very Rivers.

Before I can throw my arms around him in a hug, Rivers walks over to a set of speakers sitting on an end table. The song, "Magic" by Colbie Caillat comes on and floods me with a feeling too scary to name. Rivers steps toward me, his hand extended, asking me to dance.

I try to put my hands around the back of his neck, but he stops me, correcting my form so we're in the right position with one hand on my waist, one of mine on his shoulder, and our other hands clasped together upright. Rivers rests his chin by the side of my temple. We've been close like this before, and we've experienced energy that feels charged. I've never felt this cherished though, this seen. "How did you do all of this in two days?" I ask him, soft enough that I'm almost not heard over the music.

"I had help. It wasn't all me," he says.

"Right, but how did you come up with all of these ideas in two days?" He's thought of every detail: from finding me my new favorite flower to creating a stuffed animal I haven't thought about in months. I don't know how to process it.

"It wasn't hard, Quinny. I know you, and I love making you feel special, because you are."

The song ends, and Rivers moves me into the fort. There's a small table with the cookies, an empty mason jar, and cut out pieces of paper in the shape of stars. Rivers hands me a cookie, then sits down next to me on the cushions resting on the floor.

"Fuck, these are good!" Rivers mumbles through a bite that's way too big. "Did you do something different to them?" We've made enough cookies together that he knows what my normal chocolate chip recipe tastes like—I like that he can tell there's a difference.

"I added raw sugar to them this time," I answer, taking a small bite. "It adds a little crunch because the sugar crystals are bigger."

"Make them like this every time," he mumbles through his bite. "This is the best cookie I've ever eaten." He finishes his first cookie and instantly grabs a second.

I bite back a grin.

Rivers wipes the crumbs from his hands then moves behind me to grab the jar and stars. On his knees, he passes me a few stars and a pen. "I want to make a Star Jar with you," he says.

The look of confusion on my face must register to him because I have no idea what a Star Jar is or how I'm supposed to make one.

"Basically, we can write whatever we want on the stars, but they're mostly supposed to be wishes. Things we hope for, stuff we want to do together, that kind of thing." He smiles to himself; he looks bashful.

"What do we do with it when we're done?" I ask.

"It's kind of like a time capsule? So, in five or ten years, we see what we've done and can add more to it." I love that he's thinking about where we'll be in ten years. It gives me hope that even if we can't figure anything out right now, we'll still be in each other's lives.

"Do we tell each other what we wish for?"

"We can, or we can keep it a secret and promise each other not to look," he says.

I'm torn. One part of me wants to tell him everything I wish for; the other part is afraid that we'll hurt each other again. "Let's keep it a secret," I decide.

Rivers pulls out two clipboards from behind the small table; he seriously has thought of everything. We decide that putting the stars in as they are won't work, because they'll all fall flat, and we want the jar to seem fuller, so we fold each one in half to create volume.

I can't pretend that I'm not curious what Rivers is writing on his stars; I am. But I'm also not willing to be that vulnerable with my heart about what I want from him. I know I had a chance to be something more with him last spring break and kick myself for being hesitant to try. If I had known what type of boyfriend Justin was going to be, I wouldn't have said yes.

"What are you wishing for?" I ask, lightness in my tone so he knows I don't expect him to tell me.

"No way, you made the rule that we weren't sharing!"

I spend a few minutes writing down things I want to do: *see the Northern Lights, try the other person's sport, tell Rivers I'm in love with him.* I also write down wishes that I hope come true: *get into the same college, go to prom together, figure out how to end up with Rivers Thomas by my side for the rest of my life.*

Yeah, there's not a chance in hell he's reading these stars.

"Rivers? How are we going to trust each other not to peek at what the other person wrote?"

"I told our moms that one of them has to keep it, but I also have a plan." He pulls out a roll of masking tape and two small bottles of paint. "When we're done, we'll seal the lid and paint our thumb over the tape so we know that it hasn't been broken."

"Is there anything you *haven't* thought of?"

His smile is playful and endearing. "Nope," he says, self-assured.

I want to freeze time and remember Rivers just like this for as long as I can. The glow of the lights, his smile, how his breath still smells like cookies... all of it.

Rivers adds his stars to the jar and twists on the lid, securing it with tape. "Wait," I say. "I don't want to just have our prints on the tape because when we open it, we'll throw that out, and I want to remember this part. Can we put them on the lid, too?"

He bites down a smile; I think he likes that everything he's done has mattered so much to me. "Of course, Quinny. We can do this however you want."

We hold each other's gaze for a second, Rivers's words lingering in the air.

"Do you want red paint or pink paint?" he finally asks, holding up the bottles.

"Pink," I say, taking it from his hand. Our fingers brush, and the butterflies swoop low in my belly. I've touched Rivers's hands thousands of times. This feels different though—electric somehow. He holds out a paper plate for me, and I squeeze a drop of paint on it so I can dip my thumb into it and put my print on the tape and a few places on the lid.

Rivers does the same as me, but I see him angling his thumb a specific way. It's only when he finishes that I realize he made hearts out of our joined prints.

"It's Valentine's Day," he shrugs.

I move to stand up so that I can wipe the paint off my finger when a wet wipe materializes in front of me. "I didn't want us to have to leave the fort," he whispers.

"I don't want to leave the fort." It comes out like a confession. "I kind of want to stay here forever."

He sets the jar and paints down on the table again, then pulls me back until my head rests on his chest so we can look at the glow in the dark stars above us. "Do you think our wishes are going to come true?"

I think of what I wrote on my stars, the things I hoped to do, the wishes I made. "I hope so," I say.

"I hope so, too."

Rivers leans over and pushes play on the music again. It's a comfortable quiet here with him, looking at the stars and cuddling in this fort while the music plays around us. There isn't another person I would rather be here with but him.

"Hey, Rivers?" I say after several minutes of silence.

"Yeah?" His thumb traces lazy circles on my shoulder that send tiny pulses of electricity over my skin.

"Thank you." My voice comes out smaller than I intend. "For doing all of this."

I gesture around the room to the fort that he put together. That he enlisted the help of my parents to build. Where he thought of everything down to wet wipes to clean our hands and cut out paper in the shape of stars for us to write wishes on. I pick up the stuffed owl he made, looking at the stitching and how carefully it's been put together.

"Do you want to help name it?"

"Sure. Can I tell you my idea for it?"

Of course he's thought about naming this; he knows that it's probably one of the first things I wanted to do since he gave it to me. "Shoot," I tell him.

"I want Liz to come in and ask us a questions and if we answer it the same way, that'll be the name."

"What do you mean?"

He takes the owl from my hands. "We can have her ask us questions about food like, 'Who makes the best hotdog?' and we'd obviously both answer Big Rick, so that would be the name."

"So theoretically, I could end up with a stuffed owl named Green Bean?" I laugh.

"Quinn Clark. There are no timelines where I will answer Green Bean to a question," he deadpans.

We call Liz in and tell her what we need.

"Okay, what's the best type of chip?" she asks.

I say, "Sour cream and onion."

Just as Rivers says, "Doritos."

Liz rolls her eyes, already over our bullshit.

"Worst jolly rancher flavor?"

"Green apple, easy," I say.

"Watermelon," Rivers answers (like a *freak*).

Liz finally goes with something more generic. "Name any food you losers."

"Pizza!" I shout.

"Potato salad!" Rivers answers.

Liz looks at him with massive skepticism. "Potato salad?"

He just shrugs through a laugh. "I panicked! This isn't going like I thought it would," he says. "I kind of thought we'd knock this out of the park!"

"I don't have all day, people," Liz jumps in. "I paused *Hannah Montana* to be here, and my valentine is about to come on the TV." I furrow my brow at her, confused. "Jake Ryan," she clarifies.

"Just ask one more," I tell her. "If we don't get it then we'll figure something else out."

She rolls her eyes like having to pause her show for five minutes is setting her back decades but finally she relents. "Fine, what do you want for breakfast tomorrow?"

"Pancakes," Rivers and I say in unison.

He turns to look at me smiling wide, and I lift my hand for a high five. I pick up the owl turning it over in my hands, then give it to Rivers. "Pancakes, it is," he says.

Liz stomps away, and with her receding footsteps, we lay back down, the owl on the other part of Rivers's chest. He's squeezing us both to him, like he doesn't want to let either of us go.

I tilt my nose up toward his jaw line, breathing him in. "Rivers, I know I said it before but thank you. I don't think I've ever felt this special."

"You deserve to feel special every fucking day, Quinn. If someone doesn't make you feel like that when they're with you then they don't deserve your time. Especially Justin." He sounds angry; not at me, but *for* me, as if the prospect of someone treating me any less than perfect makes him see red.

"Who does deserve my time?" I ask him, my lips so close to his skin I can feel how warm he is. He looks down at me, mere centimeters between us. It's the closest I've ever been to his kiss. He squeezes my shoulders but maintains the space between our lips.

"Quinny," he whispers, and my heart deflates at his tone. "You just broke up with Justin. And as much as I want to kiss you right now, I also don't want our first kiss to come on the heels of someone else. I don't want to be a rebound for you."

I'm gutted by his honesty.

Rivers cups my jaw, delicately stroking his thumb along my jaw line like I could break at any moment. "If this is still something you want in a month or two, maybe we can try it then, okay? I just...I want to make sure this is really what you want."

I nod my head against him, as a lone tear escapes me.

"Okay."

Chapter Twenty-Two

Now

I decide to take a personal day on Friday since they're "use or lose." The kids grumble about having to go to school when I don't have to, but I gently remind them that I'm not going to *work*, and that's different. They also don't know that I have something up my sleeve, but I can't tell them anything about it until I know it'll work out.

When I drop them off, I text Rivers asking him to call me when he gets a chance. In the meantime, I run the three-mile loop around the lake before heading home to take a shower and freshen up. I'm supposed to meet my mom and Lianne at Parchment and Grounds for tea around eleven. Their fall flavors sound delicious. Apple pie tea? Are you joking?

As I'm driving over to meet them, Rivers calls me.

I answer quickly, not able to talk to him soon enough. "Hey," I smile as I speak.

"Hey, sorry it took a while. You texted right as I went in with a patient, and then I've been booked solid all morning."

"That's okay. What's your afternoon look like?"

"I actually scheduled this as a half-day several weeks ago just because I needed something to look forward to. Why? Do you need something?"

"Well, I took the day off too as it turns out, but I was going to see if you might want to go on a surprise adventure with me and the kids in like...two hours? I'm going to call them out early."

"Say less. I'll meet you at your house in an hour so we can load up?" He sounds excited. The man has never been able to resist plans like this.

"Perfect, then you can do all the heavy lifting!" I hang up the phone, smiling to myself as I pull into the coffee shop. I need to get a grip on my smile, or my mom and Lianne are going to see right through me.

The bell chimes as I walk through the door; varying scents from the tea waft through the air. It's delicious. I want to get my hands on every flavor being offered right now.

Katie stands behind the counter with her cool Californian ease. She's always been naturally stunning. She never wore make up in high school, and her hair had a natural beach wave to it like she was transported from a coastal town to this small mountain one. I don't see Lianne or my mom here yet; a glance at my watch tells me I'm a few minutes early. I suck in a breath, mustering up the courage to order my drink without anyone else here.

"What can I get you?" Katie is too busy to notice me initially; the café is busier than I've seen it before, and it makes me happy for her. "Oh, hi, Quinn," she says as recognition dawns on her.

"Hey, I'm torn between the apple pie tea and the apple pumpkin spice. Which would you recommend?"

"Both," she shrugs, grabbing a cup.

"Both?"

"Yeah, do half and half; I'd also recommend a caramel drizzle."

It sounds heavenly. I nod enthusiastically as I say, "Yes, I want that, please."

She laughs and jots the order down on the cup with her marker. "Anything else?"

"The pesto chicken wrap?" I know I had it a few days ago, but it was so delicious the first time, I've been dreaming about it.

"Got it." She keys the order into the tablet, then turns it around toward me to pay. "Quinn? If I had known you were with him when you came in a few days ago, I wouldn't have touched him. We broke up a long time ago; it was just good to see him."

Her candor catches me off guard. "Katie, I didn't even know you guys dated after high school. I appreciate you apologizing, but it's not necessary."

"You've always been it for him," she concludes.

I finish paying just as Lianne and mom walk in together; it halts me in my tracks for a minute. I haven't seen them together since I was eighteen. I knew they remained friends—they didn't let Rivers and I impact their friendship—but it feels like I'm in a time warp seeing them standing next to one another.

Once we're all situated and have our drinks, Lianne leans over with mischief in her eyes and tone as she says, "Bryan told me he saw Rivers's car parked outside your house pretty late a few nights ago?"

My face flames. Why did I agree to this? "Did he?" I sputter.

He's been over most nights of the last two weeks; cooking dinner and playing games with me and the kids in the evenings, showing up to Sawyer's cross-country meets (complete with snacks), and helping Wyatt with her science homework. It's felt natural integrating him into our lives like this. He hasn't stayed over though; he was at my house Tuesday and Wednesday pretty late, but we haven't figured out the boundaries with him staying the night and navigating that conversation with the kids. They're certainly old enough to understand the implications of an adult sleepover.

"Relax, Quinn. We know you two are grown; it's just an observation." Her voice borders on teasing. "Besides, you two had six years of foreplay as kids. 'Bout time that all got worked out, wouldn't you agree, Diane?"

"Lianne!" I nearly shout.

My mom laughs so hard that tears come out of her eyes. I cannot believe I'm having this conversation with *both* of them, and Rivers isn't here to suffer through it too.

"When do you see each other again?" Mom asks once she's calmed down.

"We're going to take the kids on a little adventure this afternoon. I have to meet him in a little over an hour."

They look at each other, knowingly. I know they're excited about the prospect of Rivers and I, but I can also tell that their joy extends beyond that. They know how hard my life has been the last five years, and they're excited to see me find some happiness for myself.

"Are you guys official then?" Lianne wonders.

I put my hand over my mouth, so my face is harder to read, but it only serves to make them snicker again. Rivers and I haven't had the conversation of what we are yet, but I know there isn't anyone else I'd stop to consider dating but him.

"We haven't talked about it," I say, trying to maintain some level of privacy, even though in the back of my mind I know he's probably the one for me.

We talk mindlessly for the next hour about the kids, how my school year is going, and how we'll need to meet up again soon, maybe inviting June and Liz next time if our schedules can all align.

When I pull up, Rivers stands in my driveway, leaning against his car in a hunter green henley and black jeans. His olive skin glows against the shirt, and my mouth waters at the sight of him. I step out of the car, not wasting the time to park in the garage when we'll be leaving again soon, and before I can even set my feet down on the concrete, Rivers pulls me out of the car and picks me up until my legs wrap around his waist.

I lean down to kiss him and feel him smile against me, digging my fingers into his hair while he grips my thighs, keeping me upright. He carries me toward the door, a tangle of limbs and tongues that I can't get enough of. "Well, it's good to see you too," I joke before I slide down his body, and take his lower lip between my teeth.

His breath hitches. "I really hated not seeing you yesterday, Quinny. Now that I have you, I want you all the time."

"You can have me right now," I whisper as I kiss the line of his jaw, playing with the button of his jeans.

Rivers hoists me over his shoulder, his grip over my ass tickling me as we make our way back to my room. He bounces me onto the bed and peppers kisses down my neck, my arms, and then my palm. He pulls my shirt up and over my head, then lifts up my bra so that my breasts are exposed.

"Where are we going this afternoon?" he asks as he moves his hands down my body. He flicks his tongue against my nipple, as his hands move lower, and the gentle caresses make me shiver. He moves his hand up my inner thigh to the hem of my shorts and traces his finger across the line of my panties.

"The beach," I confess; breathless as the tip of Rivers's finger moves beneath the fabric and finds my entrance.

"Hmm," he says against my skin. "Does the beach come with you in a bikini?" He slides another finger in and curls them toward him, making me gasp.

"Maybe," I breathe out.

"Maybe? I need a better answer than that, honey." Rivers places his thumb where I need him most, building the pressure in my belly higher.

"I'll wear one if you want me to," I say, willing to give him anything he wants if it means I get what I need. I sound desperate, squirming against his hand in a desperate search for friction. I'm so close to release.

"I just want you," he says, before he takes my nipple in his mouth again, pumping into me faster until my orgasm crests over, in wave after wave, pulsing through my body, leaving me spent.

He starts to leave, but I pull him down back toward me, not ready to let him go, and he hastily tugs his shirt off as I try to unbutton his pants. With his dick free, my breaths shallows in anticipation of having him again.

"Condom?" he asks me through another kiss.

"In the drawer," I tell him. "My birth control appointment is on Monday."

Rivers pulls back from me to take in my face. "Really?"

"Yeah, is that okay?"

"Okay? Quinn, are you kidding?" He rolls the condom over his length, then leans down to take my mouth in his. "Yes, that's okay. I knew in my mind that we weren't just fooling around, but I feel more settled knowing that you're on the same page."

I take his face in both my hands. "I know that we've been notoriously bad communicators in the past, but I swear from this point on I will only ever be honest with you," I say.

He moves his eyes between my own, like he needs to search for confirmation before he can believe it, then kisses me again, and turns me over so I'm on my belly. He lifts my ass into the air, with my head still pressed into the mattress, and then pushes into me easily. Rivers grips my hips so hard I'll probably bruise and increases his rhythm, making me see stars.

"Fuck, Quinn." The exertion of his movement makes him pant as he says my name.

"More, Rivers. Please, God." I'm so close to coming I could cry.

"You're doing so well," he says. "Seeing you take my dick like this? You're perfect." He slows down again, torturing me just like he knows I like only after a few times together. He still reads me like a book. It drives me mad.

"Rivers," I whimper.

"I've thought about bending you over like this for days, Quinn." He keeps moving so slowly, torturing me. "You can't rush me now."

The laugh in his voice only pains me more. His fingers brush gently down my spine; after being so tightly wound, the feather light touches of his fingers make me moan.

"Days, huh?" I manage to say.

"Give or take a few weeks," he confirms.

His pace begins to increase, and my breath hitches. "Rivers, please. I need more."

"I know you do, Quinny," he grunts out, and then he slams into me with ferocity, over and over again, igniting me like a fuse, until I burst, sending ripples of pleasure through every limb of my body. Rivers lets out a moan, and his release chases my own.

His body collapses onto mine, my back to his heaving chest. He presses his lips to my shoulder, then heads for the bathroom to cleanup.

I follow to do the same, and our eyes meet in the mirror, grins matching. Once we're both dressed, he pulls me into another hug, leaving a kiss in the center of my forehead.

"So, the beach, huh?" he says with a smile.

"Yeah, the weather is supposed to turn cold tomorrow, so I thought it might be a fun way to officially welcome fall," I tell him as I move around my kitchen, packing up snacks for the drive down. Technically, fall started a few weeks ago, but with the lingering summer heat, it hasn't felt like it.

"Hey, do we have any hot dogs?" Rivers asks, moving to the fridge. The "'we'" in his question makes my heart hammer in my chest, the small word doing such a big job of communicating that he feels at home here, that he's turning us into a team I didn't know I needed or wanted.

"Yeah, I just bought some the other day, why?"

"Might be fun to roast them over a fire for dinner. Maybe we could make s'mores, too?"

I grin, immediately moving to the fridge to put condiments into the ice chest while he gets the makings of s'mores from the cupboards. We move so seamlessly together in my kitchen, it's hard to believe we've spent so many years apart.

"Rivers?" I ask as we load everything from sunblock, to towels, to bathing suits, to food into the car. "I just realized I don't have lighter fluid or s'mores skewers to cook anything with. We'll need to stop at the store on the way to get the kids."

"I have both of those at my house," he says. His house is on the way to the school. "Plus, I need to get a bathing suit anyways."

It's silly to feel thankful that he has lighter fluid and skewers, but I'm struck by the reminder that Rivers has always been the person to have and be the things I lack, the things I need.

Rivers's house is a medium sized A-frame overlooking the water on the same side of the town as me; though my house doesn't have a water view. Its windows are panoramic, the view exquisite. Tall pines tower along the side, the lake blue and shimmery below. I've been here a few times in the last two weeks, but not as much as he's been over to see me.

He's changing into his bathing suit, leaving me to wander around his house and take in the charm that I've been too busy to properly appreciate the other times I've been here.

His space is tidy, just a mug in the kitchen sink, and the surfaces wiped down. My house has become cleaner thanks to him. Today, though, I notice a small shoe box sitting on the coffee table that doesn't belong. It looks like some high school mementos: his academic letter, a concert ticket stub, and a postcard from Yosemite. I remember him buying that card in particular because we were able to see where we sat to eat after climbing to the base of the upper falls. Next to the box, there's a photo I haven't seen since I was eighteen and packing up to leave for college. It's the one June took of us that night on the trampoline where we looked at stars for the first time.

"Crazy how time flies, huh?" His voice pulls me from the memory.

"Yeah," I say, "We look like babies!"

"I mean, we basically were," he jokes, coming over to stand next to me.

"I remember being so scared for you to come over that night," I admit. "I thought you'd think I was so weird."

"Quinn, you are weird," he deadpans. "It's one of my favorite things about you."

He kisses my head, then moves to the garage to get the other stuff we need for the beach. We leave his house and head toward the school, but all I can think about are the memories in my box of high school treasures.

***

The kids are excited when they get into the car after picking them up early. I haven't done a surprise like this for them in a few years. Kansas City had a lot to offer, but on a teacher's salary I couldn't exactly take them to Chiefs games like Preston used to do on a whim.

"Where are we going?" Sawyer calls from the backseat after fist-bumping with Rivers.

Rivers looks at me and smiles, as I say, "We're going to the beach!"

"Mom, it's like the middle of October," Wyatt intones.

"That's California for you," Rivers says.

"The weather is supposed to get cold tomorrow, so I thought it might be a fun way to soak up the last few hours of heat before it changes," I tell her.

She shrugs like this response is satisfactory, and she and Sawyer plug into headphones for the drive.

Rivers offered to drive my car so I'm in the passenger seat. He has one hand on the steering wheel and the other resting on my thigh, holding my hand. We're early enough in the day that the traffic headed down to Orange County isn't bad. I help Rivers navigate from the four-oh-five freeway to Jamboree Road, before we finally reach the Pacific Coast Highway that leads to Crystal Cove. It's a smaller beach next to Newport, and far less popular, in part because of the steep trail used to access the beach. Most people would say to ditch the hike in favor of one of the surrounding beaches with walk up parking access, but I've always loved this cove for the cliffs that secure it on each side, and the tidepools full of sea-life when the tide is out.

The kids help us unload the car then walk over to the public bathrooms to change. Rivers and I wore our bathing suits under our clothes, so we wait for the kids while taking in the sweeping expanse of ocean. It's breathtaking, the blue so deep and rich with waves of sea spray glistening in the air.

Rivers holds my hand down the steep path, steadying me as we approach the sand. I take off my sandals, carrying them between the fingers of my other hand and walk to the fire pits toward the back of the beach. They're set far back away from the shore because the tide fluctuates so much, but the kids don't like that we're so far away from the waves.

"You have legs! Run to the water if you want." I laugh as they roll their eyes, perfectly in sync. Rivers and I get our two beach chairs set up; the kids assured us they'd be fine to sit on towels. I start putting sunscreen on him, while Sawyer and Wyatt help each other.

They're about to turn away when Rivers stops them. "Have you guys ever swum in the ocean before?"

"A few times when we were younger," Sawyer says.

Rivers points out to a break in the waves, where it looks like it will be the calmest to enter. "Do you see that, right there? Where there aren't any waves crashing?"

"Yeah, rip tide, right?" Sawyer answers.

"Right. Don't go near there, but if you get pulled into it, do you know what to do?"

Wyatt looks unsure, gazing along the beach for where to enter if not there, and wondering how to stay away from what sounds like something ominous.

The kids shake their heads.

"If you get sucked into a rip current, let it pull you out a bit, then swim parallel to the shore and come back in with the waves somewhere else. You know what parallel means?"

Wyatt holds her hands up so they're facing each other but not touching.

"Good," Rivers says. "You guys should be fine, just wanted to make sure you knew what to do."

Sawyer fist bumps Rivers again, then they turn away to walk over to the water. I'm grateful Rivers teaches them what to do. Remembering to warn them of all these things that came second nature to us growing up is a bit of a culture shock.

"Thank you," I tell him as he sits down. "I completely forgot to teach them that."

"Of course. Even if you had told them, I would have talked to them about it anyways. I worry about them." He looks down as he says this last part, like it's a confession he's not sure he's able to claim.

"You do?"

"Every minute of the day, Quinn. I think about all three of you, and something bad happening."

"The feeling is mutual," I admit, though I think it's bigger for Rivers to acknowledge that my kids are starting to feel like people he's concerned for.

"Reese's cup?" he asks me, digging in the ice chest.

"Obviously! Look at this view! How could I *not* need a happy snack right now?" I laugh, unwrapping one of the large cups; we left the minis at home, obviously.

We sit in the quiet for a while. Wyatt stands on the beach, letting her legs sink further into the sand with every pull of the waves, and Sawyer collects a pile of kelp that he will undoubtedly try to chase her around with later. Rivers and I both pull out our books, his, a Brandon Sanderson fantasy, while I'm glued to a thriller Sybil recommended. His hand rests on my thigh again, like it's supposed to be there. I pull out my phone and snap a picture of it: his hand, the frayed ends of my cut off shorts, the waves. Before I can second guess myself, I post it to my Instagram story, publicly claiming this new chapter of my life.

"My ass is falling asleep in this chair," Rivers says after an hour or so. "Want to go walk in the surf?"

It sounds perfect.

We put sunblock on again before we walk toward the water and remind the kids to do the same.

Sawyer groans outwardly at the request. "We just put some on, Mom!"

"Every hour, dude. That sun is way more powerful here on the beach than it is up on the mountain," I tell him.

"When can we cook dinner?" Wyatt asks, climbing out of her knee-deep trench. "I'm so hungry."

Rivers and I look at each other, knowing we'll have to walk after we eat.

He starts the fire, and I put the hot dogs onto roasting spikes, then hand one to each kid as the flames get bigger. I pull the sweatshirt over my head that he left at my house, leaving my shorts barely visible. I'm not freezing yet, but I can tell the weather is quickly changing.

"Do you think we could practice wrestling when we get home? Try-outs are in four weeks, and I don't feel ready yet," Sawyer asks Rivers.

"Sure, we can do that. Have you been doing any weight training or just cardio for cross-country?"

I try not to let them notice that I overhear their conversation, wanting to give them this time together and still craving to hear how he integrates with the kids.

"Just cardio. Do you think I need to do weights?" Sawyer sounds nervous now.

"I think it could help, yeah. We can work out after school if you want, then I can show you how to build strength without it affecting your weight class too much."

I know enough about wrestling from when Rivers did it in high school to know that Sawyer can't gain too much weight for his class, but I also know that I'm grateful Rivers is here. This is something I'm not equipped to help with like he is.

When we finish eating our delicious—albeit, sandy—hot-dogs, Sawyer and Rivers toss the football back and forth with each other in the sand, leaving me and Wyatt in the chairs. She's been quieter today, more subdued than I'd expect for leaving school early. She'll talk to me about most things, I think, but if I press her, I know she'll shut down, just like I did when my mom used to try to get me to open up to her.

So, going against every instinct I have, I choose to stay quiet until she's ready to speak, and, eventually, it pays off.

"Mom?" she asks.

I look over at her and see tears in her eyes.

"What's wrong, baby?" I ask, my voice laced with concern.

"What do you do when the person you like doesn't like you back?"

"Is this about Keegan?" I ask.

"Yes," she sniffs. "And no? I don't know! I thought I liked him, and that he liked me back, but now he says he likes some-one else. It's all just so damn confusing!"

I tilt my head back to the sky with a deep inhale, trying to get my own feelings in line. I do *not* miss being a teenager.

"How do you feel about him liking someone else?"

"Relieved? And that also makes me feel weird because I don't know if I like someone else, and is it weird that I like two people at the same time? Does that make me a terrible person?" Her confessions tumble out of her, like she's been fighting off an army for weeks and they've finally broken through her defenses.

"Who else might you like?" I hedge.

"Will." Her voice is so quiet when it comes out, I can hardly hear her over the crash of the waves and the crackle of the fire.

Suspicions confirmed.

"How does that make you feel?"

"Scared? We're friends, Mom. What am I going to do?"

I think back on all the years Rivers and I wasted by drawing boundaries we didn't want to adhere to because we were too afraid to let each other all the way in.

"Well, I don't think you're a bad person, sweetie. I think at your age, it's really normal to like more than one person. But I also know how scary it is to like your best friend." I jut my chin toward Rivers, so she understands who I'm talking about.

He must feel us watching him because he walks back toward us, while Sawyer moves in the direction of the water.

"You okay, Wy?"

When he sees the tears in her eyes, he falls to his knees in front of her. "Whoa, whoa, what's wrong? What happened?" His concern is so palpable it makes me ache.

She looks over at me and nods, granting me permission to explain. "Wyatt is trying to figure out how to like her best friend as more than a friend," I say, trying to be succinct.

Rivers's eyes soften. "Hmm, you know, there're two people here who know a little bit about that," he says, sitting down next to her.

"How did you guys do it? How did you stay friends?" she asks.

He and I look at each other and laugh. "We didn't!" Rivers says.

"We were terrible at it," I add.

Rivers puts his arm around Wyatt to reach my shoulder, and I do the same. She rests her head on my other shoulder but doesn't shy away from him.

"But what do I do?" she cries.

"I think my first mistake was giving Rivers a letter that told him how I felt, and then not letting him talk to me about it when we had the chance," I offer. "I think if I had just talked to him from the start about my feelings, we probably could have worked our issues out a lot sooner."

"That's not fair, Quinn. I also didn't talk to you for two weeks after I got that letter which didn't help you feel like you could talk to me," he says. Shifting his focus back to Wyatt, he says, "She also dated some real jackasses before she married your dad."

Wyatt laughs, whether it's the thought of me dating a few tools or Rivers saying jackass, I'm not sure, but the laugh is a win by any standard. "My point, Wy, is that your mom and I weren't great at telling each other how we felt. We were always too scared, and I think, had we considered the fact that we were talking to our best friend, things might have turned out differently."

She nods her head, taking in everything we've said. "Rivers?"

"Yeah?"

"Thank you...for helping me. For wanting to know me and Sawyer. For making Mom seem alive again."

I squeeze her hand with mine and kiss her forehead.

"It's the easiest thing I've ever done," he says.

Sawyer walks over to us from the water and asks Wyatt to go look for sand crabs before the sun goes down.

Rivers takes my hand. "We're going to go on a walk. We have our phones, okay?" he says.

"No going into the water until we get back," I add.

We move hand in hand toward the water until a wave kisses our toes; the temperature of the water makes me shriek.

"Fuck that's cold!" Rivers says, laughing.

"So cold!" The sun sets as we meander down the coastline. It's a mile, maybe two, from one end of the cove to the other, and I bask in every second of walking down this beach with this man by my side. In one day, he made sure my kids had a water safety lesson on rip tides, promised to build a workout routine with Sawyer, and got through to Wyatt about her boy dilemma. He's made us all feel safe, cared for, and seen just by being himself, just by being the boy I've always known in my heart was the first boy I ever loved.

The realization makes my heart pound. I love him. I'm in love with him.

"Rivers?" I turn to face him. The sky is pink and orange behind him, making everything around us feel softer. He looks at me, taking me in feature by feature. I press my lips to his in the softest of kisses. His hands hold me, one at my waist, and the other behind my head, angling my mouth to deepen our kiss.

"Hey, Quinny," he says against my smile.

"I love you," I whisper.

"I've always loved you, honey. And I always will."

Our next kiss is slow and gentle but holds more meaning than maybe any other. I feel how much he loves me in every brush of our tongues, every hitch in our shared breath, every beat of his heart beneath my fingertips.

And this time, when the waves splash up and over our legs, I don't even notice.

Chapter Twenty-Three

Then, Sophomore Year

Outside of the window to the student government classroom, the leaves on the trees start to bud. It's spring now, two months since Valentine's Day. Rivers and I haven't talked about how close we almost came to kissing. It feels like neither of us knows what to say.

"...The other Junior Prom Prince and Princess nominees are Rivers Thomas and Katie Meyers."

My ears snap to attention at the sound of Rivers's name coming from the student body president. Prom court winners aren't announced until the night of the dance, but as student government, we're in charge of the voting process and gathering the nominees, as well as presenting them to the student body. Rivers being a nominee doesn't surprise me in the slightest: he's handsome, and funny, and kind to everyone he sees. But hearing another girl's name with his? That feels like someone piercing my chest with a dagger.

Justin finds my gaze, trying to decipher what I'm sure can only be interpreted as pain on my face then breaks away. We've spoken a few times, and every time he tries, he apologizes, but I just can't trust it. At least not yet.

I pull out the poster I was working on yesterday announcing the baseball game this Friday against our rival school. Justin sits down next to me, grabbing the small paint brush I brought to outline the letters in black and starts working.

"You alright?" he asks.

"I'm fine." My answer is curt, but discussing my feelings with Justin is the last thing I want to do right now.

"Fine, huh? No feelings whatsoever about Rivers being nominated for Prom Court with someone who isn't you, who he'll probably go to prom with, dance with, and who knows what else?"

"Is there a reason you're being as mean as possible about this?"

"I'm not trying to be mean, I'm trying to see if you're okay."

"Well, I'm not!" I bite out.

It's quiet for a minute while we work. I don't know how to broach the subject with Rivers about my feelings or that I think I'm ready to try with him. Eventually, Justin pulls out his iPod and extends and earbud to me while we work. It's a Katy Perry song I know he likes, though I've never been a fan.

When I finish the poster, I bring the brushes back into the classroom to clean, then find the tape so I can hang the poster up. Without my asking, Justin follows me silently out the door to find empty space for the sign. We move through to the commons, where I'd intended the poster to go, only to have to move to the cafeteria since everything else is filled up. Before we reach the stairs, Rivers rounds the corner and looks between Justin and me.

I walk straight into his arms, unable to resist the tether that pulls me toward him every time he's in the vicinity.

"Hey, Quinny," he mumbles against my hair. "You okay?" His voice is stony, and I know it's because Justin is here.

"I'm good," I answer, and Justin scoffs.

"You got a problem, Parks?" Rivers says through clenched teeth. "I mean apart from you just generally being an asshole?"

"No problem, just helping Quinn hang up this poster. Hey, congratulations on prom court, man. Hope you and Katie make it."

Rivers's confusion is palpable. "Thanks? I need to get back to class, but I'll see you at your meet, Quinn. Good luck!" He pulls me into a hug before he leaves again.

"What are you doing Friday night?" Justin asks, once we're walking back to class.

"Working concessions for the game, you?" I say.

"No plans," he answers. "What events are you in today?"

"High jump, long jump, and the thirty-two hundred."

He nods his head and opens the door for student government right as the bell rings to leave. "You'll do great, Quinn," I hear before everyone shuffles past me.

***

The thing about track meets is that you have to get on board really quickly with there always being way too much going on and never knowing where you need to be at any given moment.

I have five minutes between my thirty-two hundred and long jump, so I decide to scan the fence around the perimeter of the field for Rivers since he usually walks over right when I cross the finish line. Today, I don't see him, yet, but I do see Justin with a pair of Ray Ban sunglasses on and something in his hands. I move toward him, trying to make out what it is, and realize he's brought me...flowers?

"Hey, Quinn! These are for you, but I can keep them since you have to jump still." It's a bouquet of yellow roses, which in my mind are the flower you give to your sick grandma in the hospital, not someone you have romantic feelings for.

"I thought the color was happy, and that it would bring you a little sunshine," he says. The sentiment is sweet, though I still can't get on board.

"Thanks, Justin," I say.

"I also brought you your favorite cookies!" He holds out a box, eager to hand them to me. It's not a secret that I thrive off of snacks, I'm just surprised that Justin remembered my favorite cookie. When I open the box, I'm greeted by a dozen snickerdoodles. A top five cookie, for sure, but they aren't my favorite.

"This is really sweet, Justin. Thank you." I hand him the box again, unable to bring them with me on the field when Rivers comes running over.

"Sorry I'm late, Quinny! There was a line!" He pulls me into a hug, despite my sweat, and only then does he register Justin.

"Hey man, what are you doing here? What do you have?" Rivers asks, curious. I don't want him to embarrass Justin or me, right now, but I don't see a way around it.

"I came to give Quinn one of her favorite snacks!" Justin says, as he holds up the cookies.

Rivers looks over at them, then back to me. "Snickerdoodles? Cookies are like the worst snack for her right now. They're too heavy in her stomach." He pulls out a zipper bag full of Gushers fruit snacks, which I take with greedy hands because I am a weakling, and pop a few into my mouth. "These give her a short burst of energy without making her feel like she's going to barf."

I feel so bad for Justin right now, so instead of agreeing with Rivers (who is right, on all counts), I decide to throw Justin a bone. "But I do love to eat cookies when I'm done," I say.

"Then I'll have them here waiting for you," he says.

Just as Rivers says, "You need to get to long jump!"

***

On Friday, I get the key and cash box from Mrs. D before the baseball game starts. It's supposed to be a massive turnout because it's our rival, and because prom court is being presented to the community like homecoming court does in the fall. I have a good view of the field from concessions, which means I'll see Rivers be presented in his tuxedo with Katie on his arm. He's sworn up and down that they are just friends and that he'd tell me if he liked her; I just feel like I can't trust it.

No girl could get that close to Rivers and not fall for him.

I prep everything for concessions, and glance at the clock, wondering when my partner is getting here. I thought that it was a senior named Sam, but she hasn't shown up yet.

Mrs. D turned the nacho cheese on, so I just have to get the chips lined up. As I move to grab the plastic containers, the door opens, but instead of Sam here to help me, it's Justin.

Fuck.

"Need a hand, Quinn?" he says, moving to the counter next to me to open up the tortilla chips.

"What are you doing here?" I ask.

"I traded shifts with Sam and wanted to spend some time with you. Make sure you were okay when the fourth inning rolls around and prom court gets announced."

God, I really don't want to think of Justin as considerate, but on the scale of things he's done, this definitely isn't on the asshole spectrum.

I nod my head, not able to find words for the mixture of feelings warring inside my heart or my head. On the one hand, of course, I'm thankful that I'm not here alone, and that the person working with me understands the dilemma I'm in. On the other, I really wish that that person wasn't Justin.

And I really, *really,* wish I was immune to his charm.

"K, well let's get the hot dogs ready. God knows people can't watch baseball without wieners."

Justin laughs as he pulls the buns down from the storage shelf. "Is that a euphemism?" he jokes.

I toss a crumpled-up piece of trash at him, which he bats away with his hand before reaching out and gently holding me by the wrist. He pulls me closer toward him, and my breath hitches. I don't know if it's habit or hormones that draws me into him but his arms loop around me in a hug; I feel myself melt a little. Rivers hasn't shown a lack of affection since Valentine's Day, he just doesn't know the feelings I'm still harboring for him, or unfortunately, for Justin.

"Ladies and gentlemen, welcome to Pine Grove High School, home of the Timber Wolves!"

I leap away from Justin and move back toward the counter prepping the nacho plates while Justin puts music on through his mini speaker.

The first three innings are a whirlwind of nachos, hot dogs, water bottles, chips, and candy. We're making a lot of money which is great for funding homecoming next year. Justin and I move seamlessly through the small concession stand, knowing where the other is and what they need. He handles the cash box more than I do since math hasn't ever been my strong suit, but overall, we're working equally as hard.

"And now..." the announcer begins, "it is my pleasure to introduce the prom court of Pine Grove High School!"

My attention snaps to the field despite helping customers at the stand; I'm completely zoned out of what's in front of me.

He makes it through the first two couples from the junior class before he gets to Rivers and Katie.

"Katie Meyers is a member of the chess club, shred team, and American Red Cross. She hopes one day to own a business so that she can surf and snowboard whenever she wants to!"

The crowd erupts for Katie, who is gorgeous, with blonde hair like silk that reaches the middle of her back, and whose tanned skin accentuates the stunning pale lavender dress draped elegantly over her small frame.

"Rivers Thomas is on the varsity wrestling and Science Olympiad teams but spends most of his spare time on his best friend's trampoline. Someday, Rivers hopes to climb to the top of the upper Yosemite Falls and go to a Weezer concert!"

I swoon over his references to us, to me.

If the crowd went wild for Katie, they're ecstatic for Rivers. He's in a black tux that perfectly fits his body. His broad shoulders are accentuated, and the shirt is taut against his expansive chest and strong neck. More than anything, though, his megawatt smile blinds me from all the way over here.

Rivers is fucking beautiful.

And kind.

And generous.

And he's on the field with his arm looped through the arm of a girl who isn't me, holding her steady as she wobbles in her heels on the uneven grass.

I feel Justin move beside me, glancing in my direction. "Good?" he asks.

I give a curt nod, then school my features as I help the people in line. I can't focus on Rivers right now. It's not his fault he got nominated for prom court, and it's not his fault the most beautiful girl in his grade got nominated to be his partner in it.

All I can do is focus on what's in front of me.

By the end of the sixth inning, the line slows down considerably. Justin and I are hesitant to start cleaning things up though, since most of the time we catch a second wave at the baseball games.

We're in the middle of a game of spoons when we hear laughter approaching the stand, so I move toward the counter.

"Oh, hey, Quinn!" Rivers looks ten times more handsome up close than he did on the field. He's changed out of his prom clothes, and instead has on a pair of dark jeans, his staple lace-up vans, and a red t-shirt.

"Hey," my voice is small.

"What's wrong?" Concern drips from his voice.

"Nothing, what can I get you?"

"Can we just get two waters?" He pulls his wallet out at the same time Katie does.

"I can pay, Rivers," she says.

"What kind of prom date would I be if I didn't pay for your water?" His eyes are full of mischief.

"Well, add this to the growing list of reasons you're the best prom date I could ever ask for," she says, gripping his arm and nuzzling into it like he's a giant teddy bear.

Logically, I know she's being silly.

Emotionally, I feel like I might throw up.

"Do you guys want some coleslaw while you're here?" Justin asks.

Rivers looks at me with horror in his eyes. He just found out that I've been in this stand with Justin all night, and it feels like his eyes silently ask me if I'm okay.

"Why would we want coleslaw?" Katie asks, confused.

"Because you're being fucking disgusting all over each other. I'm sure there's room under the bleachers. Otherwise, maybe you should get lost."

"God, you really are the biggest asshole, you know that?" Rivers says, shaking his head and putting his change away. "I'll call you later, Quinny."

He and Katie turn to walk away as I walk back to the supply closet to fall apart.

Justin finds me a moment later, after I assume he's put the sign out that says we'll be back in five minutes. He crosses his arms against his chest and leans against the door.

"Why'd you do that Justin? I was fine."

"You weren't fine, Quinn. Rivers knows that you're in a sensitive place thanks to me, and having some other bitch all over him isn't going to help anything."

He walks toward me, caging my body against his. Despite the things that Justin has done to be an absolute jerk, he's always been good at reading my emotions and comforting me through the things I don't want to feel.

"Let's take a few deep breaths, okay?"

I nod my head against his chest to calm myself down. It takes a few minutes, but eventually, Justin and I go out to the stand and start to clean up for the evening. There aren't too many rules about how long the stand has to stay open other than it needs to be for more than half the game, and you can't shut it down if there are still people in line.

We make our way to the announcement stand where the school's athletic director counts the till before we're excused. We wander over to the stands to find a few friends, and I keep thinking that Justin is going to leave me, but he doesn't. Instead he slips his hand into mine, and I can't tell if it's to be friendly or flirty. I want to find Dani and unpack all my feelings with her, but she sent me a text message ages ago that said she and Brad were hooking up, and that I shouldn't disturb her unless it was an emergency, which this, obviously, is not.

I shiver as we walk, and Justin gives me his hoodie which smells like something earthy I can't name. It's oversized, but cozy.

Jaclyn, my vice president to the sophomore class, waves at us from the stand behind first and second base. We make our way slowly toward her where she scoots over to make room.

"Are you two a thing again?" she whispers in my ear, though the way Justin's hands flex, I'm sure he heard.

"No," I answer honestly.

"Do you...want to be?"

"I don't know. I think I need more time to figure it out with him."

After another thirty minutes, Pine Grove is down by one point at the bottom of the ninth inning. Everyone in the stand is on pins and needles.

Justin keeps looking at his phone, and I try not to let it bother me. We aren't together, he can talk to whoever he wants to. He's also been so much more like the guy I fell for all those months ago the last several weeks, and my resolve around him is starting to weaken. I like that he sees and understands my feelings.

"Quinn, I'm going to head out," he says. "I'll see you later."

"Justin, there's maybe like three minutes left of this game."

I'm confused. Justin likes sports and cares about Pine Grove's standing for our league. It's not like him to leave when we're in a situation like this.

"I know, there's just something I have to do."

I move to take the sweater off that he lent me, but he stays my hand before I can do anything about it. "You keep it for now, I don't want you to be cold." He kisses my forehead, and then moves to leave.

"Damn girl, I don't know why you let him go," Jaclyn says.

And I'm starting to wonder why I did, too.

Pine Grove wins by two points and the feeling in the air is electric. I wish Rivers was here to celebrate this with me, or Dani, but I end up walking to the parking lot alone, bolstered only by the swells of people cheering around me. When I finally make it to the lot, I spot the familiar outline of two people I recognize.

Justin and Dani.

"If you treat her as anything less than a fucking princess, I will personally make sure that you never see the light of day again and then, if your body is somehow discovered, smile through my mugshot knowing it's so disfigured your own mother won't be able to identify you," Dani's voice carries across the wind.

"I won't fuck it up Dani. I miss the hell out of her, but I know she won't give me another chance without your blessing. I promise I've changed," Justin says on my approach.

Dani looks at me, then back to Justin. "Do you want to give him another chance?"

Justin whirls around to see me, shock on his face.

I'm put on the spot, but still unsure. "I don't know," I manage.

"You have to earn her trust back, ass-face. If she wants to give you another chance, she has my blessing, but I have no issues castrating you if the opportunity arises, so think with your head, not your micropenis."

We get into the car with my mom who bombards us with questions about the game and the prom court—though I'm sure Lianne will fill her in.

Just as we round the last corner to my house, my phone buzzes with a text from Rivers.

> Why were you sad tonight, Quinny?

> Idk. It was hard seeing you with Katie for some reason

> We're just friends, Quinn. I swear. Do I need to beat the shit out of Justin for you? Why was he even there?

> He's not that bad. He did something bad, but he's actually been really nice the last few weeks.

> Oh. Do you think you're going to get back together with him?

> Undecided.

> Got it.

I should tell him that I'm still curious where things could go with us. I should tell him that I haven't stopped thinking about him since Valentine's Day. The problem is that Justin really has been trying.

Did he get my favorite track meet snack wrong? Yes. Did he buy the worst type of flower imaginable? Yes. Did he try though? Also, yes.

He didn't have to paint my poster with me after I heard about prom court, he didn't have to come to my track meet, and he sure as hell didn't have to work concessions with me for three-and-a-half-hours tonight. But he did, just to make sure that I was okay.

He even left the game early to try and talk to Dani and make amends.

Maybe Justin really is changing.

Chapter Twenty-Four

Then, Junior Year

The tears forge trails down my face as I lie in the fetal position on my bed. I'm being melodramatic, laying here like this, staring out the window like I'm the main character in some late 1990s music video. I think of Justin's biting words during Student Government and how stupid I feel for giving him chance after chance to treat me well.

Fuck high school dating.

A tap at the door breaks me from my humiliation. Rivers stands there, folding his arms across his broad chest, looking at me with a half-frown.

"Hey." He has a gentleness in his voice that I usually only hear when he gets sleepy.

"Hey, I thought you had wrestling practice?" He told me two days ago that he only had two weeks left of wrestling, and that he felt relieved. Senior year has been busy for him.

"Oh, I told Coach that I was, ahem, not feeling well." He fake coughs into a closed fist, clearly feigning an illness.

"Ah, so you came to say I told you so?"

His brow furrows, and then I notice that he's holding a small blue box. "No, I came to see if you wanted to eat these with me while we watch a shitty movie of your choice?"

Rivers extends the box of s'mores Pop Tarts toward me like some kind of peace offering for keeping me at a distance for almost seven months.

"S'mores?" I ask, my mouth turning up ever so slightly.

He pulls out a second box from his backpack and tosses it to me. "Yeah, and blueberry. Everyone knows you claim s'mores are your favorite Pop Tart, but that blueberry is your actual secret favorite, although you'll never admit it, because it makes you seem less original," he says, rolling his eyes.

I gape at him. Sure, it's only Pop Tarts we're discussing here, but I feel seen. I have never told anyone my favorite flavor is blueberry, but they are always the ones I buy when I'm alone. And damn him for calling me out on s'mores! They're delicious, but blueberry really is superior.

I try to recover from the expansion in my chest over Rivers's insight into my Pop Tart preferences. "What movie?" I ask him.

"*Twilight*, obviously. How else will I get you to laugh?"

I give him a little scowl, hating that he knows me this well, while simultaneously feeling comforted by both his gesture and presence. "Fine. How long can you stay?"

Rivers clenches his jaw, puffs out his chest, and says, "A while." It's an obvious callback to Edward answering Bella's question of how long he's been seventeen.

I feel the curve of my smile before I can help it, and he must notice it too.

He gives me his own cocksure grin, and says, "See, *Twilight* is working its magic already. Now scoot over so we can feast on chemically engineered pastries and watch this cinematic masterpiece."

After queuing up the DVD player, Rivers climbs onto my bed, moving Pancakes the owl out of the way, and extends his legs, the box of Pop Tarts separating us. The opening credits begin to roll in cadence with the wrappers of our treats. We don't need to say anything; Rivers knows he was right about Justin being a prick, while I wish he had been wrong. But that's the thing about Rivers, he never says I told you so, never makes me feel stupid for acting impulsively; he just shows up at my house with my favorite sad snack, the world's most iconic movie, and sits in my sorrow with me.

I feel tears prick my eyes again as Rivers snakes his arm around my shoulder, pulling me towards him. Like a broken dam, my tears begin to flow as I cry into him, letting all the ugliness I feel come free.

"Quinny," Rivers whispers with so much sympathy I can hardly take it.

"Yeah?" I answer, sniffling, my eyes growing droopy from all the tears.

"You know that someday, you're going to meet someone who loves you like you deserve right? Someone who makes you feel like there's a balloon in your chest, that listens to Taylor Swift with you in the car, and knows exactly how you like your tacos. Someone who makes you playlists and shows up to your door just because they missed you. Someone who sees how incredible you are and doesn't want to change you or hide what makes you awesome. It's going to happen, Quinny, and if it doesn't, then love isn't real, because you're the easiest person to be around, and any guy would be a damn fool not to see that."

I give a small nod, and he squeezes my shoulder. I keep my head on his chest, watching the movie unfold in all of its glory, but Rivers's words play on a loop in my mind.

Everything he said I'd find one day is exactly who Rivers is to me right now, and this part of our relationship always confuses me. I never know if he wants me to see him that way or if he's just being a good friend. If I can see that he's very obviously this person for me and to me, does he also see it in himself? I swear I can tell him nearly everything, but God, I wish I'd never let us get away with ignoring the obvious all those years ago. If I hadn't firmly shut that door on that part of our dynamic it would be a hell of a lot easier to broach it with him now.

I decide to test the boundary I always seem to want to cross by closing my eyes, feigning sleep, and bringing my hand up to his chest as I curve my body closer into his, forcing us into a cuddle. I feel Rivers inhale a shallow breath and go still beneath my arm, but instead of leaping away like I expect him to do, he takes hold of my hand, his bigger one covering mine in his warmth. I'm so content to be here with him, I quickly fall asleep to the sound of Rivers laughing under my arm and Edward Cullen leaping between the trees with Bella on his back.

***

The smell of homemade bread pulls me from my dreamless sleep as does the sound of Rivers's voice coming from the kitchen while he talks to my mom. The credits roll on *Twilight*, and I stretch my arms while yawning. My t-shirt rides up my stomach an inch or two, and when I open my eyes again, Rivers is in my door just like before the movie, but now there's a heat in his eyes I've never seen as he takes in the small sliver of skin. With a jolt, I remember my brazen flirting before I fell asleep, and worry I've stepped over the line with him.

"Are you staying for dinner?" I yawn again into my fist.

"My parents are coming too. My mom called to make sure I was here, and next thing you know, its spaghetti and game night." His easy smile relaxes me. We're cool.

"Ugh, no. I don't want to play games. That's all I need is *both* of our dads talking to me about my lying, cheating, ex-boyfriend." I grab my pillow and groan into it.

Rivers's posture stiffens at the mention of Justin, and honestly, I feel shitty about bringing it up. But I also don't know how to broach the subject of us cuddling on my bed and Rivers's declaration of what I deserve in love. Why is it always so confusing with him?

"We'll keep them in line." He sets his jaw and clenches his hands. I can't tell what he's more upset about: me talking about Justin or Justin proving he's the jackass Rivers knew he was.

"Come on, Quinn." He pulls me up from the bed by my hands, his fingers warm and strong. "Your mom wants us to set the table."

***

After my mom's famous spaghetti, our parents expect us to clear the table and do the dishes. That first summer Rivers started coming over sort of solidified our routine. While Liz clears, I wash, and Rivers dries. They're here so often that we don't even need to ask who does what anymore, we just know the role we all play while our parents talk at the table.

When everything is cleaned up, Rivers and I go downstairs to pull the games from the game cupboard, though, I question why we bring up multiple games. Our parents only ever want to play dominoes.

We're in our third round when my dad asks me about Justin.

"Quinn, your mom said you came home upset from school today?"

Lianne jumps into the conversation too, pulling everyone's eyes to me. "Rivers, is that why you came over here today? You told me you skipped practice for something important, but I didn't realize it was because of Quinn."

Rivers clears his throat a little, clearly uncomfortable to also be targeted by our parents' dual scrutiny. "Oh, uh, yeah. I just wanted to make sure she was okay."

"What happened?" Now Mom has jumped in, and I swear Liz is looking back and forth like a goddamn tennis match is taking place—which in her defense it sort of is.

A tear escapes my eye, but I brush it away. "Nothing, it's fine. I'm fine."

"You know we love you," Bryan jumps in. "We just want to make sure you're okay."

I look at Rivers, and he gives me a subtle nod telling me he's with me. He inconspicuously puts his hand on my knee without our parents seeing, and my heart rate starts to spike as his thumb moves ever so gently against my leg. I grab his hand for extra courage as I suck in a breath, bracing for the impact of what I'm about to say.

"Justin broke up with me."

The confession sends both of our mothers into a tizzy about young love and heartbreaks, while both of our fathers grumble about "young bucks" who "don't know a good thing when they have it."

Rivers and I make eye contact through the commotion, and he signals to me that he's going to put me out of my misery with a gentle squeeze to my hand.

"On that note, I think Quinny and I are going to take a walk. Liz, do you want to come too?"

"Sure! Can you guys walk me to the bigger playground?" She's still too young to go on her own.

Rivers scoffs, like he's offended she would even ask. "Obviously. Go grab your shoes."

Our parents are still too caught up in their anger towards Justin and "lying, no good, boys" to notice we've even vacated the house.

When we make it to the playground, Liz runs off to the monkey bars while Rivers and I loop around the paved walkway. He takes my hand, the first time in almost a year, since I was in a relationship. I feel fragile and exposed because I know that Rivers is going to ask me for more details about Justin, and I know it's going to infuriate him to know how bad it is.

"What happened, Quinn? I know he broke up with you, but Dani said you've been over him for weeks. There's got to be more to it than just that."

I inhale and look down to the ground. I can't make eye-contact with him when I divulge the truth. "He's been wanting sex for months, and I'm not ready for that. It just hasn't felt right."

Rivers goes still as a board next to me. I breathe in again and turn to face him.

"Did he hurt you?" His voice is low, menacing, and protective.

"No, nothing like that. We fooled around a little bit a few months ago, and when I wouldn't go beyond that, he decided to hook up with Jaclyn instead."

Rivers's eyes look like ice, and I'm not even to the worst of it yet.

"I found out about it this morning from Sophie. I confronted both of them in Student Government, but not before he told everyone..." I start to shake and cry, hardly able to speak, as a hiccup escapes my throat.

Rivers loops his arms around me. "He told everyone what, Quinn?" He whispers but his words are clipped, like he's trying to restrain himself from physically exploding with rage.

"He told everyone that the reason he was hooking up with Jaclyn was because I—I didn't shave...down there?"

I swallow uncomfortably, mortification cloaking me like a blanket. "I think it grossed him out, and I didn't know I was supposed to do that..."

I trail off, preparing to tell him the final part. "But I think the real reason he went for Jaclyn was because he has always been insecure about the relationship between... you and me. He's always hated how close we are."

My face is pink, snotty, and covered in tears, and Rivers tightens his arms around me, trying to shield me from the humiliation.

"I swear to God, Quinn, I am going to tear him limb from fucking limb."

"Please just ignore it. If you do something about it, it'll only make it worse for me."

"What do you need?"

"You. This." I squeeze him tighter to me, and he lets me. "I'm just going to lay low. I can't change what he says. But I do think I owe you an apology."

"Why the *fuck* do you owe *me* an apology?"

"You told me he was an asshole almost three years ago; I should have listened to you and not jeopardized our friendship over someone you didn't deem good enough."

"You don't owe me shit. And for the record, there is not a single thing you could do that would ever jeopardize our friendship. I just want you to be happy."

"Well, I want you to be happy too, and I think it will bring you joy to know that Dani has texted me seventeen times telling me, in extensive detail, I might add, how she plans on chopping off his balls and feeding them to him."

"God, she scares the shit out of me."

I laugh. If there is one person who does not need to fear Dani, it's Rivers.

"Me too. She could bring the whole world to its knees and not even lift a finger, I swear."

Rivers's phone rings, and I overhear Lianne telling him that they need to go home for the night. We walk back to my parents' house with Liz, hand in hand, and before he climbs into his car, Rivers gives me a final hug. "See you tomorrow, Quinn." His breath is warm on the shell of my ear, making me shiver.

"Night, Rivers."

I jump in the shower after Rivers leaves, clean up the Pop Tart wrappers from my bed, and study for an AP Biology test the next day. As I'm studying, Mom comes and sits on my bed.

"Hey, sweetie." She looks at me with so much sympathy in her eyes. I know she wants to talk about Justin, but I can't tell her, at least not everything. I give her a hug, because I need one, and by the looks of it, that's all she's wanted to do since I got home from school.

"Hey, Mom."

"Do you want to talk about it?" She looks hopeful, like I'll tell her everything.

I decide to give her a half-truth, though. I think it'll help her understand that this isn't just a stupid high school tiff.

"He cheated on me. Or I guess, I should say, he has been cheating on me...for two months."

"Oh, baby." Her voice sounds heartbroken. "With who? Why?"

"Jaclyn." I feel her still. She knows Jaclyn has been one of my good friends the last two years. "I think he was just jealous of Rivers and me."

Mom pulls back from the hug and tilts her head—a sure sign I'm about to get some Diane wisdom.

"I think people who have been married for fifty years could be jealous of you two, baby. What you have is really special."

"I know. He's my best friend, Mom."

"Is that all he is to you?" I think she's known the answer for ages but wants to hear it from me.

"I don't know. Sometimes I think we could be more, but the thought of losing him as a friend scares me more than anything else in the world. Flirting feels safe, but anything more than that I start to panic that it will blow up in our faces."

"I understand." She kisses my head, and just as I think she's about to get up, she adds, "People spend their whole lives wishing they could end up with their best friend, Quinn. Don't take him for granted."

In my bed, I'm just about to fall asleep when my phone vibrates with a message from Rivers. I read it twice and the unmistakable flutter of butterflies fills my belly.

> Justin should be jealous of my relation-
> ship with you. After all, I don't see him
> taking a nap with you on your bed (;
> Sleep tight, Quinny.

Chapter Twenty-Five

Now

B y the time November hits, the weather is cold enough to warrant starting a fire in the hearth when we're at home. Rivers brought over a bunch of firewood that he had chopped since he's been over at my house more than his. It's nice to have someone here to support a household. We grocery shop together, cook dinner together, and help the kids with homework. He still leaves the house in the evening; we've talked about how to discuss him moving in with the kids but don't know how. Neither of us is kidding ourselves, we know this is it for us.

Rivers and I snuggle on the couch with the fire going, a blanket draped over our legs, watching the snow fall outside. It's the first snow day of the year, despite being earlier than normal, so the kids are upstairs in their rooms. He came over early this morning before it started to fall so that if the roads got bad, he'd already be here.

"Should we do something with the kids?" Rivers asks after a while.

"What did you have in mind?" I ask him, kissing the pulse of his neck.

He sits up, gently sliding me to the couch from my perch on his lap, and walks to the kitchen. The sound of cupboards and drawers opening reverberates throughout the living room like he's searching for something but doesn't know where it is. I follow him in, the blanket around my shoulders like a cape.

"What are you looking for?" I ask, leaning against the door frame.

Rivers moves toward me and places a gentle kiss on my lips that makes me grin. Quietly, so as not to alert the kids, he says, "Let's all bake a dessert—we'll each choose a favorite."

It's a fun idea. The kids and I used to bake all the time, but the older they got, the less time they wanted to spend in the kitchen with me. "I like it." I kiss him one more time before calling the kids downstairs.

Sawyer makes it to the kitchen first in baggy sweatpants and a Pine Grove Middle Wrestling sweater. He made the A team, in large part thanks to Rivers working with him almost every day since the beach. His first meet is in two weeks down in Fontana, but between the two of them, I think Rivers might be more nervous than Sawyer is. It's adorable.

Wyatt trundles in only a minute or so later wearing something similar, but she has on the brightest pair of fuzzy socks she owns—a staple for any good snow day. "What are we doing?" she asks.

"A great snow day bake off!" Rivers declares, throwing his arms in the air.

"A great snow day bake off?" Sawyer looks more confused than if he'd been told that starfish are land mammals.

"Yep, we're all going to make a dessert and then we'll stuff our faces and watch a Christmas movie." Rivers starts pulling basic baking staples from the cupboards—flour, sugar, oil. He pulls out the kitchen whiteboard where we all leave jokes for each other, poised with the pen. "What is everyone going to make?"

"I'll make an apple pie," Sawyer says.

"I'm going to do homemade ice cream." Wyatt goes to grab my stand mixer with the ice cream attachment.

"Quinny?" Rivers asks.

"Chocolate chip cookies," I answer. "What are you going to make?"

"Lemon bars," he says.

And it shouldn't make me blush that he's remembered one of my favorite desserts, not even a little bit, considering everything else he knows about me, but it does.

Two hours later, the kitchen is put back together, the smells of all the treats mixing in the air. There were a few mishaps, like Sawyer breaking not one, not two, but three eggs on the floor before he finally got it right for the egg wash on his pie crust. Wyatt also forgot to cover the cream when she first started mixing, so it flew up onto the ceiling on her first go around. We've been laughing almost non-stop. I'm worried about eating anything because I don't need my stomach to hurt more than it already does.

After the last dishes are washed, we move into the living room to turn on a Christmas movie. Wyatt wants to watch *Home Alone* which none of us protest against. We know we're going to watch all the good Christmas movies anyways—why bother fighting about where to start?

Rivers stokes the fire before coming back to the corner of the couch, opening his arms for me to crawl into. When I'm situated, I catch Sawyer looking at us. Rivers and I don't shy away from being affectionate in front of the kids, but we also try to be careful about when and how we show affection. Sawyer smiles at me, looking genuinely happy to have Rivers here with us.

The movie plays, and we laugh through all the antics of the plot; between the McCallister family banishing Kevin to the attic, and an eight-year-old deceiving two burglars, it's priceless entertainment.

"Mom, what are we going to do with all of these desserts?" Wyatt asks once the movie finishes. "There's no way we can eat them all."

"Maybe we can see if Aunt Dani and Will want some?" Sawyer suggests, oblivious to the fact that his sister has turned a deep shade of crimson.

"Wyatt, would that be okay with you if they came over?" Rivers asks her. It's so tender and sweet of him to want to make sure she's not blindsided—something I wish my parents would have done for me in the past before they knew we'd be seeing the Thomases.

Sawyer looks between his sister and Rivers, trying to understand why Dani and Will coming over would call for her permission. We've seen them since we ditched school early for the beach—she is my best friend after all—I think Rivers is just trying to let her know that she can say she needs space, or at least a warning.

"That's fine." She stands and comes over to Rivers and me, pulling us each to our feet, then loops her arms around both of our middles in a group hug. It's the first physical contact she's initiated with him; the sight of him hugging my baby girl makes me feel like I really don't have to do all of this on my own.

I love you, I mouth to him over her head.

I love you, too, he replies.

***

There are few things Dani gives fewer shits about than snowy roads, so when we call her to tell her that there's a plate of baked goods at my house with her name on it, she and Will arrive within fifteen minutes.

Almost as soon as they enter, all three kids make their way to the upstairs loft to play video games which they really only like to play when other kids come over.

Dani shoves a bite of everything into her mouth as she plops onto my couch, her feet kicking up into the air to reach the coffee table. "Fuck, that's delicious," she says through the mound of food as crumbs spray everywhere. "Who made the lemon bars? I know these aren't Quinn's."

"I did," Rivers answers, his arm going around my shoulder. "How'd you know they weren't Quinn's?"

"They aren't lemony enough."

"I followed the recipe exactly!" He sounds exasperated by her already and she just got here.

"Bold of you to assume Quinn follows the recipe at all," she answers through a yawn.

Dani seems more tired than usual the last few months. I can't tell if it's because the school year is starting to wear on her, or if there's something else going on she's not telling me. After Velocity Vortex, she didn't hear from Brad again, not that she will until closer to Christmas, but still, I know it's not him.

The three of us spend some time talking and laughing—Dani giving Rivers shit about taking almost two decades to be in a committed relationship, and him dishing it back about how she missed out on a career in the CIA to teach fifth graders. It feels like no time has passed listening to them bicker, yet everything has changed. I've been married, then widowed, and now finding love again. Dani, much as I love her, has become hardened to love, not willing to give people the chance to get close enough to hurt her, and Rivers has been living what he calls a half-life until now.

I take my turn to go up to the loft to check on the kids. They're self-sufficient teenagers, not needing a grown-up to check on them like when they were little, but I can't help it. I want to make sure they're okay—safe.

Three heads turn to look at me when I reach the last step on the stairs. The game controllers lay discarded on the floor along with popcorn that's been abandoned. They're watching *Tarzan* which we've all agreed has the best movie soundtrack of all time, but instead of focusing on Phil Collins's masterpiece, my eyes zero in on Will and Wyatt, holding hands on top of the blanket all three kids sit under.

Wyatt's cheeks tinge the lightest shade of pink, and I silently vow to not embarrass her. I hope she'll talk to me about it later. "You guys good? It got quiet up here, so we just wanted to check on you," I say by way of explanation.

"We're good. We were playing Mario Kart earlier. Sorry if we were loud, Aunt Quinn!" Will says. I love that, despite holding my daughter's hand, he doesn't feel an ounce of embarrassment about it.

"Got it, Mario Kart can get ruthless," I admit. Liz and I used to play it on a Wii console, along with Just Dance. "It looks like they might cancel school again tomorrow since it's still snowing, but I want you guys to get to bed at a decent hour, okay?"

Sawyer and Wyatt both nod in agreement then return their attention to the movie before I make my way back down the stairs. Dani and Rivers sit on the couch watching a home renovation show when I get back to the living room, which makes me feel every one of my thirty-six years. "Wow, we've peaked," I joke, sitting down and curling into Rivers's side.

"I think you mean we've turned into our parents," Rivers says into my hair before he kisses the top of my head.

"I don't even think our parents were this lame," Dani jokes.

Thudding footsteps flying down the stairs startle us all.

"Mom! Mom!" Wyatt shouts. "MOM!"

I bolt off the couch to get to her, checking her over to see if something is wrong. There's no blood, no broken bones—she's tearing up, but there isn't anything visibly wrong with her.

"Wyatt, what's wrong?" I lean down in front of her, trying to figure out what's going on.

"Mom, I'm a top three finalist for my fire prevention piece," she says, her voice wobbling. Her art club submitted their pieces to the Rotary Club ages ago, but I hadn't heard anything back.

"Wyatt, I didn't even know that you were a regional winner! Why didn't you tell me?"

"It just didn't seem like that big of a deal. It's just the county," she says.

"Wy," Rivers's voice comes from behind me. "Did you know we live in the biggest county in the United States?"

She lifts her head to meet our gaze. "Really?"

"Yes, really," I say. "How did you find out about being a state finalist?"

"I got it in my email just now!" She angles her phone towards us, and we all crowd around the little screen to read it.

From: Doug Fieldman
To: Wyatt Stewart
Subject: CAL Fire Arts Awards

Dear Wyatt Stewart,

It is my privilege to inform you that your art piece titled, "Fire Flies," has been selected as a top three finalist for the California Department of Forestry and Fire Prevention Arts Program. The winner will receive the cash prize of $2500 and have their work displayed throughout the state of California next year.

You and your family are cordially invited to attend the awards ceremony at the Griffith Park Observatory on Monday, November 17th 2025, at 6:00pm.

Should your piece be selected as the winner, it is expected that you make a few remarks about the work and the inspiration behind it.

For more information on the dress code and schedule of events for the evening, please visit: CALFIRE.com/events/ARTS

Congratulations on your accomplishment!

Most sincerely,
Doug Fieldman

Communications Director
California Department of Forestry and Fire Prevention

"Wyatt, this is incredible!" Dani shouts giving her a hug.

"I'm so proud of you, sweetie!" I pull her away from Dani and into my arms.

Will moves to give Wyatt a hug next, and I watch the way they hold each other. It looks like Rivers and me; not caring about who is watching, clinging onto the other person like they're the most important thing in the world. He whispers something in her ear that I don't catch, leaving us adults in the dark, but we communicate with just our eyes that the dynamic between them looks awfully familiar.

Sawyer congratulates her, though he doesn't seem as happy as he'd normally be about her success.

"Sawyer? You okay?" Rivers asks.

"Yeah, it's just that Wyatt's award is the same night as my first wrestling match," he says, downcast.

"We'll work it out," I assure him. "We'll make sure to find a way for all of us to be there."

"It's going to take two hours to drive out to L.A., Mom. We won't be able to make both things happen." He's worked so hard the last few months to make the team, I can't disappoint him now.

Dani catches my eye, sympathizing with the fact that I can't be in two places at once and that it was never meant to be this way, choosing between them like this.

And, like magic, Rivers puts his arm around my waist. "Quinn, Wyatt, maybe the two of you could stop by the match to see him on your way out to L.A., and then I'll take him home?"

We all settle on the idea. Obviously, there's no guarantee that Sawyer will be wrestling when we get there, but at least we can see him and wish him the best before we go.

"That works, then we can both see each other!" Wyatt hugs Rivers, then Sawyer, and flies back up the stairs shouting, "Mom! We have to go shopping for a dress!"

***

Two weeks later, I zip up an emerald dress for Wyatt. As I do, she puts in the only real pair of diamond studs I own. Her blonde hair gently curled, she has mascara on, making the blue in her eyes pop, and she's wearing a low heel that makes her look at least three years older than she is.

Rivers texts me to let me know that he's on the way to the meet. Sawyer has to ride the bus with the rest of the team for liability reasons, but Rivers can drive him home later.

I promised Wyatt that we could stop at the Chick-fil-A drive-thru once we made it off the mountain since we won't have time to eat anything at home. I put a towel over her dress to make sure she doesn't get anything on the front—grease stains at an awards ceremony aren't the greatest look—and start driving.

Wyatt acts as DJ for our drive, playing songs I've either never heard or have heard a thousand times—there's no in-between. "Mom?" she asks, her voice is hesitant. "What if I don't win?"

"Hmm, you tell me? What happens if you don't win?"

She thinks about it, looking out the window and furrowing her brow. "Nothing, I guess?"

"Right," I say. "You'll be disappointed of course, but nothing else will change. You'll still be a great artist, a top three finalist for the State of California, a great daughter and wonderful friend." This seems to reassure her a bit. "The bottom line, sweetie, is that I'm proud of you either way, and you should feel proud of yourself, too."

The rest of our drive passes quickly. There's very little traffic out to the wrestling meet, which bodes well. It should mean minimal traffic on the way out to L.A.

Wyatt and I are seriously overdressed walking into this meet. Our high heels click clack on the floor, and eyes of parents waiting to see their kid compete follow us as we make our way over to Rivers. He pulls me to him, gently taking my jaw in his hands and kissing me on the lips.

"You look stunning, honey," he whispers. He glances over my shoulder, taking in Wyatt as she comes down the stairs. "Wyatt, give me a twirl!"

Visions of Wyatt as a toddler playing dress up and spinning around in her princess dresses flash through my mind in rapid succession. My heart aches seeing how quickly she's grown up.

Sawyer walks up to us from the floor of the gym in his wrestling uniform. He's almost taller than I am now, and thanks to Rivers, his muscles are starting to become more defined. I physically restrain myself from scooping both kids into a hug and instead have them stand next to each other for a picture. The juxtaposition of their outfits is almost comical; I want to remember it.

"When's your first match?" I ask, hoping we'll get to see him.

"Not for thirty minutes. Will you be able to stay that long?" he asks, hopeful.

I glance at my watch to see what kind of time I have. It's three o'clock, and as long as we leave by four, we should make it on time. "We should be able to!"

Surprising everyone, including me, Sawyer walks toward me with his arms outstretched for a hug. I hold him against me, letting him take what he needs. "I'm nervous, Mom," he whispers so only I can hear.

"I know. I think that's a pretty normal way to feel about something you've never done," I tell him. "No one expects you to be perfect at this you know. It's supposed to be fun."

He separates himself from me and walks back to his team. This is the part of parenthood that people don't ever talk about. Kids grow up and become self-sufficient. They cook their own food, clean themselves, and express what they think, but they don't ever stop needing you. It just might not be as obvious when they do.

The meet begins, and Sawyer is in the first round, going up against a kid that weighs three pounds more than he does. They shake hands on the mat, then begin circling each other. My stomach is in knots at the sight of Sawyer willingly looking to fight someone.

Pretty quickly, Sawyer charges his opponent and gets him into the neutral position, where he's on his back trying to take the other kid down to get him pinned.

Rivers shouts, "Move to a side-lock, Sawyer!"

That must be some type of headlock, because Sawyer gets his arm around the other boy's neck, and Rivers claps like that's what he wanted to see. Sawyer's opponent looks like he's trying to do something with his legs to trip him up, but Sawyer spins in a circle, dodging it, and puts his leg behind the other kid to trip him to the ground, before he rolls on top of him. Sawyer hooks the leg of his opponent with his own, then pulls the head of the other boy toward his knees.

"He's trying to pin him with a cradle!" Rivers shouts, looking between the boys and the ref, eagerly anticipating the pin. It's the longest three seconds of my life, but the bell rings in favor of Sawyer, and I can't believe it.

Rivers and I jump up and down, screaming with joy and pride. Sawyer stands up, helping his opposition up off the floor. Rivers used to do the same thing at his meets. I turn to face him, thankful that he's coached Sawyer well enough to win his first match and thankful that my son has someone like Rivers to learn from.

"Did you tell him to do that?" I ask.

"I had to. It's important to be a good sport when you're going one-on-one like this," he says with a shrug.

I hold up the *I love you* sign to Sawyer before I signal to Wyatt that we need to leave. Rivers kisses me goodbye before I make my way out of the bleachers and walk to the car with Wyatt, hoping the night goes just as well for her.

***

"Before we announce the winner of this year's Forest Fire Prevention Art campaign, we want to thank each one of you for being here with us tonight," the MC says into the microphone. "Every year, California is plagued by wildfires that harm our environment, reduce air quality, and cost the state billions."

Wyatt's foot taps anxiously as we wait for the winner to be announced. I put my hand on her leg to try and calm her, but my heart races just as quickly. "Without further delay, the winner of the 2025 Cal Fire Art Campaign is…Wyatt Stewart for her piece, '*Fire Flies*!'"

The black sheet covering Wyatt's creation falls, and it leaves me speechless. I hadn't seen it before—she wanted me to wait until tonight before she showed me—but I can see why it was selected.

Wyatt painted black pine trees silhouetted against hues of red, orange, and yellow that mimic a sunset, with small specks of color that resemble fireflies in front of the trees. Upon closer inspection though, the fireflies become embers, and the sunset reveals itself to be a fire, coming to destroy the forest with swirls of smoke dancing up toward the sky. It's striking.

Wyatt moves to the stage to take the microphone. Other people may not see it, but her hands are trembling. "When I started thinking about what to paint, I thought about my house at night. I always see fireflies outside my window, and I thought I could use them for this, but in a different way. Fires are so destructive in California because the wind is so weird thanks to the ocean; and I know about wind—I lived in Kansas until just a few months ago."

This gets a laugh from the crowd. I'm so proud of her, so astounded by her poise.

"I hope that when people see my art, they see how easily the next fire could take everything from them and make choices that prevent it from happening. Thank you."

She hands the MC the microphone and makes her way back to me—crying, blubbering me, who is so in awe of my girl. I give her a hug, but she's pulled away from me quickly by people wanting to shake her hand and congratulate her.

The photographer for the event ushers us over to the piece, snapping picture after picture: Wyatt and the head of CAL Fire, Wyatt and the art, Wyatt and me. As I watch her graciously shake hands and take photos with dozens of people, my phone buzzes with a phone call from Rivers. He's probably wondering how it's going. I've been so distracted by everything, I haven't even texted him that she won. I'm desperate to know how the rest of the meet went for Sawyer.

"Hey! You'll never believe it!" I answer.

But something is wrong. I can hardly understand what Rivers is saying because his voice is so broken through uncontrollable sobs it's hard to piece together, and there's a noise in the background I recognize but can't name. Then I figure it out; it's sirens, and I finally hear him clearly.

"We were hit by another car on the way home, Quinn. Sawyer is being taken to Loma Linda. He's unconscious." I hear him hiccup through his tears. "Get here as fast as you can."

And that's when I scream.

Chapter Twenty-Six

Now

I'm not sure what's worse. Finding out that my husband is dead over the phone, or having my new boyfriend tell me that my son is in critical condition. What's worse? Picking up my kids from school to tell them that their world is shattered or having to drive two hours before I know if mine will be again?

Wyatt and I sprint to the car once someone helps to my feet, and we've been almost silent the entire drive apart from both of us muffling our cries. Her cheeks are stained with tears, and I'm certain I look the same. Rivers calls almost immediately when we get in the car, saying that they were taking Sawyer to surgery, but I don't fully understand why or for what. It's killing me not to know what's going on. I'm trying to drive safely so that Wyatt and I don't also end up in the hospital, but holy shit if I don't get answers soon, I'm going to fight someone.

It's nearly impossible to not let my mind wander into the not knowing. I think about the first time the nurses put Sawyer on my chest, how his little body curled right into mine and, at the sound of my heartbeat, he settled, like that was right where he belonged the whole time.

I hear the sounds of his little feet padding through the tiled hallway of our small apartment, sticking to linoleum and seeking me out with his bottle in one hand, his favorite board book, *That's Not My Puppy,* in the other. We'd read it over and over and over again, and then, when the milk and story and giggles ended, his eyelids would flutter and he'd fall asleep right there on my chest just like the day he was born.

I think about his third birthday and how much he hated cake so we made him a giant chocolate chip cookie, and when I set it down in front of him his eyes went wide and he said, "I uv oo mommy," and wished everyone a Happy Birthday because he thought everyone was being celebrated, not just him.

I think about Preston throwing him in the air, making my heart stop, and the big, beautiful belly laughs that would erupt from Sawyer as he fell back down into Preston's arms.

I think about how, after Wyatt was born, it was Sawyer's breathing that settled my anxious heart as I fell into life with two kids, and how it was the cadence of his steps next to me, our faces muddied with tears and dirt, that pulled me from my grief on long runs after Preston died.

I think about the smile on his face this afternoon because I'd been there to see him compete, and I want to scream and thrash and fight the universe for trying to take him from me, too. For trying to rob the world of so much goodness, to rob me of such a fundamental part of my existence.

My phone rings an hour into the drive, Rivers's name illuminating the screen of the car. "Rivers? Any update?!"

I'm frantic, trying not to speed but absolutely terrified for what I'm about to hear. Terrified that I might find out my son died on an operating table while I'm barreling down the freeway with his best friend in my front seat.

I cannot lose him too.

"Quinny, I have a surgeon here with an update, okay?" Rivers sounds broken.

"Okay," I answer, bracing for the worst.

"Ms. Clark," a female voice greets me, "I'm Dr. Tran, one of the trauma surgeons here at Loma Linda. I have Dr. Peller here too, one of our pediatric residents."

"Normally, we'd want the pediatric surgeon to come talk to you, but she's in surgery with Sawyer right now," Dr. Peller begins. "Sawyer sustained some very serious injuries that we'd like to go over with you if that's alright?"

I take Wyatt's hand in mine on the center console, knowing we both need the other.

"Sawyer's vitals were stable when he first came in, but one of our tests found that he had blood in his abdomen and around his lungs, causing his blood pressure to drop quickly, which required a massive blood transfusion."

This is what they told me when they called the first time.

Dr. Peller continues, "We took him straight to the OR, where we found that he sustained a grade five spleen laceration, which requires that his spleen be removed, and a pulmonary laceration, requiring a chest tube."

"What—," Wyatt chokes through a sob. "What is a pulmonary laceration?"

"Forgive me," Dr. Peller says. "It means he has a substantial cut on his lung, which led to a hemothorax, or blood in his chest cavity, and the lung collapsing. He has a chest tube in now to help reinflate the lung, drain the blood surrounding it, and help him breathe. That same lung also had a pulmonary contusion, or bruising."

"Since Sawyer lost so much blood from these lacerations, he had to have a second blood transfusion in the OR," Dr. Tran adds. "So far, the surgery is going well, and we've been told that Dr. Miller should be done within the hour. Do you have any questions we can answer in the meantime?"

"The surgery is only two hours?" I ask, surprised.

"Yes ma'am. When we have a trauma like this, we're trying to get in and out as quickly as possible to stabilize the patient," Dr. Tran answers.

"Does he have any other injuries?" Rivers asks.

I can't even imagine the trauma he experienced tonight. Walking away from an accident, riding in the ambulance with Sawyer not knowing if he was going to live or die, having to call me to break the news.

"We won't know until we can get him into a CT scan," Dr. Peller says. "When there's bleeding in the abdomen and the chest cavity, we have to respond to that right away before we assess if there's anything else going on. We'll take him to CT immediately after he's finished to check for anything else."

The doctors tell us that someone will update us when they have new information and it hits me: Rivers has been sitting there alone for the last hour, not knowing what was going on, not having anyone to talk to. I may be hurtling down the freeway, but at least I have Wyatt—at least we have each other, and I want to give him that too.

"Rivers, can you call everyone and update them?" I want to give him something for his mind to focus on besides the fear and guilt I'm sure he's enduring.

We finally pull into the parking lot of the hospital, and it feels like déjà vu, running into a hospital to try and find the person I love more than anything and figure out what's wrong with him. I dial Rivers before I even cross the threshold.

"I'm here, I'm here! Where are you?!"

"I'll meet you at the check-in stand." His voice is urgent and scared. Wyatt and I are there less than a minute before Rivers strides over, taking us both in his arms. I fall apart, every ounce of undiluted terror heaving out of me in sobs I can't control.

"I'm so sorry, Quinn. Oh my God, I'm so sorry." Rivers repeats it like a chant, like if he apologizes enough for someone else's recklessness, it'll fix everything, fix Sawyer, and put him back together again.

"Excuse me? Are you the parent of Sawyer Stewart?" I pull away from Rivers to find the chaplain looking somber, and waiting patiently for us.

"Quinn Clark," I answer, extending my hand. "Sawyer is my son."

I wipe my eyes on my sleeve, trying to compose myself despite feeling the insurmountable weight that comes with catastrophe. The chaplain hands me a tissue, then gestures for us to follow him down a long hallway. I remember, when Preston died, that feeling of walking through a maze. Endless hallways and corridors leading to places and rooms that weren't identifiable. I know without asking that he's taking us to a quiet room, the rooms that feel impersonal, where you receive the biggest, most life-altering news without even a picture on the wall to bear witness to your pain.

The chaplain ushers us inside, and from what I can gather, this is a surgical quiet room; the signs on the wall indicate that we're close to the standard surgical waiting room, despite the hallways giving nothing away.

"Ms. Clark, I can't speak on your son's condition other than he was critical when he came in, and I've been told that he's out of surgery."

"But he's alive?" I say.

"He's alive, yes. I'll send someone in to speak with you more about what's going on. Just let me find someone." He excuses himself, and I take in my surroundings. Wyatt hugs herself in the corner, and Rivers sits on a chair with his head in his hands. There's no color in this room. It's lifeless. Ugly. The chairs are mismatched and uncomfortable, as if they know that the person sitting in them won't be there long anyway. That they'll get the news no one wants to hear, and wait for the next person to come along to meet the same fate.

"Rivers, what happened? Are you okay? Were you hurt?" I start to cry again thinking about losing them both.

Life is so fucking fragile. One minute you're on a cruise in the Bahamas, the next, your husband dies at work at the hands of two disgruntled employees. One minute you're watching your daughter win state level recognition for her creativity, and the next you wonder if your son is going to die.

Rivers looks like he doesn't have a scratch on him, but I'm not naïve enough to think that it doesn't mean there isn't anything wrong; sometimes mental wounds cut just as deep as physical ones.

He stands up and pulls me to his chest, breaking with the weight of what I assume is his own guilt. "The car came out of nowhere, Quinn. The light was green, it was completely clear for me to go, and then it just smashed into the back of the car, right where Sawyer was sitting. I told him I didn't want him in the front because I didn't know if you let them do that, and I wanted him to be as safe as he could, and now he's in the hospital for that mistake."

Rivers is inconsolable; I feel his grief and his guilt with each shake of his shoulders. I understand it. I feel it too. So many what ifs and questions that I don't have answers to. What was the last thing I said to him? What was the last thing he thought about? What does any of this mean if he isn't okay? How much can one heart take before it shatters?

Rivers and I pull apart from each other and sit down next to Wyatt. There's nothing we can say right now to make her feel better. All we can do is sit in this silence and wait for answers. It's like torture. There's nothing we can do but wait and hope that Sawyer is strong enough to make it through to the other side.

When Preston died, the permanence of his condition forced us to reconcile with the knowledge that he wouldn't be around for so many major life events. We knew he'd miss walking Wyatt down the aisle. We knew that we'd never take another family vacation. This feels different though, the not knowing. We don't know if Sawyer will wake up. We don't know if we'll get to hear him laugh again. Was every time before this the last time that we ever got?

Someone knocks at the door, pulling each of us from the spiral of our swirling thoughts.

"Excuse me?" Two female doctors walk in. "Ms. Clark, I'm Dr. Miller, the pediatric trauma surgeon overseeing Sawyer's case, and this is Dr. Russell, one of our neurosurgeons."

"Nice to meet you," I say with a tremor in my voice, trying to mind my manners despite wanting to scream, plead, and beg them to give me good news.

"Sawyer is out of surgery, and he did great. We removed his spleen and stopped the internal bleeding," Dr. Miller tells us.

I breathe a sigh of relief, my first in what feels like days, but has only been two hours.

"Can we see him?" I ask, itching to hold him, to feel him breathe.

"You can, but we've also come to tell you the results of his CT scan," Dr. Russell answers.

"Unfortunately, during the crash, the impact of the car dislocated his shoulder and fractured his humerus," Dr. Miller says, touching the upper part of her arm. "He also sustained two fractures in his wrist."

Broken bones I can handle. People break bones and recover from them every day. This is a minor issue as far as I'm concerned.

"Okay," I say, nodding. "Broken bones are good news in this scenario, I feel like. Isn't that good? It could be worse."

The doctors look at me like they hate that they have to deliver this news to me, that their jobs would be so much easier if broken bones were the only other issue we had to be worried about. It dawns on me then that Dr. Miller introduced Dr. Russell as a neurosurgeon, and she wouldn't be here unless something was wrong with Sawyer's brain.

"Ms. Clark, Sawyer also sustained a traumatic brain injury, a subarachnoid hemorrhage, in the crash," Dr. Russell says.

"What does that mean?" Wyatt asks. She's been so quiet, I almost forgot she was here, experiencing this type of trauma for the second time in her short life.

Dr. Russell opens her computer, turning it towards us. On the screen she shows us an illustration of a brain, with clear hemispheres housed inside the skull, protecting it. "When we're talking about brain injuries, we usually name them based on where we see the bleeding. A contusion would be a brain bruise; a subdural bleed would show us blood between the brain and the skull. For Sawyer, he's bleeding in between the squiggly lines here." She points to the image for us to visualize the injury.

"Does he need brain surgery?" My eyes flood. I cannot do this again.

"He doesn't," Dr. Russell says. "These types of injuries are more of a wait and see situation. Often, patients recover from them just by resting."

"No surgery?" I feel the smallest amount of relief.

"Not at this point. We'll give him another CT scan in twelve hours to assess the injury. We want to make sure that the bleeding doesn't worsen. And we'll do neuro checks every hour once he wakes up to make sure that he's coherent."

"He's going to wake up?" I whisper.

"He's a fighter, Ms. Clark," Dr. Miller says as she takes my hand. "His vitals look great right now, and I expect them to continue to improve."

It's not long before Dr. Miller comes to get me again, telling me that Sawyer is awake. We're only allowed to see him one at a time, so Rivers stays with Wyatt while I walk back to the surgical recovery unit, where Sawyer is coming out of anesthesia. He's groggy, moaning quietly like he's uncomfortable while tears trail quietly down his cheeks. The tubes and wires coming from his body give me flashbacks to seeing Preston hooked up to more machines than I could imagine. The first thing my eye finds when I walk in is the c-collar around Sawyer's neck. I assume it's to keep him stable until they know he's clear, but it knocks the wind out of me. He has an oxygen tube under his nose, IVs in both arms, and another line coming out of his groin. I see the chest tube connected to what looks like a small rectangular box dangling by the foot of his bed, and his left arm is taped up and set in a black sling, preventing movement.

Sawyer is a tall kid, especially for fourteen, but he looks so small under all of this equipment.

It's quite possibly the most significant opposition of feelings I've ever experienced: relief flooding every atom of my body at seeing him awake, and complete and utter terror that I'm going to lose him still.

"Mom?" His voice is hoarse thanks to being intubated earlier.

"Hi, baby," I say as I walk toward him, clasping his hand in mine like a lifeline. I stroke his hair back from his forehead, taking in the shape of his face, the curl of his eyelashes, every freckle on his nose, the auburn undertones in his hair. His face is littered with red bruises and scrapes that aim to mar the face I love. How close I came to losing every bit of it, every bit of him because of someone's carelessness.

"Mom, is Rivers okay?" Sawyer searches my eyes, silently pleading with me that he hasn't lost another man he loves.

"He's okay, baby. He walked away without a scratch. How are you feeling?"

"I'm alright. A little nauseous though."

"Ms. Clark, I'm sorry to interrupt, but I wanted to do a neuro check with him while he's awake." Dr. Russell enters the small curtained-off room.

"Hey, bud. I'm Dr. Russell, one of the neurosurgeons here. I'm just going to ask you a few questions, okay?"

"Okay," he says.

"What's your name?"

"Sawyer Stewart."

"How old are you?"

"Fourteen."

"Do you know where you are?"

Sawyer starts to cry, his shoulders shaking.

Dr. Russell turns to look at me. "This is normal. Sometimes patients get emotional realizing they're in the hospital. Often, the anesthesia makes them more emotional than normal. We'll see how he does with these questions as we go."

Sawyer continues to hold my hand. "I'm in the hospital."

"Good. The nurses here will move you guys over to the pediatric ICU here shortly, and one of them will ask you those questions again in about an hour, okay? Try to get some rest."

I step into the hallway with her, wanting to know her general assessment of his responses.

"He answered the questions well," she starts. "I've written down his responses to see if they change, so the nurses know to come get me if there are any variations in his answers. He might get frustrated answering the same things over and over, but we like to keep things straight and to the point so there's little room for alternative answers."

"If he asks what happened to him..." I trail off, not sure what I'm asking exactly, not sure if there's an answer to my unknown question.

"Some patients remember, others don't. Sometimes their brains are trying to protect them from processing the trauma of what they've experienced, other times their brain is busy healing and just can't pull at those threads. It may come back to him, it may not, but I'll be with you every step of the way."

I walk back out to the waiting room where Rivers and Wyatt are, and see that my parents, sisters, Dani, Will, and even Bryan and Lianne are all here. It brings me to my knees. The last time I did this, I had to brave that first day almost completely alone. I feel buoyed up knowing that they're here.

"How is he?" Mom asks.

"He's okay, awake. They're moving him to the PICU to recover and monitor the brain injury."

Rivers pulls me into his side and kisses my hair. It calms me.

"I'm sorry you guys drove all the way down here."

"Yeah, we're not going to have you apologize to us right now," Dani says. "What's the first big thing, Quinn?"

"Waiting," I tell her. "Just waiting."

***

Three days later, I step out of the shower at the Ronald Mc-
Donald House and quickly put on the change of clothes Dani
brought down for me last night. I put my dirty clothes in the
laundry bag the charity provided so they can be cleaned for
me to wear them again tomorrow and then race back to the
hospital across the street before Sawyer wakes up for the day.

Dr. Miller said they're going to move him over to the pediatric floor today, a step down from the PICU, which feels
monumental. It means that Rivers, Wyatt, and I can all visit
him at once, and most importantly, that he's stable enough not
to need intensive care.

Dr. Miller told us that Sawyer getting out of here is going
to depend on his chest tube, and what his chest x-rays look
like in the coming days. He did well for his orthopedic surgery.
They said his repeat CT scan looked the same, so there isn't
any new bleeding in his brain. Dr. Russell hasn't been the
one to ask him questions since that first night, and I assume
that means he's answering everything almost the same which
is good news.

He remembers some of what led up to the crash, too. That
they were on their way home from a wrestling meet, that he
was excited to hear about Wyatt's award, and what song was
playing on the radio. I can't decide if that's good or bad, if it's
better for him to remember or be sheltered from the trauma.

Wyatt is at June's house today, and she'll come down
tonight, so for right now it's just Rivers and me. My family
has been incredible, of course, with the exception of June's
husband, who heard the news, but didn't say anything or come
to visit. I just wish he'd talk to us. Talk to me.

Rivers and I help get Sawyer situated in his new room.
Rivers went to buy him a robe before he got here so that the
care team could still access his surgical wound, a vertical incision in the middle of his stomach, but not be as uncomfortable
or exposed as in the hospital gown. Dani sent the Nintendo
Switch down with my change of clothes for Sawyer to play in
small snatches, not very much, since the screen isn't great for

his brain, but some. While Sawyer naps, Rivers sits next to me on the couch that turns into a bed for overnight stays, his palm on my upper leg, taking in the space.

"Did I tell you the police contacted me about the crash?" Rivers's voice has an edge to it I don't recognize.

"No, what'd they say?"

"It was a drunk driver, Quinn." Red flares in my vision. The selfishness of a person to get behind the wheel and almost rob Sawyer of the rest of his life makes me seethe. "He's been taken into custody, but who knows where it will go from here."

"Rivers, I never thanked you for everything," I say.

"What do you have to thank me for, Quinn?"

"For getting him here, for being here with him when I couldn't. For helping him have the best time at the wrestling meet before it all happened. I could go on and on." I play with his fingers sitting in my lap, appreciating every part of him.

"Honey, loving that boy is as easy as loving you. I don't know how I spent my entire adult life without the three of you. You and the kids are the highlight of my life." I turn to face him, letting him kiss me in the center of my forehead while his strong hand grips the back of my head.

We fall asleep to the sound of Sawyer breathing, and for the first time in days, it's not punctuated by the sounds of machines reminding us of his proximity to death.

For the first time in days, I sleep peacefully.

Chapter Twenty-Seven

Then, Senior Year

I'm wandering through the grocery store hunting for heavy cream. Mom's making pasta tonight, and now that I can drive, she's always sending me on errands.

"Yeah, I got it Mom. Anything else?" I hear my favorite sound in the world behind me and turn quickly toward it, like it's a lighthouse and I've been lost at sea: Rivers.

Before I can stop myself, I sprint toward him, throwing my arms around his middle and pressing every single part of my chest to him, and squeezing with all my might like if I don't hold on I'll lose him.

He's been out of town for two weeks on a trip to Europe—a graduation gift from his parents—and then we went out to see June in Vermont for two weeks. She's been out there twice as long as we thought she would be. I miss her, but now that it's time to start looking at colleges, I understand the appeal of moving away from home. Pine Grove feels suffocating sometimes; I see why she wanted to start fresh somewhere that no one knew her.

The last month has felt like I've been walking around with a Rivers-shaped hole, and this hug, this proximity to him, fills up every crevice. I feel Rivers breathe out a sigh, like he's just as relieved to hold me like this as I am him.

"How was Europe?" I ask, holding his hand as we move toward the candy aisle. He doesn't even need to ask where we're going. If I'm at the store, I'm getting a snack—especially with Mom's money.

"Fucking incredible," he says, grabbing a pack of pull-apart Twizzlers. "Do you remember the first time we drove into Yosemite Valley in like...ninth grade?"

"I do. It felt out of body, almost."

"Europe was like that, but for man-made cities. Standing in the Colosseum and looking at how well-made it is even though it's almost two thousand years old was surreal. Like how did they do that type of math without a computer? How did they know how to measure everything perfectly, and get it to last so long? I don't know. It just made me appreciate how cool humans are, I hope you get to go someday," he says.

"Ah yes, building a fighting pit to stand the test of time is so compelling," I joke. "What was your favorite part?"

"Don't make fun of me, but the Neuschwanstein Castle." He separates our hands then takes the can of Pringles out of mine so I can grab a bag of Starburst.

"Why would I make fun of you for that? I don't even know what that is."

"It's the castle that inspired the one at Disney," he answers.

"No way? Do you have pictures?"

"On my digital camera, yeah. What are your plans tonight, Quinny?" Rivers starts walking toward the check-out stand, one hand gripped around the block of cheese I assume Lianne sent him to pick up, the other holding too many snacks.

"My mom is making fettucine, and then I was going to maybe start looking at colleges. You?"

"Colleges? Like...ones in Michigan maybe?" Rivers got accepted to Michigan State on scholarship for their biology program, and since they offered the most in terms of funding, it's where he decided to go. He got accepted to a few California-based universities, and to some others in Texas, Kansas, and one in Ohio. Lianne and Bryan offered to help with the cost a bit if he stayed here in California, but he refused. The biology program at Michigan State is pretty prestigious.

"I've been poking around the Michigan schools to see what there is, yeah." I know deep down, despite it being painful to admit, that I likely won't be following Rivers to Michigan. Whether it's because I won't get in, won't get a scholarship, or something else, it doesn't feel right. Not ready to fess up to the truth, and not ready to be away from him, I say, "You still haven't told me what you're doing tonight though."

"I'm taking this cheese home to my mom, then going to your house to look at colleges with you." He smirks, flashing his dimple that always feels like it was made just for me. "I didn't know you guys were home or I would have just come over. I thought you were supposed to get back Tuesday?"

"No, we left on Tuesday. We flew back home this morning so my dad could work tomorrow."

"Oh yeah, I think I remember my dad saying something about that. I'll go home and drop this off, then head over in a couple hours?" We exit the store and the heat of summer engulfs us, radiating upward from the paved parking lot like flames licking our bare skin.

The thought of being away from Rivers again for more than a minute feels like someone is standing on my chest, preventing me from breathing. "If I ask my mom if you can come for dinner, would you want to?"

"Probably not," he says sarcastically. "I'd rather feel like shit for the rest of the day."

I lightly punch his arm then turn to my car, feeling whole for the first time in weeks.

***

After my parents spend thirty minutes grilling Rivers on every moment from his trip, we retreat into my room to talk about colleges.

At his graduation party we hung out on his porch talking about how different everything was going to be for both of us the next year. Not seeing each other every day was a concept we hadn't mastered over the course of our five-year friendship. I didn't know how to deal without his constant reassurance just as much as he couldn't handle us not talking every minute of the day.

"What if we end up in different states permanently, Quinn? I mean I get the one year where you're here and I'm there, but what if you go somewhere else?" he asked me that night, his elbows resting on the railing of the deck, his fingers clasped together under his chin.

"I don't know," I answered honestly. "Maybe we can take the few weeks we have apart as a test run? Maybe we won't see each other but we can still talk every day? I can't guarantee that I'm going to Michigan, Rivers. You know that. If I don't get scholarship money that plan is out."

We both went quiet after that, thinking about how, for the first time since we went camping together all those years ago, there was a very real chance we'd be ripped apart, and it wouldn't be because we chose to take some space.

I pull up the list of colleges I've been making that have strong creative writing, journalism, and teaching programs since I'm not certain what I want to do yet, other than knowing I need something related to English. Rivers glances over my list one at a time taking in my selections.

"No Michigan State?" he sounds disappointed.

"They have education, but their creative writing program is only offered at the master's level, and I don't want to confine myself to a box when I'm not sure what I want to do yet," I keep scrolling through.

"Hmm. How close is the University of Michigan to Michigan State?" he asks.

"Only an hour, and they offer a lot of different English programs." It's one of my top schools, but I can't honestly say it would be my first choice. Part of the draw of going out of state for college is to experience things I haven't before. Of course, I've never been to Michigan, but I'm used to forests and lakes, so something like Kansas State University appeals to me since it's something completely different from where I'm at now. It feels like I have my whole life to do what's expected but a really short amount of time where I just get to be a selfish college student, living by my own rules and wants.

"Okay, well that's perfect then." He says it like it's a done deal, but it isn't.

"Yeah, hopefully it all works out," I manage.

***

Rivers and I spend most of the End of Summer bash in tears, either from laughing about our shared history or crying that it feels like the end of an era. He leaves for Michigan tomorrow, and I still haven't told him that I don't think I'll be going. The more I look into Kansas State, the more it feels like the right fit for me. The ironically-named Manhattan, Kansas, still has a small-town feeling, offers great English programs, and the weather isn't as extreme in winter as Michigan if you don't count the tornadoes. Mostly, though, it feels like the opposite to Pine Grove in every way.

I've been trying to come to terms with the prospect of not seeing him every day, but no matter how hard I try, my brain can't wrap itself around the idea. I heard a theory once that said our fingers are as easy to bite into as raw carrots, but that our brains won't even let us try to bite that hard on them as a defense mechanism. Saying goodbye to Rivers feels like that. I know it's happening, but my brain refuses to believe it's true; it refuses to inflict that much pain on itself. It feels more like he's going on vacation than anything else.

Rivers and I walk along the shore of the lake, trying to get to the far side where no one ever goes. As we walk, I see all the memories I've had of us here. The spot where he held my hand in secret that first summer. The cove that sits on the opposite bank where Rivers and I caught a group of kids smoking pot when I was fifteen and ran away because we were scared our parents would smell it on us.

We sit down in the sand, and Rivers unpacks the blanket from his backpack to put around our shoulders. The bonfire is on the other side of the lake, but we promised each other that tonight would just be about the two of us soaking up our last few minutes together.

"When will you be home to visit again?" I ask him. I have a lump in my throat that makes my voice come out quivery and uncertain.

"Christmas," he says. "I wanted to come for Thanksgiving too, but..."

"Yeah, I get it. Part of going out of state for school, I guess."

"So, Quinny, how exactly are we spending our last night together?"

"Don't say it like that." I nudge him in the shoulder. "You make it sound like we'll never see each other again."

Rivers sets his hand on my thigh, my shorts giving him access to my bare skin, it makes me shiver. His thumb skates back and forth across, his touch like a tattoo that I'll never be able to wash clean. "Well, it does feel like I'll never see you again, being so far away." Something catches in his throat, and when I turn to face him, I see him wipe a tear from his cheek.

"Rivers please don't cry," I beg. "You know I can't see you cry without falling apart."

"Why couldn't I get a scholarship to Cal State San Bernardino? Why did it have to be in fucking Michigan?" The drops from his eyes flow more freely; it breaks the dam of my own.

"Don't do that. You're excited to be there, and I'm excited to hear about everything you're going to do." I reach into my own backpack and pull out my speakers and iPod. If I have two hours left with Rivers, I'm not letting any of it go to waste. "Best Weezer song right now?"

"Perfect Situation" he answers without thinking. It's one of my favorite songs, and I'm curious just for a second if he says it because he knows. I get to my feet and set the speakers on the blanket with my iPod so it doesn't get ruined by sand, then help Rivers up. We do the routine through our tears, laughing at how ridiculous we must look to passersby.

Halfway through the song, Rivers twirls me in toward him but instead of his chest to my back, he stops me so that I face him, looking up into his blue gray eyes that look like an ocean of sadness.

How do we do this?

"I don't want to leave you, Quinny." His eyes move back and forth, taking me in.

"You aren't leaving me. You'll be back, and I'll be here, waiting for you. I promise." I hold up my pinky to him, a vow that however he and I are connected won't ever be severed, then let him pull me down next to him on the blanket so I'm lying on his chest while we take in the night sky that's always held us both so carefully. "Who am I without you, Quinn Clark?"

I don't know how to answer his question. The only Rivers I know is in the context of who he is to me. He's the boy who became my best friend. The boy I fell in love with and never told. The boy who called me the sun. The boy who has made high school survivable. He's the one who made Valentine's Day perfect, he's who knows why my favorite Taylor Swift song *is* my favorite Taylor Swift song. He's the one who knows that blueberry Pop Tarts are my favorite flavor, and that I would grow dahlia's all year if I could. He's my whole world, and I'm about to lose him. Whatever resolve I had to tell him I'm not going to Michigan vanishes into the night. I cannot send him away feeling any worse than he already does.

Instead, I tell him through my tears, "You're Rivers Thomas, and I know who you are without me just as well as I know myself without you."

Which is to say, not at all.

***

The snow comes down in fat clumps as I leave school for the day. Christmas is in three days, and I hope that June and Rivers's planes land on time before the weather gets worse.

Rivers and I text every day and started video chatting once a week; the distance was too hard without face-to-face contact. Nearly every time I see his face, the urge to feel his touch amplifies into a dull ache. I just want to hold his hand or hug him.

Being more than a thousand miles apart is for the birds.

To make matters worse, Dani has been beside herself because Brad is shipping out to basic training for the Army just after the first of the year. He graduated early, which I guess is an accomplishment, but the Army was the only branch that would take him with how low his aptitude test was. I'm not supposed to know that; Dani just let it slip. I hate the idea of being apart from her next year too, but she knew she wanted to go to Cal Poly at San Luis Obispo when we were sophomores, and that wasn't ever on my list. I'm not worried though—I don't think I can be with how interconnected we are. There are very few times when life shoves a friend in your face and demands that you take it: Dani was one, Rivers was the other. No matter what happens, I can't see that ever changing.

By the time I make it home, there's at least an inch of snow on the ground, and an extra Honda in Mom and Dad's driveway: Rivers.

I bolt into the house, taking the steps two at a time to get to the kitchen where he scoops me into a hug that would make our one over the summer look like child's play. It's perfect, and healing, and right where I'm supposed to be. I don't even notice my parents in the kitchen, staring at us.

"Well good to see you too, Quinn," Dad mocks.

"I saw you this morning," I say, still being crushed by Rivers. "I saw him, months ago."

"Sure, we'll leave you two to catch up." Dad's voice is laced with something I can't name. It feels like he knows something I don't.

"Actually, I thought Quinn and I could take a walk," Rivers says, looking at my dad. It feels like they're in on some kind of plot that doesn't involve me.

I put on my snow boots and grab another pair of gloves. The street is quiet, the snow muffling the sound of everything around us. I loop my arm through Rivers's, desperate to have the closeness I've been craving since September.

"When did you get in? My mom said your plane wasn't supposed to land until five?" I tell him.

"Nah, that's what I told everyone to tell you. I wanted to surprise you."

"Well, it worked!" I loop my arms around his neck again, needing to be closer to him.

"Quinn, I wanted to talk to you about something...something kind of serious?" I can only assume the reason for this walk, and the reason for my dad acting weird in the kitchen relates to whatever it is that Rivers is going to tell me here.

"Okay, sure."

Rivers sucks in a deep breath, bracing himself for what he's about to say. "Michigan is beautiful," he says. I'm not sure what I expect him to say, but it's not this. "It's got gorgeous scenery, the lake is incredible, and the campus is amazing. I really love it there." My brow knits, still not sure why he feels like this is news. He tells me how much he loves Michigan almost every day. "But...once I got there, I realized that Michigan could be the most beautiful place in the world, and it still wouldn't be everything I need because you're not there with me."

I gasp, audibly. The tears sting my eyes before I can stop them. "Rivers."

He turns to face me, not liking the tone in my voice, the break in it. "No, Quinn." He knows something is coming.

"I don't want to go to Michigan," I confess. "I know you love it there, and I know that it's what's best for you, but it's not where I want to be."

"Quinn, I'm in love with you. I think I always have been? I think that first trip to the desert closed off any other possibilities I'd ever have with anyone else because you're it. You're...everything. You're the reason I get up in the morning, and the first person I want to call when anything happens to me, and it would be so much better if you were there, experiencing it all with me. Do you remember last year when I told you that someday you'd find someone that felt like a balloon in your chest?" I nod, remembering everything he said, and everything he didn't. "You're my balloon, Quinn. I don't know how to live or function without you." He's almost shouting.

"Rivers, where was this years ago? I begged you to want me my freshman year at homecoming. And Valentine's Day when I was a sophomore, I tried to let you kiss me and then we never talked about it again. And again last year when we were in my room watching *Twilight!* You know you described yourself and didn't do anything about it."

I'm crying so hard I can hardly see what's in front of me. "You've always been my fucking balloon, and you knew it. And now, I want to go somewhere else to college and you come back here trying to convince me that you'll finally let me all the way in if I follow you?"

"Quinn, no, it's not like that. I love you, I just don't want to be away from you anymore. It feels like it's killing me, and it'd be so much easier for you to come there. The English programs

are awesome and your parents have already told me they'd help
support you. That feels so much easier than for me to find a
biology program at the same level wherever you want to go."

It would be so easy to believe him.

So easy to trust that he means what he says.

But I've been burned too many times to be able to. I believed
Justin the first time when he convinced me to date him. I believed him the second time when he seemed like he'd changed
and then hooked up with one of my closest friends. I've been
on this teeter totter with Rivers for five years. Five years of back
and forth, of push and pull. Of waiting to see if one of us was
finally going to be brave enough to do something, and now it's
too late. It's been hard, but we're still friends. If I try this with
him, if I give us a real chance, then I run the risk of ruining our
friendship beyond repair.

It's not a risk I'm willing to take.

"I can't do this," I whisper.

"Quinn, please. Please give me a chance to show you that
I'm serious. You're the one for me."

"But you're not the one for me." My heart feels the betrayal
the moment the words leave my lips.

And then I run.

***

Three hours later, Lianne knocks on my parents' door.
My dad looked disappointed when I came inside without
Rivers. I know he's viewed him and Forest as the sons he's
never had. Mom lets Lianne inside of course, but none of
them knows everything that's happened between Rivers and
me—and everything that hasn't.

"Quinny girl?" Lianne's voice calls from my bedroom door.
I turn to face her, eyes bloodshot and puffy, surrounded by
mountains of tissues. "Want to go for a short drive?"

"It's snowing, Lianne," I mumble.

"I made it over here just fine. The roads aren't bad. It's just starting to stick."

I pull my boots back on, then get in the front seat of her Ford. We don't drive far, just around the corner from my house, so that we have privacy my parents won't give us. I know with certainty this privacy is an illusion. Lianne will undoubtedly tell my mom everything I say.

"Are you okay, kiddo?" she asks.

I laugh through a sob. "No," I answer.

"Do you know what Rivers told me all those years ago, after your homecoming dance?" I shake my head. "*She feels like seeing color for the first time, Mom.*' I remember asking him why he didn't pursue you then, if that's what he thought of you, and you know what he said to me?" Honestly, I didn't even know that he talked to his parents about me at all. "He said, *Because what if it destroys what we have, and she loses her color, and it's all because of me?*' I thought he was being a little dramatic, but I understood. It's scary to think about what could go wrong and a lot harder to think about what could go right. But you know, Quinny girl, sometimes the best things in life are the things we take chances on. The things we're afraid of but do anyway."

I think about what she's saying. I get it, but I can't do it.

"Lianne, I appreciate this, I do. But I can't. I can't lose him because I want more with him. Right now, what we have is enough. It feels like tempting fate to ask for more."

"Quinn, please, just think about Michigan. It feels like you threw it out before you even gave it a chance. You'll never know and always wonder if you don't."

"No, Lianne!" I shout. "I don't want to. I. Don't. Want. To," I say, punctuating every word. It goes against everything my heart is saying, begging me to try and give Rivers the chance I know he's due. My head is so loud though, the anxiety and fear drowning anything else out.

"What's the worst that could happen, Quinn? Come on."

She's begging me to love her son back—to be as vulnerable as he just was with me—and it's not that I don't. I love him. I've loved him for years. But I can't ignore all of the ways this could tear me apart.

"Everything could implode! Why are you pressing this so much? I know you love us both, but you've always been a meddler, and if you wanted this so bad, why didn't you push him harder?! I've been begging him for years to just fucking SEE me, and you've known the whole time? You've known that I've been sitting here, waiting for him to figure it out and watching me get my heart trampled on by guys who didn't give a shit about me. And now you're going to ask me to try with him when I've given him chance after chance? It's too late. I'm too scared to do that again in a place I don't know with no way out!"

She looks down at her lap, hands folded. "I'm sorry, sweetie. I wanted you two to make your own decisions." Her voice is small.

"Well, this is mine," I say with finality. "I know that you have nothing better to do with your time as a housewife to two kids who have moved out of the house, Lianne, but I'm old enough to make this choice without you trying to fix what took you *and* him five years to name." I open the door to the car, and trudge home through the snow, my tears freezing to my eyelashes in painful crystals that make it harder and harder to see.

I told Lianne I didn't want to lose him by asking for more, and in the blink of an eye, I lost them both for demanding less.

∗∗∗

My freshman year of college at K-State is devoted entirely to my studies. I have a few roommates that like to go out, but I spend most of the year devoted to making sure I'm making good grades. Dani and I talk once a day, though most of that time is spent listening to her recounting parties she's attended and how much she still misses Brad. She's told me a few times that she thinks they'll get engaged, and I want to tell her that she's worth so much more than him but never do.

My heart longs for Rivers every fucking minute but I know that he deserves so much more from me than an apology, and I know that even though I went about everything in the wrong way, each of us going our separate ways was still the right call. My parents try to tell me about him, and Lianne has tried to reach out a few times, but I can't talk to her. I'm scared she'll tell me about Rivers and how he's doing and who he's meeting, and it'll gut me to know that his life is moving on without me.

Sophomore year is where things really start to change. One night on the phone with Dani, she tells me about her teaching program and how rewarding she finds it to think about how people learn. She's joined a tutoring service at Cal Poly where she gets to support students in their classes and encourages me to do the same at mine. I promise her I'll look into it, especially since I still haven't completely felt right about a direction for my career yet. I could go into communications, copywriting, or something more creative, but none of them have felt like I belong. I waitress five nights a week at the local Texas Roadhouse to support myself, and, eventually, I do as I promised Dani and show up at the library on a night that tutoring is scheduled.

A shorter female student with long blonde hair rounds the corner when I enter. "Hey, I'm Sybil! Any chance you're good at English? I'm short a tutor for writing."

"I'm Quinn," I tell her. "English is my best subject."

"Then pull up a chair, bitch, cause you're about to teach adults why they need to capitalize letters."

Sybil and I spend almost all of our sophomore year in the library tutoring other students. She's told me that she's in the education program, and that I should really consider declaring my major to match hers, which I do, three months later. Sybil is loud and boisterous, like Dani. In some ways, she makes me long for home. I've been back to Pine Grove for Christmas, but it's the most I'm willing to do. The prospect of seeing Rivers, even by accident, feels overwhelming.

The ache in my chest pulling me toward him begins to lessen halfway through my junior year. I'm making more friends, experiencing more things, and taking in what Kansas has to offer. Sybil and I spend weekends in Kansas City exploring local bookshops and record stores, immersing ourselves in the Kansas City Chiefs and other sporting events. I meet her family, and mine flies out to watch us run our first half-marathon of many. After dinner that night, when Sybil and I get back to our apartment, I tell her the story of Rivers and how badly I messed everything up.

"Quinn, you were seventeen, and it was so unfair of him to ask you to rearrange your whole life for him," she tells me.

After a few months, I start to believe that's true.

Sybil and I spend a ridiculous amount of time in the counseling office making sure that we have the same schedules our senior year—including our student teaching placement. We know that there's no chance of student teaching at the same school together, but we want to be close enough to carpool since we'll basically be working for free for three months until we land jobs.

It's grueling work. The students are much more challenging than our professors made them out to be. They want to be on their phones, and the growing cyber-bullying that plagues teenagers is a near constant struggle. Both of us collapse in exhaustion most nights, living off of ramen and mac and cheese because we can't afford anything else. The realization that we're each going to have to fund an entire classroom after making zero dollars is as daunting as it is unjust. I'll have to grind at Texas Roadhouse the next several months to try and salvage some things.

Sybil and I decide, at the end of student teaching, that we would rather quit education entirely than work apart from each other. We spend hours searching for job listings that have openings for two English teachers and discover that we'll have to move away from Manhattan and closer to Kansas City for the plan to work. We find a cute apartment not too far from downtown. As two young women, we don't feel like living in the suburbs and away from the nightlife that downtown offers—we may be teachers, but we're only twenty-two.

After countless interviews for both of us, we find a middle school in Liberty that offers us each a job, and it feels like a dream come true. I call Dani to tell her; she's living in North Carolina now, married to Brad. She quit college two years ago to be with him, and I've told her repeatedly to try and finish her degree online. I hate to say it, but I worry that she's going to be left stranded if he ever decides to leave her.

That night, Sybil and I make our way out to celebrate. She's in a red mini dress with wedges that are way more comfortable than the stilettos I have on with my little black dress. I haven't thought of Rivers in almost a year, and with the way my life is right now, I think I'm finally ready to start dating.

I'm standing at the bar, paying for a vodka soda when a man gropes my ass from behind, and tries to talk into my ear. The bar is crowded and I can hardly move, let alone signal to Sybil that I need help, but it doesn't matter, because just as I'm about to yell for someone, another hand, warm and comforting touches my shoulder. I turn around to see a man, handsome, tall, and sculpted. "Is this guy bothering you?" He references the man that groped me.

"Yeah, but I'm fine."

"Are you sure you're okay?" He's so earnest, so genuinely concerned.

"Yeah, I just want to get back over to my friend," I gesture to Sybil.

"Let me clear the way for you." And he does; he uses his big shoulders to carve a path for me to walk through without a single person touching me.

When I get to the table where Sybil's been waiting, I turn to thank the handsome, charismatic stranger. "Are you going to be my bodyguard now?"

"That depends," he says, flashing me a megawatt smile that awakens feelings I'd long since forgotten.

"On what exactly?" I tease, taking a sip of my drink.

"On if you're going to tell me your name." His voice is deep and rich. I could listen to it on repeat.

"Quinn," I answer, extending my hand to him.

"Nice to meet you, Quinn. I'm Preston, and if you'll let me, I'd like to take you out tomorrow night."

Preston and I fall in love almost as quickly as we meet. He's charming and funny. He doesn't take life too seriously and always knows how to lighten the mood. More importantly, though, Preston always goes after what he wants. He's ambitious and driven in his career, and he's never been anything less than upfront with me about how he feels.

The night after we met, he took me to a jazz club, and he could tell almost immediately that I wasn't into it.

"Let's go," he'd told me.

We ended up at a mini golf course, with me obliterating his score. He took it on the chin, and when we got ice cream cones from the small concession stand, he leaned over and kissed a stray dollop of cream from my mouth without hesitation. I opened my mouth for him immediately, willing him to take more.

Nine months into dating, Preston asks me to marry him. Our parents don't know why we're rushing it, we just know. Sybil fields spectators who wonder if I'm pregnant with an emphatic, "NO!" until a month before my wedding, when she finds me throwing up in the staff bathroom from morning sickness.

"My lips are sealed, babe," she says with a wink.

Preston and I get married right before my twenty-third birthday, and have Sawyer eight months later. He's the best father, the most supportive husband, he lights up every room.

And nine years later, he's gone.

Chapter Twenty-Eight

Now

S awyer is well enough to be discharged one week after the crash. He's been up and walking every day, but Dr. Miller told him he's not allowed to lift anything heavy for two weeks. He's also not allowed to do contact sports, run, bike, or engage in cardio for six weeks while his brain and incision heal, which means he's going to miss the rest of the wrestling season. He's unhappy about it, naturally, but at least he's alive. His coach came to see him two days ago and promised that he'd have a spot on the freshman team at the high school next year, possibly JV if he stays dedicated to the training Rivers had set up before the crash.

The school has been extremely accommodating for both Sawyer and me. They called in a tried-and-true substitute to cover my classes, which more often than not feels like finding gold, and my co-workers have been prepping enough materials for my students to use while I've been out so that I'm not having to come up with lesson plans.

Sawyer will start out doing half-days at school until he stops having headaches, and has to do all of his work on paper because of the TBI. Dr. Miller said to limit anything he does on the school issued Chromebooks, and they've agreed to scale his assignments back by fifty percent until the concussion clinic gives us the all-clear for him to resume his normal activities.

"I'm going to tell everyone that my doctor said cardio is bad for me," he jokes as she examines him one more time. "Actually, that should be a t-shirt. Mom, can you get one made before I go back to school?"

I would do nearly anything for this boy right now. I'm just glad he's still here to ask me to do it.

"Ms. Clark, how you deal with a hundred versions of these snarky remarks every day is beyond me," she says with a chuckle.

We've talked a bit about our jobs, and how parents are one of the hardest factors in both the medical and educational professions. Dr. Miller has it worse though. I have to tell parents that their child is missing assignments or that their kid swore in class; she has to tell them that their child might not make it out of the hospital.

"The only way I know how, Dr. Miller—by dishing it back."

"Sawyer." She gently clasps her hand on the shoulder without the broken bone. "It's been wonderful getting to know you...and I hope I never see you again."

We all laugh at her humor as she leaves the room.

One of the nurses helps Sawyer into a wheelchair before we make our way through the colorful hallways of the peds floor where Sawyer waves goodbye to some of the nurses who helped him recover, the physical therapist that helped him get to his feet to work on walking following the surgery, and his favorite radiology tech that performed his daily chest x-ray. Despite the hallways and rooms often feeling impersonal, these people took care of him, loved him, and wanted the best for him. I'll never remember all of their names, I'll probably never see them again, but I'll be thankful for them every day of my life for keeping him alive.

We make it out of the elevator and enter the final maze of hallways that somehow lead toward the parking garage where Rivers waits for us with my car since his was totaled. He's assured me I have nothing to feel guilty over, that it's just a car, but it's hard to keep those feelings at bay knowing that if it weren't for me, Rivers wouldn't be tangled up in this mess.

Our drive home is comfortable. Sawyer sits in the back seat with his head resting against the glass. Both he and Wyatt start seeing a therapist next week to process everything they've been through; Rivers and I wanted to make sure that if there was any trauma, they'd be able to work through it early. Rivers is going to go, too. He said he wanted the kids to have an example to follow on positive mental health and for them to see how being proactive about it leads to better outcomes. Honestly, we probably all need to go together. I've processed my PTSD from Preston dying, but almost losing Sawyer felt like a relapse. Between the antiseptic smell that only lives in hospitals and the constant beeping from monitors indicating life or death, it feels like it loops on a soundtrack that hasn't stopped playing in my mind.

Rivers helps Sawyer into the house while I take in our bags in. We picked Wyatt up from June's house on our way home, so walking into the house feels like I'm behind on everything. There's laundry to wash, counters to clean, grocery shopping to do, meals to cook, and more that I have to worry about, but none of it matters. All that I care about is that my people are here. That they're safe.

Sawyer sits at the kitchen table, eating a bowl of Fruity Pebbles—all he's wanted for a week—while Rivers loads the dishwasher and I move clothes into the dryer in the laundry room right off the kitchen.

My parents show up to the house an hour or so after we get home, announcing themselves by bringing in bags of groceries full of all our favorite foods, and three freezer meals I can stash for easy cooking.

"Hi sweetie." Mom pulls me into a hug, while Dad shakes hands with Rivers.

"Good to see you, Jack," he says, shaking his hand, then pulling my mom in for a hug. "Diane."

"How's Sawyer?" Dad asks, putting the groceries away.

"I'm good, Papa." Sawyer walks into the kitchen with his cast, but moves towards my parents for a hug.

"You feeling okay?" Dad's voice is gruff, but kind. He's never been overly sentimental by any stretch. The last week has been tough on him though. He hates seeing any of us in pain, especially the grandkids.

"Yeah, I'm alright. I really just wanted a way out of wrestling without hurting Rivers's feelings," he jokes, shoving licorice in his mouth.

I think it's a good sign that despite everything he's been through, he's able to make jokes. I worry he's masking his pain and fear with humor, but that's a conversation for his therapist.

"If you want to hurt Rivers's feelings, you should hear about the time your mom dumped him," my dad says.

"Jack!" Mom is indignant. I kind of am, too.

But Rivers just brushes it off. "It wasn't the right time, and honestly, I didn't help your trust issues after the stunt I pulled after Valentine's Day." He puts his arm around my shoulder, reassuring me that he's not upset. I love him for it.

Mom and Dad look back and forth between us to each other; they always assumed that Rivers and I didn't work because of my trust issues with Justin. They had no idea that part of those issues came from us being two young kids who were too afraid to lose each other.

"Jack, can I talk to you privately for a sec?" Rivers gestures toward the front door just as June and her boys walk through with Dani and Will at her heels, followed right after by Rivers's good friend, Theo, and Trevor right behind him.

"What are you guys all doing here?" I ask. I have *so* much to catch up on, I can't entertain everyone today.

"We're here to help you get your shit together." Liz comes in with an industrial sized bottle of shampoo, and my brow furrows.

"With shampoo?" Sawyer asks the question we're all too afraid to utter.

"No, June stole the rest of yours from your shower while you were gone because some crazy lady wanted it for her hair cut and she didn't have time to replace it. I'm just here to refill it." She marches toward my bathroom.

I turn to June, still confused. "That pretty much sums it up, yeah. I brought the bottle from home to refill yours; she just took it out of my car for me since I had these freezer meals." She holds up her hands, and I see she has three more meals prepped for me.

"What kind of psycho demands a certain kind of shampoo for their appointment?" Dani asks as she throws a handful of Fruity Pebbles into her mouth.

"I don't know. Some lady named Marjorie," June answers.

The drink I had in my mouth sprays all over my kitchen floor. "Marjorie Winthrop?" I ask, stunned.

"Yeah...how do you know her?" June asks.

"Her son is in one of my classes," I say, moving to clean up the mess before Dani stops me and shakes a mop in my face, like *why bother when we're just going to mop it up anyways?*

"Good luck," June mutters. "She's a bitch."

"June!" Mom scolds. It sends all of us into fits of laughter that sound like music in my kitchen. How did I get lucky enough to have so many people love me so purely? People who show up to clean my house, and fold my clothes, and bring me dinners so that I can figure out how to function after almost losing my son, my Sawyer.

From the corner of my eye, I see Will engulf Wyatt into a hug when they think no one is watching. He moves his nose to her hair like he's breathing her in, and I wonder, just for a second, if Rivers ever looked so completely content to hug me like Will is now. I can't be sure what the future holds for Wyatt and Will; they're only thirteen. I do feel confident that they'll be in each other's lives though—especially if Dani and I have anything to say about it.

Once Rivers and Dad come back into the kitchen, teams are divided into who tackles what. Mom and Dad offer to clean the bathrooms, but the empty birth control box in my trash can makes me volunteer to do those with Liz instead. Rivers and Dani tackle the laundry, Theo and Trevor offer to stock firewood to prep for the incoming storm, and June offers to do the dusting and vacuuming, leaving Mom and Dad with the easiest job: the general cleaning of my kitchen. It's not in bad shape, and I think everyone agrees we want them to do the least amount of heavy lifting since they're getting older.

The kids are all upstairs talking to Sawyer about what he missed. Banks is trying to catch him up on school, but I think that will be something we take one day at a time. Dani can help him figure out the math he missed, Rivers can tackle science, and I can help him with English. Between all of us, Sawyer has a support system that I'm proud of.

Both of these kids have dealt with more in their short lives than most people face in a lifetime, but they've met it with strength and grace that I can only attribute to the people around them.

People who show up to clean their house, catch them up on work, and fill their freezer.

Rivers finds me in the bathroom, scrubbing the shower, and pulls me to my feet. "Hey honey." He smells like laundry soap and sweat, and his muscles strain against his black thermal.

"Mmm," I say, inhaling him. "Hi." I lean in to kiss him, firmly pressing my lips to his and gently coaxing his mouth open with my tongue.

"Quinny," he groans. "I want you right now, but I cannot do this knowing your father *and* Dani are right outside the door."

I giggle thinking about him being more afraid of Dani than Dad. "What were you talking to my dad about?" I ask.

"You. How much I love you, how thankful I am for you, and how scary it is that I can't protect you all the time."

"I get that. I feel that way about the kids. Like no matter what I do, life is going to do what it wants."

We stand there, hugging for a few minutes before someone bangs on the door of my bedroom.

"You know it's rude to have a quickie while your family is out here scrubbing your floors, you two!" Dani shouts.

I cover my face in my hands, mortified that now my parents and sisters will have that visual before making my way out of the bathroom with my head held high, the garbage in my hand and Rivers by my side.

***

After everyone leaves, Rivers and I sit on the couch tangled together doing a crossword puzzle while Sawyer looks through a telescope we found while cleaning, locating planets and stars in the dark sky. Every now and then, he calls out to us to come look at what he's found.

Wyatt finds us out there, waiting for Sawyer to focus in on Saturn, holding her science homework. A quick glance reveals a catapult project. "Rivers, do you think you could help me make this? I have a couple of weeks, but I don't know where to start."

He glances down at the assignment, scanning the requirements.

"Yeah, we could do this! I have most of the tools we'll need at my house, but I can bring them over. I need to go home tomorrow and get some clothes anyways."

Sawyer looks up at him from the telescope, then turns to Wyatt. The kids communicate with their eyes, nodding like they're reading the other one's mind.

"Rivers?" Sawyer's voice is hushed.

Rivers kneels next to him, offering to adjust the knob since Sawyer can only use one hand. "Yeah?"

The kids look at each other one more time before Sawyer speaks again. "This *is* your home."

"What are you saying?" Rivers asks, turning to face them. I notice him swallow, see the way he looks between Sawyer's eyes, trying to understand, trying to confirm what I think he knows.

"We're saying if you and Mom feel ready for it, we want you to live here with us all the time, like a family," Wyatt says.

My heart races. Rivers here all the time? It's like a dream.

"Are you guys sure? You know that you can take as much time as you need with your mom and me. I don't want you guys to feel like you're being rushed just because of the crash," he replies.

Sawyer nods like he understands where Rivers is coming from, but it doesn't deter him. "We're sure," he starts. "You might not be our dad, but everything you've done for us is what our dad would have done."

"We love you," Wyatt's whisper is almost inaudible, but we both catch it.

Tears glisten in his eyes as he takes them into his arms, and it turns me into a puddle. The three of us have been through hell and back the last five years. We lost the most important person to us and had to figure out how to put all of those pieces back together without him, had to make them fit together in his absence. There won't be a day that passes where I won't think of Preston—that I won't wonder what our lives would look like if he was still here. But life doesn't always work out the way we expect it to, and the fact that life, in all of its cruelties, still offers us second chances makes me want to weep with gratitude under the constellations that have heard so many of my wishes.

Six Months Later

"**M**om!" Sawyer's voice travels from the loft down into the kitchen.

"Yeah?" I'm scrubbing the last of the dishes before Dani comes to pick up the kids for a scary movie. Wyatt said that Keegan and Theo were going too; I'll have to ask Dani about it later, since from what I can tell, Will and Wyatt are more of an item than either of us realized, and Dani hasn't dated anyone in twelve years. Maybe Theo is helping her turn over a new leaf.

"Do you know where Dad's old Pokémon cards are?" Sawyer walks into the kitchen now. He's healed well, and therapy has been going well for him.

"I think they're in the storage room. I'll help you look."

Rivers finds us rummaging through boxes, trying to sort out where the cards are. He moved in the day after the kids asked him to, and his house sold three months ago. It made sense for him to move in with us, even though he had the better view. His house was two bedrooms and wouldn't work for our family.

"Hey, what's all this?" Rivers says as he pulls a box down, just as Sawyer finds the Pokémon cards.

"You're not allowed to trade those," I tell Sawyer.

"I know, Will just wanted to see the first edition Charizard before we leave for the movie."

When he leaves the room, I turn back to see Rivers gently removing things from the box he found. One glance at its contents, and I know exactly what box this is: my Rivers stuff from high school. There're some notes and papers with jokes or conversations I'd written down that Rivers reads through: they make him laugh, they make me squirm.

"God we were masters of poor communication," he jokes, reading through notes. "Why do you look embarrassed? It all worked out."

"I don't know, probably because I was really embarrassing?" I can feel the flush creeping into my ears.

Rivers stands up, hugging me to his chest. "We were both embarrassing, Quinn. Give me a second." He moves to the closet of the storage room, pulling out a smaller box. His smile is wistful as he takes it in, remembering something. Rivers puts the box in my hand, then nods his head, a silent gesture for me to open it. Inside, right at the top sits the letter I made June deliver. The quote on the outside makes me cringe internally—I was so dramatic.

"You kept this?" I say, holding it up.

"Of course I kept it. It was the first time a girl ever liked me!" He laughs. "I also kept it to remind me that our communication issues stemmed from me, not you. You told me exactly how you felt, and I waited too long to build the courage to do the same."

I give him a gentle kiss, a silent thank you for always being exactly what I need, then move to look at all the other things I have stored in this box. Underneath my old iPod, buried beneath a concert t-shirt, postcards from Yosemite, and the birthday candles from my sweet sixteen are three things I didn't even know I still had.

I gasp when I see them.

The mood anklet Rivers bought for me at the Fourth of July parade; Pancakes, the stuffed owl Rivers made for me for

Valentine's Day; and the Star Jar, still sealed. Pancakes frays at the edges—a few of it's seams have come undone—but could likely be repaired easily enough. The Star Jar looks like it hasn't aged a day. The masking tape still covers the jar, our fingerprints peppering the surface and proving that we didn't read each other's wishes.

"Hey, Mom? Rivers?" Wyatt calls from the doorway. She looks so grown up it snatches the breath right out of my lungs. Her blonde hair is growing long, in loose waves over her shoulders, and she's starting to grow into her gentle curves. Some people wish that their kids would never grow up, that they'll stay little forever, but after almost losing Sawyer, I know better. Growing up means they're still here, still alive, and that's a gift.

"You look beautiful, sweetie," I tell her, assuming that's what she wants to hear before she sees Will.

"Thanks, Mom. Aunt Dani just pulled up, so we're leaving, okay?"

"Here, Wyatt, take some money for the concession stand for you and Sawyer," Rivers pulls out his wallet. "I don't want Dani paying for all of you."

She gives us both a hug and turns toward the front door. Unfortunately, I'm too curious and nosey to sit here without knowing what's going on with Dani, and follow Wyatt outside.

She rolls down her window as I approach, her dark hair in a messy knot on the top of her head. I level a look at her, refusing to be the one to crack first.

"Got something to say?" She's keeping her guard up, which tells me she has something she's trying to hide.

"Just interesting how Keegan and his handsome Uncle Theo are also going to the same movie...at the same time. Wonder how that got coordinated?"

Dani just stares at me, defiantly.

"Just didn't know rubber duck shirts did it for you. I hope you enjoy them," I sing-song.

Dani's face flushes bright pink before she flips me off through her window and backs out of my driveway, confirming my suspicions.

I walk back inside to where Rivers sits on the couch, holding the Star Jar in his hand. "Rivers? How worried do I need to be about Theo getting close to Dani?"

"Quinny, you and I both know that the only concern you need to have when it comes to men and Dani is that they're aware that she's not afraid of a first-degree murder charge."

I snort but still feel wary. "I'm serious."

"He's a good guy, Quinn. I wouldn't have convinced him to move here if I didn't want to be around him."

I lean my head against the wall with my arms crossed, taking him in.

After a minute, he looks up at me and tosses the Star Jar back and forth between his hands. "Are you as desperate to read these wishes as I am?"

"Oh my GOD, I thought you'd never ask. Yes, rip off the tape!" I sit down next to him, anticipation making my fingers twitch. "Are we reading each other's or just our own?"

"Why not both?" he says as he peels back the tape and unscrews the lid.

He pulls out a star, then clears his throat like he's announcing something serious. "'*See the northern lights.*' That one has your writing."

I pull out the next star and read, "*Ask Quinn to a school dance.*" The irony settles around us. What would have happened if he did ask me? Millions of timelines with outcomes we'll never know but this one.

"Damn, we were bad at this," he jokes.

"I think I had a prom one in there, too if it makes you feel better."

"It doesn't, thanks though."

Rivers pulls out the next star and unfolds it. "*Tell Rivers I'm in love with him.*" He turns to face me, but I don't feel embarrassed.

"I'm in love with you," I tell him, grinning like a fool.

His hand moves to cup the back of my head and pulls me toward him for a kiss, our tongues brushing softly.

I pull back and reach my hand into the jar. "'*Figure out how to end up with Rivers Thomas by my side for the rest of my life.*' Oof, I may have had a little crush on you back then!" I say with a laugh.

"I was pretty irresistible," he shrugs, then dumps the rest of the stars out like he's looking for one in particular.

I try to protest, feeling like this is cheating the time capsule, when he lands on the star he's been searching for.

"'*Marry Quinn Clark.*" His words linger in the air just a moment before he's on his knee in front of me. "Quinn, I know this isn't conventional, but we've never been fans of convention. I knew you were it for me at sixteen, and that's never changed. Will you marry me?"

Rivers is right, I didn't see this happening so soon. I'm also smart enough to know that the moment I saw him in his practice for Sawyer's appointment that this was an inevitability of the universe.

We were always meant to end up right here.

And so, I whisper the only word I can. "Yes."

***

We decide to wait on sharing the news with everyone we know and love until we can tell the kids. Rivers said he asked them a couple of months ago, after talking to my dad the day everyone came over here to clean when Sawyer came home. I know the kids will be happy, but I don't want them to be blindsided.

I'm lying on the trampoline with my head on Rivers's chest feeling the steady beating of his heart as *Breaking Dawn* projects against our house.

Starting our new life.

Together.

My phone rings with a call, and glancing at the screen, I see the contact of someone I've hardly spoken to the last five years. Or maybe I should say, he's hardly spoken to *me* the last five years. We drifted apart when Preston died, against my will. I tried to hold onto him, but he became a shell of himself, and I couldn't reach him; he and Preston were close.

Rivers looks at it too, squeezing my shoulder to him as I brace for whatever is on the other end of this conversation.

"Hello?" I answer.

"Quinn," Cody sobs uncontrollably and my heart breaks for him, "she's leaving me, Quinn."

It takes me a full ten seconds for understanding to sharpen my focus as I take in his ragged breathing. I knew they were on rocky ground, but not this bad.

"June just told me she wants a divorce."

Acknowledgements

I know most people will skip over this section of text because the story is over, and as readers we often don't care about who all made this story came to life. Who was responsible for what, or how they assisted the author, but it's one of the most important sections to me because often, these are the people gave the author the belief that they could do the thing they set out to do: write a damn book.

This book, by all accounts is a love story, but for me it's a love story to my hometown in Southern California. It was idyllic and wonderful, but I couldn't see it until I was older and removed from what felt like a fishbowl existence. Pine Grove is fictional, but the experiences I had in a similar town shaped me.

If you made it this far, then my first thanks goes to you, reader. Thank you for trusting me with your heart and your time, and for making it to these last few pages with me. I've wanted to write since I was a child; I've wanted people to read what I write since I was a teenager. Thank you for fulfilling that dream.

Shelbi Self, you are more than a good friend, you're a *damn* good friend. Thank you for reading this book in it's most early stages, encouraging me to continue, having the most un-hinged commentary, being honest with your feedback about what isn't working (such as all my damns), being my sounding board through this whole process, and gasping at all the right moments. You're the best unofficially official agent/manager I've ever had.

Emily and Nicole, you two have carried my vulnerability, hyped me for every win, and are the embodiment of best friendship. It's been the greatest gift sharing my life with two people who have known me longer than anyone. You two are all the best parts of Dani in this story and I'm so thankful to you both each and every day.

Tiffany Broberg, I can't even imagine this book without your stroke of genius. You are without question the best proofreader to ever proofread in the history of proofreading. Thank you for taking so much time to digest every punctuation mark. Your skill made this book as meaningful as it is.

To Shannon, I could not ask for a bigger hype girl than you. Every post, every story update, every moment you could, you did. You always show up and cheer me on and I will always, always, always be thankful for it. How did I ever get so lucky?!

Eric Self, I appreciate you're willingness to make sure I never once used the word "springs" in relation to a penis. Thank you for work-shopping the mechanics of that particular issue via Shelbi.

To my editor, Beth who was on call 24/7 and never let me get sloppy, thank you. This book is what it is because of your guidance and coaching so early on, and the tough love I needed to hear as we moved further along. You've made me a better writer, and for that, I'll always be thankful.

To my cover artist, Cortlee. GIRL. You brought my vision to life, and secured yourself a permanent slot in all my future acknowledgements (pending you're willing to go through this with me again!)

Meagan Briggs, my beta reader, this book is as good as it is because you saw the potential and called me out for where I fell flat. I told you that I was nervous because it's hard to take criticism, but you gave me just what I needed to make this work. It's a big ask to read something by a debut, indie author, but I'm so glad I chose you. More importantly, I'm so glad I listened.

To Destiny Crabb, my friend and sensitivity reader for this project: words will never be able to express my gratitude for you. I knew very early on that Quinn was going to be a widow, and that was intimidating. I've never been through that experience and the last thing I wanted was for readers to feel like I hadn't handled the emotions correctly or adequately. Your feedback and willingness to subject yourself to what I'm sure was somewhat traumatizing means more to me than you'll ever know.

To Staci Nelson who sat down with me for three hours to talk about the logistics of Preston's death and Sawyer's stay in the hospital: thank you. Thank you, thank you, thank you. Something that matters to me more than just about anything as a reader is that I can tell that the author took time to properly research what they're writing about. I will never be able to repay you for your generosity in going over every minute detail regarding these traumas. If there are any mistakes in this regard, they are entirely my own.

For my sisters Savannah and Abby, who are my real-life June and Liz, our sisterhood is the thing I hold most precious. I'd be lost without your love, support, wisdom, friendship, and guidance. Who gets to say that they are best friends with their sisters? Me. I do. And I'm so lucky.

To my parents, Jim and Debbie who have supported my dreams with unwavering love my entire life, thank you. Thank you for showing up to my second-grade assembly where my short essay on Patriotism was read aloud to the school. Thank you for being interested in my stories in the car on the way down the mountain, and for buying multiple copies of the magazine I got published in without telling you I submitted a piece. Thank you for championing me through college, for supporting my Bookstagram, and for wanting to read this (sorry about the adult content, this is embarrassing).

To my kids, who so graciously allowed me to spend so much time creating a world that I love, and who have been so supportive of my dreams. There is nothing quite like having your kids tell you they're proud of you, or that they think it's cool that you're writing your own novel. Wyatt and Sawyer's personalities were largely drawn upon from the idiosyncrasies of my own precious babies, and in my mind, are the most incredible kids I've ever known. I'm so lucky to be their mom.

Finally, to my husband Tyler who is without question the biggest green flag I've ever known. You, who encouraged me to pursue my passions without ever batting an eye at how it would impact our family. You, who refused to read a word of this book until it could be bought. You, who never hesitated to pick up take-out when I got lost in writing. I've never known a love more pure than yours, and will never be able to express the depths of my gratitude for it.

Writing Pine Grove felt like coming home to me, and I hope, with everything in me, that when book two comes out, it'll feel like coming home to you too. Thanks for reading.

Playlists

Below is a list of songs I listened to while writing this novel, along with every song mentioned within it's pages. Enjoy

1. Like We Used To by A Rocket to the Moon

2. You All Over Me (Taylor's Version) [From the Vault] by Taylor Swift

3. Ocean Avenue by Yellowcard

4. Island in the Sun by Weezer

5. Nothing to See Here by Tenille Arts

6. Pork and Beans by Weezer

7. Just in Case by Morgan Wallen

8. the 1 by Taylor Swift

9. What If I Never Get Over You by Lady A

10. One and Only by Teitur

11. 7 Summers by Morgan Wallen

12. Tim McGraw by Taylor Swift

13. Someone Else & Jesus by Ricky Manning

14. Fell in Love Without You by Motion City Soundtrack

15. Who Knew by P!nk

16. Hey Jealousy by Gin Blossoms

17. Chasin' You by Morgan Wallen

18. Bruises (feat. Ashley Monroe) by Train

19. Coffee Shop Soundtrack by All Time Low

20. Delicate by Taylor Swift

21. Deja Vu by ROM COM and Eliza Harrison Smith

22. Risk by Gracie Abrams

23. Trouble Sleeping by The Perishers

24. Beverly Hills by Weezer

25. Renegade (feat. Taylor Swift) by Big Red Machine

26. Fingerprints by Jenny Baker

27. Just Let Go by Mae

28. Ghost by Justin Bieber

29. Friends Don't by Maddie & Tae

30. Grow Old With You by Adam Sandler

31. The Black Dog by Taylor Swift

32. I Wish by Leah Mason

33. Pushin' Time by Miranda Lambert

34. Perfect Situation by Weezer

35. Haunted (Taylor's Version) by Taylor Swift

36. The Prophecy by Taylor Swift

37. Magic by Colbie Caillat

38. Iris by The Goo Goo Dolls

39. cardigan by Taylor Swift

40. If My Heart Was a House by Owl City

41. Bless the Broken Road by Rascal Flatts

About the Author

Jamie Cluff starting writing poems in her mom's car when she was four years old, and by the time she was ten, got published in an international children's magazine without her parents knowing. She spends her days teaching English to eighth graders and her nights writing swoon worthy romance novels. Jamie lives in Kansas with her husband and two children. Like

We Used To is her first novel.